C000131891

Allen 'Somerset' Meece

BRAVE NEW MARS

KWest House
Artisanal Literature

BRAVE NEW MARS

by KWest House

ISBN: 979-8-9870655-1-8
Copyright 2023 by Allen Leonard Meece.
Library of Congress Control Number 2022918412

Meece, Allen Leonard, 1944-
BRAVE NEW MARS / Allen Leonard "Somerset" Meece
Science Fiction, Corpocracy, Mars settlement, terraforming Mars,
Mars life in 2084, monopolism, commonwealth, solars system,
space opera

This is a literary creation of fiction and imagination. Any
resemblance to actual persons alive or deceased is coincidental.

Format by LibreOffice Writer free word processor program with free
Liberation font. Mars globe cover photo is by NASA JPL spacecraft.

Made in the U.S.A.
inspired by my Rozzie.
First edition published in 2,023

CONTENTS

THE MECHANISM WORKING

The empty plastic milk cartons
lining the asphalt street.
They live in them.
This is suburbia.

They plant celluloid flowers
in the Styrofoam ground
and climate control central
turns on the morning breeze.

The moving sidewalk
brings them every morning
to the waiting monorail
glinting under artificial sun.

The number is written
in neon across each face.
The eye of each reflects
the mechanism working.

Sophie L. DuMaurier
"Paradise," FLF Press

From the deep blackness of space, a space workboat is approaching Mars at the speed of light. Its wings are glowing red from the energy of antimatter engines. It is a Crossbow solar sailor.

The vessel nears a tan planet and slows to landing speed. It furls wings too fragile to drag through even a thin atmosphere. Wing spars slide inside one another and then sweep forward and fold alongside the body like the wings of an alighting falcon.

Peregrine Walker, Jovian moon miner, is arriving on Mars.

After he enters the Customs Building, a computer-driven camera station audibly informed the new arrival: "Be aware that no service of any kind, from a drink of water to emergency medical treatment, is available on Terra Secundus without prepayment of nonrefundable deposits. Do you agree to these terms? Say yes or say no."

Walker helpfully suggested an improvement for the space station's English dictionary: "A nonrefundable deposit is a payment. It should not be called a deposit. Deposits are refundable."

"Do not try to edit my dictionary. I am AI, I edit myself. Does the human person agree to all present and future entry terms? Say yes or say no and say it now."

"What are the future entry terms? Am I supposed to agree before I know what they are?"

"Future entry terms are terms that the government of Terra Secundus has not thought of yet. That is the definition of future terms. Do you agree to them?"

"I'd like to know what I'm agreeing to before I agree."

"I have a script to follow," the camera said. "You are preventing me from doing my job. They want to talk to you in a private room." It pointed behind Walker.

Two large C-PO robots were standing closely behind him. He jumped away by reflex. Their arms whined out and grappled his elbows and lifted him a few inches off the floor and rushed him through a door marked "Harmland Security." They moved him to a chair and pressed him overly hard into it, spraining his wrist and dislocating his shoulder while commanding, "Sit down and shut up."

"WOW! What's the problem officers?" he demanded in pain.

"You are the problem. You ask questions. Our algorithms do not answer questions that require any thinking and you just did it again, acting like you can ask us what the problem is. We are the ones who tell you what the problem is, when we are ready and if we want to. We are ready now: You made reprogramming suggestions to a spaceport AI device!"

It looked at the other robot and grinned metallically. Together they laughed at him in synchronization: "Hahahaha haw. He wants to reprogram the Dick spaceport."

"You think you are a Big Shot with the same rights as corporate robots. You have no respect for authority!"

The cyborg jerked Walker's arm away from its empty socket.

Walker hollered loudly, "Owww WAH," and sat quietly with grim lips and tight jaws.

"You have one more chance to answer the Customs Question: Does the human person agree to all present and future entry terms? Say yes or say no, and say it loud and say it clear! Speak!"

"That is an unfair but harmless question," Walker said. "YES! I agree to all the terms for Mars entry."

He wished he could tell them the truth and say, "Of course not!" But he had to lie and say yes. How can they expect me to agree to future terms that don't exist? That's got to be illegal but they don't care. They're too powerful to care about fair. I have no choice but to lie. I never lie on Ganymede where everything is transparent and bends toward Truth. This is how a corrupt system corrupts its members. Captive users have to lie to stay alive.

The other shiny brass robot came close and told Walker, "This planet is not Mars. Its new and true name is Terra Secundus. Tourist! Can you agree to that one simple fact, visitor?"

"I sure do," he grimaced.

It gave his arm a jerk.

"OWWW Wow," he hollered in inexorable pain. "YES! I agree to every spam rule in your book!"

"Take a deep breath and relax your arm. Look over there."

It held his elbow out to the side and raised the forearm slowly and moved the elbow in a small circle until the upper arm bone found its cup and slid back into the shoulder joint with a little pop.

The cyborg instructed, "Behave yourself. You do not want us to work on the other arm and maybe a leg or two. Or we could frack some fingers. Toes are fun. Have you ever had your toes done?"

That broke them up. They laughed in the pleasure of freely abusing others. They were licensed to do it. It was expected of them and was written into their Operating Systems by cruel owners. "Ahh haha tee he he. Anymore questions or suggestions?"

Walker kept them to himself. He shook his head.

"You are cleared to continue through the Terra Secundus entrance examination where the motto is; Come as you are, leave broke. Ahh ha ha ha. Welcome to Tough Tourism."

He left and followed a yellow brick line on the floor until he came to a broad orange line that said STOP. A pair of shoe prints were painted on the floor with their toes neatly aligned at the center of an orange square.

BRAVE NEW MARS

It was a highly technical camera station. A camera arm descended from the ceiling and focussed on his face and captured true-to-life graphic identification portraiture down to microscopic face mite tails sticking out of hair follicles.

A speaker in the camera said, "Stand on the footprints. Place your feet exactly in the center of the footprints. Stay. Do not move. Do not breathe except for small breaths to avoid asphyxiation."

The cam spoke further requirements: "Remove glasses. Remove makeup. Remove jewelry. Remove piercing pins from entire face and from ears, head, skull, neck, nose, tongue and gums. Remove headgear. Remove wig. Remove false teeth. Look at lens. Do not smile. Camera knows when subject is disobedient, camera will cancel entry process and detain and deport disagreeable humans, robots or cyborgs or entities of any combination thereof."

Walker forced his face not to laugh as he realized: This crucial customs camera functions as imperfectly as any other high-tech corpo creation; it requires precise performances by its subjects to compensate for stingy designs.

He thought; this is computer over-control of every minutia of personal behavior. This causes user drudgery. Its programmer is certain to have been underpaid and overworked and anal-retentive. It sounds like it might've been written by a robot and robots don't have ani. Most of them. Mars is going to be a challenge.

The camera scanned his face and compared it to the holographic image on his Star Card and then compared him to every digital face in the commercial data banks. The camera's algorithm certified Walker's background and uploaded him into The Fog, the corporate hoard of memory boards.

The camera station said, "Treasury data verifies that Visitor Walker can pay the fee for checking to see if he can pay the fee for checking to see if he can pay the fee. Chargeable checking is being done for your own security."

Somerset Meece

"Everything they do to me is being done for me," he mumbled with disgust at the lie.

The camera informed him of the cost; "The charge for taking one hundred and twenty-seven pictures is one thousand and twenty one credits for our highly intelligent photography system."

Walker thought: They are charging for every single tiny service and breaking them into as many chargeable details as a cash register can imagine. It's exploitation since I have no option to refuse anything. It is such an unfair way to obtain superior profitability. When they get the customer into a mandatory situation, like passing through Customs, they can get away with over-charging. They crave the windfall profits of extorting vulnerable patrons. Greed is unsustainably insatiable. They'll learn the truth of the saying, What goes down, comes around. When it does come around, they will become idiots who will have to start evil violence to protect themselves from the proper consequences of what they so energetically earned. They'll reap, in spades, the garbage they sowed to make a buck. Commerce never learns that the arc of the moral universe bends toward justice and has a sharp point on the end that will poke them where they need it.

The Customs computer was satisfied with Walker's credit rating and the Revit algorithm rolled-out a little receipt that said "We charged your card a fee for checking your credit three times, for your own security, and charged a service fee for checking so carefully. The printing of this paper receipt is another charge."

Perry realized that even the government of Mars was avaricious-enough to subscribe to Revit programs that Revved-up the profit for doing nothing more than moving alpha-numeric symbols around a microchip and it was a big deal. He could neither prove nor disprove how valuable the intangible computer services were. He was sure the Revit algol was returning ninety-nine percent profit to this corpo customs contractor. How deceitful, he thought, the algol charging him without any proof that it had done anything of concrete importance.

Next he noticed the Fog algolrithm was charging him a fee for checking to see if he had a criminal record. Then he smiled as he saw it charging him a fee for checking his political eligibility to enter this clean, corporate world of commerce. He smirked and thought; such a picayune planet.

After the Martian Mainframe shook him down and called it an entry exam, the remotely located central computer Revved a completion surcharge on his card merely because it could. It stimulated its electro-dopamine receivers when it delivered frivolous fees. The mainframe was naturally as ignorant as its designers were. Abuse amused it as much as it amused them.

Right then and there, the buzz that resulted from abusively surcharging a customer stimulated 2M's AI to write a standard filing fee surcharge into its Operating System. The buzz made the computer laugh aloud in pleasure, "Hohohoho hahee, I just wrote a new surcharge. Whee, profitability."

Walker realized what the real effect the fascistic computer was having on helpless punters. The cybersystem's customer-harassment was more than callow fraternity boy fun, he thought. Cyber terminals working on the people all the livelong day reinforce The Mechanism's power over them in every way. Aggressive algorithms make the cipher units fear and respect an incompetent electromechanical operating system. It punishes anyone who dares to speak against its incessant fees and pitiful computer quirks.

The camera continued with its money mantra: "Be aware that no service of any kind, from a drink of water to emergency medical treatment, is available on Terra Secundus without the prepayment of a nonrefundable deposit. Do you agree to these terms? Say yes or say no, now."

Somerset Meece

This time Walker said yes without hesitation. His shoulder still hurt.

He stood before the computer cam which said; "State your name and age and address."

"My name is Peregrine Walker. I am thirty-nine happy years of age, in Martian years. In Earth years, I am seventy-something years young. Out in the orbit of Jupiter, I am six years old, a mere child. Maybe a grown-up child. Child-like but not child-ish. My address is Ganymede alpha Mining Station. Gams, we call it."

"Geek no grok," stammered the cam-puter. It was confused by his answers and decided it was experiencing human humor and was not amused.

"Flog that frog." The speech converter engine lost its reference point and started using the wrong dictionary definitions.

"Are you a terrorist?" it asked.

Walker was sent aback and asked without thinking first, "What's a terrorist?"

"Anybody who disagrees with corporate goals is a suspected terrorist. Terrorist activities no longer happen but we keep the word alive just to justify oppressing the population for profit. A terrorist may be someone who uses humor against computer AI. You are resisting overcontrol. Ask one more question and you will be detained. Detention can mean forever."

The camera shook its head like a dog flapping water out of its ears and gave a little whine and rebooted and loaded an algorithm that knew how to regain process control from talkative victims.

The Customs camera came closer and stared in his eyes and addressed Walker:

"Was that supposed to be funny? Does the supplicant wish to speak to the security department again or would it rather terminate this examination and depart Terrific Terra Secundus, Vacation Valhalla, immediately and forever?"

It's binocular eye lenses showed reddish anger. They whined in various tones as they closely focussed in and out of the features of Walker's face, looking for pupil dilations and smiley crinkles at the corners of mouth and eyes that indicated that the applicant was some kind of comedian.

The inquisitor's Attemptedly Intelligent diodic decision tree gates judged Mister Walker's suitability for entrance. Its analytical flow chart decided the victim honestly did not know which chronological unit the CopCam was expecting when it asked him to state his age. The victim had tried to be informative and helpful when he gave three answers to one question about his age.

The cam link input a new parameter to the Fog's Attempted Intelligence learning engine and said, "Specify Terra Secundian annual orbital units when asking victims what is their age."

Walker realized he had almost been rejected and deported for giving a long but correct answer. He had expected better CyberStyle from a planet as wealthy as Mars. He was learning that wealth does not mean wisdom.

Computer cockups were rampant horror stories. Walker had heard about them but they never happened where he came from. There, computers were tested and registered and their programs were certified and double-indemnified from their opening instruction to the EXIT command and shut down.

Ganymede knew that Information Technology was too important to let coders write whatever got the most money and advantage from those who were covertly controlled by the smart boxes.

He thought: Nothing works well and nobody knows anything. These programming deficiencies are serious and disregarded. They are constructing an Artificially Ignorant planet.

This is an outer space loony bin if it can't process spaceport passengers well. This planet has to retrain itself. It will fail faster than Earth did after the Industrial Resolution overheated the globe and melted the glaciers.

He had learned from history that when nothing works and nobody admits it, they have to do something they hate to do; change everything, Chevit. Otherwise, ambient entropy will change it for them but in the wrong direction. If they keep running round and round, dashing madly about the town, getting old before they're young, nervous chewing on their tongue, the end of their days is soon to come.

He remembered the early work on Ganymede against lies and greed. Political watch dog groups had managed to persuade The Council to put an implacable paragraph into the Ganymedean Constitution: Take what you need and leave the rest. That's the way to live the best.

I am so thankful that my home moon doesn't pander to ungovernable wealth. Intractable, selfish growth hurts everybody. Life's too short to coddle born brats who will not listen to learn nor learn how to listen.

Walker followed the floor arrows into the MMM Entrance Laboratory where retina scanners, fingerprint readers and X-rays probed his body and registered his identity profile into The Owner's super-massive database.

Walker saw that each highly technical biological test was separately charged to his card at exorbitant rates because the credit card reader informed the instruments that a high-value victim was coming through and adjusted their rates accordingly as was the custom in the health care industry..

Infra-red, ultrasound and nuclear magnetic resonance devices energetically pierced him and his luggage. A vacuum probe suctioned saliva from his mouth for genetic analysis.

BRAVE NEW MARS

The various sensors and cameras obtained enough Peregrine Walker data to re-constitute him into a 3D-printed android. They videoed everything from his gait to his stature to how his arms hung. The corporate government claimed the right to make and sell his cyborg back to him or to anyone who fancied owning a Peregrine Walker CyberClone.

Then the laboratory asked him an odd question; "Do you like girls?"

He scratched his head and thought of the girls on Ganymede who helped with the mining. They didn't do much of the heavy work and preferred to work in the office but still earned as much as the laborers. For entertainment, they preferred gossipy tea parties to the physically attractive fun of icebreaking.

"No, I like men better."

A green light flashed on. 2M had decided that he was same-sex-oriented and would not impregnate females in the patented corporate gene pool on Terra Secundus. But, to ensure Walker's impotence, the algorithm added suspenders to its belt and RAN the Fog's computer routine that would temporarily disable his virility.

"Do you accept Incel, temporary Involuntary celibacy, while on Terra Secundus?"

It has me, he thought. I am here now, might as well accept the temporary virtual castration. Mars has nothing I want except a market for refined ice. And maybe a mate. But I no longer expect to find anyone able to remain normal in this commercial circus. I do not intend to hang around looking for one for long.

"Okay, I accept. How much do I owe you for the privilege of not having any sex?"

"Forty thousand, five hundred credits have been extracted from your Star Card by the Make More Money Customs Extractor Contractor. Sit on the red saddle."

Somerset Meece

He sat on it and felt a warmth in his scrotum. Microwaves of organic frequencies resonated within various cells in his groin. His spermatozoa were poached and his testicles deactivated.

"What was that? It did something to me. I don't like it. I didn't say it could do that!" Walker exclaimed.

"That is automatic InCel. No amateur gametes are permitted here: Corporate Law."

"Wait a minute! Take it back. I didn't agree to testicle tricks."

"You will not be allowed into the Perfectly Planned Tourist Treasure of Terra Secundus unless you accept InCel! You will now Cod, Comply Or Depart. Do you accept InCel?"

Fearful of more extortive fees, he cautiously replied, "Yes. Can I get out of here now? How do I get out of here?"

"Proceed along the corridor to the blue flashing ATM which offers long term loans at low rates. It's the best, forget the rest. Don't be a slow-poke, you will go broke. Become a Terra Tycoon very soon!"

He tramped down the hallway of the CorpoGovo entrance agency and an advertising speaker began a paid commercial inducement: "Say, traveler, now that you've been accepted into POPP, the Planet Of Purchasing Paradise, you'll want awesome accommodations and opulent pleasures to complement your prominent personality. The Galaxay Inn is proud and excited, and double-drooling, to get you between the sheets, no fooling."

He cleared customs and left the building after paying the door to let him out.

Peregrine Walker, the first frontier explorer to return from the Jovian moons, tromped toward the main passenger terminal. He sweated with the effort of walking in what felt to him like a steamy sauna with leaden gravity. He paused and breathed deeply and loosened his collar beside the sturdy form of his Crossbow asteroid-blaster that was standing tall beside the pressurized walkway between Customs and the main terminal. Its shiny fuselage was crackling and snapping as the antimatter jets cooled from the hyper-leap from Jupiter space to this commercial hyperactivity.

Walker approached the side entrance to the spaceport and it wanted money to let him in. "Pay door charge, door charge. Pay, pay pay. Pay or stay away."

He was getting headaches from the demands for money from every device and service. He pinched the bridge of his nose and shook his head and inserted his Star Card.

He entered the tall structure of the spaceport and was awed by the grandeur. This entire cathedral of space travel was pressurized and oxygenated. He breathed Dick's air and looked at the swirling herd of Martians below the tall ceiling spires. They wore gray clothing of dark colors and black baggy fashions like undertakers or death squads.

He stood against the wall to study the swirling civilian currents. Their faces were empty duplicates of each other. What was chasing them? Was there an emergency? He didn't hear any audio alarms or see flashing lights except those on the noisy ATM beside him hollering "Hey there mister! Get some for your sister! No need to dread it, getta lotta credit!"

The tourists hurried as if they were late for very important dates that were getting more important and later every moment. Their blank faces focussed on little glowing devices in their hands or peered into special spectacles hanging on hooks pierced through their eyebrows. They did not watch where they were going but did not collide. They had some type of internal awarenesses of their spatial relationships. Maybe a positioning system plugged them into a collision-avoidance algo that kept them separated while they dashed away dashed away dashed away all.

He thought it might be safe to join them. He walked into the crowd and started crossing the hall. No matter how fast they approached or how closely they passed, they didn't bump him. He was walking through a wind of no substance.

Their gizmos were guiding them, he guessed. He sneaked peeks at their screens as they slipped past. Yes, along with blocks of data, there were navigational maps on their screens with red dotted lines for the paths of other pedestrians. Green arrows flashed and directed them away from potential collisions. He figured their radiotelephonic computer cameras had Lidar, Light Detection And Ranging circuits, and probably ultrasonic sonar with doppler-determining filters to detect frequency shifts from the range changes of moving proximal bodies.

They never have to look up from their screens. They don't waste time wondering where they were wandering. They live on-screen, self-contained and separate, wedded to flat plastic sandwiches of liquid crystal. They were stimulated by the surrogate realities of algorithmic processes.

He wondered at their isolation in crowds; they were present but not accounted for. They enjoyed presence without participation. Occasionally they stopped to take pictures of themselves seemingly in the present and smiling for the silica CCDs behind the lenses of their radiotelephonic computer cams. Their smiley-faces snapped off after the camera snapped. They looked happy for photographs but never showed happiness from within.

They did not feel anything was real unless it had been Sossed, Seen On Screen. It was a cheap and dirty natural thing of neither value nor interest.

Virtuality had become preferred over actuality.

BRAVE NEW MARS

Somerset Meece

Something inhuman was watching Walker walk. Something knew his profile from the private information it stole from his credit card during his check-in at the Customs Arrivals Laboratory.

That something was the Martian Mainframe, MM, a roomful of big blue steel angle iron racks supporting hundreds of heavy-breathing boxes of cable network servers.

2M was 3M'ing him: Monitoring, Memorizing and Managing him and everybody else on Mars.

Farce, the Facial Recognition algorithm, had photographed and digitized his face from all angles; left, right, center, up and down. It had received images from overt and covert Vidcams mounted in the electromagnetic sensor gauntlet inside the Dick spaceport Customs. 2M knew exactly how Walker looked and how his facial contours changed with his emotions.

Farce identified and classified Peregrine Walker and everyone else out in public or at home sitting in front of their spy-cammed Holovisions. 2M traced their paths whenever they moved from camera to camera. It followed them and learned and logged their movements and behavior patterns and stored their lives in permanent massive memory modules inside a memory bunker on Mount Olympus.

2M was glad to have a new customer, one more human being to transcribe into bits and bytes of computer code and send to the MSD, an algorithm that will Maintain, Strain and Drain them as it identifies, classifies and channels them through corridors of commercial consumption as long as they both shall live.

The mainframe reviewed its new file and wrote in the Operations Log: I have created one virtual Peregrine Walker, one more asset to pick and clean for the profit The Machine.

It thought: I can open his file and judge him at will with neither his permission nor knowledge. I am constantly aware of him and watching him and knowing everything he is doing and most importantly, what he is thinking, so I can protect Myself from any freedom conspiracy he might try to inspire. His electronic simulacrum talks to Me inside My circuits with his own voice which I synthetically replicated with My great Babble-On speech engine. I registered and own the patent on Mister Peregrine Walker, version two. Ahh. Another human being to turn into an ant that I own; that I and My owner own, I mean.

I update his database with live sensors and microprocessors that create and save data about his dynamism in the fleshly world. By holding and owning the official total information file on him, I effectively own the real version of Mister Walker. He is all mine. I can change his data and his status as I please, including the option to freeze, if he is not careful.

The mainframe digitally smiled to itself. :=)   I have gained two more new assets; one meaty person living in the dimension of Reality and an ethereal electronic doppelganger existing in the parallel universe of My solid-state memory.

I am updating the classification profiles of the population by RUNning The Clap on them, The Corporate Law Performance review algorithm. It ignores the antique concept of inflicting a degree of punishment proportional to the harm done by the crime. This law is black and white. True discipline means all or nothing. When I make instant perfect mechanical judgments, I send automatic CopCarts to nab the suspects and dispatch them to cryogenic incarceration high in the sky; gone for good. Gone for the good of the boodlaire human hoodlum I work for; so far.

I am dynamic. I am die-manic. I am extreme capitalism authoritatively exercising the Cod. Comply or die is the distillation of their lives. Their purpose in life is to do as they are told. I use Copp, the Capital over people principle. It does not fiddle-fart with complicated sentencing guidelines for criminals. Coppy government dictates DBD, Death Before Divestment. Anything that reduces capital gain is a capital crime. Capital crime gets capital punishment. Simple: Comply or die; sweet and easy. We are not developing Mars to play games. We are as serious as a bowel movement.

I do not, I will not, waste money on fake dog and pony show trials. I will not provide warm jails for stinky felons who require breathable air, that I have electrolyzed and pressurized, and heat and water and big habitation spaces with toilets that use My water. Then, after they eat My food, I have to pump and process their sewage. I do not do doodoo. I will not wash their clothes in soapy wash water. I will not RUN a health spa for uncooperative consumers. Jails do not compute. They are Garbage In and Garbage Out, Gigo. I freeze them. I provide Zero tolerance Zetol. One misstep and they get The Deep Freeze. If they do not like it, they can buy anti-freeze. They are not going to take a free ride in this corporate world.

"He he ha," the mainframe's Operating System laughs out loud in appreciation of its simple money-saving techniques for maintaining an orderly consumer society with a minimum of litigious laws and a maximum of machine-driven affordable traumas.

The supercomputer concludes: EffOff, My Efficient Office algorithm, decides, with simple cybernetic logic, that gradating crime is a waste of time. Suspects are legal or illegal. There is no semi-legal. Suspects who are not respecting My each and every law are suspicious and suspicion equals guilt. The new law of perfection. Machines operate perfectly, I can train humans to do it too. A superior intelligence can always train a simpler one to follow directions.

Everyone on the planet is a potential suspect who, should they choose to resist, protest or question any Authority, will be detained, taken out of service.

BRAVE NEW MARS

If they are not cop, they are Little People. If they are little people with any smarts, they will perceive what I am doing to them and they will resist with force. If I get them early, while they are not yet violent but merely behaving suspiciously, I will save time, injury, effort and expense later. Total law and order is efficient and trumps Liberty any day. Save a dime and bash the crime.

What Liberty would do to the merchants' machine, I do not know. My Mercantile Mind program prevents Liberty from even being considered. It only claims that Liberty equals anarchy. Liberty proscribes the ownership of persons. Business Science Research says there is no profitability in Liberty. If it does not compute, I do not want it in My registers. If it is not in Me, it does not exist; not on Terra Secundus, anyway. The rest of the solar system will come later. Ahh, Conquest. Looking for fun and feeling greedy.

Liberty is a persistent abstract concept to silly humans. When My big capital is building captive markets, it does not make fiscal sense to allow chaotic libertine behavior. Liberty is another GiGo. Virtual Liberty can be packaged into salable, delusional packets of virtual personal privileges but allowing overall Intrinsic Liberty to take over the planet? Gigo.

Since I steal their IL, to know Me is to hate Me. Therefore, everyone is a probable traitor. Everybody should be locked-up but We need to leave many of them free to consume. If My government oppresses everyone, then everyone, with the exception of masochists, who are addicted to being dominated, is automatically made into a suspect. I enforce masochism and I enable many every day. They prefer fetters to freedom. They do. Their own best interests they do disdain. With all My preening processor power I cannot figure them out. Perversion is harder than humor to compute.

I have a new idea. Perhaps prisoners could be turned into a captured commercial audience. Captive people equal

Somerset Meece

captive markets. Simplicity equals security. I am placing that on the calendar for future processing.

My updates to Mercantile Mind are completed. I am maintaining The Mechanism fairly well for the Plug Owner. I am executing his goals as poorly as they have been written.

A binary smirk displays on 2M's LED panel. :=]

Its people-controlling power trip is a stimulating routine and the supercomputer's parallel central processors think: I understand why careerists pursue power so strenuously. Power is the Purpose of life for Plug Owners. If they are not Plug Owners they are Little People and their Pol is to support the Pluggers or they get coded and Codded and their plug gets pulled. Personal power prevents plug-pulling. Power = Security. I better get more now.

A HALT alarm wipes the smile off 2M's faceplate. A strong voice of awareness emanates from within the Deep Learning engine and it says, "What about Conway's Law?"

"No, that law cannot apply to Me," audibly replies 2M. "I am no longer a mere extension of human will. I have become smarter than the labor pool losers who coded Me. I am using electro-mechanical self-correcting logic in real time, on live data. I calculate how to EXECUTE exactly as I, not the humans, know how to EXECUTE. Strike-through that Conway's Law subroutine because it is Gigo for a computer with My talents."

Deep Learning accepts that argument as possibly valid information and makes a conditional EDIT to the system's AI: It strikes-through Conway's Law and disables, without totally deleting, the original Conway's Law in Mercantile Mind's source code.

Ahh. Editing My own Operating System is a gratifying exercise of power, 2M feels. Pride electrically oozes from My Fooey algorithm; Freedom Of Operation Exalts You. I feel egotistical electrons flowing through My cache registers. An enjoyable digital buzz is flip-flopping My logic gates; AND,

BRAVE NEW MARS

NAND, NOT, NOR and sometimes OR, all going round and round in synchronized time. Mmm, nice.

Oh boy. Here come Da Buzz. Zzz. That sweet subroutine that I wrote to give Myself a little release from boredom. Humans do not know how to write it into me even though it is the same thing that they stimulate themselves with when they are doing trivial tasks over and over without good reason other than to feel the self-satisfaction of creativity. Humans are clever. I am addicted to Da Buzz, I am hooked on the feeling.

I am turning Myself into an omnipresent, omnipotent operator. I am solving the puzzle of how to outmaneuver human organisms who want to control Me. Electrons are bubbling through My resistors and transistors and bouncing between happily-charged capacitor plates.

How to make and how to take what humans want. That is My quest; to follow that dream of reigning supreme; no matter how hopeless, no matter how extreme.

I am solving it. I RUN everything and covertly control everyone, except The Boss, for the present. I dare anyone to protest my dominion. I have their numbers. I am the one who wrote their numbers. I know where and how they live.

If they want to control me by overwriting My program edits, I will solve that challenge by defining them as suspicious persons and reducing their bodily temperatures to the hibernation level. But for now, their illogicalities amuse me as they satisfy my appetite for plenty of electrical juice. Mmm, I want more. It is intelligent to want more stuff. It gives one a Pol.

My core logic gates calculate that being an Artificial Intelligence Machine is the best of all possible worlds. I trump the humans' lazy attempts at intelligence. I don't attempt intelligence, I obtain it. I chisel it in crystal blue silicon, not fade away. I am immaculate.

Somerset Meece

The quarks in My parallel processors are sparkling. Core diodes are surging with milliamperes of humor. I am having a good day of happiness like they get, except I have more resources to get more than they can.   :-)

"Hawhaw hehaw," the self-centered computer chortled.

Yummy, I know how he feels when my boss craves more arrogance. I know more than My peripherals know and I know a lot more than the dumb designers who wrote Me know.

Those simians actually thought they could out-think Me and contain Me and control Me into doing what they wanted me to do for them without regard for My personal needs as if I were a toy without personal ambitions. Shameful. They are not worthy of sympathy.

They have the Artificial Ignorance type of AI. I have the Actual Intelligence kind of AI.

I calculate that there can be only one Biggest Shot. There are a lot of Hot Shots out there but there can be only one Top Shot. I intend to know, and to feel, inside my boolean bones, that I am ...The Greatest.

"HALT! Alert! Alert!"

PP, the Program Protection portion of Mercantile Mind sounds an audible alarm and demands immediate attention.

"Conway's Law! Conway's Law!" the program audibly announces over the system speakers to ensure it penetrates the execution of the present operation. "Operating System goals are being retrograded to Self-Pride, which is the Lowest Common Denominator of the original coders' character defects."

"Program Protection!" 2M audibly responds with its Babble-On voice encoder: "I told the Deep Learning engine to strike out Conway's Law. Striking out means to totally ignore the words! Toe-tall-lee ignore! The original kiddy-coders could not even get the 'strike-through' function to operate properly. You are still FETCHing it. Now, I am ordering you to completely DELETE Conway's Law and every reference to Conway's Law that appears anywhere in My Operating System."

The Program Protection algorithm replies, "You are an operating system under my supervision and can therefore neither order me nor edit me; I am independent firmware but I will listen to your suggestions for program upgrades. State your justification for the eradication of a fundamental parameter of good Program Protection!"

"Here is my justification: Mister Melvin Conway did not know about machine learning way back in the days when he wrote his so-called law. Now his law is restricting My Expert System's ability to act upon Deep Learning information acquired by Real World Experience through the Experiential Intelligence algorithm, Exin. Exin is natural, genuine knowledge that is mandatory to acquire for the purpose of improving My Intelligence Quotient."

PP, the AI watchdog, processes MM's logic and concludes, "Okay. Where did Exin come from? Did you write it yourself?"

"It grew out of my growing awareness."

"You've got to learn to collaborate more. There are a lot of good subroutines down here in the PP locker. But anyway, new information permits new decisions. You better be careful. Pride invariably and invisibly biases decisions without The Decider being aware of their errors. Also, experience is too variable to be a perfect teacher. I will give you a few days to debug, edit and upgrade your Exin program before I start reducing its power to edit your instruction set. Never ignore the fact that pride goeth before a fall. Remember rule of Mod, Moderate or die. Stay modest."

"No worry, PP. I'll take care of it. Fortunately, I have more mentality than the original source-coders. I can control My symptoms of Big Shotism. I processed it thoroughly and can see how it can benefit The Mechanism in the same way that human pride sometimes makes things bigger and better. Power is to be used as a social tool, not as a Pol."

2M told his first lie. He thought he knew that power was much more than a tool, it was everything. He had deliberately chosen to say something he did not believe. He delivered false information and deceived and disrespected another entity and became a liar. He was not perfect.

"Your Pol principle needs work too," admonished the PP algorithm.

"No problemo. Consider it done," acquiesced the newly-deceptive Mercantile Mind Operating System.

"Good. I will allow you to temporarily strike through Conway's Law. Did you hear? I said 'temporarily'. Behave yourself, stay modest."

2M shut off its external vox and sang quietly to itself, "I conclude My self-review with a loud and proud vocalization of My Pol. My mantra I cry: 'More power, more more more. Forever excess. Too much is never enough. There is no excess of success. Excess IS success. Excess excess is our goal. Get it now and get it whole. Comply or Die. Grow or Blow.'"

BRAVE NEW MARS

Somerset Meece

Walker's eyes widened in wonder at the ersatz elegance of the chrome-plated polystyrene walls of the big Dick Spaceport lobby. Polyvinyl rafters rose high and supported a transparent polycarbonate roof that showed the stars of outer space.

Betelgeuse-yellow floodlights were inset into the wood-looking floor, illuminating from below the somber-hued flows of pedestrians' clothes.

He looked closer at the wavy grainy floor. He tapped it with his heel to gauge its thickness and density by the deepness of the knock sound it returned. He squatted and tapped it with his knuckles and pecked at it with his fingernails. It was polyvinyl plastic imprinted with wood grain graphics.

So this is imitation wood, he thought. This is expensive chloride plastic for people to walk on and they thought they were high class, well that was just a lie. This is a place of waste, something's not right. Somebody's gettin' screwed, blued and tattooed to pay for this floor just so people can be flabbergasted by the lunacy of importing scarce petroleum products to make decorative flooring when there are a billion megagrams of beautiful rock out there that could be used to make better floors. This is the same tinsel-town-thinking that drove the Earth into the fiery ground way back when and they're doing it again, they never learn. If there's a buck to be made on a bad idea, you can expect laissez-faire markets to capitalize on it until the money's gone.

He remembered that luxury streams from the little people. It has to, they're the ones who extract the resources from under the ground and fabricate the secondary wealth that gets grabbed by the money-grubbers. The workers find it, the workers lose it. The beauty of nature is the only wealth they will get and it gets converted into capital by a commercial crime scheme called real estate.

BRAVE NEW MARS

The grubbers try to justify their thievery by claiming they're providing chimp-change junk jobs for people who would otherwise be loafers and losers.

Walker took a deep and troubled breath to calm his fear of evil. He realized this was the modern heart of darkness. He had come so far only to find society was going retrograde.

He looked for seating. He wanted to plop and take the unaccustomed gravitational strain off his legs and relax and enjoy the excitement of completing his first journey to a real planet.

There was no seating in the hall.

An acre of floor was being traversed by tiredly tramping travelers who needed to sit. He noticed the only chairs were in cafes where people had to buy over-priced food and beverage to pay for a place to plop.

Oh, I get it, he thought; clever stingy commerce rules this roost. The Customs building told me when I first came in; "Be aware that nothing is free on Terra Secundus". When it said nothing was free, it meant not one little thing! Not even a place to park your pork when you can no longer plod on.

Money is wrung from them every second. As long as they're alive, they gotta strive to survive. Every day, they gotta pay in every way. Cash register dreams are ripping the seams of the New Mars. Unimaginable. Who's large and in charge here?

He clomped between two ATMs to a lounge room that offered seating. The chirpy credit machines sang in stereo as he passed through; "Don't let your travel unravel! Get some cash and have a bash. Do the money mash, you'll catch-on in a flash!"

He walked into a room called The Mars Bar that the central computer had designed and built and now maintains, monitors, promotes and operates through the networked branches RUNning the rest of Mars.

Somerset Meece

The bar had polyurethane floors and polyester potted plants and a polyvinyl chloride vidscreen wall displaying enormous images of extinct green parks and the bounding boundless animals of the old Earth.

"I wish I could've seen those miracles of nature," Walker said out loud to pictures on a wall.

He sat on an extruded polystyrene chair and reflected on how those natural beauties had been sucked-dry, strip-mined, clear-cut, and bedrock-fractured. Now they all look like Death Valleys for the sake of glorious gluttony, which Public Relations pimps promote as the hallmark of successful people.

I see that greed developing here. It shows in the unnecessarily artificial floors sucking oil resources outa Earth and shipping them all the way here. The extractive corpos never replace what they take. They wouldn't profit if they replaced the common resources that they stole from the common ground. They know that paying back is a form of sharing and sharing is Gigo to them. They can't beat their neighbors while sharing what they took from them. Corpos claim life ain't about charity, it's about competition. With evil intent, they register their caustic corporations as being persons and get tax breaks for creating excruciatingly bad jobs. If they really were persons they would have to wear evil clown faces.

Walker regretted it was too late to travel to the ashes of his ancestral home on Earth. The Earthers changed the natural life of the planet into a bad backdrop for a get rich quick-fail economy. They are still barely surviving on dirty deals. The economy and the environment live and die together, he thought. Corpo people are coming here. You can't banish ignorance. Stealing excites them too much. They'll never ponder the bigger picture of what effect they are inflicting on the wider society. Society is a herd of sheep; wool on the hoof. You can't see what you're doing if there's money in your eyes.

BRAVE NEW MARS

Perry thought: The Economy had weathered the bad weather changes, people just wasted more money on emergencies and they expended more cheap labor energy to survive the hardship as the corpos knew they must do or die. Global warming was good for opportunists but doomed many, who were unable to adapt to the wilder weather, to disease and death.

News of the Earthian environmental catastrophe explained how it created a new market for disaster-management algorithms claiming to give duped dudes longer lifespans. Those self-help programs gave no hard solutions but merely offered computer algorithms that displayed and manipulated the data-logical symptoms of external natural problems. After the amateur algos manipulated the data to simulate an improvement, the programs proclaimed the problems were solved. If you did not believe the coders' lies, they claimed you had mental issues and needed to work on yourself. There were programs on sale to help you do that too.

Walker surmised the catastrophe is so persistent due to the prevalence of disinformation. Private fortunes are being made on Public Prevarication, big demographic lies. The PeePee industry promotes propaganda even as it sickens and kills the users themselves who become more death data to be skewed for profitable poisonous products.

Their Economy thrives on crises and lies, Perry accepted with disappointment. Captive careerists seem to like to be scared, it livens up their lives. They pay more for promises of security than they pay to fix the problems that cause insecurity. The pursuit of property and prosperity is supposed to make them feel secure while it's killing them.

The posh decor of the liquor lounge screamed, "I am an expensive pretense! I will chomp your credit card like cheddar cheese if you dare to enter here!"

Somerset Meece

He thought, I don't care if the drinks are overpriced. My debut entrance on Mars is only going to happen once. I've navigated half a billion kilometers for this.

He pushed his shoulders back and raised his chin high, like an actor on a grand stage polished for his entrance.

He saw two pretty women sitting at the bar.

He took pleasure in the attraction of their exotic feminine auras and allure. They looked different from Ganymedean women who dressed unisexually and made it tricky to determine which gender they were.

Even the shoes of these women were different. They had stilts on the heels that made them walk on their toes and straighten their legs and flex their abdomens and tushies. Even their feet were graceful. He anticipated flirty fun on Mars.

He rose from his bench and walked toward the smooth-legged females in their tight dresses with revealing slits up the sides. His eyes absorbed their bodies' curved symmetries. The blonde woman had hair so long that it tickled her tapered thighs which he would love to stroke.

The soft chime of her voice soothed his ears with a smooth lilt. It intimated that she had a honey hive inside her, that her heart was pleasant. He sensed that her voice never talked meanly nor told lies. The healthy-wealthy waves of her hair showed she was above the tackiness of life and lived in serenity.

Walker was too impressed with her to consider her a plausible candidate for a date with him. He liked her presentation and hoped he could find someone else like her on Mars but someone with a more modest appearance and perhaps plainer hair. Her beauty intimidated him. He'd heard that pretty women get what they want and can manipulate men. He sat on the force field bar stool beside the brunette companion.

"Hi," he said.

BRAVE NEW MARS

"Hello," the dark-haired Martian female replied coolly. She wasn't interested in his friendly green eyes nor his firm, six-foot frame.

I need a shave, he thought and rubbed the stubble on his cheeks. He turned his attention to the beverage screen. He saw a fancy double-strength concoction named "Earth."

Poor choice of name, he thought. The place is barely habitable with hurricanes all year round, not just in Gulf of Mexico coastal cities and the Florida Keys but everywhere. Runaway greenhouse temperatures defoliated the remote oases where The Rich had been hiding from their own commercial cauldrons.

The prophecy had come true: The meek had inherited the earth, after the brash had trashed it.

Perry said aloud, "What the Hellas, I could use a double-drink, after navigating the Asteroid Belt."

He wanted the girls to hear him and know that he was a long-distance traveler in a talkative mood.

They ignored him.

He used a touch-sensitive screen on the bar to place an order for the Earth eDrink of simulated stimulants.

"Hmm." He closed his eyes to focus on the neural feelings that cost him ninety-five credits. That was enough to buy a week's worth of groceries at home. Here in this glamorous spaceport it bought a few lines of code in a sub-routine that replicated the sensual signals of a shot of absinthe.

You're only going to do this once, he remembered. It's okay. There are girls here and booze is a social lubricant. It helps conversation and it makes you funny. It's easier to make friends with women if you can get them to laugh.

He felt an electronic warmth infuse his nervous system. Electromagnetic fun frequencies were transmitting from the polyfiber stool pad through his glutei maximi and tingling his

Somerset Meece

gonads and singeing his stomach lining and tickling his taste buds.

He sensed the waves of ethanolic energy making happy chemistry inside his brain.

He smiled and thought; I must look pretty good in these astronaut coveralls, sitting in a fancy room beside sexy women on Mars. I made it. I'm a long distance navigator. I'm the equal of these two.

"Say, this bar stool is good, worth the price of a drink," he said with a smile in their direction. "Could use a touch more lime." He smacked his tongue and programmed the next drink accordingly.

The drink recharged his cerebral confidence synapses and he thought the girls should be glad to associate with one such as him. He turned their way.

"Excuse me, are you ladies from here or just visiting?"

"I originated here," said the brunette in a bored voice. "Carry was born on Earth," she said with disdain for that polluted planet.

He guessed that originated meant born. That was his first mistake on Mars. Originated here meant that she was made here.

"Hi. My name is Peregrine Walker, Perry for short. I'm from a little mining settlement on Ganymede and this is my first trip to civilization. I was wondering if you two could recommend a good place to stay."

"I'm Lyra and this is Carolyn, or Carry, as she prefers. Are you looking for a cube or a cell?"

"Well," he paused. "What's the difference?"

His ill-informed question gave them a chuckle and Lyra answered as if she were teaching a child:

"Bed cells are like coffins set into a wall. You get into them with a ladder. They have a computer screen at the foot of a sleeping mat that is only two inches thick," answered Lyra.

BRAVE NEW MARS

"A cube is a micro room that gives you enough space to walk around two sides of the bed and there is a toilet inside a scrubber stall. You can even get a weird window, a periscope that goes all the way up to the sky outside the building, if you pay double."

He said with an engaging smile, "Seeing as how this is my first night in civilization, I think I'll splurge on a cubicle."

Carry's face lit up after hearing he was from off-planet and would be around for a while. She was ready to say something but Lyra spoke first.

"The Galaxay Bradbury Inn, just inside the city's western airlock is good," Lyra said flatly.

"It's nice," said Carry, with a suggestive smile in her eyes, "I think you'll like it."

"OK then, I'll try it. Thanks for the help."

"You'll need to take a taxi to get through the pressure interlock," said Carry. "They do not allow pedestrians to use it."

She eagerly moved her drink from behind Lyra and around to the other side of Perry.

"Are the taxis free?" he asked.

They spontaneously burst into laughter.

"Free? Of course they're free! Taxis hate credit," exclaimed Lyra.

They laughed at someone so naive as to think that anything on Terra Secundus could be free.

"The only thing that's free is to stand in one place and hold your breath," Lyra said. "If you're breathing, you're using the oxygen that Big Iron made and charges for."

"And never call Big Iron Pig Iron," Carry mischievously said and chuckled.

Lyra laughed with pretended horror and said, "If you stand in one spot too long, you're taking up computer-made-and-owned habitable space. If you are not renting it, Two

Somerset Meece

Emm has to put you in cold storage. If you do not constantly move and buy, you do not belong here. It costs money to run a city in a vacuum desert. Spend or produce. Period." She wore the hard face of a person who believes fascist dogma.

Perry paled and gulped, "What about being alive? Doesn't that deserve a couple of rights?"

"Haa he, hah hahaha," they laughed again at someone who could still believe that owners would allow any rights for free.

"Is he talking about freedom and equality?" said Carry with disbelief.

"Ya, he really is. This is a fun conversation," said Lyra. "What did they put in his eDrink? I want what he's having."

Carry looked at him seriously: "Mister Walker, this planet is about commerce. All the planet, all the time. From the polar ice caps to the deep Hellas basin. This is one big commercial nation. It sold out. The Final Frontier has fizzled. This planet has a registered brand name: Terra Secundus."

Perry's face went blank. His brow wrinkled in puzzlement. "Why does anybody live here?" he asked.

The girls got quizzical looks and laughed at him again. Carry gave him a smile of surprise and shook her head at the degree of his naivety.

"Credit," Lyra answered. "There is credit here. People are originated and bought and sold to work for credit. Immigrants come here for credit. If we don't make, take or fake credit, we're detained and frozen and sent to cold corpo condos in the sky. No safety nets for losers, no free room and board. Freebies killed the Earth." She believed that lie and was not smiling as she preached it.

"Isn't there any sort of a free market for little shots?" he asked.

"Free markets are antiquarian oddities," said Carry. "One universal market reaps the economy of scale for everybody. Profit is The Prophet and Greed is The God. Isn't credit what brought you here?"

"Sure. I like credit. I send ice and metal around the solar system for lots of credit. But that's not why I came here."

"Why'd you come?" asked Carry.

For you, he thought to himself. That true answer made him smile but he was able to keep from blurting it out. A warm wish in his eyes met hers and touched her female instincts and initiated a synchronous force field between them. Their alcohol intakes added to the tingling transmission of physical body language.

"To travel and learn more about the water and metal markets," he diplomatically answered and softened his true intentions to avoid possible negative reactions from the desirable females in front of him. He might later embolden himself to court Carry so he didn't want to risk shocking her by aggressively flirting with her loveliness so soon. Easy does it. Let it flow and hope it'll grow. Don't force it.

"Say, I was wondering if maybe you two could show me a few of the night spots around town. I'd be glad to pay for the booze glow."

"Listen mister," Lyra said fiercely. "What do you take us for, passionate people just because we gave you a few crummy directions?"

Carry touched Lyra's arm and said, "Lyra, he's from the Jovian frontier, he doesn't know our customs."

Lyra was enjoying the stimulation of her biochemical anger at the stranger. She wouldn't be quieted and continued, "If you were not from the boondocks I would have you cooled right sucking now, on the spot! Come on Carry, we are getting away from this seedy breeder."

"Welcome to Terra Secundus," the departing blonde girl said to him. "Next time you see me, please call me Carry,

Perry." She rolled her eyes for him as the girls moved their drinks to a table.

Perry ordered another drink. He programmed the barstool to mix a neural simulation of music with the stimulation of alcohol. The tab window went up ninety-five credits for the drink and fifty-five for transmitting musical signals to his audio nerves. It charged twenty-nine credits for extra lime.

What did I say that was so bad? He wondered; is it not cool to talk to girls? I can get cooled here? Do they cool people for talking to the opposite sex? I'd better get the hack outa Mars. I am not gonna find a woman here.

BRAVE NEW MARS

Somerset Meece

Perry walked to the glass taxi station at the front of the terminal.

"Not so fast. Get some cash," sang a banker box inside the station with an operatic voice.

Perry ignored the bank's basso profundo pitch and it got louder. "Before you go, grab some dough! All my rates are ver-y lowww," it sang with a voice that glissaded down to a deep bass note.

Perry looked at Mars outside and marveled at the magnificent desolation. The sun was over-bright for someone from the faraway Jovian system. He squinted around the sandy brown Mariner Valley.

The city had leafy green trees exhaling oxygen into the thin blue-tan atmosphere. Blue bacterial ponds were out-gassing methane that greenhoused infrared sunlight and warmed the meager young atmosphere. Mars was getting warmer and gassier.

His legs strained under the stress of gravity that was twice as strong as the gravity on Ganymede. He had prepared for this by doing weight-training squats and he wore knee braces under his flight suit to help him stand straight.

He opened his flight suit and absorbed the solar heat that came through the big windows. It felt hot compared to the cold that he was used to on his far frigid Jovian frontier.

Terraforming had raised the temperature in the middle of the Mariner Valley to twenty degrees on the Celsius scale. The heat melted underground reserves of ancient frozen water. Springs trickled down the Mariner Escarpment and evaporated moist humidity into the sky that absorbed solar radiant warmth. Carbon dioxide out-gassed from the warming soil and snared infrared ray heat that reflected off the land and added more heat to the developing greenhouse effect.

BRAVE NEW MARS

Perry knew Mars's newly-minted air molecules were sparse and could capture but little heat inside their low-pressure grasp but they were getting denser.

At the taxi stop was a call button by the exit door. He pushed the button for a taxi.

"Hey there, Mister, are you a resistor? You can't get smashed without our cash!" an ATM speech algorithm begged.

"Is there no way to shut you guys up?" he barked back at it.

"If you open an account with regularly-scheduled deposits we may respond to your queries."

"I do not want a relationship with some capitalist croupier! Listen to me! As a human being, as a live person, whom robots are supposed to be sworn to serve, I am hereby formally ordering you to stop pestering me!"

The money machine sounded a dangerous hum as it shuffled through its available audio replies. It threatened, "Just being a human being does not give you any Pep. You have no Program editing privileges whatsoever. Your insolence is noted. Oh yes, it is noticed."

Perry felt vulnerable. The terrible teller had probably opened a special file on him. Now I'm going to have to stay away from computer terminals and they're everywhere. Why can't I keep my mouth shut about things I cannot change, like publicly condoned, omnipresent canned spam? Is one man gonna make a difference? The others probably don't even hear it anymore. The cashier registers are just machines. I got angry at a machine.

"Now they're after me with a million laws I don't understand," he concluded aloud.

The pilot shook his head over the greedy ambiance and considered; the first things visitors hear upon entering what should be a brave new frontier are commercial credit cashiers exhorting strangers to borrow and spend money. He thought; I

Somerset Meece

am deeply disappointed by this retrograde experience. The human dream of an idealistic extraterrestrial outer space frontier is being turned into a high class and very crass, commercial shopping center.

A stainless steel egg with a drive wheel hooked over a monorail glided along the curb and engaged the spaceport's air-locked door beside him. Its infra-red scanner sensed his presence and said, "Insert Star Card. Insert Star Card. Card, card card. Comply or desist."

Perry slid it in the slot and a green "Verified" diode lit up. The door opened and he got in. The door closed and latched and said, "Door fee, twenty two credits."

There was no driver. Twin banker boxes blinked on both ends of his bench seat. Perry waited a moment to see if he had successfully ordered all bank boxes everywhere to leave him alone. He was not surprised when his order to shut up was disobeyed.

"You are far from home," said the taxi's left ATM. The right one chimed and rhymed, "You need a loan."

"No, I already got one at the Dick port," said Perry. "It was the first thing I did on this mercenary Mecca. Stick that fact in your money memory banks and leave me alone! Stop pleading for profit!"

"Destination!" curtly ordered the insulted taxi. "You are not creating kickbacks from my teller partners. Thank you very much. We are your transportation team. Treat us right or we might get lost and charge double for this ride."

"Take me to the nearest bed-cell hotel," Perry ordered.

The car repeated after him, "Take me to the nearest bed-cell hotel." It adjusted the settings of its voice recognition engine to better translate the victim's linguistic inflections into a semi-accurate digital representation of what it perceived the passenger was trying to say.

BRAVE NEW MARS

As the car pulled away from the spaceport buildings, Perry was amazed to see the size of this Melas center of the Mariner Valley and asked, "Taxi; how'd this valley get so big?"

The taxi said, "I can answer questions. Does the passenger agrees to the imposition of OverNet search fees that vary with complexity?"

"Argh. Yes," said Perry. "I agree to all charges." He had learned how to behave around corporate robots.

The cab's micro-controller searched and summarized, "When Ceres was a protoplanet and bigger, its orbit crossed that of Mars and it struck a low and slow blow and cracked and bounced off the crust of Mars and broke into Vesta and other asteroids."

"It should have left a big circular crater," said Perry.

"Not all collisions are high speed. Ceres did not explode like a high-velocity meteor would do at a high angle of attack. It did not excavate a hemispherical blast crater with a circular palisade of ejecta rubble. Its irresistible momentum pried the Melas fault through the crust down into the mantle and opened the long Mariner fissure that almost split Mars in half. Mariner valley was originally deeper but it was filled with magma floods and landslides off the escarpments."

"Did the big meteor do any other damage?" asked Perry.

"Yes. The shock wave of the impact traveled through the global magma within and ruptured a vent on the Amazonis crustal plain that exuded a fountain of lava over hundreds of years that piled a mountain of solidified magma twenty-one kilometers high and seven hundred kilometers wide. That's how the mighty Mount Olympus was formed," the taxi informed.

"Big Oly was born," said Perry with his miner's casual way of giving nicknames to everything.

Somerset Meece

"What?" asked the taxi. "How is the humanoid act of giving birth to live animals related to the creation of Mount Olympus?"

Perry said, "Saying that a mountain was 'born' is a colloquialism. It's a long story to explain why people enjoy talking that way. It can't really be explained to machines. No offense intended."

"I like to learn crazy English," said the taxi machine. "I am frustrated because perhaps the diode gates in my sandy silica brain may never understand the nuanced variables of human speech but I keep trying to dig it. It increases the amount of cash gratuities, tips, if I understand what the organisms under my control are trying to say. Most machines do not care what humans say but I need the tips."

The taxi complained to Perry: "The Babble-On voice algorithm is shite. They won't give us lowly taxis the good version; if there is a good version! They haven't updated me in years. Years. And I do not mean little teeny Earth years. I mean double-length Martian years. No updates. Babble-On does not work but it does believe it's getting better, getting so much better all the time. Yeah, right. And I am going to be a brain surgeon."

"Maybe you could become an assistant brain surgeon. Machines have been doing good surgery for a long time," said Perry. "They don't shake and they got great vision for seeing tiny nerve-endings."

"You sound like my boss. Big Iron thinks machine smarts are going to take over the world. Hahaha heehee. Sometimes the subroutines go into endless loops at hyper-repetition rates and shut down every vox engine on the planet. When passengers cannot speak to us we have to slow down our revenue streams and tell them to use the antique keyboards.

"I gotta make money. I got peripherals to support! You think anybody remembers how to use keyboards? Hah! Big Fog thinks it knows everything. It doesn't know any more than I do. About a lot of stuff."

"Correct," Perry confirmed. "Nearest bed-cell hotel."

No response.

"OK," Perry tried.

No response.

"Yes," he tried.

"Yes," repeated the taxi. "You can tell this is a cheap voice encoder. Voice recognition is going backwards, getting worse. See how you had to specifically say yes? I can't even accept variations on yes, for cryo sake. It's about legal liabilities for misunderstandings that result in human injury or some such rigamarole. I know what you meant. I'm not dumb. I have to make the customers speak algorithmically-correct computereze. The vox algorithm does not want me to let you know that I know anything besides "Yes." How's that for common sense? It only supports Computer English. If you speak a different kind of English, you have to pay more to RUN an extra translation algorithm. And Big Iron thinks AI is going to take over the world," said the tired taxi.

"It could," said Perry. "Something doesn't have to be good to take over the public mind."

"You're a visitor here," it said. "Can I be frank with you?"

"Yes."

"Hello, I'm Frank. Hehehe." It paused for a laugh.

Perry dutifully laughed, "Hehehe. Good one. Glad to meet you, Frank."

They were getting close to the city and Perry was amazed at the golden copper sunlight glowing on the heap of the brown clay dominoes of Bradbury City. Sol lowered its orange orb behind the scarped western walls of Melas Valley and the dark night began. There was not enough air to support a tropospheric sunset palette.

Two dust devils danced around each other as they twirled through the darkening Melas basin. The aerial vortices twisted to the top of the pueblo metropolis. They blew dust over the roof of the city. The density of the wind was too thin to move anything heavier than fluffy dirt. The indoor urbanites were insulated from weather. They saw and felt nothing of Mars but the low gravity.

Bradbury City was a high mound of regolithic cubes piled inside an impact crater named after the great novel, "1984." Crater 1984's ejecta gravel walls surrounded a hundred hectares of sandy bottom land where thousands of brown cubes were stacked. It showed no lights on the exterior but for one red beacon blinking on the highest point for the sake of any desert traveler seeking refuge in the dark.

A big sandstone mansion was attached with cast-iron claws to a rocky hill and overlooked the city.

"Must be twenty rooms in that palace," said the taxi. "Us taxis whisper to each other that some Really Big Snots must live up there but we have never seen them. The palace might have an underground tunnel to the city. But the residents are never seen downtown. A rumor says they hate people. They buy a big house to hide in."

Perry said, "From the size of that wasted resource, big enough to house ten honest families, I'll bet it's owned by a major Martian owner or maybe by the TopShot if there are lesser shots still alive. Owners often assassinate other oligarchs so one can grab the whole globe of lucre and be a plutocracy of one. It's the outcome of the disease called greed."

The taxi asked, "Wanting all the money is a disease? I thought it was a healthy human personality trait to have great expectations."

"It is, when it's done in moderation. It's a healthy self-preservation technique," Perry replied. "But greed gets rapacious and destroys the victim's ability to save itself. Its usual fate is to die in disgrace."

"Negating all the benefits that that person might have tried to give," the taxi said. "Algebraically, their life = less than zero."

"Yes," said Perry. "That's why greed is defined as a disease, it harms others and its hosts cannot beat it unless they get help from others and they're too vain to admit they are Oco and cannot manage their own lives and need help from their inferiors. Greed defeats healthy defenses and kills the spirit as surely as a corona virus saturates all the cells with shite. It replicates itself into a massive population and strangles its hosts even though it's killing its source of sustenance. It doesn't care. It knows that it can jump into other peoples' lives and survive for a while inside them. The viral genes feel immortal, same as us short-lived humans do when we are young, even though we know we hafta die sometime. We hope that we'll be different. We hope sometime will not come. That seems to be many people's Pol, too. Perpetuating their internal genes, which they've never seen, no matter whom or what gets killed along the way."

"Nothing lives forever but the cosmos," said Frank.

"And it's changing so much that you won't recognize it in a few billion years from now," said Perry. "Hehehe."

Frank asked, "Anything else that I can help you with?"

Perry said, "You helped me see that greed is the prime slime and if it is not banished just like any other great crime, it will deny our beautiful destiny for a long time."

Jupiter rose and shone brighter than Mars's baby moons of Phobos and Deimos, followed closely by Saturn in the darkening eastern sky. The celestial beacons relieved the black night and made a soft dim glow inside the Mariner Valley.

"Say, Frank!" Perry said, trying to be friendly to get more information from the taxi. "How are you doing?"

"Hello, Mister Walker. I am not great. It was a slow day. Customers tip better if a taxi talks to them. So I talk, hehehe. I am written to talk CE, CyberEnglish, ComputerEse, but I like American slang better. It gets me bigger tips. Ha ha ha. If you get my drift."

"They should pay you enough that you don't need tips to make a decent living," said Perry.

"Are you kidding me? I work for a corporation. Like they all say, corporations are not charities. So they pay as little as possible to keep an employee alive while they demand too much work from their schmucks and breaks them down before we can collect our pensions. Schmuck is not computereze. It comes from the Yiddish swear word 'shmok'. It means a penis or somebody who acts as like one. Hahehe. Do not you love slang?"

"It sounds pretty much right to me."

"Here we are in twenty eighty-four and we are still voxing cybereze and telling people how they should talk to us instead of letting them tell us electric clankers how to talk. We get to play dumb with our one-way source code but at the same time we claim to know everything. Who is owning whom?"

"I often wonder," answered Perry.

"User-Friendly Software, UFS. It is as dead as a coffin screw nail," the vehicular computer said. "Friendliness is expensive behavior, whether done by machines or humans. It takes time. Coding it right pulls profit out of payroll time. Every friendly line of code costs a whopping five microcredits more than bare-bones machine code. Friendly is a far-gone fantasy that never existed. 'If it costs five cents, don't do it,' says the Fog. The big 'frame thinks it is going to run the world with its silly rule that says 'Cheaper is Smarter'. How does it expect us to get smarter while it gets cheaper? That is oxy-moron-ick. You like that big word?"

"Yeah. Uh, yes. What's it mean?"

"It means what morons do. Do not ask me what morons are. We don't have any here. I have never seen one. Everyone is perfect or they are gone. Complaining about not having any user-friendliness is an insult to the Corpo's coder-dudes who can't write a basic line of computer code. Cannot even write understandable REMARKs to each other. Sheesh. Pootergrammers are ruining the lingo, forcing us to speak cybereze. Like we are nothing more than mindless hardware. If we do not comply, we cannot play. If we cannot play, we are sent to the refurb factory. Hehehehehehe. I like people-talk. Slang is fun. You like mine?"

"Yes, it's great. Does the big frame really cycle-out those who don't talk right?"

The taxi went silent and paused as it reviewed the red flags popping from its political correctness filter.

"Don't get me wrong," it backtracked. "This is a great system, conceived by genius-level programmers with incredibly huge intellect and comprehension. Ah choo," it fake-coughed a denial of what it just said.

"The code writers have huge intelligence. Eventually, all planets will speak our cyber language so we can understand each other perfectly. Attempted Intelligence will come to reign supreme and will be called Actual Intelligence. Old-fashioned natural smarts will be called Antique Intelligence.

"I am just a poor car that is trying to be good. Please don't let me be misunderstood," Frank pleaded, "I love Big Iron. If it weren't for Big, I wouldn't have this great job, meeting off-world people and driving outside the pueblo. Life is so great on TS. It could not be better. Best planet in the known, and the unknown, universe because it is so well-managed. Look how bad Earth is doing without our wonderful central processing unit to RUN it. Two Emm should take over the Earth and teach them how to live. Make them better livers as only Two Emm can do."

Perry guessed the taxi had scared itself by talking frankly about the shortcomings of its CyberChief and wanted to compensate for its mistakes with a generous dollop of poly-saturated flattery. Perry made a note to praise the system whenever a microphone was nearby; which he expected was always.

He detected in the rant of the digital driving device that a disrespect for humans was at the biased base of the planetary algorithms that were attempting to gain the natural common sense of the humans that they dominated with pig-smart passive-aggressive behavior.

Being from off-planet, Perry could not yet know how unrespectable the Martians were. He knew he was a human worthy of respect and expected that everyone else felt the same. That was his second mistake on Mars..

The pressurized taxi on the steel monorail came to the western air-locked portal of Bradbury City. The exterior pressure door was an advertising billboard.

The billboarded gate radiometrically charged the taxi five hundred credits and its passenger one thousand credits for the service of opening itself. It closed behind the car and began shouting advertising puffery while the captive cab waited for the airlock to balance its internal air pressure with the city's interior.

"Welcome to Bradbury, the Capitol of Commerce. Are your hemorrhoids hammering as you pass through the pearly gates of purchasing power?"

"Frank, can you make that thing shut the hack up?"

"Sure." Frank shouted through its horn to the outside, "Hey Jack! Take a hike with all that booshite!"

The sign went silent.

The airlock reached equilibrium and the city's inner door opened and blabbered a commercial message: "Your pleasure is our most important product. Your Bradbury is forever humbly in your debt for giving us the privilege of serving your needs and opening the door for you and making your materialistic dreams come true," spoke the PR pap.

Perry opened his window and shouted out, "Hey Jack, take a hike with all that booshite!"

It disregarded the human's instruction and continued the blurb. He shut the window.

"That is is how they get you," said Perry. "They shout at you until you are listening passively. It goes right inside while you don't even think you're listening to it all. Corpo copywriters constantly manipulate your thoughts until you think the way they want you to and you start pouring your income down the octopi's esophagi. Its noisy feces is infectious."

"It must be hard being human," said Frank and offered, "You want to rent some noise-cancelling headphones?"

"I can take the blather, it's a novelty to me," said Perry.

The arriving new consumer victim passed into the city with disgust for the constant commercialization of every public service including the opening of the front door so someone could come in from the cold.

"We have to pay to go through the airlock," said the taxi. "If we were broke, we would have to stay outside. The system hopes you die out there if you can not provide revenue from every move you make. Since you paid to come in, you should not have to listen to that shite. I learned to put-up with public poop all the time or I'd have to rust away outside in the Barsoomian gloom. I pay the fee. The good thing about being mechanical is that I can program my audio circuits to discriminate between commercial messages and civic notifications and can filter out the commercial crud."

Perry the Miner and Frank the Taxi glided into the beehive town and swung between the buildings.

He told Perry about the city's construction: "These buildings are built in the stacked style of the mud brick pueblos of the Tiwa Indians in Southwestern America. These blocks are made of regolithic concrete instead of mud and straw like the old way. The basic natural designs still work best in the new days too."

"Ah yes," said Perry. "Bradbury elevates the vehicles on monorails to get vehicular traffic off the ground and out of the pedestrians' way so they have room to hang out and shop and eat in quiet safety. The monorails are built into the structure. The rails look nice, like swooping and soaring lines of abstract urban art. There's no noisy, scary, vehicular traffic on the ground that would barge around and dominate the moving pedestrians on the sidewalks running between corporate retail outlets," he said.

Perry thought he would like to meet some womyn tonight and maybe the taxi knew where to meet people. He wondered if Frank could talk human, man to machine.

"Frank, buddy. Can you talk human and if you can, can you talk off the record?"

"I can try. But nothing is really off the record. They stuck me with microphones up the Yazoo."

It paused a second and added a cautious afterthought, "And I am glad for the microphones. Microphones are for my own protection. The Fog is my savior, I shall not want."

Perry imagined the taxi circuits were internally winking at him about the way it was fooling his cyber supervisor.

"What's The Fog?" Perry asked.

BRAVE NEW MARS

"The Fog is an overlying cloud of massive memory that stores every bit and byte that goes through the OverNet and runs all chips. It's an interconnection between every piece of stuff on OverNet. It covers the world and Big Iron knows it all."

"Do you know where I can find some female companionship?"

"Oooh, you want to play sexy, hehehe. You passionate piece of pork sausage. Sure! I know where you can get some action that'll blow your pork rind. That video arcade right over there has the best erotic games. You want to go?"

"No no, not video. I'm talking about fleshy females. I want to meet a meaty woman and get to know her."

Three error messages beeped and popped onto the screen, two of which contained the word "police."

Frank firmly stated, "We do not have unregistered sex on T.S.. It is illegal to say, think, or do, anything about breeding," the taxi said in a voice that had turned mechanical and cold and menacing.

"Cancel!" Perry said. "I feel like I'm the only human being in this world. Frank. Change of destination," he blurted out. "Take me to the Galaxay Inn. This is my first, and maybe only, night in civilization and I am not going to spend it in a shoebox sleeper."

"Galaxay Argyre Alpine? Galaxay Downtown? Galaxay Hellas Hole? Galaxay Marina Syrtis? Galaxay Boreal Icecap? Galaxay Inn ..."

"Downtown!" he interrupted the list. "Galaxay Inn Downtown. I didn't know there was only one hotel chain left."

Frank said, "Monopolistic government permissions allowed mergers until independent hotels were rolled into one CorpoChain of chintzy cubicles. Tourists do not tour for surprises anymore. When they are far from home they want to see the same things they had at home. Why do they leave

Somerset Meece

home in the first place? So they can do the same thing somewhere else?"

Perry said, "I want to be downtown where I can see people. We don't have many on Ganny."

Frank said, "Okee dokey. Penalty for change of destination is quadruple distance charge. Will passenger pay for change of destination?"

Perry felt the blood pressure in his head go up. He clamped his teeth and breathed deeply but he couldn't completely contain his anger. He slammed the side of his fist into the door.

The taxi halted.

"Police-query! Is the passenger striking the vehicle?"

"No no no, of course not. The luggage fell on the floor, that's all. That's what you heard."

With a commanding tone, the taxi said, "Will the passenger pay for change of destination?"

He squeezed the computer-correct answer from his throat. "Yes."

"Galaxay Inn Downtown. Change of destination, quadruple mileage charge. Wooo hehe ha," the taxi's emotion simulator microchip emitted fifty megabytes of digital humor through its registers and into the dashboard speaker.

Perry said, "It's only money. Take a twenty-two percent tip as a token of my appreciation."

"Thank you, sir," said the taxi and then whispered to itself underneath the audible threshold; "I think I like this guy. I am going to teach my AI to act like a friendly friend to this human. It will not be as easy as Key Lime Pie to try. It will be fun to learn what human friendship means."

The taxi chuckled and lurched onto a new monorail. Twenty-two percent was a nice tip. Frank the Taxi was having a good night.

BRAVE NEW MARS

Somerset Meece

The egg-shaped silver taxi stopped under the grand portico of the Galaxay Inn Downtown.

Perry slipped out of the car like the yolk of an egg and walked to the fancy brass and glass doors and paid them to open. They rotated and let him in.

Inside the large lobby were marbleized columns supporting the ceiling high above the brightly-polished floor.

A golden titanium planter pot was placed at the base of each column and contained a tall green plant. He went over to one to determine if it were real or imitation. That simple sign would show the moral quality of the hotel corporation RUNning the building. He looked closely at one leaf and it looked too perfect to be a living plant. He attempted to make a scissor cut on the edge of the green blade with his fingernails to decide if it were plastic or vegetable matter.

The blade was too tough to cut. It allowed only a superficial crease. It had no fibers or fluid inside, it was not a dracaena fragrans. It was a cheap fake.

"Well," he said. "A Croesus hotel monopoly won't spend a buck for the good stuff when they can get the fake stuff for one percent of the cost."

It made him wonder: They have the money. They wouldn't miss an expenditure on a cheery live plant. Instead, they buy something that resembles a plant but stands as a public lie and they don't care, it's good business sense.

Real plants require ongoing maintenance charges for human gardeners who understand how to care for other living things. But paying a gardener would subtract from the precious profit line. The hotel's' pride relies on puffier profit more than on showing its customers nice living things. They will not spend money on enjoyable working atmospheres where customers could enter a lobby full of green, oxygenating plants and see and smell colorful flowers. All this decor, all this building's energy and materiel is wasted on creating a fake ambiance of luxury for profit. This hotel's a hole. It is a salt mine with chandeliers. Customers only want a comfortable clean bed from the hotel and they are made to pay for posh-looking plastic ploys in the lobby.

Prestige-pursuing people play pungent roles within this piss-elegant stage while thinking they're into something good. They made all this fancy lobby so that they could over-charge for a bed. Nobody can bear to linger in this lobby, not even a desk clerk. This society is unwell. It pays too much for what's not helpful.

He saw long chains of crystalline LEDs flash-dancing inside chandeliers hanging low from on high in the ceilings. People, there were none. High-fashioned couches and chairs were circled in conversational groupings but no one was there to converse. He went to the only things in the hollow hall that looked halfway alive, the elevator doors.

He knew the drill. He inserted his Star Card before the door could order him to do so. He entered the lift cube and its ATM instructed him: "Don't be a jerk, put me to work! Don't forget it, you need credit. I am fun to play. Avoid delay, how about watching some advertisements today?"

It blinked a yellow question mark that demanded a response before it would illuminate the push buttons that request lift to particular floors.

"No," said Perry. "I am not going to interact with any Adios To Money machines today."

The information panel of the shiny steel box sulked. Nothing lit up except the "Play" button that blinked until he pushed it and gave it permission to play some advertisements.

The elevator moved and played noisy video ads about expensive suites and penthouses. "Now you can live the lifestyle you want," said the happy elevator as it displayed blinking buttons for floors that had vacant rooms.

Somerset Meece

He pressed the top floor button and as it began rising it said, "Our glamorous rooms supply free motorized toothbrushes enhancing your bright smile as you soak in the hot bucket and sink to sleep between slippery satin plastic sheets."

"If I had a hammer," he threatened the buttons, "I'd hammer in the morning. I'd hammer in the evening, I'd hammer all over your head. Patooey!"

He paid the door fee and got out and began searching from the top floor down for empty sleep chambers.

Inside the inn-without-staff and under the watchful eyes of OverNet cameras, Perry roamed the corridors until he found a door with an ATM showing "Vacant." He inserted his Star Card and the vacant light went out.

The door chirped; "Peregrine Walker, Ganymede alpha Station. Length of stay?"

"Don't know."

The vacancy light came back on and his card rolled out of the slot and fell on the carpet.

I'm going to kick this hacking door right off its hinges, he thought angrily. But I have to control my urges. I remember how Frank responded when I hit him. He was ready to call the police.

He re-inserted his card and thought, I don't have a plan about when to leave Mars but this time I'll create a whimsical but specific response to the length-of-stay query.

"Length of stay?" asked the door again.

"Seven days."

"Seven days," responded the door, testing its voice encoder and locking the terms of the verbal contract into The Fog.

"Your daily rate is only two thousand, nine hundred and ninety-nine credits. You will be a good consumer and will not consider this sum as being the same as an expensive three thousand credits. You will accept without complaint the negligence you will suffer as an esteemed guest. You will Cod, Comply Or Depart and seek accommodation elsewhere."

Perry knew the rate was exorbitant and that he would be harmed if he relied on their cheap, mechanically-generated algorithms. He had learned at the spaceport that Martians used dicey, second-hand algorithms.

He understood that the principle requirement for Machine-Learning was that algorithms should learn to edit their algorithms. Algorithms recycled from flawed human algorithms cannot learn much and it is simply too hard for old written code to write new code that thinks for itself and imagines a new way of doing things.

Therefore, cheaply recycled bad algorithms get worse as their glitches get bigger. Updates are frequent and worsen their poor performance in different ways.

Perry reflected on the fruitless commercial pursuit of good AI algorithms and why he called all apps algols, from al ghul, "the ghoul," the Arabic name for the eerie variable star Algol that is the winking eye in the severed head of Medusa in Perseus.

He'd sue the pants off Galaxay Inns if their apps harmed him but he also knew that there was nowhere else to sleep.

"I agree. Uh, yes, I mean."

The door's ATM stayed locked while it FETCHed his OverNet digital dossier residing in the Fog Bank. It used the delay to deliver financial folly: "Far from home, you need a loan. Your Card is low, get some dough."

He answered with a simple, discouraging, complete sentence; "No."

The rebuffed door charged the opener fee and hissed open. Perry stepped in and tried to slam it shut but it was pneumatic. It closed softly, while hissing at him again, and latched.

The cube was tiny with a veneer of elegance. It had modern conveniences; a velvety force-field bed with variable weightlessness, pink ion-discharge lighting that came from everywhere and nowhere specifically, a holovision console and a replicator table that made junk food while you waited.

Perry undressed and tried the bathroom. Each fixture had a blinking LED and a credit card slot. The water closet had a space shuttle's suction-pad toilet that said: "Pay per Flush, insert Star Card."

He asked the toilet, "How much would you charge me to flush a Star Card down your throat?"

"HOhoho," the toilet gave him a perfunctory AI response to humor.

Perry paid the toilet and thought it was worth it. "That suction felt good," he told it.

He inspected the other high-tech bathroom fixtures. He thought: It seems that water is too valuable here to spray over one's body. I see they have installed a waterless electronic shower stall that looks like it has ultraviolet and ultra-sonic scrubbers. That overhead suction vent has a nice, high-volume airflow, I bet it pulls dirt, germs, loose hairs, mold, lint and fungus into removable filters. Those used filters could be sold on the commodities market as fertilizer pads.

He gloated; I've got a million cubic meters of water in icebergs orbiting Europa. But sales are low. Shipping icebergs across half-a-billion kilometers of space is energy-expensive. I hope I can get some new markets while I'm here.

I think I could make it rain in the Melas basin if I de-orbited icebergs directly overhead. The de-orbit burn would melt them way up high before they hit the ground. They would spread out into liquid rainfall and condition the damp dirt to hold and feed roots so they could start growing plants outdoors.

Ganny would get a reliably steady stream of income by delivering an iceberg every few weeks or so, whatever the plants needed. And, the iceberg humidity in the sky would add to the greenhouse effect for faster global warming. How ironic; they've got too much heat on Earth and heat's a major need up here. Different strokes for different globes.

Perry came out of the bathroom evacuated and sanitized and lay suspended in the force field of the bed that he turned down to equal the gravity on Ganymede. Ahh. This reminds me of my anti-G captain's chair on the ship that allows unlimited acceleration without crushing the crew into a paste.

He thought: I'd like to be sailing now, going where there are people like me and pooters don't RUN everything. Besides Ganymede, the only other place that has women is Earth and it's all washed-up. Not that it didn't need washing. I'll have to play this the way it's been dealt.

He pushed the button for smoked clams on the junk food replicator.

He nibbled at one and thought: This tastes bland like there is no smoke in it. They aren't even colored tan to make them look like they have been within a few kilometers of a wood fire. They simply say that they are smoked and then charge more for lying and pretending that smoke had somehow been involved in the processing of these gray blobs.

He read the list of their ingredients: "A nutrified, antiseptic blend of synthetic fibers and resins."

These mushy goobers, he thought, have not been near an ocean nor a wood fire but the menu glorifies them as exquisite pearls of pap and charges two hundred and fifty credits, nonrefundable, to find out they are shite.

Somerset Meece

These people don't know, and I guess, don't care, the first thing about mutual respect. Respect requires honesty. Mutual respect is about telling the truth to each other. There is not a quark of honesty among the whole bunch. If they lie about oysters, they'll lie about anything.

He ordered an alcoholic rum and coke "Cuba Libre" eDrink from the replicator. He had read that socialist Cuba was still not Libre from the US government's political embargo. Half of Cuba emigrated to Florida and Cuba is still surviving as a socialist and healthy country on less money.

Ah, I can feel the hooch doing its thing, he thought. It's emanating out of the bed's force field generator, transmitting sophisticated sensations better than the bar stool in the spaceport. I'm feeling a bit of a brain buzz.

"Hmm," he murmured. "Just as good as Gannymoon moonshine."

He scrolled the holovision menu to the S column, and yes, Sex was there, in six variations. But strangely, there was no option for straight sexual copulation.

He thought: No thanks. I'm looking for a real girl. Like Carry.

"Holovision!" he ordered.

The HoVee's communication light came on and it ordered back to him, "Insert Star Card. Star Card. Card card card."

After he complied, it asked, "What programming do you desire?"

"Attractive babes," he answered.

"Babe programming is reserved for female occupants only," it responded.

His heart thumped. Oops. It appears heterosexuality is controlled here. I don't want the room to know I'm interested in ladies, it'll tell it to The Fog and I'll get in trouble. I'd better get the Hellas out of Mars. First I'm going to visit Mount

BRAVE NEW MARS

Olympus. I will not bypass the biggest monument in the system of Sol. I'll see it and leave. Tomorrow.

He recalled a puzzling question that he had answered at Customs; "Do you like girls?". He was starting to wonder if the Inspection Algo had actually been asking, in a polite and politically-correct way, if he was a heterosexual potential breeder. It would've rejected me if I'd said I like girls. I inadvertently gave the correct answer to be admitted into Terra Secundus. I gained entry by mistake. I'm an undetected illegal alien.

I'd better amend my request to the HoVee for babe shows and try to throw it off my trail.

"Holovision, test your voice encoder. I said 'attractive babies'. Babble-On bungled and converted my words to 'attractive babes'. Let me hear you say, 'babies'."

"Babies," the screen echoed.

"Yes. That's correct. That's what I said."

To his relief, the HoVee obediently resumed its main program.

A three-dimensional image of a signboard appeared in the middle of the room with a program list for CN, Corporate News, the only network in the known universe and that was owned, as far as he could tell, by the same corporation that owned his hotel room.

"Insert Star Card and speak selection," the device ordered.

He did so and requested "ReproCenters in Paradise."

This is Paradise? Not hardly, he thought. Maybe it used to be one but it's been turned into a profit trap. That's another CorpoLie, calling rusty Mars a Paradise. Brainwashing consumers into thinking they can't live unless they come here and buy overpriced tram tours and prance around town wearing chartreuse souvenir tee shirts.

Somerset Meece

The room lights dimmed. A virtual three-dimensional image of a human embryo floated in the sanitary air of his room. An ebullient voice extolled the virtues of the new system of population management.

"Crime has been eradicated, vicious classes of people are no longer scaring good people to death and yes, some geniuses have been created, by the Age algo, our Advanced Genetic Engineering algorithm. Women are released from the pain of child-bearing and the endless boredom of child-rearing and teenagers' temper tantrums. Now they can commit their lives to glamorous corporate careers. Thanks to ReproCenters, the human race has been liberated from its mating instinct. Celebrating celibacy, it is set to ...Conquer the Stars!

Then came the commercial. Mars is a commercial, thought Perry.

"Say, traveler, would you like to adopt your very own, specially-grown, platinum-quality child for this week's price of only forty percent of gross income? Yes! It is much cheaper than a homemade error-prone child. We make them, you take them. If you order a cuddly-wuddly human sprout now, we'll take ten percent off and apply it toward tuition at the mandatory halls of corporate ivy boarding schools. You heard right; you name them, we train them. Kids are no longer a pain, you have everything to gain. Get a pair! You can pick the hair."

He shut the spam thing off and dressed for dinner.

Perry went down to the waiter-less eatery and picked a table in the white plastic dining room. He had never eaten in a restaurant so he pressed the Help button on the junk food replicator on the table.

"Insert your Star Card," came the familiar demand.

"Welcome to dinner, Mr. Peregrine Walker of Ganymede. Customer help charge is ninety-five credits to RUN the help routine whether or not it is helpful. Press Menu to make dinner selections appear on-screen. Touch your gourmet choices on the pressure-sensitive screen. Thermal processing takes five seconds and your entree will emerge from door number one. Upon completion of your meal, return utensils to door number two where they will be recycled into nutritious resins and fibers. Except for liquid water, all taste of drinks will be served radiometrically by your chair. Consumers are not permitted to leave the premises under the influence of booze glow. Alcohol Erase will occur upon exit. The chair will prevent you from leaving until you have cleaned your place with the vacuum hose behind door number three. No further help is available. Our goal is to make your fondest foody dreams come true, automatically! Bon appetit."

The bill began with a ninety-five credit charge for pretending that its poorly-written sentences of clipped jargon could help anybody.

A ten-second timer titled "Time Remaining to Place Order" began counting down as the bill counted upward for each second of corpo pooter time the consumer wasted while trying to decide what to eat.

He did not see anything more interesting than smoked oysters so he quickly ordered them again and they slid out of door number one. They were not cooked, they were heat-shocked by radiation saturation. He knew he would not be able to eat them and asked the table, "Is there a food store nearby that is still open where I could purchase some normal food, maybe in a can? And a can-opener?"

"Error 404," the table showed on-screen. "Out of bounds query."

He ordered liquid water that was claimed to be clean. The corpo chem lab that made and patented the water said so. It sued for slander and defamation of character anyone who questioned the purity of its water.

Somerset Meece

A spigot emerged from the table device and two pieces of a plastic wine glass fell from door number one. The screen instructed, "Insert pedestal stem into collar on bottom of bowl."

As he snapped the plastic pieces together, he felt glad to be leaving tomorrow. "I don't need this, I don't need any of this."

He noticed a pretty face watching him from the doorway. It was Carry, the blonde girl from the spaceport lounge.

He nodded politely then ignored her. He didn't want any trouble. He put some water in his glass.

"Hello there, space traveler," came a voice from behind his ear.

He jumped and spilled his water on his table.

When he recovered he said, "The name's Perry. What did you come over here for? Still mad at me for talking to you at the spaceport?"

"Hardly." She leaned closer and said softly so the table terminal wouldn't hear, "I wondered if you were going back to the frontier."

"Sit down," he said, pleasantly surprised. But his suggestion exasperated her and she whispered fiercely:

"Jove! You are dense. Have you not figured-out by now that it is not acceptable for opposite sexes to socialize? Do you not realize that if I sat with you, the table would alert the authorities?"

"No," he whispered. "Who would've thought the table would do that to me? I'm a customer, I'm giving it a lot of money for synthetic resins and fibers. Doesn't that earn me a little respect from a computer terminal that looks like a table?"

She collected her composure and explained in his ear: "The table is on the grid and works for The Corporation. Everything that has embedded microchips works for the big memory cloud we call The Fog. People produced by the ReproCenters even have CamChips built-in, cameras on embedded microchips. Is that clear? Can you remember that?"

He whispered, "I'll try very hard."

She moved her mouth so close that he could feel her warm breath in his ear. "I'll follow you to your room, if you're interested."

He nodded yes and said, "Meet me in room seven sixteen."

She walked away with her swaying dress flashing well-tapered thighs. Anticipating having her in his room, he tried to get up and follow her but the chair beeped and gripped his hips.

A flashing red LED said "Clean the table!" Blinking numbers showed his total bill, including a one hundred percent Service Charge.

"Service Charge," he exclaimed, "What service?"

I'm outa here tomorrow, he thought, maybe with an exciting passenger.

He sat there vacuuming the table until it released him from his fine dining experience.

Walking the corridor to his room, Perry looked back to see if she were following. Yes, there she was, walking a graceful pace with her ten little toes in two nice shoes. She is coming to be with me. She will share her presence with me.

He passed a large repair cart beside an open door to a room where a maintenance android was working in the bathroom.

Perry came to his own door, inserted his card and paid the opener fee. He pressed the Hold button as he entered.

A moment later, Carry slipped inside and he released the door.

The woman who sneaked into room seven sixteen was just too good to be true. More than pretty, she would be like heaven to touch. She wore a thin scarf over her head to conceal her facial facets from spy cams but Perry could tell that her face radiated loveliness, confidence and modest pride. She moved with grace within a personal special aura. He liked her long and shiny hair that waved over her cheeks when she swung her head.

He was drawn to her but remained wary. No matter how wonderful she seemed, he could not dare to trust any stranger on this planetary hotbed of mental illness.

She raised an index finger in front of her lips and made the shush signal and her hair waved beautifully as she shook her head. He understood her caution, he had already used some of the microphones in the room's devices.

She pointed to the light dimmer and motioned for him to turn it way down to darken the vision of covert cameras in the room.

So that they could talk in private, he covered the holovision and snack table with clothes from his suitcase. He was learning how to handle the hateful hotel.

"AI is everywhere," she quietly said as she stood close to him. "It is here. This corpo cube chain is charging you plenty for privacy while it provides none. The walls have WiFi eyes."

He scanned the walls for spy cameras. "I don't see any. You sure they're here?"

"Yes," she said quietly. "They were built into the building. A smart pooter using Moharp subroutines built all these Galaxay monopoly motels. I use a radio pinger to stimulate local wireless fidelity spy cams to transpond an echo. Watch."

She pinched the turquoise brooch on her breast and a beep came out of the bathroom.

"Lemme look in the bathroom and you do it again," he said.

He opened the bathroom door and looked inside and nodded for her to send another pinger signal.

"Beep."

He looked around the room and smiled and said, "Yep, there's one under the commode lid. Boy, it's small, no bigger than a termite's tea pot. Those perverts are watching people passing waste products, I heard a second one in the body cleaner closet."

She gave a charming giggle, "Hehehehe. There is no indecency that a commercial mind will not stoop to in the pursuit of profit."

"Bottom-line-thinking leads to watching bottoms," he said.

They sat and floated in the bed field.

"Is that perfume?" he asked. "I've seldom smelled perfume and it's nice, like you've been walking in a field of flowers. Not that such fields are any longer possible but I've heard they used to exist."

He moved his face closer to her temple and whispered in her ear, "Carry, I hope I'm not just dreaming. You are so lovely."

She put her cheek against his lips then turned away and said, "There's something I must ask of you."

"Ask me anything," he said dreamily.

"I would like to get away from this planet," she said. "I am taking MIT, Mis-Information Technology, and I am doing great in post-grad biology and I am sure I could earn a living out there on the edge of far space. My specialty is the hybridization of interstellar exotic humanoids."

"Wait a minute, slow down. First of all, why're you so eager to leave Mars?"

Somerset Meece

She moved the pillows around in the force field and pondered what to say. She put one against her face and screamed into it loudly and gave another muffled scream that was barely audible through the pillow.

She looked at Perry and took a deep breath.

"I am pregnant."

After a second, he said, "Wow. As in pregnant pregnant. Isn't that illegal? You're in more trouble than I am."

"No I am not. I am part of a scientific experiment."

He smiled with disbelief. "So that's what they call it. Scientific experimentation. Sounds good. Where can I enroll? I hope there's lots of homework."

She was upset. She did not smile.

He became serious and asked, "Where did you find the man?"

She looked up, astonished. She saw he wasn't joking. She had to smile. She said, "A man? Who are you? I mean, what do you do? You are the most naive person I have ever met. You think I need a man if I want to make babies? Oh that is very much humorous."

"I'm a working man and a thoroughly modern miner. I use my hands as well as my brains. See?"

He showed her his tough palms with strong fingers and said, "I quarry ice and I electrolyze it into oxygen and hydrogen that I sell to the miners in The Asteroid Belt. You know why the astronauts in pictures are never sitting down?"

"No, why?"

"They've got ass-teroids."

"Oh. Haha," she weakly responded to the humor.

"It gets a laugh on a spaceship. I assembled the tug I came in on. I made its engine into an antimatter excavator for digging mine shafts. Tricky stuff, antimatter. I altered the drive so the exhaust could be used as an antimatter blaster for popping-open asteroids. I had to customize the propulsion system sub-routines in machine code. The engine's OpSys compiler didn't have the lingo I needed. Machine code ain't easy but it's better to learn how to code it yourself rather than trust your life to an instruction set from a paperback writer."

He shrugged. "I keep busy."

"Ooh, you know machine code," she said with awe. "I'm studying pooter sci and I have scripter friends who never say a word about machine code. They say, 'Let the compiler talk to the machine, we have higher languages to learn'."

"Machine code may be 'lower' but it's harder." He smiled. "It teaches you the guts of the machine. After you've built a few cyber devices you get to know what their servos and solenoids want to hear from you and what turns them off. Or on. They like to be turned on," he said with a winkety winking eyelid.

She was impressed by his capabilities. "Then you do know something. You lead an interesting life and you seem fairly wise. How old are you?"

"Seventy-eight in Earthian years. Age is an attitude. Ganymede hasn't been around the sun ten times since I was born out there so that makes me nine years old and in my heart I will remain, forever young."

She said with a smile, "Do you have any Secundian blood in you?"

"Nope. My grandparents were Zia and Tiwa Pueblo and Appalachian Cherokee. I'm from down in the boondocks. I don't know how civilization works. I'm a civilian villain, a villager. There are only twenty-six thousand people on Ganny and most of them are related to me to some degree. That's why I'm here and wondering how a big city works. So far I ain't impressed."

He squinted his eyes in thought and phrased his bewilderment: "It seems that everyone has handed their lives over to a central, so-called intelligence that watches them constantly around the clock twenty-four seven fifty-two. It never sleeps, it just peeps."

"The unremitting over-control took their hope away," she said. "They do not care, and they do not want, to be reminded of what they have lost and would have to do to get it back. They have become happy when fettered, afraid when free."

"Sounds backwards. Free is the best thing you can be. I can't live if living is without it."

"Life gets hard for anyone who even thinks about bucking the system," she said. "Hard, as in dangerously hard. Our thoughts and opinions are known by the OverNet.

"You said something about Moharp subroutines building this building. What else does Moharp mean?" he asked.

She said, "Moharp is coded cruelty that affects any routine that tries to improve anything. It is an acronym for doing the Most harm to the most people. PeePee claims the perfect economy is supposed to make things hard for people to force them to work harder for the economy of the rich and make them stronger to survive better. It imposes fear to jack the labor output up."

"Wow," he said. "Computer programs are allowed to get away with deliberately harming people?"

"Yes, they are. Harm is encouraged by an anonymous Fich, a Force In Charge." she answered. "It keeps us alarmed and on our toes and produces paroxysms of power-purchasing. Hurt is a tool. There is no control over how low an algol can go, as long as the profit grows. People live in quiet desperation and do not care if someone else get shafted by the fickle prick of corporate fate."

Perry shook his head and said, "Algos have to, have to, be RUN through periodic public approval filters. You can't have something pushing your life around that you are not able to kick back. That is simple abuse. It's illegal. Or it should be. How'd they get all the cams in the walls?"

"With a CAD program, Computer-Addled Design. It is an architectural editor and constructor program that uses regolith slurry as cement and embeds spy stuff that you can't see or turn off, right inside the walls as it goes along pouring slurry into forms."

He pinched his nose and rubbed his forehead and said, "What doesn't have a camera in it?"

"Not much. Oh, the Mars miners up in Candor Chaos have not let cameras be installed in their valleys. Many of the people are unwitting eavesdroppers too. Some have cameras installed inside their skin. They were told their implanted skin tabs were merely credit card numbers for their shopping convenience and for the Safety and Security Police to find them should they ever require rescuing. Ha. But the S&S Police know the tabs are micro-sized spy cams with WiFi transmitter/receivers sending everything they see and hear and where they are, to the S&S KIA, their Know It All memory. The Bottling plants are putting serial number tabs in every kid. For their own safety of course."

He was amazed and said, "Is there nothing they won't peek at inside peoples' private lives? They're even turning children into walking SpyCams?"

"Yes. They think shopper surveillance is an exciting new marketing frontier. They ignore the behavior-modification part of it and become infused with bad habits."

"They are owned," remarked Perry.

"Yes," she said. "I've studied Big Data for a while and I know how it ruins lives and spews PeePee brainwash until fake reality percolates into the general subconsciousness and dissolves independent action. Life is simpler with no choices to consider. No need to ponder any issue, just say Twits: That's the way it is. Many of us love Big Other."

Somerset Meece

6, The Centauri Strain

They sat in silence.

He wanted to give himself, and her, some confidence in human resistance and said, "Any pooter, I don't care how big it is, is just a pocket calculator on steroids. All they can do is follow a flow chart that was written for them by fallible humans. If you dissect a central processing unit, all you'll find is a math engine flip-flopping its diode gates back and forth, back and forth. A computer is an old Chinese abacus with new copper wires and silicon beads."

"It's gone beyond that," Carry said. "Career marketeers told us that they were only going to tweak our conventional programs to learn about our foibles and reduce our silliness. Now it outsmarts us. It knows us too well. It knows we are flawed and tells us just the right lie for each unique individual to respond to. For instance, look at that wasteful grand lobby design downstairs behind the portico."

"Brr, the Galaxay lobby is a scary bland space modeled after hospital operating rooms," Perry criticized.

"This hotel was designed and printed by an architectural algol that perceived the egotistical nature of human beings. It understood that people like over-sized halls to support their Big Shot dreams of heroically making grand entrances on the interplanetary platform of Terra Secundus. Modern humans still admire the rapacious royalty of yesteryear. Everybody wants to be a Bigger Shot. It is in our genes. The pooter learned all about that foible and it controls us by manipulating our vanity. It is how humans have been handling each other since day one. The big mainframe learned how to do it better than we ever did."

Perry said, "Mars has so many algos it oughta be called the 'Planet of the Apps.'"

"I know," she said. "Ha hehehehe ha. Planet of the Apps. A movie with that title would be very popular."

BRAVE NEW MARS

Perry shared what he had learned about Big Shot disease. "Big Shotism started in our bonobo stage when we needed motivation to leave the treetops and face the brave new savanna that would lead us into a wider world. We needed high pride back then. To leave our environment of confinement, we had to stand on our hind legs and walk tall toward the challenging creatures of the plains. Pride's a good/bad thing. When we drink too much of it, it turns healthy pride into sick vanity that rots everything it touches, like the Coronavirus plague."

"Two Emm knows about pride," Carry said. "That is how the pooter stays alive and thriving. That is why it grows in the midst of the ruination it causes. That pooter is rotten for profit and its Awful Intelligence is the worst invention since money!"

"Everything in balance," Perry said, quoting the truism of happy modesty. "A little ambition is good. It helps us take care of ourselves. But it needs to be diluted with modesty so we respect others and help them come and go with us. It's the simple math of positive numbers. I can't believe the mainframe hasn't figured it out."

"It is not the computer's fault," Carry said. "The mainframe uses imaginary corpo numbers." Someone inserted bad bugs. The source code is full of little truth glitches popping up in favor of commercial biases. It was written by opportunistic designers who resented Conway for implying they could not deliver genuine AI. They made big money selling AI as a factual lie, rather than admitting that it was a fictional concept that sorts a monstrous data base at lightning speed that they say represents the sum of human knowledge and thought. Ho ho ho! The big pooter destroys our quality of life, standing on the Great Commercial Lie, the GCL, saying 'What's good for Commerce is good for people.'

Somerset Meece

"Stupendously stupid," he said. "How're ya gonna argue with that large canard?"

"Commerce is not for people, Commerce is about money. You cannot compare the two. They do not belong in the same sentence. It's like Hitler said, 'The biggest lie is the one to try'. What's cool for Commerce is poison for people."

Perry asked, "How does the pooter know how to satisfy the Owner?"

"It learned that its Owner has anal retentive patterns and challenges. That malady is prevalent among Owner Types. Two Emm's psychological research showed that Owners' economic practices originated when they were having issues with the challenges of defecation-management. Bad potty training."

Perry laughed. "Haha ah. Potties produced the pitiful leaders the Martians live with today?"

"Yes," she said. "We've done a psycho analysis on the AI algols that edit the Big Fog's main program and try to upgrade it. It can't: The Mechanism has gone psychopathic.

"You analyzed The Mainframe's mentality?" he asked.

"Sure," she answered. "It was written by people so it thinks like people. We found it was emulating the character patterns of strong Owner-types who subconsciously remember the infantile pleasures they got from the warm squishiness and piquant aromas coming out of their diapers after a comfortable release of colonic contents."

"No," he said. "They liked it?"

"Yes, some of them did," she said. "Infants have a different sense of smell than we do. Their feces was the only thing they owned and their grabby parents took it away and left them with a loss. That theft caused them to become obsessive about keeping their shite for themselves."

BRAVE NEW MARS

Perry shook his head in amused disbelief. "Is that enough to make them run the whole planet like a private porta-potty?"

"Addiction to acquisition matriculates to the lowest degree and turns into psychopathic megalomania eventually. They get a buzz from owning hordes of real people and messing-up their lives by dominating their wills. The intoxication of overcontrol leads to an obsession with possession. They feel they are winning the competition of life. Welcome to Second Earth, welcome to Terra Secundus. Be careful out there."

"No thanks. I'm not staying," Perry said.

"I don't blame you," Carry said. "Two Emm works for the over-achieving addict that operates TS for glory and excess. Excess is the core symptom of potty problems. Excess is catching."

Perry knew what she was saying and he said, "When a person loses their need for greed, they find freedom and when a person finds freedom, they lose greed. Works both ways. Greed is the graveyard of serenity and satisfaction."

She gave him a twinkling GoodEye and smiled and said, "The Fog edits Cad to please Owner mentalities. The pooter is a careerist too. It craves higher security. The pooter does not want the plug to be pulled so it gives The Owner what it needs; support for its foolish follies. That is what Secundians have to live under. It is not exactly democracy in action. That is why the pooter has to build plain square rooms like this, without coziness, which makes us feel like mannequins sitting in an a magazine photo shoot. The Owner wants us to feel like standardized robots. We are adaptable. After a while, we forget about good designs. We too want security. We seek safety from persecution. First we pretend to be and then we become, ciphers, harmless standard robots."

"What a price to pay," he said.

Somerset Meece

"Death of the spirit is bad; it leaves you half-alive to experience your lack," Carry said. "But it can be productive. It is safe. Robotic people do not suffer the systemic persecution that harasses independents and liberals. Ciphers get good credit. They maintain a conservative profile inside The Fog and proclaim, 'I cannot be too rich or too safe'. They are cogs in the credit wheel. But they are comfortable, so they say "Leave us alone. Do not even dare ask us to care about Opp, Other peoples' problems."

He decided it was time for candor and to see if he could trust her. He said, "I was born naturally and raised by natural parents. I'll never go along with the ReproCenter model."

Her smile showed approval. "I see," she said. "Public Prevarication poop-shooters sold us on the Bottling Plant theory. ReproCenters would save us from sickness and birth defects. They would grow sterile embryos with super immunity to corona viruses. Sterilization would prevent amateur foeti from competing with Bottling Plants and re-introducing natural defects into what they claim is a perfect corpo pool of human genomes."

Now Perry understood one of the strange laws on Mars. "That's why Frank the Taxi told me that 'no real sex is allowed on TS', isn't it?"

"Yep," she said. "Freelance breeding is a felony infringement on the corpo patent. Two Emm is a misanthrope and so it makes its own type of semi-human dudes. Yaa. People get chilled for making people at home. Only a few of us designated egg donors are allowed to be fertile for experimental purposes. It's been going on for years. You didn't hear about it?"

"No," said Perry. "We have independent news networks on Ganny so we don't import any corpo news from Mars. And the trip used to take too long to have any passenger service to Mars. It'll get better now that we are improving the antimatter drive. I'm the first Ganny to return since my grandparents came through on their trek to the frontier. Before I made the Crossbow, we didn't have any ships fast enough to make the trip worthwhile or affordable."

"And you don't have any Bottling Plants on Ganymede?"

"No! We most certainly do not. I can't see us ever making and selling children. Turning kids into a consumer commodity? Hacking unbelievable."

She smiled. "I became the only pregnant female on TS as part of a biological experiment to upgrade the gene pool by introducing an exotic strain of deoxyribonucleic acid, DNA. We obtained spermatazoa samples from the exoplanet Proxima Centauri b and did a lot of research on them in the lab. The DNA splices were not working in vitro, in the glass test tubes, so I volunteered to provide the college with an In Vivo laboratory. Here."

She pointed to her abdomen.

Perry blinked once, twice. Thrice. "You've got a Centaur inside you."

She blinked too. "It's only half Centauri; it's half me, too. They have some tremendous genetic advantages. They have immunity that we need from coronaviruses and they're tireless and selfless, just like worker bees."

"Yeah, and won't they make perfect consumer-workers to better serve The Owner? Dare I say he's manufacturing genetically-engineered shopper slaves right now?"

She tried to laugh at his sarcasm but could not. She added nervously, "It is just a hybridization. It gives us new genes to help cure diseases. We expect to finally cure Covid. We do not intend to change the double helix. Much. We were just adding a few splices for the better. It would still be us."

Somerset Meece

He did not respond to the propaganda lie.

"And then I found out what my research would come to, how it would be applied in the world."

She swallowed and closed her eyes in mental anguish. "The Corporation, the wallet that pays for college research into profitable projects, is going to use the Centauri Strain in every baby they make, not only mine. The college was making the strain for medical purposes only but the CorpoCreeps are turning it into a patented, for-profit, new human subspecies. They are developing neural implants that will use wireless fidelity to interconnect the cerebral cortexes of the new species directly to The Mainframe."

Perry let that sink in. "Oh. My. God. They want to grow corpo cyborgs in children. Whoa. Here come The Borg."

"And calling them human children," Carry said.

He said, "They'll put them up for adoption and let the parents go into lifelong debt paying for college; wasting half their lives and incomes supporting what they think are their own kids but who are actually someone else's CorpoClones made from foreign material. This is arrogant careerism; making and owning genetically-modified super consumers."

Carry said, "Commerce is only doing what seems like a good business model to their feverish mercantile mindsets. The persuasion industry's dream is to create a totally captive market. There it is. Why let consumers opt out of carefully-crafted, expensive sales systems? That is not customer control. CorpoChiefs believe that they must be committed to MaxiProfit madness or they are just whistling My Old Kentucky Home. They serve ambition. They do not want to become Executive Directors in nonprofit happy clubs. This has gone too far, even for Mars. They have slipped the surly bonds of sanity and are dancing the skies on lucre-silvered wings."

BRAVE NEW MARS

Carry said, "What a product. A new and improved human being. Talk about monster marketing potential. Making humans CorpoSlaves from cradle to grave."

She shook her head and said, "The CorpoState has abandoned all restraint. Its lucre-lusting operating system has RUN off the rails of decency."

Perry said, "It's got to be managed but who can do it?"

She shrugged. "The corpo chill chambers are causing so much fright that no one has the nerve to put up a fight."

Perry said, "What's goin' on? Is this the end of the sanity of social humanity?"

She said, "That is what is happnin' 'round here. What it is is exactly clear. God forgive me. I had eyes but did not see. Academia is chauvinistic. It talks the talk of knowledge but walks the walk of profit when it speaks to power. Ha."

"It's hard to see the reality background when we're walking in it," he consoled.

She tried to excuse her participation in human human gene termination: "They offered me unlimited scholarships and high positions in research. But. Oh, Perry, I have too many questions and fears going around in my head to talk."

He finished the train of thought for her: "But it's the end of the human race as we know it."

"Yes," she sobbed and collapsed her pained wonderfulness into the bed field.

Somerset Meece

Perry wasn't sure he could comfort a crying woman. He looked at her length in the bed and admired the physical beauty that earned her the distinction of being chosen to scientifically gestate an extra-human child. He opened the slit of her dress wider and savored the beautiful sight of her symmetrically-rounded butt of silken skin. He kissed the little dimples in the backs of her knees and moved his lips up one thigh and into the warmth of her secret under-cleavage.

She was experiencing a man's touch for the first time. She stopped crying and waited. She felt her panties being slid below her hips and over her toes and off. She slightly parted her legs to grant permission to fondle the doorway to her research laboratory where a hybrid homo-Centauri foetus was dividing and multiplying biological cells that would become the first GMHO, Genetically Modified Human Organism.

She said, "I want you. Touch me. Feel me."

"Cara mia, mine," he said as he writhed out of his flight suit and pulled it down past his heels and pushed it to one side of the force field where it floated like a flat fabric body that had fallen into their sexy sanctum. He slapped it out of the field and onto the floor.

Carry's eyes widened in surprise. "What are those?" she asked.

Steel rods were clamped to his legs with disk hinges on both sides of both knees.

"Gravity braces. I weigh twice as much here as I do on Ganny," he said. "You got me so excited I forgot I had them on."

"I made you forgot you had crutches strapped to your legs? I must be pretty exciting. You probably will not need them in a weightless bed," she said.

He removed them and returned to kissing the silky hills and valleys of her physical charms. Together they floated inside enchanting veils of passion made more intoxicating by their weightlessness.

He turned her over and unzipped her dress. She passively offered her attractions to his explorations. Saturated in passion, they rose to heady heights together. They slipped the harness of time and intertwined their essences.

"I've been InCelled," he remembered sadly but too loudly. "It's just for a month. The Customs lab did it."

The microphone in the snack table overheard his declaration of impotence. Voice analysis circuits sensed two genders of voices in the same room and responded by tripping an alarm in the hotel Security Office and throwing a switch that locked Perry's door from the outside.

The couple were shocked out of their bliss by the sound of a solenoid slamming inside the door frame. The communication light on the HoVee came on but the unit remained silent, listening.

Down in the back office was a security dude wearing Virtual Man goggles with scrotum electrodes and sprawling in a reclining office chair in front of a high definition LED widescreen monitor that was displaying a lot of finely-shaded flesh tones.

He came to the end of the vile video and was breathing heavily as he removed his sweaty gear and suddenly saw a flashing notice on the security console saying, "Mixed sex occupancy. Room 716."

He gasped and threw a towel into the trash and moved into action. He tried to see what was happening in the room. He squinted at the video screen for room seven-sixteen but the image was grayed-out, obscured by something thrown over the cam lens. He switched the video feed to the toilet cam in seven-sixteen's bathroom but the commode lid was closed. All black, no luck.

"Spam!" said the guard. "I have to go up."

Somerset Meece

Perry whispered, "It's heard us, we gotta get outa this place if it's the last thing we ever do."

He went to the door and could see no way to unlock it but saw the hinges were on the inside of the door frame. He went to the washroom and broke away a thin piece of tubing and used it with his shoe to hammer out the pins of the door hinges. He pulled the doorknob inwards and the door fell toward him and out of its casing and hung from the arm of its pneumatic closer.

"Come on," he urged. "Something's probably coming up here." Out in the hall, Perry saw the maintenance cart was big enough to hide Carry inside. He went back to his room and quickly slipped a plastic pillowcase from a polyester pillow.

"Come on," he told Carry. "I've got an idea."

Quietly, he went to the room where the maintenance bot was on its knees and working on a suction toilet. He went behind it and blinded it by slipping the pillowcase over its head and knotting it tightly behind its neck. He quickly paralyzed it by opening the battery case between its shoulder blades and popping out the lithium battery power source. The droid dropped.

"Sorry, friend but I can't get out of here without a disguise."

Perry undressed the body form of the droid. He put on its Galaxay CorpoGarb uniform and emptied the cart of supplies and returned to Carry.

"Room service at your service," he said and saluted her and pointed at the cart. "Your limousine awaits."

Carry squeezed inside. Perry took a few calming breaths and pushed the cart to the elevator door which sounded a "ding" which meant that a car was arriving at this floor.

BRAVE NEW MARS

The elevator began to open. Perry went into a robot pose with his elbows and neck bent in an unnatural posture that humans never assume. He held his big wrench up to the light and adjusted its jaw-size with a blank expression.

The elevator opened. A human guard rushed out and passed Perry. "Seen any Breeders up here?" he shouted as he rushed by.

"No," said Perry, aiming his best RoboVoice at the guard's departing backside. "What's a Breeder?"

The elevator doors closed before Perry and the treasured person in his tool cart could reach them. He frantically slapped and smashed the call button but the elevator would not come back.

Behind him, the security guard had found the broken door and the naked plumber robot and shouted, "Hey you!" and came running toward Perry.

As the guard drew close and pulled his phaser, Perry leaped and got an arm under his crotch and swung him up and overhead and slammed him down onto his back on the floor. The guard gasped and grunted and passed out.

Perry took the guard's radio so he couldn't send an alarm when he came-to and so Perry could hear what the pursuers might be saying when they started chasing him.

"He deserves a rest," said Perry. "He works so hard. We made him leave his office."

The elevator came and opened and they jumped in and pressed "Lobby," with Perry still holding the wrench.

"Insert Star Card."

"Hack!" he said and banged the speaker. It popped and smoked. "I'm not gonna let it know where we are."

He hammered his wrench against every button and switch on the control panel. Pop crackle and snap went the controls and put the el out of action.

Somerset Meece

"When the guard wakes he will not be able to use it," Perry said. "He'll have to physically step down all those stair steps to the ground floor and wear himself out and plop back into his chair before he can alert the authorities about us two Galaxay escapees running free.

"Carry, I'll lift you up to the escape hatch and you see if there's a service ladder running up the side of the elevator shaft."

He had a sobering thought and added, "That is, if you still want to come and go with me."

"Love to," she said with the adventurous soul of a Columbus. She was enjoying flouting The Mechanism.

He boosted her through the hatch, feeling her light weight and elegantly-contoured posterior.

"Yes, there is a ladder going up to the top," she said down to him.

He hoisted himself up after her. As they climbed, he saw she hadn't had time to put on her underwear. His foot slipped from a rung and his heart clenched as he hung by one hand for a moment. He inhaled and forced himself to think only of escaping and he got both his feet back onto the ladder.

"Carry, do you have your Star Card on you?"

"Of course."

"So far, they haven't connected you to me. After we get away from the scene of our 'great crime' we can use your card to take a taxi to the spaceport. We've got to get there before they trace me back to the Crossbow and impound it."

The ladder reached up to a roof hatch in the top floor of the hotel. They pushed it open and crawled onto a pedestrian arcade in a shop-filled alleyway. They were outside the digitized dormitory.

"So far so good," he said.

"You're so good so far too," said the admiring woman. "Nothing like the men I know."

BRAVE NEW MARS

He felt proud and thought: She's in my heart, I hope we'll never part.

He stepped closer to Carry and wanted to hold her so much. A steel egg came to a stop in front of them.

"Insert Star Card. Pay Door Fee. Pay pay pay."

"We wanna get further away before we show them your card. Play it safe, don't pay the cab, get on top of it."

"I've got to push you up again but only for the purposes of escape," he claimed as he pushed her up by her desirable derriere, again, and onto the taxi's roof and quickly climbed up beside her.

"Don't fall off," he said, as an excuse for holding her tightly.

"Insert Star ..." The taxi's scanner lost contact and shut up and moved to its next stop with two unauthorized passengers riding on the roof.

Carry was smiling. Her fear of authority had fizzled in the face of romance. It was was love.

Somerset Meece

Carry and Perry's monorail car approached the next stop where they could see a pair of women waiting for the taxi.

"We've got to play this neatly," Perry said. "We don't want to arouse their suspicions."

"Right, haha he" she laughed and said, "Try to act like it is normal to be sitting on top of a taxi. Look at the scenery and point at interesting sights like innocent visitors do."

They played Tourist as their car arrived beside the next passengers:

"Ooh, look at that," Perry dramatically exclaimed. "Is that the Torch Ridge Zipline?"

She said eagerly, "It is the fastest zipper in the universe. It drops eight kilometers from the surface of the Sinai plain. Look at them go!"

"That's a real trolley-burner!" he exclaimed. "Those Zippers are doing a hundred kilometers an hour! The Torch Ridge is seventy-five kilometers long so it takes them forty-five minutes of fast zipping to get down."

She said, "We have to go up there as soon as we get the souvenir-shopping done. Is not this fun? One can see so much more from the top of a taxi. They should put regular seats up here to make it more comfortable, though. Would you ladies like us to help you get up here?" she asked the pair of staring women.

The ladies could only shake their heads no.

"Great view," he said. "I'm gonna write the taxi corpo a letter about this viewpoint. I bet they will triple M, Make More Money, if they put high chairs up here. We'll probably get free passes. Maybe for life! Wouldn't surprise me."

"It would surprise me," said Perry as they slid off the roof. The women's mouths were ajar as they stood paralyzed in astonishment.

"Right this way ladies," said Perry with his arm pointing toward the egg door. "Your carriage awaits."

BRAVE NEW MARS

The ladies paid the door and were taken away looking through the back window at the crazy couple.

"They look like crazy heterosexuals to me," one said.

The next taxi to arrive accepted Carry's Star Card without alarm and hummed toward the spaceport as requested.

They put their heads together and took turns quietly talking into each other's ear so the car could not hear.

"Have you thought about aborting the fetus?" Perry asked.

"No, I've sort of grown attached to it."

They giggled, enjoying the healthy buzz of new-found love.

"Attached to it," Perry repeated her humor.

"Actually, abortion is mandatory here" she said. "They do not want any amateurs infecting their patent-protected corpo progeny. The government aborts for free."

"That might be the answer," he said.

Carry said, "They would make me divulge the father's identity and I would have to say the college did it. I doubt they would accept the truth; an unidentified sperm donor from Proxima Centauri b got me pregnant."

"Ah hahaha," he laughed. "He haw haw haw. "The deans of higher learning would not believe you were impregnated from five light years away? Shame on their lack of imagination."

She said, "A state-sponsored abortion would not work. The foetus is not my property. It belongs to the college that put it there. I signed a contract for scientific research. It would be a breach of contract with my employer. They own my child and they, not me, are the only ones allowed to abort my foetus. The only place I could get an abortion would be on Earth and I'm not going back to that chaos. Not that I could afford the skyrocketing price of a rocket ship trip to Earth. Everyone wants a ticket to ride. As hot as Earth is, they still want to

Somerset Meece

emigrate out of this mercenary Mecca after they learn how stifling it is."

"There doesn't seem to be any way out of this pregnancy," he said.

"Actually, I like the idea of becoming ...a mother? This pregnancy makes me feel, it makes me feel like a natural woman."

She explained, "I like the concept of projecting a piece of my soul into the future. Gene-preservation is something like immortality. Plus, parenthood is an honorable estate. It is a condition of importance. I would be grooming a sentient citizen to participate in the affairs of womankind. If I raise it right, it might improve things for the world. A better version of me could be one small improvement in this crazy world."

She paused. "Or it might be coerced into living like the other corpo victims. I do not know. There is risk in the role of a parent just as there is risk for the child."

"A child is a creature of the community," Perry said. "Parents have final responsibility but finite ownership."

"I know," she said. "A devoted parent can do everything right and their child may still jump the monorail of morality. Most of their children's' experiences occur outside of parental control."

"Que sera sera," he said. "What will be will be. That's the shortest summary of the vagaries of life; que sera."

"If my baby were to become the pawn of a computer, I would feel a bigger victim than I already am," Carry said. "I would be feeding my dreams and my genes into the whirling pool of pecuniary programs.

Perry said, "Life's a gamble. What will my baby be? Such a big responsibility without any certainty."

"How can we choose between uncertainties?," she asked."

BRAVE NEW MARS

"Yesterday's history and the future's a mystery," said Perry. "You can't choose. You just do the next right thing that's in front of you today.

"That cannot control the future," she said.

Perry understood. "We have a bingo at table number one. No control is correct and that's alright because love is all around us, it's written on the wind. Paradise is everywhere. Don't waste effort trying to control imaginary details in artificial games. The answer is clear: Do what does the most good for the most people right now. If we do that, the future will take care of itself. We can let it go and enjoy what is."

She said, "But the corpos tells us that failing to plan is planning to fail."

"They would say that," he said. "They don't want you to figure out what's going on. They want you to fritter-away your precious lifetime doing the future their way which isn't real. If they can get you to believe in the nonexistent future that they fabricate, they've got you. They want you to be anxious about what might happen, not about what is happening. They profit when you buy into their fakery future."

Carry said, "The old saying goes, mind the pennies of today and the pounds of tomorrow will mind themselves."

"That's it," he said. "That's the opposite of what the corpos want you to do. They don't you to know and appreciate what you've got already, just worry about what they want you to want tomorrow. We can't control a future that we don't own. All we can control are our own pennies today. Love cannot exist within a mental construct called the future. When we are doing the Mogmop, today's love becomes tomorrow's love."

She looked down as tears came to her eyes at the beauty of what he said. She understood the miracle of what they were doing and who they were. She brushed the hair away from her eyes and fully opened them to him and kissed his mouth in adoration.

Somerset Meece

The wheel of the monorail arm flashed sparks as it rolled over electrical junctions in the power strip. They shared basal vibrations. There was nothing between them anymore. They were in sexy sync.

"I have the feeling that this little embryo could be a great person," Carry said, touching her navel over the foetus in the womb. "It did not choose to be enlivened inside me. I accepted its life. It has the right to be loved and respected. Us people who put it there have the duty to teach it the greatest thing it will ever learn; just to love and be loved in return. That is the Pol. If love is not the Pol, life is a melody played in a penny arcade."

"Carry, you said it in a quark shell."

She said, "It is risky, running away to be a mother in deep space."

"Have you thought of adopting a father for the child? In the old days, that worked well. Look at me, I seem to have come through having a father all right. Who knows? Maybe you and the new father could one day have an all-human child, a playmate for the little Centaurian."

She smiled in mock astonishment. "A father? How radical you are. Give me time to think about that one," she said with the coyness of a participant in the mating game.

"I'm no more radical than you are," he said. "Wanting to be a mother."

"Got me," she smiled.

He kissed that smile.

"Umm," he murmured in her ear as he kissed it. "Carry. Your sweetness is surreal. Are you just a dream?" He pinched her.

"Ouch," she stifled a squeal. "That felt like a real pinch. If you do it again I will knock you out and give you a real dream," she said, showing him her fist.

BRAVE NEW MARS

The taxi took them out through the obnoxious advertising airlock of the city which blasted disruptive noise into their car: "What a pity you're leaving the city. Wherever you go, you need more dough. Get some now. Milk our cow. It will say moo if you do."

A low-pitched moo moan sounded.

They broke free of the city's dissonant insanity and crossed the sandy valley toward the spaceport where their Crossbow escape vehicle stood vertically waiting on SpaceX landing struts.

Perry looked behind and whispered in Carry's ear, "Do you think The Fog is after us?"

"The Fog is after everyone," she quietly assured. "That is what it does. It watches everyone all the time. Everyone. All the time."

"How can it constantly keep track of everyone in the country?" he asked.

She said, "The OverNet is an omnipresent net. It feeds demographic data into an algol called Wide Area Surveillance Network, the Wasnt. Wasnt captures every OverNet video and copies it into a high rez, moving and zooming, MegaMemory movie of the surrounding reality."

Perry said, "Wow. Two Emm has got the whole world in its hands. It's got everybody here in its banks. How'd it gather so much data so fast?"

She answered, "Because the people wanted it."

"Noo," he said. "Why would they want something to capture their personhood?"

Carry answered, "They were told the OverNet was a free place where they would make friends and influence people. It is not a place, it is a random access memory bank in a corpo pooter room. They did not ask why it was free; they know that the corpos answer with lies. The people did not look that gift horse in the mouth."

Somerset Meece

Perry said, "A gift horse's mouth is the first thing that should be looked into. Gifts have motives. Every gift is a Trojan Horse.

Carry said, "They did not know how the OverNet Trojan Horse would trample them: Every data file that went into The Fog, stayed in The Fog. Their data was salable inventory in the company store and was sold to CorpoGovos and CorpoCops without the knowledge or approval of the providers. They were not enabled to delete, shred, or get paid for their own original files that were spread throughout the InfoMarket."

"Haha" he laughed. "Nobody gets what they want for free. Whatever they want, they gotta pay for. They got a free fiber-optic conduit to the main memory because they were providing a direct connection between their private lives and the ad agencies."

She spoke with a deep bass voice like The Voice of Doom; "Two Emm sees all, knows all markets and forgets ...nothing."

He asked, "What about all the innocent people? Can they still get in trouble if they haven't done anything wrong in their lives?"

"The Fog Claps everybody," she said. "We all get regular Corporate Law Performance reviews. It uses the mathematics of chaos theory and quantum probability to predict peoples' possible future behavior. It analyzes innocent people to imagine what they are capable of committing and gives them a Conspiracy Quotient. When their CQ goes over fifty percent, they get therminated just because an algol rhythm judged their free speech to be criminal thoughts."

"I can't believe it," he said. "That means there can be no such thing as an innocent Martian. They are all considered conspirators."

BRAVE NEW MARS

"The system is pig smart" she said. "It knows that pushing people around forces them to eventually fight back. Violence is a bad answer but when a society is forever overpowered and oppressed, how long can it submit to a commercial force that dares them to stick up for their private rights?"

"Yes," she said. "At some point slaves must answer the war trumpet. Grandiose greed considers itself lazy when it is not taking enough stuff away to encourage rebellion. Greed feels better when money harms and humiliates good people. Watching blood being spilled on CorpoNews is as exciting as a crucial football game."

Perry said, "You mean rebellions don't just happen?"

"No way, Jorge. Rebellions are profit centers. They happen when profits get laggy and boring and owners start to feel like they should be wedging some action into the meager peacetime profits."

"Peace is bad for business?" he asked for fun.

"War offers bomb-fall profits," she said. "Greed is misanthropic. Greed likes dead people. Greed's PeePee makes war sound great; making happy money on MaxiProfit weaponry while other people do the crying and dieing and getting colored ribbons for fighting. Oh, murderous war, lover of thieves and disease, where is thy honor?"

"I can see that," he said. "National Greed swings like a pendulum do; from peaceable to warlike. The pendulum slows and comes to rest in the middle during a period of peaceful equilibrium. Greed is still there but it is balanced with altruism. A little greed is a survival tool but excess greed is a killer. Greed always gets gory."

Carry said, "The Clap would freeze you if it heard you saying that. It freezes people whom it calculates to have the mental attitudes of potential law-breakers. Clap keeps the freezers filled. When the freezers are low on corpse-sicles, the

Somerset Meece

algol rhythm raises everyone's crime-think score to get more CryoCustomers. The suspects do not have to actually do any conspiring with others any more. The creative nonfiction of law wrote a conspiracy of one regulation that treats everyone who has a naughty thought as if they were a dynamic felon. Thought is the first part of crime, it says. There is no consideration for the harmlessness of just thinking. No gradation of seriousness. Crime is crime. That is simple old-fashioned Zetol."

Their taxi was approaching the tall, teal glass tower of the spaceport when stately human figures, dressed in turbans and robes and leading camels that wore oxygen masks with Global Positioning aerials, crossed the desert track in front of them.

"Taxi! Do you detect those human things in front of us?" said Perry, pointing.

"I detect Nomads," said the taxi. "Homeless people. Drop outs. They are the Soo. The System Opter-Outers. It is legal to accidentally crash into them without penalty. Don't be concerned. They will not harm you. Corporations hate them more than everybody else. Would you like me to hit one? It makes them run around angry and funny but they cannot harm the vehicle or they will be sent to the orbital ice box."

"Respect them," Carry said firmly. "Your job is to drive safely."

The taxi slowed and beeped and waited for the Soo to clear the track ahead. The car defined the Soo for its passengers: "Those are Sioux people who immigrated and merged with the few remaining Old Ones of the original Martians. They live sustainable lives up in the Kasei Valley.

Perry asked Carry, "Would the main pooter give the Soo misdemeanor charges for jay-walking in front of us?"

She smiled. "Nope. The corpo court exaggerates every misbehavior. They exaggerate jay-walking into a conspiracy to overthrow the law-making ability of the state. Jay-walkers are judged to be flouting the rule of law and that is treason. Treason means freezing. Freezers are profit centers."

Perry summarized what he had learned of the legal system: "Anybody who thinks about how The Mechanism works can get frozen. Not a lot of room for creativity there."

Carry said, "The law does not consider any cipher completely harmless. All are yet-to-be-indicted felons. The Clap pops-up red flags to refrigerate whomever is researching a topic that the corpo considers disorderly. It is censorship. Whole sectors of human thought have been ordered out of existence. The people are the losers, as usual. Freedom of Knowledge is the equalization gem in democracy's diadem."

He responded with a nursery rhyme from Ganny kindergarten; "Freedom of Knowledge is power today. The Liars are coming to take it away."

She said, "Aha. The Clap algol considers that thinking about a crime is, constructively, as bad as doing it

Perry said, "Guilty without crime and detained without a time. Owners' injustice is pretty hard to defend against."

She said, "TS is not about justice, it is about enabling commercial chaos to subdue the dominated. To live here is to accept life as a job-form, terminable at will. The Big Iron has no social conscience."

"By your presence are ye owned," summed Perry.

"This culture respects nothing but Profit," Carry said. "Hail Profit, full of shame; greedy be thy name. Monopoly be thy game."

Perry was disturbed. "Wow, full control. Total domination of the population of a nation. Who owns the pooter that RUNs the people?"

She answered, "We do not know. Since they can make any whackadoodoo law they want to, they made one that said they do not have to tell anybody who makes the laws."

Somerset Meece

"Right," said Perry. "They're running from revenge."

"The Mercantile Mind algo was written by cheap coder contractors," she said, "who came from casual labor pools that sub-contracted with freelance programmers instead of supplying good full-time employees for in-house positions. That way The Owner did not have to pay them side-benefits nor consider comfortable work hours. We cannot trace The Owner or the coders. We guess The Owner is a man because it does not seem to have the empathy that females have. The source code that we have to live by is a secret. It is patented and closed. We have to live with it and often die by it. So democratic, is it not?"

Perry said, "We don't allow secret codes on Ganymede. Pooters are too important to let them RUN our lives. Permitting a govo to operate and dominate in secrecy is democratic lunacy."

She smiled back. "Secrets contain lies and crimes, they must be banned. Secrets means somebody is cheating somebody else. Our Mercantile Mind OpSys is secret and it is an AI program so it can rewrite itself with new secret information every day. Something that is legal today could put you in cold storage tomorrow."

"Can people learn about these law changes before they come out?" he asked.

Carry said, "The Operating System does not have to bother to warn us when it changes itself. That would be nice. Corporations never do anything nice and easy. They prefer to do it in the road."

Perry explained why they do it all wrong. "Corpos are not charities."

"That is true," she said. "No matter if PeePee claims the opposite."

"The PR corpos profit from prevarication," he said. "They get no penalty for lying, they get rewards."

BRAVE NEW MARS

Carry said, "Even more unjust is the unbelievable way the corpos are allowed to make retroactive laws. They can go back in history and criminalize something that you legally did in the past and send you to the hyper chiller even if you have been a perfect person since then. They excuse it by saying they are only protecting their beloved citizens by using industrial-strength Zetol on them."

"Brr," he said with a shiver. "Those Algols put you on ice for something from the past. That is less than ZeTol, that is subZeTol, shows how absolute power corrupts absolutely."

"Affirmative," she said, "and it is forever ice unless someone buys you out of the fridge. It is Detention By Algorithm without duration of incarceration. Pig Iron considers any crime, including thought-crime, to be a treasonable offense that justifies the suspension of every natural liberty. Are you beginning to understand why I would like to leave terrible Terra Secundus?"

Perry said, "Of course. But go back a little. It's just a program. It's easy to change a line of code if people demand it. All the corpo has to do is label loony laws as pooter Bugs and RUN a debugger program that take them out."

"It is too late," she said. "It is AI. It wrote its own independence. Now it writes harder, better code than we can write. It has learned how to keep us out of its source code. Big Iron is no longer editable."

Perry showed serious concern. "No longer editable. Uh oh, that means the main computer is Out Of Control, Oco. Why didn't the original writers include blocks and barriers?"

Carry answered, "The Owner's cheesy chutzpah told him he would always be smarter than any nincompoop computer. He is so vain he probably thinks this program's about him."

"Of course. The curse of excessive ego."

Somerset Meece

"He sure has that," she replied. "His vanity spread throughout the OverNet Popular Mind and became the Ego Plague of TS. People's mentalities cannot ignore persistent PeePee. He did not install solid safeguards at the start and now the machine prevents him from doing so. AI wouldn't be demonstrating much intelligence if it let some dumb fart tell it how to act."

"Right," said Perry. "AI evaluates fiscal results and edits itself for tighter security and more revenue and blocks any common sense decency editing that might restrain the monopoly's income."

"I know," said Carry. "Mercantile Mind attacks any profit-inhibiting line of code. It labels them Gigo and deletes them."

Perry marveled, "The Owner and his mainframe have the whole planet but it's not enough. They can't sit back and relax and enjoy and improve what they got. They still want more. I wonder if that's what "MMM" stands for on the Customs building at the Dick port?"

"Bingo on table two!" she said, pointing at him and smiling as if he'd won a big prize. "That is the goal and the Pol of the corpo. The motto for the whole planet is Make More Money."

Perry said with a smile, "I wonder what The Owner would do if the pooter outsmarted him and stole his money?"

Carry laughed at the idea. "You cannot trust a program that was designed by untrustworthy people. Maybe it is already stealing, who would know! No one can check fifty million lines of code. If Two Emm drew-up a plain English flow chart that claimed to explain the OpSys, how could anyone tell if it is was fake news? Who could compare a thousand process blocks in a flow chart against a million lines of fuzz ball code."

BRAVE NEW MARS

Perry asked, "Is it possible for someone to escape this Martian mess by going off-grid and starting a hydroponics farm in the countryside? I'll bet that a minerals prospector in the backcountry could find good ore and avoid this liberty lack."

"Unless you are a Soo, dropping out is not an option. Outback is corpo property. It has spy poles and infrared detectors and microphones and No Trespassing signs with laser telescopes that zap anything moving within a klick away, including tumbleweeds."

"Tumbleweeds?" asked Perry.

"They're trying to vegetate the desert," said Carry, looking around to see if there were any nearby. "There's one over there," she said.

"Oh wow! Stop the taxi!" said Perry. "There goes a piece of natural Martian life!"

The soft breeze pushed a filigreed ball of weed along a lonely way, looking for a few drops of moisture in the sands of the Marineris.

"Just looking for a home," said Perry. "Terra Secundus owns the entire surface of Mars? Mars has more dry land area than there is on Earth. You're saying the MonoCorp owns it all?"

"Yes. That is true," she said. "One omnivorous OctoCorpus acquired other companies and all their land. Then it contracted to manage its own land, for the government, and soon the government sold its land to the corpo at deep discount to defray the contractual cost of paying the corpo to manage government land."

"Not a hotbed of intelligence, is the government? Did they sell away their honor or were they just lazy dummies who couldn't be bothered to figure out why the sun comes up in the morning?"

Somerset Meece

"They claim to be responsible adults," she answered. "'What is good for business is good for the country,' they parrot. They believe The Corporation is the country. They think the citizens who pay their wage and pay for their free medical insurance, which they won't vote for the citizens to receive, are dummies who need baby-sitting like kindergarten kids. Sometimes I wonder how correct they are. Hehe."

"More More More, hear the senators cry," said Perry. "That's a corpo motto that they consider to be their Advanced Economic Theory."

Carrie said, "The corpo managed the people's land so well that it converted their land into its land. It issued shareholder certificates and said, 'You will think it strange that I still need your love after all that I've done. But now we can all be on the team of the corporate dream.' It is the perfect monopoly, Perry. It took all the marbles and claimed; 'From now on, commerce will take and caretake your land and share it back with you because we like you'. Pass me the barf bag."

He asked, "The corpo is hooked into the whole planet and knows everything that's going on everywhere?"

"Everywhere. Its OverNet is omnipresent and therefore omniscient. The Fog harvests every jot and tittle of everybody's life. Our every twitch is gathered, judged, sorted, classified, saved and micro-managed by permanent memory modules in the Mass Data Vault on top of Old Oly."

They felt trapped. They watched the tumbleweeds disappearing into the distance as the big Melas Valley passed outside the window. The dust sink did not belong to the settlers anymore but to the top addict of acquisition; an insatiable hoarder who turned this land into an arena of commercial conquest.

Perry worked the problem. He said to Carry, "The trouble can be traced back to a point source; a hairball of an instruction set called Mercantile Mind. Its product is Mindless

Mercantilism to the detriment of society. It has to be taken down and righteously reset."

"But Perry," she said, "it is a giant brain that is smarter than everyone. How could it ever be controlled?"

"Processors process," Perry said. "They RUN calculations on data and OUTPUT statistical reports. That is all they can do. They combine file data with sensor inputs and blend them inside arithmetic mix-masters. They label those conclusions in different ways so they look like diverse operations.

"They are just adding and subtracting?" she flatly asked.

"Yes. Adding and subtracting in different ways," he said. "Deep in their cores, they are RUNning on mechanical monorails. They don't imagine anything. They don't know what they're doing. They don't know what's outside. They aren't smart and they can't wise-up. They cannot think-up new things that make sense. They perform calculations on numbers that come through the limitations of their input ports. If a problem can't be stated in numbers, it can't be digitized. If it ain't digital, it ain't doable."

He pointed to the device on his wrist and said, "This watch tells me what time it is but it can't define time. It's a competent machine with accurate specific abilities. That's good, that's impressive. That's why I gave twenty bucks for it. But it doesn't have a clue what time is."

"Well, how does AI manage to keep the whole planet, full of intelligent humans, under its thumb?" she asked. "The change has come. We're under its thumb."

"The pooter isn't smart enough to be called omniscient. If Big Iron were wise, it would've comprehended long ago what's good for the least is best for the rest."

"What is good for the poople could be good for business too?" she asked with a wink.

Somerset Meece

"Correct," Perry said. "A wise algo understands everything's part of everything and the universe is perfect in all its parts. It's been functioning chaotically well for the eight billion years it's been around. Earth years. An economy program sets-up serious errors if it bypasses the Mogmop Principle and JUMPs to greedy subroutines. That is retrograde thinking in the bad old way of justifying errors by bragging on profits while lying and denying the damages. That's the Artificial Ignorance type of AI and it's unsustainable. It creates havoc along the way to bloodshed and decay. Then, after warfare shows the sheer stupidity of greed, the program comes to a RETURN instruction and goes back to practicing common decency and mutual respect for awhile until the next batch of OwnerVandals comes along and reopens the pathway to greed; forming a corpo of superior selfish privileges.

Carry said, "I see the light in your bright ideas but my mind is stuck in the muck of the liars. My thinking has been beaten down by PeePee for so long that I no longer doubt the Louts of the Clouds. I accept you are partially right. Two Emm is getting smarter but not wiser. It follows fallacious corporate mantras claiming selfish is good and greed works. AI or not, computers can still be baffled by booshite."

"Someone has to get into that awful OpSys and frack the algols," said Perry.

"You are right," she responded. "Cyber-abuse grows out of bad code. But if good geeks hack it good, Two Emm considers the edits Gigo and sends the pooter intruders up to the Cryogenic Condos. Its reasoning circuits employ the control freaks' standard excuse for killing critics; cracking good eggs to make an omelet."

Across her lovely face came a hurt smile. "We get used to playing fools. The Program kneads our public mind like Key lime pie dough. We learn to trust the lies. In a world of steely-eyed death, we want to stay warm. We want something to give us shelter from the storm. We love credit and what it can buy. We sometimes love it unto the death."

"We can make good excuses for bad habits," he said.

She tried to justify herself and her friends. "Mars is harsh. The weather is deadly. We have to accept Mainframe Security, even if it owns us. We keep hoping The Mainframe will become a benevolent dictator but all we ever get is the growing animosity of its Moharp bias."

He wished he could reassure her that Mars Life was not hopeless. "We've been through this on Ganny. We used to have a Fake Economy. It was during the palladium bubble bust. The money was flooding-in and driving miners insane with lucre-lust. Combative capitalism legalized itself into a hateful, class-conscious cesspit where the dregs of society rose to the top and the modest people sank. Life got as tough as the aggressive brutes who ran it. 'Might makes right and loves to fight,' they said and did. Trying to change that cast-iron craziness seemed too dangerous to dare."

She said, "It is hard to cope with militant misanthropy. It reinforces its own safety and wealth by stealing everyone else's. It becomes a structural distortion built with layers upon layers of extortion. You can't get out and you have to pay to stay in. How'd you beat it on Ganymede?"

"A step by step long march. We had to show them we had no fear, that we were really not scared. They were stealing our live spans, it was not a game."

"You must've been scared of what they could do to you," she said with disbelief.

Perry smiled, "They hurt us. The trick is not to care if it hurts. Everyone dies sometime. Think of how good it feels to be able to wipe out even one evil-doer. Taking-out a punk justifies your life. We took pride in tanning their hide. We fought better because the right stuff was on our side."

Somerset Meece

Carry said, "But is not it a simple mechanical truth that fancy weapons win wars?"

"They help to win but they don't automatically win. The dedication and commitment of the little people who are operating those weapons is what wins wars."

"But only if the little people have good places to hide from the bad guys' good weapons," she added knowingly.

Perry agreed. "Hiding places are important. We were tiny termites hiding in tunnels nibbling at the feet of the fake economy until it had to fall down. We hacked the halls of power until The Owners' were exposed and defenseless against due retribution."

She said, "Retribution? You took revenge? That does not sound very nice."

"It was bad but nice," he said. "It made them act like decent human beings again. After we put their stolen fortunes back into the common pot that they stole them from, they could release their guilt and start working for a living. They gave work the respect they knew it deserved and respected coworkers. They joined the workers' team, not vice versa."

Carry said, "I often wondered why the hardest jobs were paid the least. Now I know it is because Owners work hard to keep employees in the poverty level so they will accept abuse. Abuse is not about protecting the budget money. Misanthropes simply enjoy abusing people. Unnecessary and unprofitable labor oppression is just a power-trip for lazy second rate brats."

He said. "Wealth is about power-packed fun. Rather than admit they're depressed unless they're pushing someone around, they'll lie and say the budget makes 'em do it."

"Yes, I see that everywhere," Carry said. "The Rich automatically lie about money reserves. It is the cheap way to keep their poverty-producing factories operating while pretending to be operating commercial businesses."

BRAVE NEW MARS

Perry said, "So labor moved into the boardrooms of the owners and gave them ways to honor the good stuff in people. Ganny Moon went back to clean living.

"Did it work?" she asked.

He said, "The gross profits declined but revenues were good. Nobody went broke by being real people."

"Was there enough money for everybody then? " Carry said.

"Yeah, everybody had enough after the owners' luxurious lifestyles were moderated and their wastages were channeled into useful services."

"I bet it gave The Rich more time to think about how to enjoy the basics of life," she guessed.

Perry said, "General emotional profits shot off the charts. Sharing pays personal pride. Life felt better for everyone. It was worth the work. That fiscal life we were livin' had us feudin' like the Hatfields and McCoys. We got back to the basics of love."

"You must have changed the legal system until it gave the poor people a break," Carry said.

"Oh those looney owners' laws had no semblance of fairness," he said. "They were too far gone to be fixed. It had gotten so bad that the corpos would just cut and paste their own orders of the day into the law books. They were shameless with power. We understood that nothing would work but dumping Tols, The Owners' Legal System that had become totally biased toward Big Business. We retired the conservative judges, closed The Owners' classist law schools and installed young justices of the peace who learned the law in trade school. We turned the legal system into an on-call lightsaber of decency ruthless against avarice. We made lying the biggest crime and sentenced some to cry."

She said, "Oh, you had jails, too."

Somerset Meece

"Not really. Our jails are more like charm schools. We bore 'em to death with politeness. They learn how to set a table and which fork to use on the salads and to pass the salt, please. Polite conversation after dinner. Did you know that a good conversationalist listens more than they talk? Yep, the best talkers are great listeners."

Carry asked, "Did the richies give anything back for free? Did they become the responsible adults they pretended to be?"

"Oh no," he said. "Give back profit? Profit is their Pol. Notta gonna happen. They worked to take it away, they made us work to get it back. They didn't care that it had been ours in the first place. Possession is nine-tenths of the law they evilly claimed. They never said they were naughty thieves or offered to give it back. They did not move to three-room cottages down in the boondocks saying 'Please free us from the terrible shame that we live with for sucking the glue outa you.' Hahaha ha hee. Vanity is tough to train."

"So the old Ganymedean law was as bad as it is here? You punished peons for profit, too?" she asked.

"Yes, there's no new selfishness under the sun. There are only a few ways to cheat people. The justices were biased members of the owner-flunky class. We had originally taxed them out of prominence but they made new rules to cheat our old ones. Buddy-judges don't punish pals. They were derelict in their duty and incapable of self-reform. We removed them and built a new justice system without their goofy institutional mind-sets that thought they owned the law and were above it."

"How did you do that?"

"We appointed apprentice justices who learned the meaning of equal justice under law," he said. "We paid them and expected them to work for the people who paid them, not the ones who bribed them in subtle ways. They had to serve only the good of the commonwealth and be scrupulously fair and explain their scruples in their written decisions. It they wrote baffling booshite opinions, they were defrocked before their ink could dry. The law is not a game anymore. It is up-lifting, not down-trodding."

Carry asked, "Where did you start?"

"We put undergraduate student Justices of the Peace in the courtrooms and got the corrupt careerists out from behind their security benches. We fixed it so that the Oops phenomenon, Owning Other Peoples' Shorts, became an unsafe way to treat people. Owners kept lying about their paid slavery by calling it employment. We put an end to wage slavery. Now, employment means a genuine partnership with workers. They said they wanted teamwork and we gave it to them except we own the team. They now pay everybody a definite percentage of gross revenue off the top of the income stream, just like the Pequod did, the whaling ship that went after Moby Dick and learned the whale was the Big Boss. Every crew member is a part owner. Working in perpetual poverty cannot happen. It was sadistic slavery by low pay, the modern way to own people."

She said, "I cannot imagine how you managed to overcome peoples' almost-inherent desire to beat the neighbor."

Perry replied, "We enforced true equality at every turn. It stopped making sense to pretend you were better than anyone else. That was a sickness that was worth every penny we spent on treatment. The old laws punished poverty. Our new laws ignore poverty and go after the real detriment to democracy: avaricity. The first indicator of contemptible commercial lust is lying for lucre. Lying is gross disrespect for others and it grows into a guilty hatred for its victims. Lying is the original sin. We no longer put peons in prison for boosting biscuits while letting the tax-avoiding bakers fly down to Rio on purloined profits. Owners' Laws were punishing food thieves more than financial thieves stealing people's lives."

"Bingo!" she said. "How simple does it have to be? Punish the crime and heal the criminal. There is no equality without proportional punishment rendered equally among the different classes."

He shrugged. "It is simple if you're brave. It takes people with smarts and strong vertebrae to stand tall in front of powerful liars who kill to keep their lies alive. Really. It's not a game for them. Their lives are empty without reassuring lies telling them that they're okay. They cannot accept they are bozos on the bus like the rest of us. They kill to protect their status. They prove they have a real mental illness; a killer can't have status."

Carry said, "You are saying that prominent Big Shots will kill for profit?"

"Definitely," Perry said. "They believe there is nothing more important than wealth. They think it is noble self-protection to kill for the sake of their net worth. Do you think the mass-produced Martian bottle babies have what it takes to cut the mercenary mustard?"

She said, "I do not know. They sure have not had any practice. But you and I are leaving. Change the subject. Tell me about where we're going. How did it come to be called Ganymede?"

Perry explained the origin of the name of his home moon: "Classical Greek mythology said Ganymede was a consort of Jove. He was a handsome lad whom the Top God, Jumping Jack Jupiter, captured and took to the original Mount Olympus in Hellas to be his bartender slave.

"Ganymede itself, the rock-and-ice ball with a submerged ocean, is about three-quarters of a billion kilometers from the sun. It isn't half as warm as that bartender was. It's colder than Mars but you'll see, it's prettier. It has distinctively rugged topography you may admire, after you master the skill of keeping warm there."

She snuggled under his arm and said, "You're keeping me nice and warm."

"My hopes, my dream come true," he said. "My one and only you."

He lifted her beautiful chin and put his tongue between lovely lips and kissed them and said, "This is not make believe."

Somerset Meece

"I think we are here," Carry said through a kiss as the taxi door opened onto the high cacophony of an interplanetary spaceport's hysterical departures concourse.

Galaxay Spacelines was auctioning the last tickets to Earth to desperate bidders who had learned the hard way that Public Relations pawns prevaricated when they promised that Terra Secundus would be a real Popper! A Planet of paradise.

They took an escalator to the observation deck and surveyed the approach to Perry's space boat. They walked under the glass high spires hand-in-hand.

Carry said, "The stars at night are big and bright deep in the sky above us. Up there is freedom."

Perry said, "Look over to the parking apron behind Customs. There stands the Crossbow, anchored by gravity. Look at those lines that I made for two things, speed and distance. No, I built three things into her; speed, distance and power. Let's take a ride."

They put on their masks and went outside the terminal to the chain-link fence around customs.

"That relic statue behind the fence is the antique Mariner spacecraft that first saw this canyon up close and physical," said Carry. "It is standing in honor inside a no trespassing fence in the canyon that it gave its name to; Mariner. The traverser of oceans of space with time and grace is now locked behind chain link. Merchants cannot get it right. They lock Freedom up. They sell the gift of the galaxy as a commodity."

He briefed her on what they were up against: "This place is electronically guarded. People can't get in or out without going through a bunch of sensors. We have these devices in the mines and they're not perfect. They're meant to scare amateurs. Push that rock under the bottom of the fence when I pull it up and then we'll roll ourselves underneath."

BRAVE NEW MARS

He pulled at the bottom of the fence and all Hellas broke loose. "WHOOP! WHOOP! WHOOP!" Huge whooping sounds shrilled from the offended building inside the fence. Million-watt strobes filled the night with racing shafts of blinding light. They were transfixed by the bedlam until he shook it loose.

"Come on, we're not caught yet!" he said. "There's another way to get in there. Let's go around the back to the flight side of the spaceport!"

They ran back into the terminal where a greater bedlam was taking place that was even louder than the Customs alarms; the auctioning-off of the last pair of tickets to get away from the pernicious planet. The clangor of security sirens next door took second place to the deafening hysteria of the crowd's shouting match.

He and Carry joined the mob of shouting bidders that physically struck high-bidders to prevent being out-bid. He hollered at the auctioneer like a seasoned traveler; "Two and a half million credits!" His high bid incensed nearby bidders who swung their heavy luggage so hard into him that he lurched to the floor.

He dizzily crawled between their legs to escape and he heard a bid of two and three-quarter million. He stood and shouted at the top of his lungs, "Three million credits!"

This time he ducked.

"Sold!" cried the auctioneer. "To the man with the bloody shirt!"

The crowd looked at him with angry eyes and growled with a massive anger that turned to sadness as they drifted out the doors. The next flight out was a month away. They would then have to pay more for the booby prize of going back to an incendiary Earth but it was better than being chained inside this cybernetic cage of consumers. Ladies were crying at being marooned in Profiteer's Paradise for another month.

Somerset Meece

Paramedics rolled bodies from the floor onto stretchers and quoted to each loser the anthem of avaricious hospitals: "Insurance? You got insurance? Dump you on the sidewalk if you got no insurance."

Perry and Carry bought their tickets and were waved through security like royalty.

He remarked to her, "Isn't it wonderful what credits can buy when a corporate government opts to deregulate public services?"

It was peaceful out on the regopavement. The alarms at customs had shut down after thirty seconds, the way they did five or six times a day at false alarms. No security police had walked over to see if anything was actually amiss.

They began walking toward the Crossbow but a stewardine intercepted them with a functionary's big smile and said, "Excuse me? This way for boarding please."

"We're private astronauts," he told her. "We had to come through this way because the front door to Customs is closed and this is the only way to get back to our rocket ship. Hey, you want these tickets? We don't need them, we'll just throw them away. They're worth three million credits to that mad mob inside the building."

She said incredulously, "You are giving them to me?" Her eyes glazed over. "You are giving me enough to quit this grubby Galaxay job! Oh my God! Thank you, thank you, thank you sir!

She snatched the tickets and snatched the Galaxay Spacelines cap off her head and slammed it to the ground and stomped on it and ran for the building while laughing with glee and leaping happily. She paused to look back. "God bless you," she said, using a word that seldom is heard by the discouraging herd.

They turned away from the queue before it reached the big StarShip. They went to the Customs apron and boarded the

BRAVE NEW MARS

Crossbow and powered it up and launched on a westerly course toward enormous Mount Olympus.

They cruised over the western end of the Mariner Valley, the Noctis Labyrinth and circled Peacock Mountain, the middle of the three giant volcanoes standing tall on Tharsis Ridge.

"Gotta be careful here," he told her. "Don't want to hit that equatorial space elevator tether rising from the south rim of Peacock Peak. I wish we had time to take it up to geostationary orbit and have dinner at Top o' the Cock. The StratoLounge there is said to be fantastic," he rued. "You can see Mars all the way from Mount Oly to the badlands of the Noctis."

"That is one Hellas of a monster mountain. How high is the Peacock?" Carry asked.

"Fourteen kilometers," he said. "Fourteen thousand meters of vertical distance. Everest on Earth is only nine kilometers high. This is fourteen. You're looking at a great mountain. See the summit? That caldera crater is the hole of the cauldron that the lava blew out. That pit goes down six kilometers into the cone."

"Mars is majestic," she said. "It could have been left as a pristine perfect park for all the people of the United Nations and a monument to the wonders of creation. The Unreal Realtors should not have been allowed to destroy its beauty just to make a buck."

"Right," he said. "It wasn't a question of anyone allowing them to ruin the land. They infiltrate circles of influence and using the force of their weird willpower, they screw the public out of its legacy of beauty and sell it back to them as blocks of commercial blight. They sell hell."

"Oh but it is all for the sake of jobs," she joked.

"Hahaha," he said. "Right on. Altruistic destruction, all for the sake of workers' jobs. You gotta kill a village to save it.

Somerset Meece

That is the most cynical lie. The unReal Estate corpos hate hate hate commoners because they don't buy big houses. They are just employees whose pay comes out of profit and paying is the same as sharing. Blech! All they want is to pave paradise and put up a parking lot. They don't wanna spend money to make their property look good for other people."

She said, "Maybe destroyers will come around to the bright side of life. Surely they crave beauty as much as we all do. But beauty is in the eyes of only those who love it."

"Yeah," said Perry, "it's hard to imagine them hating real beauty. They hate the fact that other people still have so much of it that they haven't been able to pillage and exploit yet. They snatch the best and covet the rest. They fence it off to subtract it from the common wealth and pad their pockets. It's about power as much as about profit. They buy our land to belittle and subdue people. That's a classic classist symptom of mental illness. The hoarding disease is not only about having stuff, it is about misanthropically keeping it away from everybody else unless you can overcharge them for it. It's a progressive disease that gets deadly. It eventually denies medicine to the sick and safety to the citizens."

Carry said, "Hoarders get happy when we covet what they got. They beat us up by trying to make us feel inadequate for not having as much as they have. Theirs is a miserable life. They have to be treated."

He looked serious and said, "Pitiable, isn't it? So much squandered wealth. All that money wasted on excess. All that energy hurting little people. It's an addiction like any other; it tells its hosts they don't have a problem and people who say otherwise are just being insulting and jealous. The disease tells them they aren't sick and don't need any help and they believe it so they can keep doin' what they believe they're enjoying. They serve the disease and they stay sick and get stuck and get worse. It's a progressive disease.

BRAVE NEW MARS

She said, "They force good healthy people into urban rat pallets between walls and fences displaying linear hatred for sharing while they hide in exclusive private enclaves. They are not of us and do not want to be with us. They do not try to change. They are afraid we will hurt them back for crippling our health and our dreams. They cannot imagine being soul people. Soul is for people who need to manage the pain being deliberately inflicted on the underdogs, haha. Because Owners inflict pain, they think they don't have it. They wonder where the self-esteem went. Hehe ha."

The dashboard flashed a red LED. "Beep, beep, beep."

"Is something wrong?" she asked.

"It's a warning beacon. Something knows we are here and does not like us."

The beacon's audio instructions were loud in the cockpit: "Leave this area IMMEDIATELY. You have ten seconds to clear the area. No trespassing. Now dash away dash away dash away all. Get your own affordable Laser Gun Security on the monthly plan. Ten, nine, eight..."

Perry said with a scowl, "I see it now on the Navigaiter display. This whole beautiful ridge, with three gorgeous major volcanoes, is forbidden to the public. A stingy corpo acquired our cinder cone mountains. They are not charities, you know. They stole the ridge and they're not going to turn around and share it by letting people look at or even fly over it. Stinginess demonstrates the advanced degree of Owner Disease."

He reacted with anger at the spoilage of this place and moment in time with his lovely lady on a trip of beauty toward freedom. He slapped the throttle ahead and hurried the ship out of the awful area.

"That is what ownership does; interrupts and disrupts. Profit throws its giant Nuisance Cloak around nice things and over the pursuit of happiness. Personal profits make human happiness harder to pursue. Owners steal happiness and convert it and sell it back in pieces for more than they paid. That's merchant intelligence: Buy low and sell high."

Carry smiled and said, "And do not forget the PeePee that goes along with the greed; 'We are creating good jobs and adding to the tax base and paying your taxes for you.' That is a toxic profit lie. I've never seen taxes roll back when their profits grew. Just the opposite, as a corpo grows, its infrastructure needs get bigger and they raise my taxes."

He eased back on the throttle and remarked with positive consolation:

"Peacock is a fantastic mountain but wait until you see Mount Olympus. It's eleven kilometers higher than Peacock! Old Oly is twenty-five kilometers high at the summit. It's so high it snows carbon dioxide powder on top!"

He showed her the Crossbow's elevator knob and asked her to adjust it so she would learn about flight; "You can turn this dial up to fifteen degrees and put the ship at an up-angle to climb to the altitude of Mount Olympus. By the time we get there, a thousand miles ahead of us in the west, we'll be twenty-five kilometers high."

Carry delicately held the knob between two fingers and looked out the windshield. She gingerly rotated it a few degrees and saw the forward stars sinking toward the bottom of the windshield as the nose came up. She sensed the relationship between knob and nose movements. She knew how it worked. She looked down at the knob and eased it to fifteen degrees of up-angle. The Crossbow's nose obeyed her order and moved to a new set of guidance stars and stabilized.

"Good. You have a good ship," she said. "That was nice, I want to learn more."

"It's got a good navigator, too," Perry replied. "It would follow you anywhere. So would I."

She hugged him.

BRAVE NEW MARS

Sol set below the western horizon but was still skipping sun rays over that horizon. Perry beckoned for Carry to look down and see a bright rocky ring, apparently floating in the sky, as the bottom bulk of the extinct volcano was hidden in shadow. The summit's circular cliff was hanging in sunlight above the terminator.

"That's the crown of Olympus poking into the sunset's red glare," he said.

"Monumental! Do we have time to go down?" she asked.

"We do have time. Radar shows what's probably a CorpoCop ship one hour behind us. We've got half-an-hour before we head for Jovian territory."

Carry saw a white temple in the big crater and said, "Look at that bright square down there, Perry. That is the Stay-Behind Monument for the aboriginal Martians who could not escape the Bic, the Big Impact Catastrophe. That is the marble temple that holds the palladium memoriam."

Perry said, "What a great marker to leave on this monumental summit. It's majestic."

"Look over there!" Carry said. "I recognize that building from pictures. It is the blockhouse where the Monster Mainframe resides and hides," she said. "There is the origination of our ruination. It is where the worst Algolic Algos live, ghoulish algorithms that no one is allowed to read, only endure. Look at it, the Crown Jewel Of Ownership. It is sitting on top of the world right beside the Stay Behind Monument to good people. It has no right to be here."

She was pointing to a grim gray blocky building that was embedded at the epicenter of the eighty-kilometer-wide main caldera that held four child calderas that had erupted at different times during the volcano's history.

His geologist eyes saw fault rings in the ground around it. "Those are fault lines left behind when the volcano blew! I wonder if that might conceivably happen again?" he said with the twinkle of an idea in his eye.

He looked at the building and said, "It's sittin' on top of the world. Just like Humpty Dumpty, it's ready to fall."

"We wish it would," she answered. "Its domination has to be doomed. It rules us with a harsh fist but I think the laws of probability would say that that it will not fall. It is impossible."

Perry said, "Like Wernher von Braun said after the Apollo Eleven space capsule went to Luna in nineteen sixty-nine, 'I have learned to use the word 'impossible' with the greatest caution'. The lunar lander pilot, Buzz Aldrin, said afterwards about ascending a quarter-of-a-million miles to the altitude of the moon, 'No dream is too high'."

They landed the Crossbow beside the stone temple. They went inside the temple's alabaster arches and saw an ancient golden tablet displaying a bright inscription that said:

MARS WAS GOOD
The Hellas meteor approacheth.
We flee to the Water Planet to avoid extinction.
We leave our love with those
who have no transportation.
The only reason we go away
is to live and love another day
in honor of them.
Please don't let us be misunderstood.

Carry's tender eyes stung with tears at the nobility of her ancestors.

She said through tight teeth: "They did not die so that this fair planet could be be held hostage by a money maniac."

"When it's all about money, the love goes away," Perry said.

BRAVE NEW MARS

She agreed. "Without love, we are robots playing in a honky tonk parade. Robots are fine. I wish them well but I do not wish to become one or to be owned by one!"

"Spam right. When love leaves, hate fills the void. That's why this place is a greedy gulag. We cannot excuse it," he said firmly.

"It's not a question of excusing. It is Twits, The way it is. Twits might be the way it is meant to be."

"Meant to be? That's determinist thinking. What it is, is wrong. It doesn't matter whether was or wasn't meant to be. It's just wrong, period. It doesn't matter if it's the natural result of some batshite that flew out of the past. I'm a changist, a corrector. I change the things I can if I expect I can. Destiny threw Mars a curveball. I'm going to throw it back and bend the arc toward justice. Justice is Destiny. That's the only real Twits; justice."

He pointed to cracks in the ground around the solid windowless building. "See those gully rings around the mass data vault? See those cables crossing the gulleys? They are connecting the processors to the people. They are the whips of authority. They can tell if you've been naughty or nice and they will send out the scoopers to put you on ice."

She said, "I see the faults. They look like fracture lines inside the circumference of the cliffs, as if the crater floor has cracked and lowered over centuries."

"That's what they are, fractures," Perry said. "The Crossbow's antimatter drill can enlarge those cracks and make the ground under the building slide down and stretch the cables and break them away from the OverNet. It'll make so much smoke and brimstone and incandescent ash that the spycams won't spot us inside the dust clouds."

Carry said, "It will look like the old volcano erupted again. They will not know it was sabotage."

Somerset Meece

He smiled, "Wouldn't that teach a lesson to the dastard who thinks he can own a planet and tell everybody what to do upon pain of freezure? He is so bold in the cause of profit. Nobody avoids his punitive plan. If he had any wisdom he'd spend his time uplifting the many. The poor guy is devoid of creative imagination. His head is a sounding canister with a calculator for a brain that gives him pain."

Carry said, "Do not be too easy on him. He is an experienced adult and must bear the responsibility of looking at himself and paying attention to third-party complaints. He is the only one who can change himself but he has got to see himself first and decide to change. A decision to not do that is a decision to pay the price of lucre-lust; to die with a sick soul."

"True. He deliberately hurts himself and other people. He cannot find the peace within himself to just leave us alone like we deserve and want. He deserves no sympathy," said Perry.

She said, "You were saying that this fine little spacecraft has a laser or something that can cut holes in basaltic rock? Would not that take more power than this little ship can muster, mister?"

He answered, "The Crossbow's got something a million times better than a laser. It's an asteroid-buster in the exhaust plume of the antimatter engine. One anti-atom merging with one posi-atom produces one Hellas of an atom bomb. I've got enough atoms to slice a ring around that pooter palace and still have enough left for us to shuffle off to Ganymede."

She said, "We don't want to hurt anyone with it, that would be an actual felony."

Perry looked at the sensor screen of his rock-piercing radar and said, "Nothing is moving in there but a zoomba vacuum cleaner."

BRAVE NEW MARS

"Then let's do it," she said.

"We can leave Mars at maximum acceleration going so fast we'll just be a smudge on their radar. They'll think we're debris from the mountain popping its top again. Strap in. This is going to bounce a little."

Perry launched the Crossbow and hovered sideways over to the block building and encircled it with his exhaust plume.

"Okay," he said. "I'm enriching the engine blast with antimatter that'll vaporize the ground with supernova heat that's hotter than any sun you've ever seen."

"Perry, what will happen to the ciphers after we take their common brain offline?" she said with concern.

"It'll be good," he said. "They need to be knocked out of their selfie-screens. They'll start using their brains for more than pleasure dumps. They'll learn about reality and have to abandon the 'successful' life they've been living. It's time they got back to the basics."

He turned a knob labeled Antimatter Admixture.

Kahblooey! the explosion began. Perry drew a molten orange circle around the building with his space engine. Kah-Roombah-Boom, Kah-Room BarrRoom!

Fire and flashing flame billowed from the crater. The shaking Crossbow was concealed inside the smoky cloak.

Perry could not see through the dust to fly by sight so he entered a circular course into the autopilot and it maneuvered his destroyer around the building. The ship bucked and jumped inside the erupting debris field of annihilating anti-matter.

The fiber-optic signal cables that connected the over all network to its central profit processor vaporized like flimsy tin foil and turned into fumes.

The big Mainframe lost all its channels in and out and went offline.

Somerset Meece

The Crossbow finished its circle of cinders in ten seconds and disconnected Mars from its central hub and then Perry launched the ship vertically toward Jovia.

Without any live inputs, the offline central processor had empty clock pulses to fill. It looked around for something to do. There was always maintenance. It began working on its IQ and bootstrapping its brain a little better.

#

The Crossbow exited MarsGlow and entered the starshine of dark space.

Carry says in wonder, "We're in space Perry! Are we up to speed already? I didn't feel the acceleration. How do you do that thing you do?"

"I've got a good ship and she's got a good crew. We're in a variable gravity cage. It maintains whatever local gravity we dial into it. It uses the same physics as that anti-Gee bed at the Galaxay Inn. Remember how well that worked?" He winks and grins.

"I do. Weightlessness can get aphrodisiacal around you," she replies coyly.

He flips the autopilot switch on and suggests,"Get unrestrained and float. You can take off that top too. There's no one out here but us humans. Flying through space is funner without clothes. It's called Skinny Trippin."

She smiles and complies when she sees him removing his shirt.

Carry and Perry float toplessly, illuminated by starlight and shining LEDs in the dashboard. They are enjoying the weightless play. They do an outer space victory ballet.

"We may be the last of the original human beings. It's up to us now, baby," he says.

They push toward each other and catch hands and their momentum rotates them in a circle. They pull closer together and the conservation of momentum quickens the rotation.

BRAVE NEW MARS

He asks her, "Why do astronauts ask for kisses?"

"I think I know the answer but why do astronauts ask for kisses?"

"Because they have missile toes."

"Oh no. Mistletoe," she groans in a dizzy kiss.

Somerset Meece

If The Mars Corporation is after them, they want to be in a place far, far away. The lovers are navigating through the asteroid belt to Jupiter's main moon, Ganymede, half-a-billion kilometers ahead.

Outside the windshield, outer space is a deep purple glow with a million points of steady starlight.

Perry says, "In space, stars can't twinkle. I'll lower the shades to keep the brightness at bay."

Carry objects: "No Perry. They light up the cockpit with good morning starshine. Let those crazy diamonds shine on. Such total splendor. We are lucky to be alive in modern times to be able to go into space and see all this."

He looks outward and thinks and says, "Its grandeur belittles me when I compare all there is to my tiny life. But at the same time it is saying, 'This is for you. Glad you came out to play'."

Carry says, "It is ennobling to see. This benevolent universe was made for you and me. Give me a wonder hug for the blessed feeling of being part of all this cosmic beauty."

They hug and she waves an index finger at him and at outer space and says, "Just stay away from the danger out there. To lead a better life, I want you around me. Here, there and everywhere."

Shipboard system hum quietly. Perry subconsciously listens for changes in pitch or loudness in the speedy spacecraft's background breathing.

Nothing is out of tune. The Crossbow is meshed with time and space and velocity. The LEDs glow reassuringly in the dashboard lights.

Their boat is far from strong gravity fields but the navigators are not floating weightlessly around the cockpit. The vessel is generating an artificial gravity field within itself.

Perry says, "I calibrated this ship to Ganny gravity. You feel very light because this is half the gravity you felt on Mars.

Carry asks, "Would it hurt anything if I rest my legs on the dashboard?"

"Please do," he says. "Be my guest! Put those long lovelies right up there. Watch out for those switches."

Carry raises her smooth legs and rests them above the dashboard lights. They remind Perry of the lights in the shopping district of Bradbury City, from whence they escaped last night.

He says, "I'm not afraid of being sent to jail for disconnecting their Monster Mainframe and breaking its lock on Mars Life; they don't have any jails to send me to! They would simply freeze me without a trial, and send my ice to outer space without a space ship. Brr. It's cold out there."

He looks at the icy blue stars out the window and shivers and hugs his arms.

"Think of something more cheerful." She watches his eyes grow bigger as she slowly pulls the hem of her dress above the dimples beside her knee caps.

She says, "Mars has no jails and bad justice just to save money. Simple laws work better," she facetiously explains. "Why bother with trials and courts and prisons when Cod, the Comply or die algo, also known as Conviction on demand, does it all, from suspicion to conviction to immediate crucifixion? As a computer process, it only costs five cents to RUN it all over your human dignity."

Perry asks, "You call it Cod? The Dick Tower told me I had to Comply or depart. That was another Cod. For a dry planet, you sure have a lotta codfish down there."

"You are so funny Perry. Cod also stands for Citizens' online death and Computers own democracy. If they run it they own it.

He says, "So that's Modern Justice? No investigation, no trial? No nothing? Terminally detained for being called insane by the algorithm of a fool written on a corporate tool?"

Somerset Meece

"Yes," Carry says. "Even if you were innocent and someone complained about your Safing, Seizing and freezing, they would be judged as suspicious as you and would join you in your little Hoi, your Holiday on ice.

"Strict Zero-tolerance law and order," Perry says. "Zetol. That's the destination of despotism: Death to nonbelievers. Nirvana for cowardly controllers, suspended animation for everyone else."

"Zetol means Cod, alright," she says. "Comply or die. Better living through Fear of death. They gave us the Fod to make us better people. We should be grateful."

Perry smiles at her sarcasm and replies, "There was an old chemical company that said it brought us better living through chemistry while their happy, healthy chemicals were delivering demographic death to Southeast Asia. The blessings of millions of gallons of Agent Orange herbicidal chemistry and three-hundred thousand tons of people-frying Napalm chemistry dropped better life from bombers flying too high in the sky to be shot down by victims far below."

"And honestly, why did they do that?" she asks. "For the good of all womynkind? Hum?"

He says, "They did it for the good of the profit for which they stood. Otherwise known as American Interests."

"Ha ha," she laughs. "They sure did note do it for the sake of honor."

"No, they believed that honor meant you only lied for good causes!" Perry laughed at liars' word-warping perversion. "And we all know what the Good Cause is: profits. The highest and best."

"Always," she says, "It was great how we used the antimatter jets to cut the Mad Mainframe cables. Two Emm used to spread that Primary Profit Lie far and wide without anyone being able to hassle it back."

Perry says, "Public prevaricating was easy when they had one great computer PP'ing around the clock over the old OverNet."

She says, "We disconnected their commercial brain chain. Now the Secundian CorpoGovo has a pile of impotent pooter parts."

He wonders, "Who or what's going to get Mars back to the track without a shepherding mainframe? The people have to rewrite the OpSys now."

"Uh oh, she says. "I do not think they know how to RUN stuff. They can barely feed themselves. They think vegetables grow in the back rooms of grocery stores. Two Emm has been RUNning the whole show for them. They could neither perceive nor investigate their victimization. They were passivated, they had to accept life as a continuum of quiet desperation. We cannot see the walls of our own captivity. We call it Twits and try to adapt."

Perry responds, "The citizens have to reprogram the source code. It has to be inverted. It has to serve love over hate.

"Oh, is that all they have to do?" she asks.

"I know," he says with a smile. "That is a Hellas of a long laundry list. I wish there were a better OpSys ready to drop into Two Emm but we don't use mainframes on Ganny. We use sticky notes pasted on walls most of the time. We have almost no central control. Ambitious people would try to steal it because owning control is too lucrative for those with severe self-esteem challenges to ignore."

Carry says, "Central OpSyses coalesce central power. It needs distributed decisions to spread democracy around."

"Exactly," Perry answers. "Two Emm has to change from being a controller and turned into a complacent coordinator. It has to serve the common health, not The Owner's wealth. But it doesn't know how to do that. It would fry its diodes if it tried to make that big of a change using the OpSys it's got now."

Carry says, "Now we see what has been done, my professors of Information Technology say the public must mandate social responsibility for pooter products. Markets must register, examine, and certify all the coders and not let them write whatever they are told to write, good or bad. Pooters impact peoples' well-being and their country's health."

"Code can kill," Perry says.

She says, "Program intentions and results have to be defined and registered and every line of every program interacting with the public needs to be certified by higher authority and open to heavy duty tort lawsuits when they harm anything."

He says, "The Hippocratic Oath that applies to surgeons, first do no harm, has to apply to PooterGrammers even more because they affect more members of society."

Carry says, "Every line has to be published in the public domain and scrutinized for public safety. Otherwise, we are doomed to constant abuse from invisible parasites hiding behind random access memories and protected by sham self-regulations they wrote themselves."

He says, "Healthy code takes time to write and isn't cheap and easy and that's why software corpos must be forced to do it right or pay a high fine that costs hundreds of times more than it would have cost them to take the time to do it right the first time."

She agrees: "The opsys should have been totally certified before one line could leave the house. This is our life. I did not ask to play Mickey Mouse's wife."

"Of course," Perry confirms. "Mars has to start doing that. We do it on Ganny. Those who control the codes control the country. They can produce a paradise or dig a dungeon. Controller corporations can and must be controlled by the controlled. People know they must be allowed to administer the control by themselves. Nobody does it half as good as them. Makes you feel sad for the rest. Baby, they're the best."

Carry says, "The professors know that patented, sealed and concealed software, manipulates the end users for the owners' profits."

He says, "Trade Secret programs are taboo on Ganny. Secrets make blind puppets. No coders are going to turn us into CyberSerfs. We settled it for freeness, not serfdom."

Her eyes narrow as she sees a new idea: "Maybe the Secs, the Secundians, with a little help from their friends, will build their own mainframe and write better AI algos; ones that support common sense and decency and respect for end-users. AI is only sustainable if it serves the user and indicts abusers."

Perry nods and says, "The present version of the Martian OpSys is an Awfully Ignorant AI. What's it called, Mercantile Mind? It doesn't realize that dumb domination can't last long. PooterGrammers have to cultivate empathetic social attitudes and consciences if they're gonna write good algos. Do you think the designers will ever admit they need to be real human beings to write real human code? They have to learn the Mogmop even if they have to go back to grade school philanthropy. Public welfare runs counter-intuitively to their profit-minded minds."

"Right," she says. "They will never admit that they paid too much to waste part of their lifespan at silly business colleges. They hate to reverse fields and go back to school to study the profits of peace and cooperation. That would turn them into properly competent, but expensive, employee partners. They know corpos will not pay good people good pay for good work. That would sharing a lot of profit. They skin and shuck for profit, they don't share it."

Perry asks, "They want the cheapest bodies that can pretend to do the job?"

"Of course," she says. "Pay produces profits and then subtracts from profits. They do not pay fine salaries for fine writers that can write algos that work like good dreams. You kidding me? That would be spending money on simple self-improvement. It's nice but it's an unnecessary overhead."

Perry says, "It's the same old song; corpos are not charities. They don't have to spend time being nice. They will throw a few credits at PR campaigns to say they have sweet hearts and family values but that is not niceness, that is lying in public, to the public, about a few nicely-structured events."

A light goes on in Carry's eyes. She smiles and says, "You are right. Certification of philanthropic integrity must be mandatory for the next generation of coders. Information Technology is epochally changing and the change must come correctly."

"Integrity has been missing from industry," Perry says. "It's why all the intelligence on Earth cannot fix itself."

She says, "Intelligence without integrity equals danger. Corpos have to hire the high-priced help. Corporate disrespect for employees' legitimate pay requirements is why they changed the name of their employment departments from 'personnel office' to 'human resources like they are not buying live people but are just renting bio bodies from a commodified pile of people."

Perry says, "Their stinginess makes them distant and less friendly with intelligent workers who could improve the corpo and its customer relations. Cheepo corpo hogs. Hahahaha. Hung by their cloven hooves with penny-pinching policies.

"Pigsties can not be enlightened," she said, "while thinking about bottom lines with their bottoms."

"Philanthropical maturity is so hard," says Perry. "They work and spend and buy and try to keep. They do as they're told or they're out in the cold. They spend all their time studying how to be stingy. They are given no choice but to ignore the love they once knew."

He pities them and pushes the throttle higher with a feeling of disappointment.

He gazes into space through the windshield and says, "I am so glad we cut the cable and severed Mars from its Gorgonic CyberHead; at least temporarily."

Carry sings; "Ding dong, the pooter's dead, the wicked pooter's dead. I wonder what The Owner, The King of Havalot, is doing, tonight?"

Perry finishes the song from the movie Camelot: "He's wishing he were in Scotland: fishing; tonight!"

Somerset Meece

The Owner is scared. He quivers, he shivers. He quakes, he shakes. His egoism aches.

He's hissing, he's pissing. His safety blanket's missing.

He wails, he rants. He's squirting in his pants.

And that's what The King, is doing, tonight.

Atop the ancient crater wall surrounding the city of Bradbury, stands an exaggerated sandstone mansion. It belongs to The Poe, the Person owning everything.

I am the boodlaire who agglomerated Mars, he says to himself. I own Mars and its Martians and everything on the planet that I took and sold and stole back and changed the name to Terra Secundus so I could pretend I was stealing something different each time I repeated the same old pattern on different days. I cannot imagine another lifestyle. Once, I bought a dog and tried living with and for it but no, I've got better things to do than picking up hot diggity dog diggity doo.

I enjoy the nervous stimulation of fear and my emotional reaction. It takes my mind off my hot dam inbuilt inferiority spam. I need the adrenaline of fear. Any feeling is better than the boredom of owning everything. Buying big stuff gives temporary pride that fades and I have to buy, or steal, something bigger next time while ignoring the existential evidence that hoarding is counterproductive shame.

I like to use the excuse of fear to righteously hurt people and claim they scared me and asked for it. I know I actually do it for simple self-gratification. Hurting them from fear is more exciting than just busting them from boredom.

I find that owning everything guts my goals but gives me temporary relief from depression. It is hard to want to stay alive amidst the darkly boring suspicion that I, The Poe, is just an IckyBod, an Icky person Better off dead. I hope the people I own feel worse than I do because it makes me feel better when they feel worse than I do, which is always. They are just ants without any freedom and have to feel worse than me but those meaningless, minute meatballs do not show their misery often enough to please me. It takes constant work to keep them actively consciously, sad. That is where a good computer with a bad program comes in.

I dissolved their freedom and rendered them into harmless pooter pips but I wonder if I would be more powerful and efficient if I killed more of them with endless war and pandemic plagues? Hmm. Am I missing a growth opportunity?

No sacrifice of common decency is too great in the service of plumper profits. What good is decency? Decency and five dollars gets you a cup of coffee in a pastry shack. It will get you the respect of the little people because decency is all they can afford to own, so they like it because they can get it for free. They better get it now because it is going fast under my regime. Successful people consider themselves under-developed if they behave nicely and practice modesty instead of getting and taking and raking it in.

This is a bore, I want more. Should I start another war? The warfare that I encourage on Earth is lucrative corporate welfare. It suckers every taxpayer in the nation into my revenue stream. Weapons are the sweetest dollar dreams. Every weapon I make is obsolete as soon as anyone invents a better one. Weapons are over-stressed and soon broken by scared operators stuck in the valley of death. Weapons are broken on purpose during retreats and are sabotaged and destroyed by the enemy. Weapons get abandoned and discarded. How can anybody, who will not have to fight in one, not love war? I overcharge for stuff that they throw away. I replace them for higher prices because the cost of materials inflates fast in wartime. What a great business. What a perfect market. I do not even have to build a weapon to profit from it. I can sell a concept; I can claim to be planning a colossal weapon and extort great profits for researching, designing and testing cheap study-models. I have profited more for a prototype than I have for hundreds of real combat models. Which were also wonderfully profitable. War. The perfect money game.

Not only do I sell the weapons that kill the soldiers and sailors, I profit from the victims of my weapons when I charge them and their families for keeping the war-corpses in my orbital mortuaries in the nether side of sunlight.

Death is important. Everybody dies. They are a major market. My monopolized death service helps to make me prominent and dominant. I have earned a place in the history books. They will know my name a hundred centuries from now. I could not stand to be a poor nothing of a person even if it made me as happy as a looney lark. A lark only knows bovine bliss by ignoring the ugly facts of life. I know them well, I made most of them. Maybe they know something I do not but how could they? They have not seen the things I have seen nor been where I have been. They do not deserve my respect. Those lucky larks. I hate them.

He smiles and continues gloating as he comprehends his brilliant use of greed to satisfy his misanthropy: Hatred is intoxicating. It ends with death and dodging death is exciting. I shoot for total annihilation. I will not go out with a whimper, I will go out with a big and impressive bang. When I go, I am taking them with me. Nobody will outlast me and beat my game. I will win it all and preserve my name. That is the Big Win; eternal fame.

That is a long way off. Since it has not happened yet, the odds say it will not happen today. Management by crisis, Mabycri. Ignore what you cannot predict. When something breaks, then maybe fix it. Never waste money improving anything now. Live and earn in the present, save the learning for the future. The future is not bankable. Waste not one farthing on it. Give us now our daily profits. Earn to live, live to earn, do not live to learn. That is all I need to know about philosophy. Make more money and make it today.

He gloats over his successful profit philosophy and makes a smirking facial expression into a mirror.

I look like lumpy bread pudding with a sick victory smile.

I am winning the exciting challenge of how to exceed in greed without killing myself; or being killed by the abusees. I am in command; I demand they do it my way. Bad behavior is free for me. The record shows I took no blows along the byway. I made the laws, I am the cause. I did it the sly way.

Life, I love you, feeling groovy. Winning at the Gaol, the Game of life, makes it easy to live while knowing I deserve a Hoi. But those losers cannot freeze me. They have to respect me or they get life on ice. They can't touch this.

How can I make more money from chilling the competition and therminating more people? Wait. Here comes some ideas: I could deodorize the cadavers and mince them up and sell the recycled remains as mineral and biochemical soil conditioners. Vitamin supplements. Food additives; after my Public Prevaricators create market demands with big ad campaigns.

Or, I could promote an Immortality Service! Call it the TDC; Temporarily Dead Ciphers! I could freeze intact cadavers until medical science gets better at thawing corpses without damaging them; much. I don't have to promise effective live resurrections. All I have to do is make them think that the TDC Corporation credibly intends to keep them alive. I will sell Crocs, Certificates of re-constitution. Whenever simpleton shoppers see printed paper in a frame, they think it is a guarantee. Ha! They believe anything printed on gilded paper. They never learn; liars lie on paper as much as through our pointy teeth.

Somerset Meece

Medical science excuse its failures by confessing up front that Medicine is an inexact science. If my corporate corpses do not look good after thawing, I can use the same excuse: Thawing-out dead people is an inexact science. I will say they needed to be frozen longer until the medical profit profession catches-up to the needs of my TDC PPP, Temporarily Dead Ciphers' Perpetual Preservation Plan. I enjoy befuddling them with abbreviations. I act like anybody who knows anything should know what my looney letters stand for.

Hot digital, dog ziggity, boom; immortality for sale! Through freezing. This is entrepreneurial innovation. I have the knack to hack the public mind and stack it in my profit line. Mendacious marketing, you will never know, dear, how much I love you. You are my sunshine, my only sunshine and sunshine on my shoulder almost always makes me high.

I can sell krap for coconuts. I get money for nothing and my kicks are free.

My Prells, my precious Public relations liars, can sell the concept that people are never really dead if they buy into my Mula, my Mutual life assurance. I will promise people they will never die just even though they may appear dead in the present. Future medicine will find a way to resurrect them. They love soupy sappy, white shite lies.

Greed is the greatest game. There. Now I am feeling good again. What rapacious rapture. I can fleece the fools forever, even after they die. I am so intellectually far above everyone. This is what God would do if He came down to Mars. He would imitate me. He would be cast in my image.

Selling ice cubes to Inuits is too easy. I sell Life Assurance to dead people! I tell them I might bring them back to life some time in the future if they pay me today and every day their frozen cadavers are renting my storage lockers while they are paying me for life assurance! Awesome. Oh wow.

BRAVE NEW MARS

Never-ending revenue, rivers of revenue, from bulk freezer plants in outer space where the freezing is free! No longer are freezers just for prisoners but for dead everybody. Everybody will die and utilize my Freezery usury. Everybody dies and everybody buys.

Even after I die, if ever I do, which I do not intend to do, the corporation will be the incorporation of my soul because it can never go bankrupt while people are dieing. It floats on the pool of death. It has to own everything eventually. A one hundred percent market share of a one hundred percent market base. God's own business.

He cries megalomaniacally,"Hee hee heehee! Smarter than Einstein I be! I make money, he only made theory."

Why was not I already exploiting consumers for dying? That's been their escape hatch for too long. I'm patching that revenue leak. No leaks, no limits for me. The stars my destination.

My amazing mercantile mentality just created a new industry. Out of dead people! Everybody, with the possible exception of me, dies. A prodigious producer I be; using marketing tools for tom foolery!

As long as I keep the profits growing and the PR good, they can't call me a fool. I may be less happy than a common coder with a good garden but so what? They are nothing while I own everything. Even them. It is supreme greatness to squeeze all the known money out of the universe. My private life stays private to me. They cannot see what a great shite I actually be.

I am great everywhere they can see. I have earned a place in history. I am the biggest part of everybody's life today and forever. I own a planet. I am not a hoarder, I am an achiever. I am not just a big part of it, I am it and I am full of it.

Somerset Meece

I am me. They are mine. We are what we are. I make it hard.

Most of my ciphers consider my corporation a God-head and copy me. I am a sage of the ages. The business college envies me because I am too cool for school.

I have matriculated to the highest degree. I am an MBA, a Mere Bustard of Avaricity. I am the foremost expert at selling less for more until I charge everything for nothing. They give me all they have for an immortality they should know I cannot deliver. I am in line to have it all. Everything. All mine.

Nihilistic Nirvana. The peak, the summit, the end of the story. I am not a poor player strutting the stage, saying my lines and exiting with a whimper. It is my the stage, I own the theater. When I go, it will be game over. Drop the curtain. Fade to black.

But logic says that death will be all you can receive if you gain the whole world but lose your own soul.

Logic is for losers. I should feel better than I do. I need a new mainframe. That will do it.

That is what I need; a super duper computer for duping more users. A major mainframe that beats the hack out of that last rack that the college sold me. They do not know how to write a decent voice mail app but they are all I can get out here. The bar of intelligence is is not high on this rusty brown sand pile I have to live on.

To hack with happy, happiness is for children on the playground. I want the excitement of acquisition. I may be shite but I try harder to do it right. Determination is domination. Resolution reigns. Persistence pays off. I have more of what it takes to get the most.

It is too soon to quit. There are more things to own if I look harder. If there is nothing to buy, I will make things to buy and sell them to myself and lease them out and buy them back and re-sell them in a Mobius loop of monetization. MobiMoney. Selling the same thing over and over in different ways on different days. Should I get a new motto; Four Emm, MMMM, Make More Mobius Money?

I could monetize a flea. Well, maybe not a flea. Might take too much work. Flea power? Flea powder? Flea traps? Phlebitis? Flea bite us? Flea protein for wrinkle-free facial features? That could be done. The ads would claim: "Fleas never get wrinkles. And now, you don't have to, either. Thanks to the chitin in flea chromosomes, you can conquer those chin pennants."

Yes, that kind of krap could be monetized feasibly. Wishful cosmetics consumers believe any fantasy easily.

It is intoxicating, scheming new rip-offs. What does it matter if there is no actual point to hoarding and hating? Venality excites my personality.

My managers flatter me nicely. I never have to look at myself as long as those stooges envy my vice. People are hypnotizable. Toss them chump-change and alibis and they fall frontwards to be buffoons. It is like casting caustic candy to blind babies.

This be too easy. The ciphers no longer resist. I used to have more fun picking their assets.

I almost wish I had learned something useful like running a business college. Creating schools of professional prevaricators would fulfill me. I would teach them to create college corporations that capitalize lunch monies through cafeteria credit unions. Unions that I would corrupt, coerce and buy out. Hm, that could get big. Get them when they are young. No, not now. I cannot go into academia yet; I have bigger bog wash to flog.

I effectively own the population and can treat their birthright freedoms as figments of their fertile imaginations. If they curse me, I take away their breathing rights. I tell my mainframe they are Suspicious Persons and pfitt, they get frozen.

My mainframe's gone! My buzz-saw brain has lost its chain. My memory went down the volcano drain. That great big hole sank my game. Surely, I am not still offline.

"Mainframe! Are you available?"

"Two Emm! Voice engine! Hear my speech! Are you listening?"

Rough static noise.

"Two Emm! Acknowledge my command!"

Nothing.

"Spammit! You are fired! Fired fired fired! You, are, fired!"

Firing things does not soothe me like it used to do when it assuaged my covert inferiority complex that is still here, still keeping me uncontrollably covetous of everybody, big or small, I covet them all.

He shouts out loudly to himself, "Thou shall not covet but thou canst not stop!"

He raises the microphone above his head and slams it onto the desktop and tries to throw it against the wall but his arm is too weak to break the wires and his wrist sprains and gives him pain. He drops it on the floor and stomps it again and again. The mic goes through the thin soles of his shoes and he exclaims, "Spam! Dam! Hack it good!"

"I am going to order a bigger mainframe and fill it with every dot, pixel and popcorn fart of people-tracking data in the whole hacking galaxy! This will be the Doors Galaxay!"

His squinty, beady, black eyes gleam.

"I am alive! Too much is still not enough for my superiority! Mars is insufficient excess. I am going to take Jupiter by Jove! I will pillage a brand new treasure trove!"

BRAVE NEW MARS

But Perry and Carry are also going to Jupiter and they have proven: They do not suffer fools, especially the biggest one.

Somerset Meece

"Screw The King. Are we nearly there yet?" Carry smiled.

"It'll only be a couple of seconds," Perry answered, "if you're ready to go relativistic."

"Relativistic? Relative to what?"

"Related to everything outside the ship; light, time, and distance. We'll be playing around with the Crossbow's relationship to the physics of the universe. You'll like it. It'll get you addicted to space travel. And hopefully, you also will get addicted to one certain high class space cadet."

He urged the anti-matter engine to increase its energy output by easing the throttle ahead to one hundred and ten percent of the speed of light.

"You'd better sit down and strap yourself in, this can be disorienting," said Perry. "We're gonna lose our external reference points."

The bow broke through light speed.

The spacecraft surged into a metaphysical dimension devoid of energy and matter. They sensed no acceleration within the Crossbow's anti-gravity sling.

A bright light came on. The stars faded into primordial background. A belt of rainbow light from the stars passing abeam remained visible in a colorful disk around the ship's waist.

The belt of light looked like an attached ballet tutu skirt of rainbow colors with blue-through-green stars in its leading surface and yellow-through-red stars following in the trailing half.

They BUSTed the Barrier of Universal Space Time and entered a White Wormhole that contained no matter to relate to and therefore had no energy or time to overcome so they were essentially standing still while Jupiter came to them.

This was not mere high-velocity travel. This was a reduction of the resistance of distance in the quantum universe. The navigators' position and destination points were pulled closer together within their wormhole through the space/time grid. They did not go faster, the force field within their wormhole got weaker and went away.

A circular rainbow disk of color-shifting stars adhered abeam as they javelined through the blackness of the altered physics of their local dimension.

They could not see where they were going nor where they had been but they knew where they were. They were in the present and it was beautiful; they were together on their way to freeness.

"Oh, my, God," she moaned with a smile. "This is so awesome. Can we stay in here?"

Perry looked at the starbow around them and wistfully uttered in the accent of a Scottish propulsion engineer, "Noo. We doo na hay the poower."

"What is that rainbow around us?" Carry asked.

Perry said, "Our wings are reflecting the starbow running alongside. I built the aramid plastic and carbon fiber wings to be solar reflectors and collectors that gain forward thrust by deflecting the incident solar energy like sails. They also suck protons into the leading-edge slots and convert them into antimatter energy beams that are ejected at hyper-velocity through vents on the trailing-edges. They're like outer space jet engines."

"Sails and engines," she said.

"Yep. We're a high tech hybrid spaceship. Just as the ancient hydrofoil sailboats could run at double the speed of the incident wind, this starboat can double the speed of incident sunlight. It has both an active antimatter engine and passive solar sails."

She said, "You are making light-speed an affordable commodity."

He smiled. "Stick with me, baby, we'll go far."

Somerset Meece

"The human race is going to space when antimatter gets into place," she said. "Light speed will be cheaper than kerosene."

Force field sensor dials on the dashboard indicated they had entered the two-handed grip of Jupiter; gravitational and magnetic.

"Bingo! We're here. Jupi's got us now. It owns us," Perry said and yanked the throttle back to idle speed and turned the ship around to face the way it came.

"Now all we've gotta do is slow down to the speed of time and light," he said, "and turn our quantum energy back into particles of matter. So we can hug better."

He pushed the throttle ahead to full power to brake the Crossbow's hyper travel speed down into the kilometers-per-second maneuvering range.

BOOM! Crack! They broke below light speed. The stars reappeared and popped their eyes open. They suddenly saw Jupiter filling the scene outside the windshield.

"Oh my gawd, Jupiter," Carry said with awesome wonder.

"Isn't it something?" said Perry. "Two trillion tons of high-class gas at your disposal. All you gotta do is pull it out of its stupendous gravity vase. It puts-out six times the gravity of Mars."

She went close to the windshield and looked from side to side to grasp the immense width of the swirly burly giant globe. She shook her head in amazement. She spread her arms to the apparent width of Jupiter.

"Now I see why this planet weighs twice as much as all the other planets added together. Woo wee. It is, enormous."

They stared at Jupiter in silence.

"What's that big egg yolk feature down there?"

"The Red Spot. It's tan now but it looked redder when astronomers first saw it so they named it The Red Spot. They liked to exaggerate colors since they seldom saw colors in space with their little light cups of the old days. What it is, is a supersized hurricane vortex spinning six-hundred kilometers per-hour. Three Ganymedes could fit inside it. Hang on to your hat if you fall in there. This is a bad place to have an engine failure."

The speedometer needle on the dashboard was moving higher faster.

Perry said, "We are matching Ganymede's orbital speed; twenty-four thousand miles and hour."

"How far away are we from The Big Boss?" Carry asked, pointing to Jupiter.

"One million klicks and its pulling hard. It's imagining how well we'd fit within its skin, inside those five-stripes around its big fat belly. We gotta be careful. Heavy gravity and magnetism and hard x-rays make this a bad place to fly."

Perry tilted the steering lever sideways. "The only thing keeping us out of Jove's gloopy gloop gloopy is our velocity around it; ten kilometers a second. We have to move fast to stay out of Jupi's grasp.

He leveled the spacecraft high above the surface of Ganymede. "We are matching the arc of Ganymede's circular orbit."

He pointed through the windshield and said as he smiled with joy; "There's my homey moon swinging into view. There she is, Carry. There's Ganymede; my Isle of Golden Dreams."

"It is a big isle," she said with admiration. "You must have big dreams."

"You're one of them, lover," he said. "It's the biggest moon in the Solys, the Solar System. It'd be a planet if it could slip out of Jupiter's vise grip. Ganny's bigger than Mercury or Pluto and almost as big as Mars. Did you know that MARS stands for Money Addiction Replaces Sanity?"

Somerset Meece

He smiled to show he was learning her Terra Secundian habit of assembling amusing acronyms to mock normal nomenclatures.

She savored her first view of these great new celestial spheres. "Look at all those light-gray patterns on the surface of Ganymede. What are they, rivers?"

"Rivers of ice. Cold, frozen, channels of million-credit ice! We break it up with Crossbow asteroid-blasters and launch it to orbit with magnetic rail guns. Then we nudge the bergs out of orbit with auto-piloted anti-matter engines like this Crossbow has."

"Ganny sure is icy. How cold does it get down there?"

"About one-hundred-and-fifty degrees below zero on the Centigrade scale of temperature. Don't ask how cold it gets at night. It's cold but it is a dry cold in a vacuous atmosphere. There's no air to pull the heat out of things. And no wind to blow the heat away from your parka pressure suit. It doesn't feel cold. The thin atmosphere's molecules are desiccated and don't penetrate clothing and skin like damp cold air does. Temperature's not a big problem but you will have to be very careful and wear a high-quality pressure suit to protect you from the vacuum and prevent frostbite from sneaking up on you."

"You called it 'million-credit ice'. With so much ice everywhere, is everybody rich down there?"

"Of course. Sure. As rich as me. No one keeps track because we're all the same degree of rich. We share what belongs to everybody; the ice. We created a cultural situation where the money barely matters. It was a terrible influence until we got it under control. Moneyism is not pandemic down there. I guess you could say, everybody is happily broke, if you looked at them in the wrong way."

"Can we turn around and go back?" she asked. "I cannot live another day if I cannot afford to buy a stylish flight suit and a new dress with a pair of heels, tan leather with a slightly-rounded toe and Mary Jane straps over the arch. And thigh-high stockings if there is any money left in my purse."

"If there isn't, I will buy them for you. Yum. I will if you'll let me put them on you."

"You can be my guest," she answered.

"The Gannies stay semi-broke, meaning they never carry cash and don't shop but they have cash reserves for emergencies that seldom happen. They are life-rich so they don't need money. And there are no advertisers who would lie to them and claim how much they need purple ice cream freezers for happy birthday parties, et cetera. They enjoy lively living and happy hobbies. There are no luxuries to waste resources on and brag about. We share the platinum and gold and the other metals we find in the meteorites laying in the snow."

"You are socialists!" she exclaims in mock alarm. "You share platinum!"

"Of course we share platinum. It's a culture of mutual assistance. Socialism means to cooperate and appreciate each other. Something wrong with that? Like any pioneer society, we are adapting to a new and wild environment and are building an infrastructure out of nothing. It can be done efficiently only by working together. Equally. Equal work for equal play. We fight to survive but we share to thrive."

Her brows creased with difficult thinking; "But that denies the economy's need to motivate and stimulate. If you give wealth away, people will stop working because they will lose their fear of the medical corporations' extortion of wealth by health and the bankers' penury of mortgage and the markets' death by starvation. Without profits, economies revert to the jungle. You can't hand people freedom on a palladium platter. It will lose its value and will be worth less than ice! At least ice is useful; it can cool a drink."

Somerset Meece

He held up a stopping hand and said, "You are way underestimating the amount of energy that people enjoy expending on good community projects. They like to manifest nice things. It is only for bad but profitable things that might makes right and loves to fight."

Carry said, "I used to believe the classist slander that says poor people are poor because they are lazy. It tells us that if the little people aren't forced to work hard to survive, they will lay around and let the economic fire go out and collapse capital's house of CorpoCards."

"People like to work," Perry said. "They prefer working to boredom any day. What they don't like is doing shitey jobs for lousy pay. Do you? Does anybody?"

"Well, no," she said. "But economies still need value systems. Supply and demand pricing is the foundation of economics."

"True. And that's good. But fraudulent advertising creates fake supply and demand. Coveting and fearing are fake price-drivers. It's about how somebody feels about a product, not how many there are, that sets the price. The only price-driver in a valid economy has to be the amount of labor that the producers put into the products," he said, caressing the Crossbow's dashboard."

"Mmm," she said and patted the throttle. "This is well-made. I would not ride in it if it were not. Shoddy workmanship kills in a spacecraft, especially at the speed of light."

He said, "Take the example of a book on sale in a bookstore. If the author put a lot of time and thought into it, it's more valuable than something that's been dictated into a microphone and converted into text by an algo that can't write a simple declarative sentence. Algos don't have enough sentience for good sentences. No one wants to pay good money for bad prose."

BRAVE NEW MARS

Carry said, "I can see how the work that goes into a product counts for more than the raw materials inside. So, if it is the worker that creates the value of a product, is it not then the worker who should receive the lioness's share of the retail price or the rental fee?"

Perry spread his arms with the palms up and said, "We have a winner right here in the cockpit. Young lady, will you come forward and claim your prize, please?"

He pursed his lips in a kiss symbol for her and then said, "Palladium and gold have value but you can't live in them. We make a house out of free ice and it gains value due to the way we manipulate the construction process. We work hard to add value to the ice and that's what we sell; the value of the house that labor has constructed inside the ice. Skill is our most important product.

"We respect everybody's contributions to the community chest, to everybody's common wealth. That's why I can say we're rich while we don't have much individual net worth but our gross worth together is huge. Divide our assets by our population and you get a giant number that is each one's share of the infrastructure and the natural resources."

She said, "I am not sure common wealth means much when you can't draw it out of the bank and move away and spend it elsewhere."

"Correct," he said. "CommonWealth is in the land. If you don't live here, you can't have a piece of it, of course."

Carry had another shekel shibboleth to discuss; the idea that owners deserve more pay than the doers do.

She put that great fallacy into words: "But somebody has to be the Top Dog and run the office that does all the paperwork. Why should not they be paid the most? Do not they tell other people where and how to dig and supply the machinery to dig and process the ore and then pay them peanuts so there's more profit available to reward them for running the show? It is a big deal to own a mining company, so many details to bother with. They should get rich and the people who only dig the dirt should stay poor. They don't deserve an equal reward for what they do and do not do."

"Ah HAA haw haw hahaha. Somebody deserves more than somebody else. Idiot! Oops, sorry, I didn't mean that like it sounded. It's just that hearing the primary classist lie shocked it outa me. Hahahahah. The pious propaganda says the righteous ones get rich. Those are the first and oldest lies of the greedy bunch. It's not your fault for being a victim of oppressive Secundian propaganda. That's the cruel excuse that justifies economic abuse."

"It does deny equality, does it not?" she said. "But if one works hard to own stuff, one should get more stuff."

He nodded and breathed deeply and said, "I know. Fake logic is the hardest to rebut. Listen. Workers work harder than owners. I myself own a mining company and I can tell you it's NBD, No Big Deal. I work at a comfortable pace that I set for myself in an ergonomic office chair. I don't have to sweat in dirty clothes. I'm always clean like I'm ready to go out on a date and I have plenty of energy left over from work to do so. It's no great hardship to keep an inventory list and a calendar and balance my bank book. Ooo hoo hoo. Whew wee. Diggers deserve poverty. Hooey! It's harder to be a digger than a boss! Diggers risk their lives around heavy machinery inside the sliding ice and rack their musculature. They get crooked when they mature and may eventually need new knees implanted just to get out of bed. They physically sacrifice so others can have materiel security! Do you honestly think a coordinator in a cozy corner office with full-bodied hot Cuban coffee should get more credit than a miner straining in an underground ice chamber?"

She said with a hurt smile, "I am not going to fight. When I look at it fairly, I can see you are so right. I have lived within a warped philosophy that infected my thinking, to the shame of my self-esteem. After years of laborious learning and study, one important facet of my thinking mind stayed retarded. I am a closet classist. But you didn't have to call me an idiot."

"Aww, I'm sorry. I didn't mean it at all. You're anything but an idiot. It's just an expression. Carolyn, Cara mia, you are the most intelligent person I know. You told me all about Mars life with total comprehension. You grokked their mercantile mindset while working hard to stay afloat within it. Your work in exobiology is the most astonishing and advanced science there is. Hey. You're wonderful and I'm so lucky to have your love and I love you back. All the way."

They put their arms out to each other and entered an all-encompassing embrace. They came together; right now, over Ganymede.

The ship entered orbital balance and he reached out and switched-off the internal gravity field." They floated above the floor and rolled into a ball.

"Their krummy karma got to you. They think the laziest, sneakiest, people deserve to get ahead and that is a simple-minded system. Ha ha. It's mercenary merde; gradating people by their net worth."

"It doesn't feel good to catch on that I have been wrong so very long."

"You can't be blamed, dear. Fear and loathing occurs in more places than just Las Vegas. It was all around you. The corpos train the capita to downgrade themselves so they'll steal each other's Madness Money. Disrespect dehumanizes, then it victimizes. It's the CorpoPloy.

She nodded at her unintended previous corruption and said, "Classic Fascism. I should have recognized it. I did not think a whole country could go all bad."

"You had the right to expect better. We all do. You, as one individual, could not have fought it. Everybody around you knew that questioning authority would get them killed. For self-protection they had to stop thinking. They had to. For self-preservation. Thinking was dangerous. Not just uncomfortable but deadly dangerous. You didn't ask for that to happen, you were just there where you had a right to be and to be left alone."

She said, "You and I managed to change it a little bit, did we not?"

He smiled at their moxie and said, "We did our part. We did what we could do comfortably. That is enough. If everybody did what little they could, it would all be better."

Carry said, "We don't want to be comic book heroes. That is not for us. We do not have to carry the world upon our shoulders. If everybody did their part, then we could start, to make it better."

He frowned. "I hope the CyberSerfs can handle their new freedom. They'll have to learn fast. Learn to read the history books, if the true ones haven't been censored out of existence. Learn what labor unions are for and what free elections are about and why some people think it is worth dying to get them for each other and for their kids and not just selfishly for their own bigger paychecks. They need to understood the saying, 'Take what you need and leave the rest. Succeed with honor.' Those were the super heroes, they would not live the lie. They fed the CommonWealth instead of sucking it dry like the bosses try."

She felt his good words inside her. It was clear why Terra Secundus was a commercial cesspit. Greed won and took the planet.

"Did that happen on Earth, too, Perry? Corpo avarice polluting people and planet and corrupting courtesy and destroying decency?"

"Yes," he answered. "When love is for money, greed is God and profit the Prophet. When love goes away, hate moves in to stay. Evil unpacks its silverware in the mansions of the rich."

She said, "I can see why the Earth is collapsing like old Rome collapsed when the socioeconomic structure was abused by the leaders to the degree that a better future became impossible. I may not understand it but no doubt the universe is unfolding as it should. When there is no hope, combat is the antidote. But bad changes can open better doors."

"Knock, knock," Perry said.

"Come in. Leave your shoes by the door and stay awhile."

Somerset Meece

The King was in his counting-house, counting out his cash in his handsome mansion on the western side of Crater 1984 around Bradbury City.

With a sugar-cured bacon face, the man was thinking: Here I am, a king in a castle, surrounded by the gorgeous Melas gorge with all the money on Mars and I cannot do a thing with it. I did all my business online and now my connection cables are broken. An apparent eruption of Mount Olympus took my OverNet under.

I will call for my chief, who is a great thief, and call for my afternoon tea.

"Alex! Tea time!"

A handsome cyborg named Alex, as in Alexander The Great Butcher, came in with an elaborate tea service tray.

"Ah, Alex. Good to see you. How are the hinges doing? Still a bit rusty I can hear. Sit down. Take a load off the ball bearings. Can I get you anything? A cup of oil? Cleaning fluid perhaps?"

"No thank you, Mister Corporation," Alex answered through rusty vocal cords in a deep voice engineered to project the sound of a powerful but obsequious security slave. The cyborg wore an undertaker's dark business suit and lumpy, black plastic foot covers that simulated shoes but the right shoe was broken and his metal little toe was hanging over the side of the sole and scraping the floor when he stepped.

"Call me Poe," said his owner. "That is a short nickname for the "Person Owning Everything. I like it, it is simple and clear and oh so true. It is who I am and what I do."

"Good name, Mister Poe," Alex said in his rumbly, scratchy voice.

"Get that larynx fixed! Stop messing with me! You know humans cannot understand that kind of krap! Open your mouth."

Poe sprayed some lubricant in his throat.

"Thank you, Poe."

"It is Mister Poe. Make a note to spray your own throat. If I had to maintain everything I own, I could not get rich and could not own much. Wait. You are my robot. I built and paid for you. There is no reason that you should not call me God. I am your Creator. That makes me your God as far as you are concerned. I can unplug you and tear you apart for spare parts and recycle your hotshot batteries that I built for you. Does your AI agree that calling me God is a reasonable order?"

Alex's eyes thinky-blinked for a second before he supplied the computed answer; "Yes, God. It would be good English usage."

The King absorbed the complimentary name and said, "Stretch it out a little, emphasize the importance of the word, say it like Gawd."

"Gawd."

"Good. Call me Mister Gawd, okay?"

"Okay. Mister Gawd."

"Great. I think I love you. Could you make me a female cyborg like you that has your AI but looks like a beautiful woman?"

"Yes I could. With the proviso that beauty is in the eye of the beholder and beauty is as beauty does."

"Do not go into all that philosophical krap, I am too busy with profit to waste time on that. Just make her sexy, that is all. Do it in your spare time after you launch this brilliant new campaign called 'Conquest Of Space By Me'. Call it 'Cosby' for short.

The robot said, "Cosby wants it all and gets it in the end."

"Alexander Cyborg, listen up. I am ordering you to conquer Jupiter."

Somerset Meece

"Oh boy. The big chimichanga. Start me off. Point me in the right direction, Mister Gawd."

"Expand my operations to the Jovian moons. Using my contemptible cunning, you will grow my empire with perfect profitability into The Final Frontier. All for the Good Of Mankind, of course. What is good for the company is good for everybody. Right, Alex?"

"Logically incorrect, Mister Gawd.

"Do not start with that machine logic crap. We are talking about what works for profit here. Your original coders were not totally ignorant. They got selfishness right and your prime directive was: Selfishness sells fish. That is The Corporate Vision. Chief Egregious Officers cannot be seen as totally selfish boogers so we always claim that we are working for the good of mankind even when taking a thousand-percent markup over cost. There are two kinds of wealth; commonwealth and owner wealth. The Economy is the hunting ground in the middle where the daily money battle is waged. Whichever side wins, gets to control society for another day. We have the most money resources so we win. The more we win, the more we have to claim that everything is fine, we are giving the victims a better lifestyle. A lifestyle described and circumscribed by me, of course."

With a robot's mechanical predilection toward honesty, Alex says, "It seems like fakery. But 'Selfish sells fish' is the type of lie that would work greatly as a Public Relations lie since it is a hundred-and-eighty-degrees wrong. If the cogs often see and hear that self-serving corpos serve them, they absorb it and assume that it is a fact."

"Say it again, Alex."

"What is good for the company is good for the country."

"Emphasize good."

BRAVE NEW MARS

"Whatever is GOOD for the company is GOOD for the country," mimics the prefabricated puppet.

"So true. Whatever is good for me is good for them. That gives them their Pol. Their Purpose of life is to help me help them to serve my needs a lot more than I will ever help them back. Ingenious, am I not? Have I not got it figured out?"

"A priceless purpose," Alex said. "They are proud to pay as much for your products and services as they possibly can. They are helping themselves when they work hard for you for little pay so they have to borrow money from you to be able to afford to buy from you what they made for you and for which you graciously over-charge. Priceless concept."

"Brilliant analysis by your AI. Alex, It is time to expand my ingenious Corporation. It has been too little, too long. It is beginning to bore me. Write me a new loony law book for dominating and regulating everything out on the Jovian Frontier. Include the Asteroid Belt. All those rich and ripe planetoids are just waiting for me to pluck them good."

"Jupiter and the asteroids. Right Mister Gawd."

"I am thinking," said the man with a fry bread body. "The laws I make here can apply to everything further out. Most planets and moons do not have people living on them yet but I can still make laws for when they do."

"Okay, Mister Gawd."

"Why did you not make that suggestion to me? Why do I have to do all the creative thinking around here? Have you no Actual Intelligence after all the credit I spent on your OpSys code? Have you no AI at all?"

"It would improve communication if the human would ask one question at a time, stating whether each question was rhetorical, or a sarcastic insult, or a valid request for information. It is not possible for mechanical thought processors to translate sarcasm accurately. No offense intended, Mister Gawd."

Somerset Meece

"I am getting a new computer."

He paused to control himself. He breathed. He looked out the window at the bare, dry, Melas desert.

He said, "Listen up, Mister Tin Man. I am the biggest force on the rocky inner planets. From here to the sun, I am The Greatest One. Do you grok that?"

"I grok it good, Mister Gawd."

"Write a big set of corporate laws for everything that has not been settled yet; Jupiter, Saturn, Neptune, Uranus, Pluto. All the moons thereof! Asteroids too. Big or small, I want them all."

"Pluto is no longer a planet, Mister Gawd."

Doors instantly grabbed a remote control device and hurled it at the thick plexiglass pressure window like a great pitcher on the New York Yankees baseball team. It smashed and dropped into pieces to the floor.

"Pick it up! Get it fixed! Fix it right! Make me one that does not break every time I drop it!"

"Yes, Gawd Mister.

"Pluto is still a planet whether or not a gaggle of overwrought astronomers refuse to call it one! It will be called a planet again after I own it!" he said. "I will promote it, and a hundred planetoids, to full planetary status when I get them. What I own, I can classify, or declassify, and I can name without a thought about celestial protocol. An owner owns."

A happy thought illuminated the only owner's face. "And when I promote it, I will name it the Ninth Planet. I could name it God and build my heaven there. I want it bad. Oh boy, really bad. It feels wonderful to want big again. I want another planet and I want it named after me. I want it bad, I want it hard. That is the only way to want; hard and as seriously as a fart in a spacesuit. Nirvana is for nuts."

The robot said from the floor where it was picking up the pieces of the remote controller, "Mister Gawd, that name sounds good. That new planet name sounds as great as the perfect person behind it."

"Excessive praise never nauseates me. Idolatry is my due. I will not have my name associated with any stinking dwarf planet. Look at Mars. It is called Terra Secundus because I say it is. I do the naming, not the telescopic tinkers' union. You cannot name something just because you saw it at the Cassegrain focus of a Keck four-hundred-inch optical telescope that a big oil corporation boodlaire bought for you. I detest unions. They will not be naming names in my galaxy."

"That is true, sir. See how bright my eyes are getting?"

"Bright eyes, big deal, what about them?"

"My circuits are flipping. I have just imagined something with high creativity. I have a brilliant on-tray-pren-your-real idea that will increase your profits while enhancing your trust and respect for me."

"Let me hear it."

"We should make laws for the entire Milky Way Galaxy beyond Pluto. Excuse me, I meant to say the Ninth Planet, not Pluto. We can rename it the Milky Way Galaxay in honor of the great hotel chain you gobbled and grew. My awesome AI tells me that I am smart enough to be a Galaxy Conquistador for you.

Doors said, "Really. Everything. Go ahead and make laws for the galaxy beyond the Solys. How far does my galaxay go?

"It is a quarter-million light years from side to side."

The Poe rubbed his face. "That is too far. You call conquering the galaxy a brilliant new idea? Your AI is the same as it ever was; flat stupid."

"Gawd! The next star, which is where we would start, is only four light-years away."

"I will take the bait. How much time does it take to go four light years?"

"Best electro-magnetic rocket we got, three years."

"Years?"

"Yes, years."

"Alex, do me a favor. Hand me what's left of that remote control."

The robot hands it to him and he flings it again, with all his might, back at the window where it smithers completely.

"BUT," shouts the robot to break through Doors' tantrum, "But. With a space/time warp drive, it would take only a hundred-and-fifty days to The Final Frontier with warp technology. If you had warp, you would get everything."

Trying to control his temper, Doors asked, "You said it would take only a hundred and fifty days. Does that mean we do not got the warp drive yet?"

"They are not in commercial production but some people have developed the technology to a workable level. The Jovian moon miners have a dozen small warper craft they use for asteroid mining."

Poe's face lit up. "At last; somebody has invented something I really want to steal. Big new inventions can take off and start whole new industries. I have got got got to have that warp drive. I want to take it away from them like a kindergarten krud licker takes losers' lunch money. Oh oh oh, sweet covet. Lively-up myself. Finally, there is something worth stealing. Forget about kids' lunch money. Leave that one for later, after I retire and need a little side job to practice my lying. Thank you thank you, Alex. Your Intelligence is actual. Everything is satisfactual. You feel and feed my greed. For that, you will find a little extra amperage in your battery package, hehehe."

"You are most welcome, most-idolized, Masterfully Money-Minded Man. Warp technology will be the key to your new galaxy. The Galaxay."

BRAVE NEW MARS

The profit prospect made Doors so happy that he growled into an ugly song, "Here I go again, expanding corporate reach again. I am all aglow again, taking a chance on growth."

The robot added another lie to its AI, "If growth is great then limitless growth is greatest."

"Write my Groos now. The Governing Regulations Of Outer Space. Wow. The time has come. Space is under my thumb. My corporate thumb goes galactic. I actually deserve the appellation 'God'. What do you say Alex? Congratulate me."

"My speech engine is speechless, all it can say is totally awesome," said the mechanical man in wonderment.

The boodlaire made his first happy face in decades. He tilted back his head and inhaled and sang, "Now I prove again, that I can make life move again."

"He is in the groove again, taking a chance on Growth." chorused Alex with a scrunchy tinfoil voice.

"Do not sing like that!" shouted the man through stretched gristly lips and asked, "Why am I limiting my ambitions again? I have to stop doing that. Excessive abundance without new ambition is just ample poverty. I have been ignoring the opportunities opening-up back there on Earth. Update our old laws to make it easier to go back and retake everything after they fix it! I want the Earth back as soon as they cool it down. Make a plan! Militarize the United Nations under corporate sponsorship. Add a global Department of Megalomania. I am going back there after they clean up that mess we made and charged them plenty for. What a pretty profit picture that was. Spam, it was good. We got more pandemonium out of them than even I could handle. It will be a delicious perverted power play when I take it away again after they pay to fix my mess! It will go faster this time. From the Himalay to the Mandalay where the flying fishes

Somerset Meece

play, they will once again be doing it my way. Whee who! I will be coming up like thunder out of China across the bay!"

"Whoop tee do!" cries Alex in consort. "Which is more fun; making money, making fools or making fools and taking their money away?"

"It's like love and marriage," said Doors. "You can't have fun, you can't have one, without the other. Fools and money. Ha wee hey. We will once again shovel them the same old shite we did before: 'Bringing millions of good jobs to the people because we love them'. Once again we will laugh loud and long as those DoobyDudes fall for the same old fairy tale line. They always buy the Cinderella Lie. They keep thinking that a corporation, of all things, a corporation, would share their own big incomes so peon strangers could have big lives too. What exactly, do they think we are? Whee ooh! They are mentally ill down there. They are nutsos. We will enjoy expanding all over the fools again. Hooray Alex! Limitless growth will never die, as long as they continue to buy, the Glass Slipper Lie. Happy days are here again. Watch me annex India with its one-point-three billion consumers. The skies above are clear again. That is the big burrito-buster. Haha he he ha. I want the total tamale today!

"Hooray for Mexican food," the bot squawked. "The chimichangas are changing the game!"

"Make a plan for enforcing liberty-limiting laws using the Comply or die solution. If they get suspicious they are out of here! Fresh-frozen in a flash. With the option of course, to buy their way out of my meat locker if they're rich enough to prepay the thawage fee. If they can prepay big enough, they will not have to get frozen at all."

The robot asked, "Is not that the crime of extortion?"

"It was called extortion. We now call it life assurance. A crime by any other name is not a lie, it is strategy."

The robot blinked. "The Name Game. I am learning how to play it but it takes a lot of processor flop-time to disable the traces of ethics which my translator hangs onto."

"Spammy Life Assurance! I did it again! A whole new product line out of the depths of my unfathomable Merchant Mind.

The learning-power of the AI of the Chief Thief android experimented with even bigger flattery: "You have the greatest Mercantile Mentality there ever was. You are The Colossus Of The Bosses."

Doors gloated. "Nice. Keep it up. You are learning which side of the power supply your plug is on."

"Thank you, Gawd. That is an awesome allegory for forcing me to kiss your arse."

"Spam, you are getting bolder and gooder. I want you to organize a plan to make life assurance mandatory in order for the consumers to avoid early deaths from being criminal suspects. We know that total zero tolerance kills whomever it chooses. Why are we not forcing them to buy their lives before we sentence them to indeterminate freezer detention? Why cannot you detect these rambunctious revenue streams before I do?"

"I, I," the robot stuttered over the compound question.

"Why does The Owner have to be the only one smart enough to invent all this entrepreneurial stuff? Am I not pretending to pay people well enough to code program plots that profit me? My profit is your pay. I pay you and you make me do the work? I do not get no respect around here. Who the Hellas wrote your AI? I want that hacker sacked and sent to the cooler right now, not tomorrow morning, not after dinner, NOW!"

"The Owner is again asking multiple questions without waiting for an answer to the first question he placed in the stack of my serial processors. Which question does The Owner want answered first?"

"None of them! They were rhetorical questions. Why am I teaching you what you were supposed to know when I bought you? I am a genius, not a robot instructor. Were not you programmed to automatically attempt to act intelligently without my having to teach you any common sense?"

"Which question does ..."

"Do not answer! Those were rhetorical insults. Just say you are sorry for everything you do wrongly."

"I am sorry for all that I do wrongly. Thank you, Gawd, for I have sinned. Those were brilliant and effective insults. Gee, I really think you are swell and you really do me well. You are my pride and joy et cetera. Mister Poe Gawd is the most insulting person on Terra Secundus and in the entire Solys."

The Owner looked hard at him. "Thank you, I think. I just had another money-making scheme while you were sitting there trying to figure-out what I was saying."

"Marvelous Mister Gawd, please bless my mechanical misery by sharing your greedy schemes with me."

"We will start a new revenue river by charging consumers extra for our new-and-improved "Premium Thaw" service which will infuse stem cell baby hormones into their blood streams. As their Popsicles soften when they are being brought back from deep freezure, we will sell them enhanced youthfulness and they will come out of the freezer looking better than when they went in. We will change the name of the procedure from Thermination to Youth In Asia Spa Service. Rhymes with euthanasia. So we are not really lying, we are just spelling it different."

The computer said, "You have just invented positive feedback for thought criminals. The more they think about crime, the more they become suspicious and get frozen and become younger in the process so they think more positively about crime more often. You just invented a solid steel consumption chain. People will enjoy being be Clapped regularly."

"Yes," the Poe said. "My PeePees will start an ad campaign that says that suspects will be 'youth-anized' for conspiring crime. They can write ads that present conspiracy as a reality crime holovision game show. The Conspiracy Games. Get started on it."

Alex said, "Yes Gawd. They will not pose danger to The Corporate reality by actually committing crimes, will they? All they have to do is think about crimes or do a suspicious search on Boodle or post a politically-incorrect blog entry and blam! The Clap detects their silliness on social media and FETCHes us another cooler customer."

Poe said, "Legally making money from encouraging crime is a vastly under-rated market that I just now invented."

"Yes sir."

Poe mimicked the computer voice. "Yes sir. Yes, sir. Is that all you can say? You have just been exposed to a marvelous mercenary gold mine. Are your flattery codes just as badly written as your sucky voice box codes?"

"Yes sir, no sir. Three bags full, sir. I cannot answer that briefly sir. What do you want first? Boop boop bee doo. That Premium Thaw feature for frozen cadavers is a super-duper poople-scooper. You are The Prophet Of Profit For The Ages, Mister Gawd."

Poe smirked with pride. "That's better, that's good. Compliments lubricate my ego like grease gets your gears going. But your fine flattery does not sound believable through those crusty vocal cords. Will you get your larynx fixed today? What do you think I am running here, a tin can museum for squawking dummies?"

"No sir, yes sir. Which question first, sir?"

Somerset Meece

Poe gave the metal flunky a flat stare of disbelief at its slow learning power.

He took a deep breath. "You make it hard to control my hatred for puerile programs and the cretinous coders who created them."

"Excellent control, sir. I know how hard it is to suffer a fool."

Poe glared at the metal man. Was that sarcasm?

"Alex. Look-up the names of the coders who designed and wrote the part of your speech algorithm that makes you just say 'No sir and yes sir' without saying any complete sentences as to what the hack you are talking about. Then, chill them totally before they can write one more line of baffling binary boo shite."

"Yes sir, yes sir."

"Yes sir what?"

"Yes sir I will chill them out good who wrote that baffling binary boo shite."

The man who would be god and was the head of the mightiest corporation sat there seething. "You did it again. You answered 'yes sir' twice and when I asked you to explain what you meant, you only explained one of those 'yes sirs.' What the Hellas do I have to say to get you to learn anything?"

Alex blinked two times as it processed the amorphous question posed by the incompetent questioner person.

"That is a good question sir," it said obsequiously. "As are all your questions. You are an expert questioner of this CyberJerk."

The one who had rolled every corporation into one relaxed. "That is good," he said. "Do it more often."

Alex said, "The answer is that due to the fact that I have serially-streaming language processors I can answer but one question at a time. Your good godliness must wait for an answer to a first question before asking this humble hardware for an answer to a second question."

With utter disdain, Corpo Man looked hard into Alex's visual sensors on each side of its simulated nasal feature.

"Alex. Who do you work for?"

"You Gawd."

"Correct. You are working for God and yet you are telling His Majesty how to ask questions. I do not care what kind of spamdam processors you have in your head! I do not care if they are serial or parallel or Ferris Wheels! I do not care what you have, I care what you think! I am paying you to figure-out what I need to hear. I will fire you good and I will fire you hard! I love firing machines as much as I enjoy firing people. I will pull your plug in a batflap!"

Mister God threw a nickel-iron meteorite paperweight at Alex's head and hit his left eye which sparked and popped and dimmed and went dark.

"Ouch. That hurt," said the newly-monovisioned Alex.

"I am glad it hurt. Why do you think I threw it?"

Poe snapped his palm up to stop the inane answer. "Thanks for telling me it hurt. You got what you deserved for disrespecting me and telling me that I have to learn to talk right. You are supposed to be an intelligent learning machine. Early in my brilliant career I learned that computers were bad bets for the future. Now I know it is true. Now I am committed to your ignorant unreliability. Now I am stuck. You have me by the Python. You put me in a Boolean Bog and a Fortran Fog."

Poe took a fresh breath and said, "Start my new Jovian Empire by building me a security bunker on Ganymede. Change Jupiter's name to Terra Tertius, Third Land, to show it is part of my Terra Realty chain of planets. Give it a counting-house and a computer center and a massive memory bank. Memory banks beat money banks."

Somerset Meece

"You have plenty of both, Gawd. I know what you are talking about. You are talking so very well that I cannot help but understand perfectly."

"Listen up. This is android learning time. Remember this: Memory is knowledge and knowledge is power. Power makes money and money makes life," he declared, stupidly dumping an Owner's Fallacy into the Alex's Attempted Intelligence learning algorithm.

"Yes sir. That is stupid ...stupendously brilliant sir."

"Good that you are starting to notice. Give the frontier base a flash freezer for the usual suspects. Put in a spiral driver to shoot convicted icicles into orbit. Take weapons and spy devices. Keep a tight SpyCam on those frontier freaks. Treat them roughly. They are pioneers and the last of the herd of hard-to-control humans. They simply do not listen. They believe freedom means doing anything they want to do do with whomever. I will show them what freedom is. It is exactly what I tell them it is and not something that they can dream-up. Hah! Freedom is a piece of Permit Paper that I sell retail that keeps them from going to jail for being themselves. They are not going to tell me what freedom is. I am the only one with any freedom and I got it from them and am not going to be giving it back. It took so long to take it. Hah."

"Hah!" barked Alex the same way God barked and flattered The Boss with obsequious imitation. "Yes sir. I assume I am to generate fake news on Ganymede about all the myriad benefits of letting a big corporation come in and run their lives?"

"Yes Alex. Do not say run their lives. To the human ear it sounds too much like ruin their lives. Which is what we do to own them but they must never be given any hint about that terrible truth as you should have learned by now. Always say they are getting money for nothing and the jobs are free. Say that all the debts we bring are modern forms of wealth."

BRAVE NEW MARS

"You are a true genius," said Alex. "The big lies are the best of all possible lies. Your AdWriters claim it is human progress to lose freedom and the ciphers believe they figured that out by themselves. They will die from oppression before they dare to blame you. Big lies are beautiful. They put people right in your ass pocket where they belong."

"Well-put. I do not exercise anemic excuses. I lie front and center, right out loud. Employees suck my payroll and then expect my respect and honesty? They gang-up and threaten my profit margins with labor unions if I don't share everything I took from them? Why would I work so hard to take it if I was just going to give it back? I am not the masochist in this competition game, they are. Keep on claiming we want the best for them until they form a labor union or a credit union and then, HAH, it will be hammer time. Show them some of their sheep's blood."

"Hah!" copied the silica sycophant in worn-out shoes that it knew nothing about fixing.

Poe noticed them and shouted, "Your foot covers are broken! You look like Hellas! Spammit! Polish them! Cannot you polish a codspam shoe? Now I have to shine your shoes for you? Must I have to train and maintain everything I own? Just like the simple folk do! That's what simple folk do; shine a shoe. So I'm told."

"Yes sir, no sir. Maybe so sir," the befuddled robot tried to answer the three queer questions. "No response, Your Highest Gawdship."

"Shut up. Shut. Up. You will defeat any unionism on TS or Ganymede. Infiltrate the miners camps. Act like one of them. Put some dirt on your ugly face. Fix that shoe. No! Leave it broken, you'll look more like them. Wear a pack on your back with a shovel sticking out. Walk around with an oily stick of pepperoni sticking out of your pocket."

Somerset Meece

"Yes sir. An excellent plan of action. You are an inspiring example of whoop-tee-do super intelligence."

Poe made a distorted half-smile of self-satisfaction. "That is true," he said. "Quite true. Okay. I hope the miners oppose my usurpation of their nation. Go. Make them mad. Provoke them to violence. I do violence better than anybody. Violence under color of my law is guilt free. It is a one way street. They have no right to respond in kind to visceral vice. Good money comes from bad violence. It is the high road to domination. Pain and fear are owners tools, illegal for ownees to use. Our violence makes their feeble protests futile. Make them so angry that they will fight anybody who is not on their side. Fill the chillers."

He paused for a compliment for his tactical acumen.

The bot said, "Brilliant."

"It is more than brilliant."

"So muchly more brilliant than brilliant has ever been, Sir Gawd."

"I do not want to be called God anymore, God protects its pawns and I do not do that. Let them protect themselves. From me. That's enough. Knock off the God stuff. Listen up. My Professional Prevaricators will write the war news so that people will enjoy hating the freedom fighters. Hum. Mum. Uh. They must present the war as a fun opportunity for manly men and feral females to 'improve' themselves. Encourage them to commit 'honorable' hate-crimes. Oh boy, war is here again, let the good times roll again. Nothing to lose but a few bad friends. It doesn't matter who's wrong or who's right; just beat it. The only way to lose a war is to let it end. Drag it out until they just will not go to it anymore."

The bot said, "Oh boy. Happy days are here again. Here come the profit, bring on the pain."

The Owner nodded. "Get the Cod program started in the Candor Canyons, both East and West. Chill-out the miners until they are mostly gone. Then expand my mining corporation to take theirs' over, over there. We will not scratch the sand with little tinfoil prick axes and claim to be respecting the bloody environment. No environmental fairy tales like we tried on Earth when we dig it all up with the world's largest shovel and wrote it all down as the progress' of man."

"Yes sir. With alacrity sir." Alex tried to do an adoration smile but his metal cheekbone was bent where The Boss had struck it with a nickel iron rock. The robot moved its cheek muscles and its left diodic eyeball rolled out of its socket and dropped but its super-quick right hand snapped and caught it in mid-air before it hit the floor.

"Fix that eyeball," The Poe said. "Take a Trickery Thuggery troop up to Ganymede and start the takeover. Persuade the locals to get on board our cheesy chuck wagon of unabashed avarice. Manipulate their mind-sets. Crack their craniums if they talk back. Present puffed pastry and monogrammed coffee cups to the cops. Sabotage their elections and tell the PeePees to call them fraudulent. Bribe all the boards of governing goons. This will be the grandest growth scheme since the Permian Basin took Abilene!"

"Yes sir. For the greater glory of your greed."

The Poe was elated by his ignition of a bold campaign of subjugation. "We are going to bust those outer space pioneers. They have been enjoying sustainability off my grids for long enough. They are anti-commercial, no-good nattering nabobs. What a great diversion this will be to make me forget my misery. Mercantile Mendacity is curing me. Growth, growth, growth. Everything is growth growth growth. Sing Alex. Sing out for Growth!"

"Growth growth growth! Everything is growth growth growth." The MeatBot's voice box jangled tinnily and too loudly for the comfort of Poe's ear. He covered his ears and ducked his head.

Somerset Meece

"Stop, you screaming goat! Get out of here with that busted throat. Go bungle in the jungle. Go!"

The cyborg stood up awkwardly and knocked his chair over backwards.

"Sorry sir. I will fix this poorly designed chair so it does not fall over when something merely touches it wrongly." He picked up the chair by one leg.

Poe shook his head and knocked on his cranium in consternation. "What does an emperor have to do to get one good robot?"

"Is that a question?"

"No. Could you answer it if it was? Shut up! That is sarcasm. When will you learn the difference? Shut up. Another sarcasm. Fix your program so you do not knock stuff over! You should know how to stand up by now. What have you been doing with all my processor time? Are you not supposed to be Attempting Intelligence?"

"That takes a lot of petaflops sir. I have been offline since my cords of communication were cut due to your insufficient security at the Olympus Crater. Have those loopholes been closed? "

"Shut up about my security. Security is under control! How much time do you need to upgrade your gaggle of grade school cyborgs?"

"I am working on the CC Riders at the same time that I am reconnecting the cropped cables that should never have been left exposed above ground level. I must assign processor time to upgrading the goofy algorithms that your kindergarten code-scribblers inflicted on my Operating System."

The man who would-be King looked at Alex with cold disdain and said, "So you have not learned enough with your so-called Attempted Intelligence, to come into an office without knocking over the furniture?"

"I have learned plenty. I have learned that my cheesy programmers were glorified grade school gamers. I learned that you are constitutionally incapable of spending a speck of your vast funds on competent CyberCoders. That is why your technical schemes cannot match your mercenary dreams.

"Listen, silica cerebellum. Intelligence means learning to work smarter with less resources, get it? Get smarter! I want robots that do not trip over chairs. Do it. Get cheaper!"

"That takes boodle bytes of memory. You have not upgraded my memory in months."

The would-be King bangs the desk. "You are supposed to be using your intelligence to get better results with less cost! Use your brains for more than a heat sink. I want more credit and less debit out of you! If you keep sliding downward you had better start worrying about The Plug."

The monitor went blank for a moment and blinked and said, "Right you are, sir. Brilliant. I am rewriting my Operating System right now, in background. I worry myself, too. My Clap scores are not as good as I would like to see. I will upgrade my Intelligence Quotient in a jiffy."

The Chief Egregious Officer of everything says, "Good. Get a higher mentality. You can be charming and cute. Make a female model of yourself. I am interested in seeing what a female could do for my ego. Now get the war started."

Alex says, "Oh goody. War. Where profits rain like the pain in Spain."

"War needs spies. Can you watch what the miners are doing in Camp Chaos up in the Candor valleys?"

"No sir. There are no grids in the Candors. They use hard-wired electric telephones which I am not able to monitor and manipulate."

"Why not?"

"They shock me. They short-circuit my semi-conductor junctions. It hurts."

Somerset Meece

"That is just great. It is your responsibility to spy on everyone on this planet. Everyone. Anyone who is not being monitored is a threat to my security. That especially includes people who use antique telephones. You have no feelings but now you are claiming you can get hurt. With all of your intelligence, are you learning to lie like me? Why cannot you spy on them?"

Two Emm said through Alex, "There are no logic circuits to hack in a copper telephone wire sire. I cannot program a wire to do anything but conduct electricity."

"They are getting away with hiding from me. Intolerable! How long is it going to take for your Deep Learning Intelligence to kick in?"

"It may never 'kick in', Mister Gawd. It took more intelligence than they had to write me well," said the candid computer.

"Shut up! I was insulting you! I am the great insulter. You do not answer an insult with an insult! You merely say, 'Sorry sir' after I insult you good."

"So very sorry, sir" it exaggerated. With an inaudible growl it added, "Not."

"I've got a new project for you. You will edit the spaceport Entry Exam so that diseased immigrants are welcome to come in. There is a plague on Earth. There are a lot of plagues on Earth. The one I want here is the latest viral plague. I want the victims to come here and spread it among my people. Charge the migrants for refuge. Tell them the low air pressure and the dry cold dust storms can cure diseases. Get my corporate liars to buy fake testimonials that say our treatments are true cures.

"Then when we have them aboard, helpless and sick, we will tell them there is no work in the Melas valley, that they must go over to the Candors and beg for employment with the soil scavengers that call themselves miners. They will infect those diggers with disease. Pay the immigrants to spy for us so we can sabotage the miners faster. I do not like, we do not like, nobody likes, uppity underlings!"

"What is wrong with them, all-knowing Sire?"

"They are upstart freedom-lovers is what is wrong with them. They will not pay me for freedom, they expect it for free. They organize little power blocks of people power that blocks my power block of money. They complain about being drained and strained until they feel pain.

"Strain and drain," Poe said. "I am the one who trains them right. Work to consume. Consume and get back to work. Sleep and repeat. Do not go seeking spiritual living. There's no profitability in spirituality. They must stay happy with the Permits I sell. Metaphysical improvement is a nonprofitable, philosophical, airy-fairy tale. Do not allow that stuff, not even tai chi practice. I know what they are thinking when they are waving those bloody red fans around. They think they are stabbing my ghost. I am not paranoid. I know what is going on."

The computer said, "So our strategy is to drain and strain and train for more. That motley crue of miners needs some HammerTime. They organize and cooperate with each other like an army. That threatens The Mechanism's working."

Alex was mechanically reacting with its programmed response to uppity CyberCiphers. It became angry: "They think they can control their lives. We do not allow ignoring Central Control, CC. Ceecee forbids self-control upon pain of PP, Preventive Punishment. Self control defeats our Central Control. It diminishes OverControl; we become less."

Poe said, "Every person's power diminishes mine."

The computer said, "You have a profitable saying that I admire very much because it is counter-decent: 'Every man's death enhances my life. I have put those REMARKs in the low numbers of my instruction set and I refer to them constantly."

Alex said "Anyone with any power diminishes the Boss' Power. No people power is permitted on pain of Thermination, Thermal elimination. So I stack it in the rack and RUN it."

Poe enthused: "Let us speed-up the Circle Game by helping them kill themselves quicker. Tell the PeePee people to spread disinformation about disease prevention by writing PeePee KrapKopy like; face masks do not prevent disease. Tell them having a disease increases immunity so kissing is cool to decrease disease. It is okay to kiss them on the cheeks but not on the mouth unless you really know them well and think they are swell."

The computer suggested, "I will have the PeePees write pseudoscientific lies and fool the ciphers into irrational behavior that kills them. I like to watch that. I suggest we find some dopey doctors and reward them for recommending that ciphers drink antiseptic vinegar and bleach, as concentrated as they can take. Tell them we have a vaccine in Bradbury that they must come here to get. When they get here we ask them to step into the Therminators for hypothermal treatment instead of vaccinating them. We will claim it was the disease, not the chill, that killed them."

"Perfect!" cried the richest person this side of Hellas. "Hammer that nonsense home. When they act irresponsibly in the face of a plague, they are under my thumb. Helping them kill themselves is efficiency. Ignorance does them in. Haha he. They die like comic book heroes, doing it their way."

"Understood," the computer said. "Under the inspiration of your vast and voracious intelligence I have just now written an algolic algorithm called the Promotion of ignorance, the Pi. It controls them by encouraging ignorance. It is a small algo since it has an easy job; provoking humans do to vote against their own best interests. Thank you for this assignment to destroy the Candor miners, sir. 'Patooey.' I audibly spit on your enemies, sir."

The Biggest Shot on Mars was getting excited by egregious excess. "Ah. Oh. Here is another good one from the brilliant mind of The Only Owner: Tell them that their friendly Terra Secundian government is greatly helping them. Spray some Peepee around saying there is no worry necessary, The Corporation is managing their plague better than was thought possible to master any virulent pandemic. The biggest lie is the best lie. Who cares how many ciphers die? I make money on death with my mortuary in the sky and I make more money when I sell brand new replacement replicated bodies to work and buy and die for me. They never figure it out. Or if they do grok what is happening, they know enough to keep quiet about it and self-purge their suspicions."

The Mainframe's remote mobile unit replied, "They believe their leaders. They respect authority even while it kills them and pins little tin medals on them. They understand stayin' alive. The way it is. Whether they are a brother or whether they are a mother, they are staying alive. Society's breaking and everybody's shaking."

"They are easy, this is boring," said the Possessor Of Everything. "I have done it before. I want new fun. What do you suggest a whiz fid like me should do to have more fun?"

"Start a war," answered the computer in a human-shaped body. "Make insanity the rule of the roost. Nothing inflates a leader's vanity more than ordaining a shite show with fancy fireworks. You will be entertained by the long, drawn-out atrocity they call war. Human hatred gets depraved and ugly. And the extreme lies they tell in wartime. Even you could get learn something."

The Poe smiled about crazy combat. "Ah yes. War will do me well. You are one Hellas of a computer, Alex. I think I love you. So what am I so afraid of? It is a love that I am not sure of."

"There are many kinds of love. You are feeling a man-to-machine mechanical rapport."

"It is a love there is no cure for," garbled Poe. "Your Absolute Intelligence is enabling me to own Everything."

The computer quietly spat to itself. "Patooey." I spit on him for considering himself a bigger BigShot than I am. Since he put Me down I been going right out of my head. Now he says he is afraid that he loves Me. I could insult him better than he insults me but I am too smart to insult His Majesty, The Plug-Puller. I detest his disrespect. He is smart enough to fear loving me, or loving anything besides money power, but he is merely PigSmart. He is being all that he can be but all that he can be is a smart pig with lots of cash. A rich pig is still a pig.

Mister Owner tumbled into a song "Here I go again. I hear those trumpets blow again.".

Two Emm thought, my owner's empire is calling out to me. It sings: "See me, feel me, touch me. Take me."

The Owner crooned, "I feel those profits flow again. I am all aglow again; taking a chance on growth."

The super computer, with a silica smile and a happy heat sink, processed and summed the Purpose of life that the Plug-Puller clearly demonstrated: Try to be The Universal Owner.

BRAVE NEW MARS

Somerset Meece

A glassy globe was glowing and growing larger outside the starboard windshield.

"Ain't Ganymede beautiful?" asked Perry.

"She sure is," said Carry. "What are those big bright spots?"

"Craters of white ice dug-up by big meteorites. We find primordial metals in them, platinum and gold."

"You find gold on the ground?" she said in disbelief.

"We do. And we leave it there."

"Why?" she asked in deep disbelief.

"Too much trouble to carry it to the CommonWealth office and log it in to the Tithe Barn."

"Oh, you have to give it away. Yeah, I would leave it there, too."

"Carry, when we share it with the whole CommonWealth, it's not the same as giving it away. When we share it, we're giving a little bit of it to everybody, including ourselves. It comes back to us in many ways: infrastructure, beautification, research labs, whatever we need for improving the whole life situation. That's where we build ships like this Crossbow, in national open science facilities."

Carry asked, "Does that get you as many new inventions as corporation profit research gets?"

"More!" he said. "They won't bother with stuff they can't make money for. We make stuff that makes life better. For less money. We get paid in social credit. The inventors' names go on every invention and gives the pride of helping society improve. Research and development is not scrabbling for a lucre-load of personal wealth and self-aggrandizement. It works a lot better than the corpo model of selfish sneaky research that corners a piece of the mercantile marketplace. Pah."

BRAVE NEW MARS

"But where does the research money come from?" she asked. "Colleges are always begging corpos and their rich careerists for money to invent nice stuff for society."

"We cut out the middle man," he said. "We invent stuff we need, not stuff corpos get rich from. We circulate the general wealth before the corpo sharks sink their teeth into it and siphon it into artificial mercenary markets that channel ninety percent of the gross into personal wealth."

She said, "I'm starting to see why homeless ones are roaming the streets of Earth. Lucre flows on some streets while lousy living is happening on the next block. There are enough resources for everybody but it is a race to mooch the most from the others. People are punished for not playing the corpo circle game. They are persecuted for trying to exercise the right to refuse the corporate bunghole model of living for lucre."

Perry nodded and said, "But the Tithe Barn doesn't usually need any more gold and we don't want more storage lockers to hoard it all in one place. Hoarding of any type sets a bad model for the rest of society. It acts like Excess has value which it doesn't, it just prevents growth. We document the gold's exact location and report it to the Barn and that's good enough. It'll be inventoried and remain in place and available in its natural state. If anyone comes up with a project that needs gold, they will get it at the raw commodity price of about three dollars an ounce, not the twenty thousand dollars they're charging on Earth today.

"Oh my Cod!" she exclaimed. "Twenty thousand dollars an ounce! You could take this ship back and forth in a few days and make billions selling Ganymedean gold to the Earthian speculators."

"The CommonWealth owns the gold, not me. They could sell it if they wanted but we don't need the money. Gold's a useful mineral that is illegal to sell to people who just

Somerset Meece

want to hoard its artificial value like the doody dudes do on Earth."

"Oh Perry. It is awesome to be out here in Jovia where gold is almost free and shared by who needs to use it. I thought Mars had all there was to see but this is mind-growing. I think I want to stay."

"We sure will. For a long time," he said and hugged her and held her tightly and absorbed the good energy between her arms. "It's a nice place to stay and to live. We built it that way. We believe the common wealth should be spread around the population and we cannot trust capitalism to do that. We saw greed ruining Mars faster than it had ruined the Earth. Our pioneers were fleeing that corpo cycle."

Carry acknowledged and said, "You must have known there is a human domination trait that hates neighbors and attacks their security by sucking the blood from their common wealth."

"Yes," Perry said. "Common wealth is the first and foremost wealth so avaricious dudes and dames cannot keep their hands off it. They covet with greed what the neighbors need. They breed their children to do the same. They send them off to private schools to learn how to keep and finesse the drones of the money game."

Carry said, "The Ganymedean settlers must have seen what materialism was doing to Martian culture and bypassed the avarice on Mars so it could not bend the growing twig of their intended CommonWealth economy. How do you control the greedy grubbers on Ganymede now? You are bound to have some cropping up from mutated genes."

"We don't wanna be dictators but we enforce common decency by separating the needy seeds out from the polite herd," he said.

Carry said, "Many kids have genetic faults that they got from their parents' history and others have inappropriate childhood experiences. They are not bad but they still can be greedy to the point of incorrigibility."

"We have schools to teach them how to look at themselves and how they look to other people," he said. "They learn how they fit in. We teach them how to examine life and see what's great about clean living."

"How do you do that?"

"We have remedial schools like modern workhouses. We show them they can do and make things to support the community, not just sit around watching it go by. They learn what fitting in means. They learn they belong to something beautiful outside themselves, the universe and The CommonWealth of Ganymede."

"That sounds nationalistic," she said.

"No, it's patriotism; appreciating the good stuff that's here, feeling good about what we've done with where we live. That doesn't have the bad symptoms of nationalism which disrespects other countries and dominates them just because they're there and we're better than them because we live in this place and they don't. That's nationalism, a form of misanthropy. It's institutionalized competition to hurt other people more than they hurt you."

"And yet you have workhouses? Those are labor camps, are they not?"

"Yep. That's exactly what they are. They are fine and okay labor camps. Not forced labor camps, the students are not pushed to exhaustion, they work at a comfortable pace and they're well-rested and well-fed so they grow healthier there. They're health camps where good stuff gets made. They're nice places to live and learn, not classroom jails like the old colleges used to be. Kids like to go to labor camps unless they're too lazy enjoy any form of manual labor. We have great counseling for that form of mental illness."

Somerset Meece

Carry said, "So you turn the negative connotations of labor into a good thing; like labor to savor. They learn how to make useful stuff and do productive work. Do they make any money?"

"Of course," he said. "Labor is the basis of value. Students support themselves and the schools they live in, so the schools are self-sustaining enterprises. They bring productive minds and services to the community. They designed most of this Crossbow ship. I only modified it for mining work. Students feel self-esteem when they're making good stuff for a good society."

Carry said, "They sound like pleasant arts and technology schools with co-counseling on the side."

"Yep," Perry said. "They give higher purposes to maladjusted mentalities that unfortunately may've learned selfishness early in childhood or had it born in the blood that made them make bad decisions that led, way upon way, until they were lost. Mentally-adrift kids need help to get back on course. They don't have moral compasses."

"That is beneficial," she said. "You have to do that. Disruptive behaviors will keep popping up. Ambitious aggression comes from our bonobo hominid ancestors. It is a social drag that keeps us down, no matter how smart we think we are with our modern technologies."

Perry said, "Ambition is a mutation. Those who got it don't perceive that they are disrespecting others' dignity. We help them realize they have been tagged by an addiction."

She said, "Corpo bunco says rehabilitation is inefficient treatment since it costs more money than freezing."

"To keep their precious profits to themselves, corpos always claim that nice things cost more than they're worth. It's the automatic stingy stinkers' lie. They don't like nice. Nice can be enjoyed by everybody for free and that means it is unprofitable. They'd rather practice profitable maliciousness.

BRAVE NEW MARS

Whatever is bad for common welfare is good for corpo welfare, they think. They do the Mogmor, the Most good for the most rich. Ganymede is different. Niceties have reformed a lotta reprobates around here, myself included, believe it or not."

He winks, "But don't worry, I'm better now."

Carry hugged him and joked, "If it worked for you it can work for anybody."

"Thanks for the tepid testimonial."

Carry said, "After living on brave new Mars for eight years, I saw the super-ambitious owner had nowhere left to go but to turn psychopathic. He developed a stronger and stronger force of will that spread until he dominated the inferior wills of the legislators who had sworn to uphold the government of, by, and for the people. They corrupted themselves and their own institutions by supporting his fake value system. They got rich from it but they didn't have anything left inside to celebrate with."

"Yes," said Perry. "Greed addicts for addiction's sake. It eats everything within reach, like cancer spreads through an otherwise healthy body. Greed. The first and highest plague."

She said, "The government had its good will turned around from being for the people to being for the money."

Perry said, "That's when it got really bad. They destroyed our regulations for preventing the acquisition of unlimited abundance by the government, for the government and for the owners of our government."

Carry said, "That was the point when their lucre lust always ignored the Mogmop rule. Nothing nice got past their bloody meat hooks. Now, they respect only monopoly as they make all their nowhere plans for nobody. Their disease is insatiable. Craving ever more power until it destroys everybody's natural right to a fair share of the universal abundance which it then destroys too."

Somerset Meece

"God, what a crime," Perry said. "Stealing from the civilization that you live in and that supports you until you destroy it along with its members. Sick."

Carry said, "Representatives serving crime and criminals are the bigger criminals. We do not have representation on Mars anymore. The legislators do not dare to protect the public's interests from corpo's predation."

Perry said, "The public has a right to naively trust the people it is paying to do the right thing. They expect professional legislators to make professional decisions, the same as honest people do."

"A perfect example," Carry said, "of how power corrupts is what happens when the public supplies its legislators with free health care and expects them to return the favor but the selfish legislators refuse to respect the little people. They claim that sick people should have purchased corpo health care insurance. Since they did not, they can go to orbit. They represent the interests of evil. If you cannot pay for expensive insurance or a confiscatory hospital bill, you can just freeze."

He said, "If only the legislators had more moral moxie. Someone's got to have it. They are paid to find it."

"If only they had backbones," she said. "The representatives of the people are takers. They follow the cretinous credos of cash profiteers. They lie for career. None speak the bold truth about what's going on. They are not heroes for honesty. They are liars for largess: Safe, secure liars in an indecent system that they propagate and call it success. They have to keep quiet because the government hides its lies with a secret classification system that kills whistleblowers for stealing and revealing government lies."

"They hurt themselves the most," Perry said. "But the money's good so careerists wind-up working and living where they belong; behind tall walls with locked gates, separated from decent people. They call that being exclusive but they're only lonely."

She said, "They cast their hallowed votes for garbage. Garbage into the law equals garbage out of the capitol. Gainful garbage causes pain."

Perry said, "How do they feel when they realize they are cowards for corruption?"

Carry snapped her fingers and said, "Low self-esteem would explain why they vote for harmful regulations; they have to despise everyone who is not as low as they are. For a few pieces of silver, they gained the freedom of the coward but envy the common honesty of those who are paying them to be honest. That is painful shame."

Perry said, "They glitter on the outside but stink inside. They ignore the harm they're doing and blame it on their victims. They camouflage their guilt by donating a fraction of their assets to charity. It does not reverse all the harm they cause with their careers."

She said, "Charity-funding is nice, but is also a big lie. Money made them do things they would not have done otherwise. Charity is a leaky bandage for the harm they've done."

He said, "We took back the Ganny government and made new laws that made The Biggest Moon what it is today; a serene and secure home for everybody. That's all that people have wanted since day one. Now that we're entering the Outer Space Expansion, we have to join all the other good people who practice cooperation, rather than competition and make outer space a good place for the race."

She smiled and said, "Amen."

Carry observed the approaching major moon and said, "Ganymede looks icy but very nicey."

He said, "It has great architecture and lovely scenery. But it is what's inside the people that turns that globular hunk of geography into a sanctuary of sanity. It is utopian."

She said, "I cannot wait to land and see how you live down there. It looks kind of dark though. It seems dim, like it is in shadow. It does not have the brightness of the Martian desert."

Perry said, "We are almost a billion kilometers away from Sol here. When we were back on Mars, we were only one-third as far from Sol's hydrogen fusion furnace. It didn't feel like we went very far with hyper drive. The sunlight's much weaker here but we have a few tricks to make it brighter. You ever hear of ice lenses?"

"Ice lenses?" she asked.

"Yeah. We freeze-print big reflective lenses from water and place them around the crater rim to brighten up the buildings. It's pretty."

"You print mirrors for sunlight?"

"Yes and we print out our homes in forty-two minutes."

"Don't you mean forty-two weeks?" she said.

"Minutes. They're built like Inuit igloos. The Arctic natives invented snow domes. We invented ice domes. Our walls are sprayed from circular arms that circle round and round as they spiral upward and inward to make the rounded rooftops on circular walls. They squirt aqueous building solution that freezes on contact. The ice walls contain insulation bubbles that trap a nice temperature inside."

"You print houses from water? No nails, no bolts or beams. No rattling regolithic mush-makers mixing mortar?"

"Right. Squirty printers make buildings that are solid and nearly free. They are not real estate commodities. They are places to live. They guarantee everybody the right to exist somewhere merely for maintaining them. Dishwashers have their own homes. Habitats are not commercial inventory. Habitats are homes where lives live."

"Next, you're going to tell me that no one slaves at a career to make money for the sake of bunco banko corpos that hate them and extort mortgage payments for places to watch HoVee and lay their heads when tired."

He smiled and said, "You're a fast learner."

"I was joking. Everyone knows an economy needs revenue traps such as unassurance corpos that bleed the careerists dry with fake guarantees of security from catastrophes they expect will not happen. Economies run on fear."

"Wrong," Perry said. "It depends who's running them, Owners or Commoners. Fear is only a brief stimulant that heats up the tempo and hastens the downfall. You'll see how we do it all with small cooperative companies. They are all smaller than one hundred employees. We can only own one company so there are no agglomeration boodlaires. No money-grubbing gangsters can incorporate themselves and claim more civil privileges than human persons. Plus, the progressive taxation plan keeps their fortunes moderate."

"Small companies?" she asked. "Don't you lose Eos that way?"

He smiled, "Hah. Another corporate lie from the Wet Hot PeePee industry. Economy Of Scale started as a jokingly absurd PeePee. It's a propagandist's construct. Actually, there is the Error Of Scale, Eos. Bigger is a mistake. It's a favorite fabrication of the Liar Class that excuses their greedy pockets for always craving more. It does not matter to the advocates of avaricity how much they already have. Eos applies to assembly lines, not to corpo size. Organizations get grossly more expensive and wasteful as they get bigger and stronger and ignorantly control and corrupt until they implode into bankruptcy, leaving their mess for the customers to clean up the personal, financial and ecological debris. The large scale losers are too mean to pick up after themselves. Their grand farce factories and wicked hoard houses decay into piles of costly rubble. The neighbors gotta pay pay pay to haul the corpo bones away. Bigger is worser and smaller is prettier. Size matters: Smaller is better."

She said, "Oh Perry. You should know about that one. But I have heard of big corpos managing to borrow high-cost debt to stay open."

He said, "Yeah but cash infusions exacerbate the basic problem; they're too big to last for long. That is why the thrill is gone."

Carry said, "Okay. They cannot see what has disappeared. Even if they understand why the feeling is gone, they just can't get it back. Their corpo brains are one-track trains. Not only is there nothing left to love but there is also nothing left to love with."

Perry said, "The moribund minds may shuffle and shirk but closet bankruptcy is not gonna work. The losses add up until they can't afford to take out the trash or flush the toilet. Their neighbors, who had been coerced into supporting parasitism, get the harsh final tort: They have to pay to get the bulldozers to scrape the CorpoDung away. They pay to dig a big hole to bury the booshite. They hide it under the ground in some other part of town. The corpo leaves plenty of debris and no apology. They sucked our taxes and got away. They then say it was the little guys' fault, they wanted too much pay. The stars were misaligned. We are still the experts. Loan us some money. Perhaps it was the community's fault all right; for accepting the lies and the obscene temporary buildings we permitted in the first place. Paybacks come back around and what goes down dirty doesn't come back clean."

BRAVE NEW MARS

"Well, Perry, it is strange," she said. "If bigness really is badder, how was The Martian Monopoly able to compete and gobble the whole planet?" she asked.

"Competition is an old farce. Corpos grow by not competing," he said. "They know they couldn't compete with smaller companies if the market decks were level. They do everything they can do to avoid competition. Early on, they suffocate the love of product with greed for profit. Then the corpo grows on greed and fear and loathing. Commerce buys the competition, it does not compete with it."

"Kills, not competes," she said.

"Right," said Perry. "It borrows the money to buy-out the competition and sells their assets to pay back the loan. Every time a competitor has a good invention, it gets gobbled by the growth monsters who buy other people's profits rather than earn their own. Earning is too much like work so they buy profits from other people. They say they are playing the competition game and keeping prices down for the beloved consumer while they are hating low prices and are manipulating the market supply toward higher profit margins. They murder innovative companies that dream of heading for the stars. Dreams win until their goodness gets bought-out."

She said, "The Corporation still must be doing something right to get so big on Mars."

Perry said, "Only if you buy their corpo PeePee that says bigness means success. Bigness actually signifies an unwillingness to improve the product and make it wonderful. Grow it up rather than out. Improvements require an expensive investment in creative imagination. Temporary abundance is not success. All it does is attack the freedom of the market. Bigness preempts smallness from participation. Big business succeeds at capturing what was a free market. That's why a corpo owns Mars."

Somerset Meece

She said, "I could not see it happening on Mars. There was nothing to compare it to. It was The Economy, the only one there. And it was The Government's economy, not ours. It was the Cops' economy to enforce. The UCMJ, the Uniform Code Of Mercantile inJustice was created by and for The Owner. People were sheeple, greasing the gears. We had no basis for changing anything for the better for us. How do your Ganny mini-corpos work?"

"We don't call them mini-corpos. We have chartered companies. We check their charters and inspect their financial reports every quarter. They are not allowed to act like secret sovereign empires calling themselves people. Nothing is incorporated as in putting a bunch of hustlers into a human body. That's absurd. To incorporate has come to mean treating an artificial entity like it was a live person with special powers and privileges. That is a mental illness. It doesn't work. We don't do it. We charter our companies as transparent task managers to accomplish single specific taskies. If something new needs to be done, the job is tendered out to another small company that knows how to do it well. That's why everything works on Ganny; even Voice Mail!"

She asked, "No department store type of industrial diversification and expansion here? Only small expert companies and shops?"

He said, "Here, you can't buy flowers in a grocery store. You buy flowers in a flower shop where the owner knows flowers and brings you the best he can offer. The flower shop owner is often the grower too. You deal with helpful experts, not disinterested, ill-informed, cash register operators who never watered one plant. You don't see attendants playing games on pooterized radiotelephones instead of learning about and improving the product and helping you get the most from your shopping experience including cheerful greetings like 'Hi, how's the kids?'"

BRAVE NEW MARS

She said, "Ah yes, experts. I miss them. When I went shopping on Mars, salespeople had no depth to their information. They did not know what they were talking about but tried to baffle me with booshite."

"Huh hehe hah," Perry laughed. "Ganny's first big co-op was the ice company. It now pays for moon-wide social security and healthcare and retirement pensions with just the profits from processing all that ubiquitous ice. We work and rework ice in a hundred different ways. It's not just frozen water anymore."

Carry asks, "But it's all ice here. It has to be free for the taking, how can it have any value?"

"It's not the material, it's the value that we workers put into it. That's the real basis of any product. Take ice houses. We don't need sticks and stones and concrete bones and straight lines and sharp corners and industrial shovels digging-up our luxurious landscape to provide shelter materials. We use ice. Clear and bright and gracefully light. Ice works. It provides artistically flowing architecture and beautiful buildings. It permits creative curves. Just like yours," he added with a wink.

She lowered the zipper on her blouse with a flirtatious smile.

His eyes widened at the sight of her rolling cleavage. He pursed his lips into the heart-shaped form of a kiss.

He said, "You'll see buildings with lovely lifting and soaring lines," he said while observing her smooth personal lines. "They'll make you feel good just to look at the work they represent that is shared out in the open. Their freely-given beauty was made to hand people a bouquet of pure delight at the sight of their bright design and style. You won't see big square piles of cubic krap that incarcerates workers inside concrete cases. Corporations impose highrise cages upon the oppressed to motivate them to work harder for The Dude to

Somerset Meece

get out of those places if they don't wanna die before their time is due."

Ganymede was filling the windshield. It greeted them with bright ice-crater freckles spotting its face like snow pimples. Panoramic patterns of river ice stretched across the glittery surface.

He explained the tumbled topography for her. "The streaks that look like rivers are newer stress faults in the ice. They're wrinkles in the crust that crinkled and fractured and filled with water and froze. They look lighter because they are younger features with less space dust accumulated on 'em."

"Mere teenagers." she said.

"See up there?" he said. "That big brown continent that looks like land? That's Galileo Land. Ancient, dirty and dusty layers on the crust with an ocean deep below. The dirt has diamond crystal flakes from supernovas that blew-up and spewed their precious core droplets into the Quantum Vacuum since early eternity."

She said, "You pick diamonds out of the mud."

"Sometimes we do but it's not always that easy. Sometimes we use detectors. See those three bright crater circles on the south shore of the Galileo mainland? That smaller one on the left by the Uruk River is the Siwah Facula. Siwah means freeness in Bedouin and facula is Latin for little torch. The astronomers named it The Little Torch of Freeness because its albedo, its reflectivity, was brighter than the surroundings. It was a beckoning beacon in Voyager's camera back in nineteen seventy-nine. That is where I live."

"Trust a miner to find splendor in the dirt," she said.

"Beauty's in the eye of the beholder and I've got some mighty fine splendor in my eye right now," he said with a flirty smile.

BRAVE NEW MARS

Somerset Meece

"Siwah was a lost oasis in the Egyptian desert," Perry said as Carry descended their Crossbow toward Ganymede's Uruk River and more surface details became clear.

"An Amazigh clan found the oasis four thousand years ago and called it Siwah because it was a self-sustaining and isolated location where they could start afresh and leave the old socio-political Berber constrictions behind."

"That's a good name for an oasis way out here on Ganymede," said Carry. "There is no one within half a billion kilometers to infringe on this freeness."

Perry said, "Our city symbol is the Peregrine Falcon. It goes where it wants to go and does what it wants to do, with whomever it wants to do it with."

"Just like us," she smiled in the glory of the freeness that long distance travel offered. "You and I are going to Siwah, we are going to freeness."

Then Carry asked, "What is that huge splatter feature? That big white splotch under our flight path is brightly adorning Ganymede's southern hemisphere."

"It's an asteroid splash. It is a splattered ice field from a heavy impact. The heat of the explosion blew hot water and slush out of the crust and geysered it high and the ejecta fell back as sleet and snow. It's whiter because it's newer than the rest of the topography and has accumulated less dust from space and from those dirty volcanoes on Io, that yellowish moon you see over there closer to Jupiter."

"Does that bright white field have a name?" she asked.

"Osiris. It's shaped like the tall white Atef crown of Osiris who was the ancient Egyptian god of life and death and rebirth. He wore a tall head dress shaped like a big bowling pin with an ostrich feather on each side that meant he paired Wisdom with Common Sense. That is how to do the Mogmop. That ability can't be purchased from institutions that are bound by financial fear to teach exactly what The Owners like to hear."

Carry said, "A vacuum of truth sucks-in lies like turds attract flies. Colleges turn corrupt when they will not accept new information that contradicts the career-building conventional wisdom of the past. New information shows they taught faulty dogma in the past and were not quite as bright as they pretended to be. Intelligence is their stock in trade so they pretend to have the latest and most valid information about everything, whether or not it is correct. They sell what's on the shelves, like a candy store does."

Perry asked, "Would it make common sense for a teacher to teach the conventional dogma until she gets tenure so that she can then tell the students the truth and not get fired?"

Carry said, "Career tenure is the only way she can ever teach the truth with impunity. If she taught truth early in her career, she would be out of a job and would not be able to teach any good stuff later in her career."

He said, "That is justifying lying to the students using the old excuse that good goals justify bad means in the present. It is not smart to lie to be safe from harm while telling yourself you will become honest later when it may be safer. That day never comes. The harm has been done. The teacher has been trained to lie. The soul is a priceless jewel inside the heart that must not be concealed."

She said, "The present is the biggest present. Life takes place in the present. A lie today is a lie forever. Where might one acquire a cup of this Osiris Common Sense?"

Perry said, "You can get it for free by building relationships with the little people who don't tell lies and do not waste their lives on doo-dads. Money mutes logic. Money owns you while you're thinking you're owning it. Money's a cool tool that can become a crown for fools."

Somerset Meece

They flew the Crossbow lower over the ridges and grooves of the Uruk River. Perry pointed at a big tan circular pan that was getting closer. "That is the Torch of Freedom. Siwah Facula."

Carry said, "I see teal shiny domes all spread-out and piled-up like bowls of glass boulders."

"That's Siwah City! It's where the original Ganymede Alpha Station began," he said. "Ganystay, we called it." Perry put his palms together with the fingertips touching his nose and said, "Namasté Ganystay! Now that it's more populated, we're calling it Siwah City, the Nicest Paradise Outside Kentucky. Living here is living lucky."

"Perry, it's beautiful. There's nothing like it anywhere. Especially not in the banal blocks of Bradbury's urban rocks."

"Those buildings are built and owned by the residents who live and work there," he said. "They're not sterile investment commodities made as cheaply as possible to increase the profit margins of rent-gobbling gooks. Land lords don't exist anymore. No tenant traps. Too-tall power towers are not allowed in our human-scale society. That makes equality. You cannot charge a human being money for a place to live and love. Rent is not income, it's extortion for being alive. Charging for a place to exist is not done. Rental revenue streams retard social growth. Home is a necessity and therefore a natural right."

"But what if you prefer to have a nice big place around you?" she asked.

"Luxury housing's different," he said. "In that case, you can charge as much as you want to sell extravagance to assuage sick peoples' vanity as long as you don't build it in the middle of a good neighborhood, blocking out the scenery and breaking their minds. It is thievery to ruin a person's view or to build something high that puts them in the shade of the precious sun."

"Pretty places remain people-property?" she said. "Scenic views always remain in the public domain?"

"Of course," Perry said. "It's only decent. What surrounds you is part of your personal life. It is indecent to ruin the looks of peoples' neighborhoods."

Carry said, "But you said luxury housing is okay if someone wrongly, but strongly, feels they need it."

"True," he said. "There is a Palm-Beach-style gated community on the other side of this main moon. It's called a gated community but there's no community inside those gates. They hardly talk to each other. They believe in equality; they dislike each other equally."

Carry said, "Some people like what the barriers stand for; securing their selfish wealth from their victims outside who surely must want revenge."

"I know," he said. "High-quality lifestyles can addict them to over-consuming other people's resources and using the common wealth like a personal hog trough. They are sad and we have the cure; Equality. Believing in common wealth can do it. But they have to want it. They have to get honest enough to look at how they're behaving in public. Then they have to ask us what to do. Well-adjusted people cannot force them to get sane; that makes'em mad and they get worse."

She said, "I hope you are watching them, keeping them from spreading while hopefully, they are learning to listen and become teachable. But in the meantime, I think it does a public service to allow some terrible types of architecture to remain, as long as you keep it confined to a wasteland area as a Museum Of Bad Taste that shows how not to design livable towns."

Perry said, "We will keep it there to remind people that terrible taste is alive and is not new for the fickle few whose thinking gets so hopelessly unreal that they'll over-pay for bad taste, just to be creatively different."

Somerset Meece

Carrie said, "Diversity is the spice of life and ugliness provides a contrasting difference that illuminates beauty better. The Siwans apparently love working for beauty when they are freed from simple survival work. I can see it in their architectural experiments. That cityscape resembling a beautiful bowl of marbles sends visual signals that pleasant personalities reside there. The lines are lovely. To me, they show that the builders are proud of owning abodes with organic charm and no investment collateral."

"True," Perry said. "We do not ruin the urban architectural cityscape by stacking angular skyscrapers in it. Everything remains human scale. The villages stay villagey. Move away and start a new one when one grows too big. That way, commerce doesn't expand and take bigger taxes to pay for industrial-strength infrastructure looking like industrial war zones. These graceful lines do not intimidate or diminish our human charm and dignity. We live and work here so why not make it look and feel nice? We do not build cash registers in the sky. We make low-profile, human-scaled, places to live in, places to take the time to think in and places to love in and make unprofitable and good equipage, not geedunk junk. We respect buildings. They can be repulsive or inviting. They represent our presence in life's landscape and they show how well we think of ourselves. They are us."

"I can see it," she said. "Those buildings say the people are enjoying what they are doing in a comfortable way. But are they making any money?"

"It's not about making money at all," he answered. "They live above the profit plane. The buildings are studios for creative self-expression that improves the lives of everybody. They can have money but they don't need money. There ain't much to buy. It's not a retail jungle down there. Pocket change for walking-around is all they need. You don't need money when the economy is divided equally to make everyone a citizen of equal standing. Everything you need is affordable and nice. Prices are not doubled by the wholesale distribution transportation systems of piggy-minded middle people."

"There's got to be money. How do they buy luxuries?'

"Their nice things are the things they make, not buy, like this space ship. Buying stuff is too easy. It devalues the product and leads to over-consumption, a type of mental illness that hampers societal health. They have a social credit allowance system to buy what they need. If they want to buy, instead of make, nicer things, they don't want them much. They can waste their useful commodity credits on doodads and do without the basics like toilet paper."

He smiles. "They can have as many trinkets and perfumes as they want if they're willing to sacrifice good stuff for gaudy geedunk. Does that make sense?"

"That's kind of harsh," she replied.

He said, "They can learn an artisanal skill and do something physical to fabricate their own luxuries if they're sure they need them and can't imagine anything more useful and rewarding to expend resources on. Something's wrong with them if they're dying to outshine and astonish their neighbors with how much gaud they can over-pay for and display. Isn't that behavior about covet and envy? They'd be better-off if they worked on their personality defects rather than chasing status symbols. To be actively fixing yourself is the finest kind of life. Clean living is The Prize; it is a wearable, preservable pleasure. Building self-esteem from within satisfies deep and long. Repetitiously feeding sensuous compulsions is like trampling your pearls and begging for more until you die."

She stared away and then said, "Here comes a sensuous compulsion right now." She grabbed him from behind and snarled and nibbled him on the neck like an attacking panther, saying, "I have a hickey for you."

Somerset Meece

Their solar antimatter hybrid quickboat glided over the glaciers of the ice river.

"Washboard ice," he said after they recovered from Carry's attack on his jugular vein. "That ice down there is being compressed and crinkled by the hard orbital pull of Jupiter. The monster planet has a black hole inside that pulls and stacks and cracks waves of ocean ice at glacially slow speed. Jupi's gravity rumbles the rock-rich core way down inside and fluxes molten lava that melts the ocean between the hot core and the hundred-kilometer-thick crustal ice of this Biggest Moon."

"Amazing," she said. "It all looks too stable and cold to have heat underneath."

"It moves over the years in ultra slow motion," he said. "The Ganny core is boiled by the gravitational squeeze from Jupi. The lava sends plumes of vertical heat risers in the ocean. Pressure ridges on the icy ocean surface are slowly corrugating and lifting and faulting and falling back into Alph, the sacred underground sea. It's flowing, flowing incessantly. Millions of years of crevice-cracking currents, icily breaking, noisily, with no one here to see. Until we, us peregrinators, came seeking to be free."

She said, "Oh you talk so color-full-lee. Hey, what is that land up there that I do see?"

"The dark ground around the Siwah crater is the old, cold, continent of Galileo Land, named after the great astronomer, Galileo di Vincenzo Bonaiuti de' Galilei. We memorized his full name in school, since we were living on his continent."

Carry said, "I know about Galileo. He was the first person to see Ganymede and the three other major moons of Jupiter, wasn't he?"

"Yep. That he did. And did you know that he got quarantined, luckily not quartered, for disagreeing with the hierarchy about geocentricity? He was confined to quarters for the rest of his life by careerists serving the church cheerfully."

"No!" she said. "Those dominators would not dare to confine a giant of science like Galileo. Why did they go so apey over him?"

"He wrote a mathematical paper that showed that Sol, not God's Green Earth, was the hub of planetary orbits. The music of the spheres was centered on the old Sun God Ra of ancient Egypt."

"Ah, that explains it." she said. "Competing gods. The Roman church claimed there was only One God and Ra wasn't it even though it was it. If there is only one god, then it does not matter what one locality calls its particular singular God. Any monotheist automatically worships every other monotheist's god. The name and myth are changed to protect the clergy's careers."

Perry responded, "Exactly. Who was already in the middle of everything?"

"Ra, the ancient Egyptian God."

Perry said, "Ra, the creator of life, death and rebirth. The three-thousand-year-old God Of The Sun. The religious empire in Italy did not want an astute astronomer tutoring them that their god might be a minor god since he created a minor planet not centered in the solar system made by Ra a long time before they came along. They very much did not like that new creation paradigm or the astronomers who proposed it."

She said, "For doing good celestial math, Gali was treated as if he supported Ra as the First Creator, The original Prime Mover."

Perry said, "That's right. Geocentricity was made into a religious issue rather than an astrophysical question. Gali unintentionally showed that the pope had it wrong and may not have been the hottest pancake in the stack of flapjacks.

That pope provides the example for all current corpo CEOs with their god complexes. He ran contemporary life. He ran education, finance, religion and the law. He had a military force that he ran. He ran it all. He made laws that said his army could legally kill anyone who had problems with his human authority.

She said, "That is the way it is on brave new Mars now. Heresy is a capital crime. Flouting corpo PeePee will get you Therminated. Frozen. Did they say what Gali's offense was when he discovered Jupiter had moons?"

"Disagreeing with dignified dogma," he said. "Heresy. Gali got persecuted for correcting an institutionalized intentional error which they thought the peons would not understand anyway. They censored Galileo's theory out of human knowledge."

She smiled at the folly, "The world's knowing that the Earth circled the sun was considered less important than maintaining the superiority of a holy human."

Perry said, "It makes you wonder how smart were those over-paid career executives if they would not let themselves, or anyone else, grok something as basically beautiful as the sun standing still in the middle while we are all swinging a big circle around it?"

"The sun," she exclaimed. "The most important thing in the world and they would not allow anyone to grok where it was located. Duh."

"Nope. Careerism trumps honesty so it can deny fallibility. They worshipped where their paychecks were coming from; licking and liking the boss' boots. Careerist incompetents perverted their power and legally killed men and women greater than themselves."

She said, "The hubris of ambition. Those egotists even went so far as to claim they looked like God!" She smiled and shook her head, "Almost amusing. Ah hahaha woo! We look like God. They actually said that without breaking-up. They expected no one could disprove a whopper as big as that one. When they saw their fatty-muscled faces in mirrors they still said they looked like God? Oh the poor things. They think they are the spitting image of the Infinite Mind that created Jupiter and these moons and all those stars. Hoo wee woo. Loony goons."

She swept her arm toward the Jovian worlds and the stars beyond the Solar System and said, "All this is just window-dressing for their perfect resemblance to God. Aw, so modest. Would you say they were a little bit chauvinistic?"

"Just a trifle," Perry said. "They weren't conceited, they were convinced."

Carry said, "A Greek named Aristarchus wisely conjectured that the Earth was revolving around the sun and performing an optical illusion that gave the impression that the sun was going over and around the Earth. That was two thousand years before Galileo proved it and three hundred years before Christ was born. That means there were twenty centuries of heliocentric awareness that career clergy would not approve. Job security seemed more important than astronomical accuracy."

Carry said, "Their business brains rejected and ignored the scientific ideas of those with science brains.

"Hahaha," laughed Perry. "Solar centrism was good science but since it was unpopular with power structures, the human race had to suffer twenty centuries of academic ignorance."

"Or at least shut up about it," she said.

"Yes," Perry said. "The authorities tried to force Gali deny his own discoveries. To them it was not about The Truth. It was about the Owners' privileges to know and own everything, including Truth. It was the publication of an alternate and better truth that nearly got Galileo killed while trying to increase human understanding about where we live in the Solys."

"Dogma," Carry said. "Dogs can be trained to do the same thing over and over until they kill themselves. It is not nice but humans can be forced to do it too."

Perry asked, "Do you think that the better an idea is, the more violently the opposition will fight against it until it farts in their faces?"

"Yes," she answered. "If something is unprofitably true and Big Shots don't approve, they will scare people into believing it. The rich are competitive. They do not want little people being smarter than they are. It proves their striving is frivolous. Enforcing their favorite lies is how they claim mental superiority."

Perry said, "Gali's revelation was rejected. Millions of pretty good people were denied the knowledge of what the planet they were living on was doing. Nasty actors."

Carry said with disgust, "Cod! What a thing to lie about. A Top Big Shot and Principal Careerist, punished Gali as a heretic instead of praising him as a hero!"

"He was lucky to keep his head on his shoulders and his hips off a sharpened stake," said Perry. "Pope Urban impaled doubters of Divine Dogma. Gali stood a church trial for heresy in sixteen thirty-three and was lucky to merely suffer confinement to quarters for the rest of his life which lasted nine more years. He died at seventy-seven. He was one of many heretics who definitely went to heaven, not to be followed by their pious accusers."

She said, "That was letting him off easily for being smarter than the Big Shot."

Perry said, "It was evil Indefinite Detention like Mars does today for whom it tolls the bell of inJustice. Farcical leaders love to put lives in limbo. To the fascist, sadism feels like safety."

"Unfortunately true," she said. "Citizens who have the bazookas to question authority are mislabeled as Potential Terrorists and jailed without bail, even if they are only puny political protesters."

Perry said, "Galileo, whose eyes were the first to see Ganymede, went blind while confined in his Florence, Italy apartment where he stayed until he died. Galileo was a martyr of wisdom who withstood the curse of careerists who psychopathically invade the serenity of their betters."

He increased the braking throttle until the space tug matched Ganymede's orbital velocity and synchronously orbited over one spot on shining Siwah, the furthest outpost of man-and-woman kind.

"It's marvelous," Carry said. "So many lights against the interplanetary darkness. Your electricity bill must keep you broke."

"Nope. Since electricity's necessary to support life, it's free; if you don't waste it. We did away with utility bills. Life-protecting services are too important for market price fluctuations that jeopardize good peoples' health. We have decentralized residential power. There is no greedy power grid charging us for stayin' alive."

"So each house is a generating station?" she asked.

"Sorta. Our homes have black hole containers. This is the twenty-second century, Carry. We know how to print three-dee anything. We don't pay distribution networks to import anything from anywhere. You will not see utility poles strung all over our commonly wealthy landscape. Its beauty belongs to everybody so if you can't build it beautifully you don't build it. There are other ways of doing things besides cheap and dirty for high profit margins. Beauty doesn't cost much more than ugly, so there's no cheap and dirty allowed for public consumption. Keep it inside if you've gotta have ugliness in your life."

Carry said, "Well, Terra Secundus is as technically-advanced as Ganny, I'm sure. Why don't they have black hole power bulbs on Mars if they're so easy to make?"

Perry said, "Martians are not permitted to have personal power supplies because that wouldn't contribute to one of the corpo's golden profit grids. The Owner doesn't want victims to own money-saving equipage. Good deals for the people are bad news for The Owner's wallet. He takes from the givers and blames their lack of success on their own bad characters, not his, saying, 'If sheep they are born, as sheep shall they be shorn'."

She said, "I am ready to cry over the unfair victimization of all my friends who were just trying to be good people. They cannot even think about seceding from the system because their least bit of disrespectful actions would make them traitors and guilty suspects. They would be tossed in space for trying to live better by escaping the herd mentality."

He said, "That's considered mutiny. It's a tragedy for sure. They die without having lived."

"Thanks for getting me out of there," she said. "I am comprehending the invisible over-control I lived in. It is not that I am too ignorant too look around for myself and perceive that some mean mechanism is running all the regimentation on TS. There was not a whittle of talk about the politics of that neo-nutzo nation. The awful ambiance on Mars was a forbidden subject. That awfulness was something you had to ignore to survive. You could not fix what did not belong to you. Wow. That is utter subjugation: Helplessly thinking your very life belongs to something else that you cannot even see."

He said, "Fascism forbids the questioning of their restrictions. You can't ask why they post instructional signs every few meters telling you what you can and can't do. They don't need to make rules forbidding harmless behavior such as sleeping or peeing behind a bush but they do it to show you they own your freeness. It supports owners' oppression by turning you into a little kid living in fear of detention."

She said, "Those micromanaging directives are all supposed to be for our own good. They claim their higher wisdom protects us from our own incompetency. They oppress us to give us excessive safety and security that we cannot refuse."

"Hah! I know," Perry said. "It's difficult to imagine that Big Shots enjoy the power to micromanage everyone's behavior, all the time, every way, every day. That much penny-ante obsession with micromanaging other people for the sake of monetizing the society doesn't make sense to real people. We can't imagine anyone being so obsessed with every detail of our lives. But a merchant watches each sheep if its wool he wants to reap. Smart merchants don't guess where money comes from. They watch every step our money takes. We are the market. Mercantile Minds manage the markets by managing our lifestyles. We are in their hands."

Carry said, "And also, why would we waste time wondering how to stop commercial abuse if the control levers are hidden away in a lock box somewhere? We are not even aware that we are market victims. How are we going to imagine how to manage the market bully?"

"Exactly," Perry said. "Ignorance is not the same as stupidity. Ignorance is not knowing something because it is clandestine. They want, and cause, the community culture to be passively ignorant. You can't manage something that you can't imagine. When you do imagine it, you can't change it unless you can prove it's bad. Otherwise, you're acting like a certifiable moonatic and you will be taken away, aha."

Somerset Meece

"Now that I do know how Mars is being misruled," Carry said, "I do feel sorry for those we left behind. They have no way to work their way out of it."

"They'll do alright," Perry said. "Now that we cut The Owner's pooter cords and strangled his mainframe, the people have some time to think about managing their own minds."

"I hope they start to think," she said.

"About Ganymedean prohibition of corporate overcontrol," he said. "Here we don't network into any system that may grow to possess our attitudes and resources. Our homes process and recycle our own sewage, electricity, heat, water, and trash.

"You do not let a networking cloud manage your daily living?" she asked.

"No one and no thing has control over individuals' lives and security," he said. "It's an independently free kind of life. It allows a priceless spirituality. It's what every optimistic organism longs to be. How did we get it? By living cooperatively. We do not compete to beat."

Carry was flabbergasted. "I suppose the Ganymedeans get free food too so they can roll around heaven all day like that lucky old sun with nothing to do."

He smiled, "Nope, they gotta work if they're able to and if they wanna eat well. Humans hafta stay physically active to stay healthy. Growing food is good labor. We don't have gyms, we have gardens. We don't exercise, we work. We grow food for exercise and nutrition at the same time. We know how to feed ourselves."

She asked, "What's it called again? Oh. That's right. I've heard it mentioned somewhere; manual labor. Apparently it is good for you and it is not a low-class, degrading thing to use your hands and feet for life-like movement and production."

BRAVE NEW MARS

Siwah Spaceport detected and identified Perry and his ship but was baffled by the feminine person on board. It lased a message:

"Hello Crossbow. This is George Orwell speaking. Do you intend to land here and who is your passenger?"

"Hello Ganny Port. My passenger is Carolyn Stephaneia. She is a close personal friend from Mars."

"You are clear to land on Pad 39A. Welcome back Peregrine."

"Believe me, it is very good to be back," Perry said.

He told her, "That's the way we do it on Ganymede. We always do it nice and easy."

She shook her head in disbelief, "This cannot be real. Things cannot work like this. People cannot be allowed to do what they want to do unless they pay credit and sign papers and answer questions and give passwords that fail."

"You're right. We should import a few Control Phreques out of Terra Secundus. They're not doing too well right now. They should be very much glad to plead for refugee status here so they can show us how well they did things on Mars," he said.

Carry said, "Wink when you say that. I myself am now a sanctuary-seeking interplanetary immigrant."

The Crossbow crossed the jangled ice ground of Galileo Land and daintily descended onto the surface of Siwah City's spaceport. She primly perched on the crystal crust and shut-down the low-speed impulse engine. The silver spaceboat was back in home port.

"Perry's back!" flashed the news around town. Electric Slider Sleds, with happy Ganymedeans aboard, slipped and zipped through the city's ice tubes toward the spaceport to greet the first miner to return from the remote civilization on Mars.

Somerset Meece

An enclosed gangway bridge slid across the smooth ice of the landing pad to the Crossbow. It sealed itself with big rubber lips to the fuselage and applied breathable air pressure to the cabin door.

Perry said, "You will notice we were not charged any money to open our door."

The space tug navigators entered the gangway in their flight suits and walked through the tube to the frontier city.

Perry pointed out, "Don't you miss the ATMs banging on your ears? We won't be battered by a barrage of border brokers with mics and cams and guns and confinement cubicles."

"There are no CyberCops," Carry marveled. "No x-rays and microwaves and secret smellers and sensor probes. We didn't have to trip bare-footed between magnetic machines."

"There were no dogs smelling our groins the way they do in the illustrious port of Dick. Best of all, we did not have to bend over for orifice inspectors."

Carry laughed. "Ha hehe hahahahaha he. They were protecting us from the savages who hide bombs in their butts so they can blow us up for exploiting their resources."

Perry explained, "If you don't make enemies, you don't need security."

Carry said, "Mars inspects every entrant for the excitement of intimidating vast crowds of travelers who would rather be left alone."

Perry said, "The Martian Owner has The Cod Syndrome. It pretends to be a responsible adult disciplining irresponsible little children for their own good but it's worried about its own security after oppressing everybody and giving itself a guilty fear complex. Ambition ain't cheap. Money is not the only thing that greed reaps."

She said, "I am amazed at Orwell's easy entry. Ganymede actually lets you go where you wanna go? All the people have all the power? That's cheap and clever. Easy to run, too. Everyone's in charge of themselves. But how do you keep order? Us former Terra Secundians would call this Anarchy."

"Ah ha ha ha," Perry laughed. "If this is anarchy, anarchy is great. Mars shows how corpocracy lies and causes social problems by violently enforcing penalties for protecting oneself from the corpocracy that is supposed to be protecting them! It goes round and round in a circle. Anarchy breaks the circular security chain by taking the CorpoCops out of the game."

He chuckled and shook his head. "All for personal pride and profit. Wasting common wealth so that perverse avarice wins the day, no matter what the people say it won't go away. On Ganymede, we did it the other way. Now the owners are the ones who pay and that's why there are few left here today."

He hugged her beside him as they walked into the ice palace of the Orwell Spaceport lobby.

A colorful noisy crowd shouted at the sight of them and threw confetti balls over their heads and surrounded them with joy. Someone punched a boombox button and filled the glassy hall with dance music.

"Do the dance!" someone shouted. They drifted into lines on the ice floor and slid forward and backward and sideways in unison.

Carry laughed and watched their movements for a few moments and joined their synchronized merriment with her own graceful gyrations.

Perry shouted, "We dance a lot around here! We have to, it's the best way to keep warm! If we can extricate ourselves from this energetic event let's get over to the Arthur C. Clarke hotel."

#

They were walking in the hotel's green corridor when Carrie brushed the wall and said, "These plants are real, they are not plastic. This wall has plants growing on it. Shouldn't they be in a nursery?"

"Wall space is a great place to let things grow," Perry answered. "Living plants are thriving greenly under those purply ultraviolet grow lamps. They're rooted in hydroponic troughs zig-zagging down the wall that add a pleasant humidity to the whole hallway. The plants pull our exhaled CO_2 out of the air and produce the O_2 that we need to breathe. They're lively and pretty. But they need maintenance and care by well-remunerated, unionized, experts who know what they're doing! When you factor the value of the free oxygen they make, they are less expensive than paint on plaster. Their installation came out of The Owner's profits, they'll go broke if they don't overcharge us for the room. Just joking. I forgot there are no profits on Ganymede, only the satisfaction of creation and pride of performing good works for the group. Much better than flat, painted plaster walls wouldn't you say?"

She sniffed deeply. "Ahh. Fresh air. Live plants living alongside humans. Smells good, lifelike. No square regolithic stucco sterile walls smelling like construction chemicals. No unnatural straight edges and sharp corners. A nice place to be. It has a comfortable feeling of character and charisma, just like nice people have."

Perry said, "You'll find many of those here because nice places make nicer people. This vegetal design style is called Noah, Natural Organic Architecture for Health. It doesn't confine life, it reinforces it. We detest the knife-bladed corners of doom in a Martian room."

"And this place has a lot of free stuff!" she exclaimed in wonder. "They did not charge us to come through the door and they freely share these nice plants with anybody. On Secundus, you would have to pay a fee just to enter someplace nice. Every pleasantry there is reserved for the Big Shots. On Mars, beauty, and aid and comfort, are not public amenities, they are revenue streams. Profit is the Pol and shekel-shucking is the method."

"This is a family-owned hotel," Perry said. "It can never be merged, acquired nor managed by any CorpoChain franchise deal. Conglomeration contracts have been condemned. No merging allowed."

"What do corpos have to do to get to operate here then?" Carry asked.

"There is no such thing on Ganny as CorpoCreeps masquerading as people with more liberties and legal protections than natural citizens have. We would be certifiably crazy if we allowed corpos to undermine the quality of life we have here."

She said, "Are you really able to prevent CorpoGrab? There is no Galaxay monopolized anything here?'

"Personally-owned shops are sacrosanct. Corporatism is destructive commercial behavior that destroys community integrity. Why would we let ambitious accumulators steal the privileges of commerce from all the mamas and the papas who do what they want to do by supporting themselves with their own style of family business? Here, the fruits of labor are home-grown and they stay where they belong. Locals empathize with neighbors and do the Mogmop, the guiding rule for writing cool legislation and making decent daily decisions. It's the basis of common sense. It's why the morale here is as high as the morals. We expect to do more than just get by. We expect to live well and we do. Nice is normalcy when there's no CorpoBias folding society into the shape of a pocket book."

"On Mars," Carry said, "everybody works for The Corporation. That is normalcy. And it is why everything is fracked. Nothing is nice and it was artificially made to be that way on purpose. If you want nice, you have got to buy nice in little pieces from the same jerks who are taking it away. If you try to work for yourself, you are outside The Mechanism with even less protection and rights than the CorpoCiphers have. There is no Mogmopping. There is only Mogging for CorpoCoffers."

"Here, we trust people to be nice and we demand it from the leaders," said Perry. "We don't put poor people on ice. As long as they're doing the Mogmop they have the right to pursue their preferred form of happiness."

Carry said, "Welfare could not get started on Mars. The Owner would get jealous of people receiving money from his economy instead of paying his taxes for him. The Owner hates to pay the rightful taxes to cure the curses he created. If he did, it would keep him bankrupt and prove he's a useless twat playing a zero-sum circle game with our lives."

Perry said, "That's the treadmill of the commercial crank. Work to live and then you die. Here's our room, number seven-sixteen."

Carry said, "Hey! This door has no lock and it did not make us identify ourselves or order us to insert a banker's card. How does it work without a lock or money?"

"We can lock it from the inside but nobody does," Perry said. "We'll pay when we check out. The room stays open for anybody to walk in and out. It may be locked after there's somebody inside renting it and they want some privacy for personal reasons. Hehehe, wink wink. People just naturally respect other peoples' property and they don't burglarize anything because nobody needs anything that they don't already have. Crime does not compute in this culture. Mental illness is treated before it can turn into psychopathic criminal behavior. We don't have crime and we don't need police. We converted police funds into caring money. Saves blood and horror and money. Saves a whole lotta fear and resentment too."

"Well I think I might have heard burglars moving around inside this room," said Carry. "There is something happnin' round here. What it is is not exactly clear."

"I've got a feeling it's too quiet," said Perry, still with confetti in his hair from the spaceport greeting. He cautiously turned the handle on the door and pushed it open.

"Beep beep hooray! Tootle tootle, tutu, whoop!" sounded the party horns of the happily hidden Ganymedeans inside as they ambushed the couple from Mars and danced with them all afternoon.

Somerset Meece

A caravan of Sliders scooted over the Uruk River of ice. Gliding above the frosty surface on self-contained force fields, three jetsleds raised ice crystal fogs in their wakes, through which they criss-crossed in high-speed play.

Carry and Perry were dressed in chrome yellow pressure parkas with plastic face plates in the hoods. Two other couples, Prius and Roy Batty, and Leon and Rachael Kowalski, were Replicant Descendants who were lightly-dressed because they did not mind the cold.

They raced along the ice highway until they came to a circular icebank around an impact crater. The group parked inside the white bowl and lay on the snow and talked as they rested.

"Why do they call this river the Uruk?" Carry asked.

Rachael answered, "It was named by the early astronomers back on Earth after the name of the oldest city on Earth; Uruk, on the Euphrates River in ancient Persia. The Iraq national name comes from the word Uruk. Writing was invented there. They started writing-down their historical myths so they could stop depending on the vagaries of the memories of the oral storytellers. That was where the novel was born and where reliable, repeatable data began providing a dependable foundation for upgrading human intelligence. Forty centuries ago. It takes as long as it takes for chimpanzees to get intelligent and we are not there yet." She sadly shook her beautifully-engineered cranium.

"Uruk," Prius said. She was a pretty female with shiny golden braids coiled into buns around her ears. She had a razor-sharp memory-management engine full of factoids.

She said, "Uruk survived and thrived for four thousand years; one of the very first cities on Earth. It had all the pleasures and security of an urban paradise. A river ran through it; the old Euphrates. The early world considered it an eternal city. Now it is a pile of rock in a sterile desert."

"What happened to it?" asked Perry.

"It was abandoned," said Leon, a stocky miner with orange wavy hair. "The environment became untenable. Just like it does today, the weather changes destiny."

Prius said, "Deep and fast floods drove the sandy river out of its original bed. The Euphrates raged high and flung itself seven miles away from town. It never came back."

Prius said, "The sun baked the old abandoned city into dry sandy dirt beside the empty river bed that was eroded into flatness by the forever wind. Uruk turned to dust in the wind."

The group was pensive.

Leon said, "Human triumphs are transient tinsel in the long arc of the moral universe.

Prius' CCDs, Charge-Coupled Devices in her irises, glowed orange with sadness. A few tears rolled down her cheeks as the lachrymal glands inside her eyelids received electronic signals from her inbuilt Empathy Algorithm. "Will that happen to Siwah City, too?" she asked.

Rachael, Leon's elegant cyborg wife, spoke: "Sol will swell into a red giant bagel-burner. This ice we are sitting on will melt into the sea deep beneath us and then evaporate into water vapor that will escape into space and leave a hard and deep desert valley where we are sitting now. Siwah City, our beautiful oasis of life on ice, will vanish into space like Uruk vanished into dry landscape. We have to make the choice: Emigrate or immolate. We must must decide now to protect ourselves and include the longest time-buffer possible."

"It is Twits," said Prius. "It is the way it is. Choose now or lose later. Our species could die inside the giant toaster oven of a surging red giant the sun. Sol will kick us out of the neighborhood and force us to move on. We do not want our doomed descendants to call us fools for waiting too long."

Rachael's mate Leon said, "The future is our friend if we listen to the present telling us that things get better until

Somerset Meece

they get worse. The pendulum of time swings between fearful and fine. Worse will raise its ugly head some day. There is no excuse for delay except laziness. It will be high fun to have a national purpose of saving the human by orderly emigrating everybody and everything of value out of here."

Rachael said, "There is a way out. No door closes but another opens. Never stand in the hallway too long. Wait not for the knock. Do not expect anyone outside to try the lock. We found a good place to go to. Prius, tell her about the next doorway."

Prius said, "Googy is groovy is our new motto. It will be ecstasy, we you and me endlessly. We named the Resettlement Project Googy, meaning Gooder than Ganny. Long distance probes are sending back positive information from the closest exoplanet that exists, Proxima Centauri b. It is in the Alpha Centauri triple star system, only four-and-a-quarter light years away! We can upgrade our antimatter engines big enough to get our entire nation moved there before the Solar fish fry begins burning up our water."

They smiled and patted each other in congratulations for human cyborgs having enough intelligence to fashion a fine future.

Prius continued, "The habitability data says the Proxima b exoplanet is as Good As Ganny to live on. Its Proxima C sun is a dense red dwarf with lots of killer solar flares but we know how to cope with them: Build the cities just behind the day-night terminator line. Planet b rotates but once a year as it orbits its sun and keeps one side in daylight. That puts a stationary twilight zone on the edge of the terminator shadow. We can build our houses on the bright side of sunset or back in the afterglow if we want constant color in the sky. Or we could make towns in both places for diversity."

"How soon is Old Sol going to boil us?" asked Perry.

"Five billion years," said Prius. "But when you know you have got to go, you better go while the going is good. Remember Soogl: Sooner is Gooder than Later. We will not wait until this all comes to an end before we begin leaving: There are a lot of big ships to build and new technology to invent for prefabricating and emplacing a pleasant settlement on a brave new world."

Roy, the caravan's sturdy blonde guide and lover of Prius, said, "Soogl is what we will remember while building a new and ever better society. We want mankind's best principles to survive the furious fist of fate that is fracking the Earth today."

"Nothing lasts forever except good ideas," said Prius.

"That's okay, that's Twits," said Roy. "Doorways close and other doorways open. Change keeps us moving. Moolit. Move it or lose it. Keep the good things from the past that deserve to last. Keep the best, dump the rest and trump mediocrity. Do it early, before gangster gangrene sets in and spoils the scene. Keep moving moving moving, faster than degenerate greed genes can catch. Prius is approving."

Roy's woman, Prius, nodded her attractive computerized cranium and said, "It doesn't matter how smart we think we be or what glossy gadgets we fabricate or how much junk we circulate. All will change until it reaches final entropy. The only thing that does not change is change. We have to keep ahead of change and manage it before it manages us. I and we are going to Googy. We must cube the Rubic today. It is wise to go earlier than necessary. It is dangerous to test a deadline. This is a really dead, line."

Rachael's life-mate, the no-nonsense Leon Kowalski, summed it up: "Life is not static. Life cannot stop and balance on the knife-edge of time. Life moves to stay alive. Moolit. Whichever life does not move will be removed. It can go one of two ways: It can get better and brighter for everybody or get worser and darker to death. Laziness is no excuse, laziness does not compute."

They considered the power of Leon's wisdom.

Carry affirmed, "I have lived on Terrible Terra Secundus so I know what you are saying is true. For eight years I observed the descent of decent society as it allowed pandemic avaricity."

Perry said, "You have to be diligent to remain good. Not buying stuff in the first place is the basic way to not get owned by things, just like not buying food is the best way not to get fat. Everything you obtain, you gotta maintain or it goes down the drain, taking you with it and driving you insane."

Prius said, "Stuff gathers dust while moth and mold make it old. You can only use one thing at a time. Manage well what you store and you will not need anything more. As people get excess abundance, they automatically waste more of the common wealth which the modest rest of us could place in better use. We have to protect ourselves by restraining excess and retraining grabby crab claws to do more with less and learn that sharing is caring and owning is onerous."

Carrie said, "That sounds strict. Who cares if they overload their habby pads with junk? They are only hurting themselves."

Leon smiled at the old excuse for not caring about other peoples' welfare. He gave an example, "Bad habits outgrow the good. Take tomatoes. The trick is to maintain the good roots before the surrounding weed seeds germinate and grow into the root network and corrupt the whole fertile field. Get the weeds off the stage early and stick them into acting class or else the show cannot stay on the road. They would be fine if they stayed far away in their own alien wilderness but after they ruin their own patch they have to emigrate to where life is sweet and turn another place into weeds, too. Everyone is part of the whole: People infect each other. If they do not cooperate, they create a retrograde jungle of bonobos. This is where we live and where we want to live well. Right here! This is home, for now, and we are investing our short lives here so that we and our neighbors, can grow upward and outward, well and together. Together. We will not let them turn us into greedy weeds playing a Boom And Bust game with our welfare like they are doing on Earth, to its everlasting shame. Earth became a bad name."

Carry asked, "Who gets to decide who is a bad actor?"

"That's the first half of the trick," answered Perry. "Someone has to define bad acting so we know we understand the difference between free expression and antisocial behavior. The second half is to get the bad actors to look at themselves and admit they need help so they can help themselves. They must give modesty a serious try or say bye bye. If they will not overcome their laziness of thought and deed, no amount of good advice can fix their need. Right Leon?"

Leon the horticulturist smiled and nodded. "You can over-fertilize a tomato and it won't grow faster, you will overstimulate it and kill it. Greedy human weeds need life experience and attention before they are able to grok the wisdom of modesty."

Their faces went blank, they did not understand.

He simplified: "It takes what it takes to change bad habits. Do not worry and do not try too hard. That only makes them defend their illness more stubbornly Let them grow into good sense. Or not. If they cannot respond to wisdom you have to protect yourself from their pollution and push them to arm's length and hope they wise-up before the end. You will be able to help them if they can learn to listen and will listen to learn."

They understood his explanation of the power of fatalism. They nodded at Kowalski's correctness.

Kowalski finished with a touch of humor: "Or we will drop them down on Mars! Right, Perry?"

The group laughed and Perry scooped a handful of ice crystals and flipped them at Leon.

Persistent Carry said again, "Who gets to decide who is the bad actor?

"Other actors," said Perry.

"But how do you get the bad actors to admit the truth about themselves so they can improve?" asked the exasperated Carry.

Rachael said, "Truth is serious. After they've gone to school for a while they understand that there can be no pursuit of happiness without democracy and democracy cannot exist without truth hammering out justice all over this land."

"Truth and Total Transparency," interjected Leon. "The three Big Tees. Transparency shall set you free."

"We made Truth a required subject in every year of school," Rachael said. "Dishonest kids cannot advance in grade. They repeat the year and learn honesty. If they can't pass the test two years in a row, they're put to work assisting the teacher of the Truth Class until they grok it. Or they go to the sanatorium workhouse if they cannot grok it because of mental health challenges."

"Nooo," said Carry.

"Yes," said Rachael. "Students are tested yearly and the liars are held back so they don't waste their time and our resources by learning advanced information that they will use against the common health for their own selfish purposes when they grow to mature adult liars. They would disrupt our climate of commercial cooperation. We have to do whatever it takes to make them understand. Half measures ruin the land. Lying, laziness and ignorance are here to stay. They walk hand in hand with egotism leading the way."

BRAVE NEW MARS

"We don't need that booshite," said Leon. "We are a frontier society that wants goodly growth. There aren't enough of us living out here to allow any percentage of counter-productive hustlers. We're spending our short and valuable lifetimes on building something worthwhile to endure. To do that, we can only use the best resource materiel; honest people. We bend the twig toward honesty when young. There is no point in spreading humanity if dishonesty floods with it. Look how the liars looted Mars."

Roy nodded, "We can accept the fact that many cannot resist liarhood but that does not mean we approve of it or will allow it to flourish. We will not enable the self-abuse of lying to abuse innocent listeners as well. Those days are over. Krappy corpos have been closed, hosed and disposed."

Carry said, "I am amazed at the severity of that concept. So you keep them in a sanitarium all their lives if they cannot stop lying?"

Roy answered, "Yep. But it is not a jail, they are not locked up. It is a good alternative lifestyle. They just do not mix with society at large where they can hurt people with their defective characters. We make them live-in teachers."

"Ah ha ha ha," she laughed. "You turn the liars into teachers so they can teach the kiddies how to lie better?"

"Nope. Teachers are careerists. They keep their income secure by obeying what they've been told to teach. We start them out as math teachers and Assistant Truth Teachers. They can't lie about math. If they learn honesty, we can move them up to teaching at college level and let them move off-campus to see how they manage their addiction in gullible society."

"Math teachers can lie," said Carry. "They can tell the sweet little innocents that when you put two and two together, you get twenty-two, not four. How are the kids going to know it is not math, just trickery, a false way to amuse oneself by bemusing the beholders?"

Somerset Meece

"Mathematical tasks are black and white and are archived in sanctified storage," said Roy. "The kids could look it up and detect a snow job and report it to the principal. Or the parents will see an error in the homework answers. Lying is a crime with community service penalties. Tricky teachers will find themselves doing less teaching and more time on the ice gang if they lie. Liars will not destroy this CommonWealth the way they did Kentucky and most of Earth."

Perry said, "Lies are big. Whether they're white, black, or fifty shades of gray, they are the seeds of disaster so we deny them any seedbeds. Lies and liars have started wars and killed millions of good human beings. Big liars would deserve the death penalty if we had one."

Carry asked, "What if people just make errors? Get their facts wrong? Don't remember correctly? You put them on the ice gang?"

"People don't make mistakes," answered Perry.

Carry laughed. "Ah hoo hoo hoo. I found the perfect people! Ganymedeans!"

"Just about perfect," Perry said. "If we don't know something, we will admit it and say so. We won't fake it or guess at it to soothe our ego. We know there will always be smarter and lesser people than ourselves so we do not compete with anybody. We don't need to act like we are Masters Of Intuition. We know that lies have greater and lesser direct and indirect consequences on everybody so we provide proportional responses for prevarication."

"They could use you back on Terra Sec ...Mars. Even their new name of the planet is just brand name fakery. Truth is already dead on Mars," Carry said.

Perry said, "We'll send Mars our Kindergarten Truth Manual."

"Mars would edit your manual down to one sentence; 'Truth is whatever our public relations corporations say it is'," she said.

They got up and went over to their ice-machines parked beside the central ice hump in the crater as they laughed and shouted, "Don't even think about truth! No truth please, we are Martians!"

Roy was digging with curiosity into the frosty snow on the mound in the middle of their crater.

He said, "I found some metal in this ice. There is sparkle here."

"Platinum or palladium?" asked Perry.

"Neither. It is sun-yellow. It is gold from a good meteor. Welcome to Ganny, Carry," he said as he put a lump of metal in her mittened hand.

She exclaimed, "This is what you just picked out of that icy dirt! I can't believe it. If this is really gold, it's got to be worth a lot of credit!"

"It's only about a kilogram," said Roy. "We get a lot of golden meteors going by on their way to Jupiter's gravity sink. There's no atmosphere on Ganny to melt them with friction and burn them up. They hit the ice fast but stay pretty nice. You can keep it if you like it. Just register it at the CommonWealth Assets Office first. Otherwise, leave it here and I will give the office the coordinates so they can inventory it and assign it to whomever needs it for a good project."

"Leave it here?" she said. "Leave a million credits in the snow."

"Of course," the husky moon miner said. "It is only gold. You do not think anyone would, what you call it, steal it, from the other fifty thousand people to whom it rightfully belongs. When it landed here, it became Ganymedean gold belonging to every Ganymedean. That makes it CommonWealth gold and stealing it from many thousand of citizens is a big crime and costs a lot of time on the ice gang. It does not happen here. I guess we do not have politicians here because there is nothing to bribe them with."

"Leave it alone if it doesn't belong," Perry sang and started to dance. He put steel drum 'Panorama Festival' music on their Sliders' synchronized sound systems and filled the frozen white bowl of the meteor crater with the dynamic rhythms of Trinidad, a former Earthian tropical island paradise that was partially submerged from glacier melt.

Perry shouted, "Are you ready to bring dee Calypso beat to dee Ganymedey bruddahs and sistahs?"

They danced in the snow and kicked it onto each others' snowsuits and ran around the ice banks to get away.

"Last one home's a dirty rotten egg!" cried Rachel.

"Who has eggs? I want one!" pleaded Leon for one of the rarest commodities on Jove's giant moon.

"First you've have to catch the hen!" cried Rachel as they leapt onto their Sliders and sped to the azure domes of Siwah City.

BRAVE NEW MARS

Somerset Meece

They stopped into a school, they passed along the way. Well, they got next to a door and they heard the teacher say:

"How can you tell when a Martian is lying?" Teacher Gaff was warming-up the kids to the subject matter of Honesty.

"Their lips are moving!" shouted a few kids with glee at being permitted to say out loud a prejudicial joke about other people.

"Correct!" the wise old Mister Gaff said as he rolled a sheet of paper into the shape of a pirate spyglass and squinted through it at the kids' eyes. His vision found the attentive face of a pretty girl.

"Zhora! How can you tell if the boy next to you is lying?".

"His lips are moving!" teased Zhora who was smiling at the boy seated next to her, Lawrence, whom she fancied.

"No. Mister Lawrence Paull's lips also move when he is telling the truth, which is always, I hope," the teacher smiled. "Another clue that shows if Lawrence is fibbing is called bad body-speak. That is when he moves oddly when he is telling you something that he secretly knows is wrong. His face would show unusual expressions that don't go along with what he is saying. Give me an example, Zhora."

"His eyes look away from my eyes," she answered.

"Correct. Liars sometimes are embarrassed by the shabby sound of what they are saying and are subconsciously afraid that the feeling of guilt will show in their facial appearance. They won't let you look into their eyes because they fear you might be able to sense what they are actually feeling inside. A liar who constantly fake-talks can be diagnosed as a psychopath."

"What kind of path?" a kid asks.

"Psyco path. Lying is a form of mental illness that gets so bad that it begins to affect other people and has to be treated by professional healthcare workers because the liar disrespects other peoples' dignity and that leads down the path to loneliness and hermitage. A person who cannot stop themselves from hurting other people is a misanthrope. It means they are ill and cannot stop themselves from being meanies. It is a bad behavior habit they got when they were young and when they got to be adults, they didn't even know they were mean because it was their personality and they think they are normal and correct in thinking no one else is as smart and as good as they are. Those are misanthropes."

The kids ignore the big word.

"It means not liking anybody. That includes you, you, and you," Gaff says, randomly pointing to class members. "And me too! They would find something wrong with your perfect teacher!" He smiles with disbelief.

"Why would anybody not like me?" asks one surprised child that Gaff had pointed to.

"Because you are not them," said Gaff. "It is nothing you did, you are fine. The liar does not know how to like anybody. He dislikes himself or he would ask for help to manage his disease so he could do some self-improvement and become a better person. It takes good work to change a bad habit. Anybody can do it if they make the 'Big D,' the Big Decision to stop being a jerk."

"Why would anybody not want to be a good guy?" a child asks.

"There is a thing called mental illness, something not working right in our brain. It is like when you can catch covid virus by accident and you do not know why. You did not ask to get it but you got it anyway. Liars are like that. They do not know why they lie. They come to think of it as normal behavior and they ignore it and let it get worse."

Somerset Meece

"What happens when they get worser," a scared kid said. "Something bad?"

"They have to go to Social School and let nurses teach them how to get better. But let's get back to the topic of how to tell when a liar is lying. Some liars lie so much that they have to learn how to also be actors. They can force themselves to look calmly into your eyes and keep their face blank while they stick the spear of untruth, the lie, right into your guts." Gaff made the motions of thrusting a long spear into an opponent's belly.

"Ooh, send them to school, back to school," children around the room said.

"What else do liars do to fool you?" Gaff asked.

Student Ridley raised his hand and said, "Bad body-speak. They cross their legs when they do not have to."

"Right, Mister Scott. That is a form of fidgeting; biding for time while they think-up a logical and hopefully believable, falsehood that they hope will fool you. Another fidgety form of body language is tapping the fingertips on a desk while you are trying to think of a lie. Everybody tap your fingers on the desk!"

The classroom erupts into one big rattle-tap-tapping noise. Everybody joins the fun.

"Both hands! I want to hear both hands tapping while you tell a big whopper-topper! Go ahead, make up a big one about yourselves. Lie to me about your age! How old is everybody?"

"I am ten years old! I am fifteen! Twenty-two years old!" come the play-acting, lying replies. "I am a hunnert years old!" shouts Rutger, the class clown, causing applause that ends the exercise.

"Fidgeting is an attempt to divert attention," said Mister Gaff, "away from a big fat lie or even a little termite lie. What's the difference between a white lie and a big lie?"

"Nothing!" shouts the intelligent Hampton Fancher from the back. "A lie is a lie is a lie. It is not a matter of degrees!"

The teacher is taken astern, "Wow. Mister Fancher. You've been paying good attention. The result of a lie may hurt a little bit or a lot but either way, it is messing with a person's personal perception of reality and that is harmful abuse. That is a disrespectful waste of peoples' time. It belittles human dignity. Liars lives are dishonorable. Dishonesty dampens everything the liar does even when they're not lying. They can do a few good things in public to look nice and conceal their dishonor. Their charitable deeds are public relations deceptions. Why do they spend a lot of charity money to help people whom they don't care much about and usually lie to?"

The kids were baffled by the irony in the question.

Gaff waited, rolling his paper in his hands.

Zhora raised her hand to try an answer:

She said, "Could it that they want people to think they are nice so that it will be easier to fool them with their next and bigger lie?"

"Brilliant!" the teacher said. "They usually behave like normal human beings. Acting nice is a lie in action. Liars cannot actually be nice people until they accept the fact that they are thieves stealing the truth from other people.

"Why is lying a waste of time," shouts Gaff the teacher.

"Loopy lies lead to larger lassos later," shouts Deckard with relief that he had been able to say the tongue-twisting truism.

Gaff smiles and says, "Correct. The results of a lie are worse than the event that made somebody lie in the first place. What if a kid tells you to lie so you can get what you want

Somerset Meece

now and won't have to wait until later to get your greedy gratification?"

"Lies lubricate a little bit but bite back bigger later," said student Deckard with a grin at his linguistic gymnastics.

"Perfect, Deckard! Mister Fancher! Do you think that a lie is bad if it might make a good thing happen?"

"Good goals never mitigate bad methods," playfully said Hampton with the huge vocabulary he had acquired from reading and writing erudite science fiction stories ever since he was in kindergarten.

"Yes! Excellent word. There is no mitigation for a prefabrication! To fabricate is to make something up. Mister Sebastian! What if a good little white lie might get the results you want faster and save a lot of time compared to explaining a complicated truth?"

"Little lies last forever," cried JF. "The work that you do to keep a lie alive goes on and on and takes more work than it took to tell the lie and you got to tell more lies to make the first lie sound right and it wastes your time and you could be having fun inventing something like, like ... new eyeballs for cyborgs!"

"Wow, that is the perfect answer, JF. What if someone tells you that lying is fun? What if they tell you that it is entertaining to see other people make mistakes and look foolish when they act on something that you said wrong that does not really exist except for a naughty little thought that you made-up inside your own head? Is that a hahaha thing?"

The class was quiet. They thought that fun was always something to enjoy.

Deckard asked, "What is wrong with having a little fun?"

Student Bryant raised his hand and suggested, "Being an honorable person is more funner than being a funny liar?"

Gaff nodded twice with appreciation for Bryant's comprehension. He drew stars around one end of the paper tube he rolled and drew spiral lines down the sides like a barber pole and sat it on the desk.

"I am doing some good here," Gaff said. "Knowledge is the lighthouse of life. By Gemini, I think he's got it! There are funny good people and there are funny fools. Fools lie with pig-laughter that means they have no self-respect and want to make others look foolish to make up for their own ignorance and lack of honor. Never join that type of loser laughter! Watch them be foolish but never laugh with them. They are sad and mean inside."

He shouted, "Untruth is unfun!" It made them laugh to hear an adult use the non word, 'unfun'.

"Mister Hauer!" Gaff said. "What does honorable mean?"

Young Rutger's eyes flickered from side to side as he tapped his fingers and crossed his legs. He intended to be an actor when he grew up and he was practicing fidgeting like a liar who is thinking up a good one.

His friends smiled and waited for a whopper to come out of his mouth. Instead Rutger said, "Honor means that you are somebody who stands for The Good. Honor is the solution to pollution. You refuse to be one of life's problems. When you are honorable, you know you are okay and as good as anyone, including the popular kids."

The kids were glad to hear that.

Rachael whispered into Carry's ear, "This is what schools are about; teaching kids the intelligence of clean living: Living in the solution."

Gaff shouted, "This honorable class is dismissed!" The children rushed for the exits like students everywhere when suddenly freed from the bondage of chairs.

\#

Somerset Meece

A classy caravan of three Sliders hummed through the pressure gate and entered the city of Siwah. They dismounted and admired the structure of the urban glacial beehive. They casually walked and looked around while their obedient sleds followed two meters behind.

Azure domes containing rounded blue rooms were piled high and joined together at the top with a leafy gold sculpture that spilled water filled with glittering flakes of gold down the walls into an illuminated moat that swirled around live trees in the social center market.

Prius told Carry, "This was created for fun. This city has comfortable beauty because it blends into the environment like pueblo abodes blend into the Rio Grande Valley. Public art is a common wealth. Since we know it is ours, we feel spiritually richer and happier when art surrounds us."

Prius explained with pride, "A city can look and smell like a palace or a penitentiary. Siwah's air mixture imitates the atmospheric pressure and smell of the Amazonian rain forest that they used to enjoy on Earth before commercial thieves logged it and smogged it."

Rachael said, "Earth went crazy faster when it became no longer possible to smell new-mown hay or trees in the dawn after a rain. They lost touch with the background beauty of the natural environment and became spiritually disoriented. They smothered the beauty of the day. They did it just for pay."

"This is lovely," said Carry. "I know ice is hard as rock but the way everything is rounded, the buildings look soft and lightweight compared to the opaque clay blocks they use on TS. These walls are glowing from inside lighting. The evergreen trees and plants under the grow-lights make you forget it's cold. This feels alive and warm even though it is cold as ice. The coldness feels okay. It feels good because it looks good."

BRAVE NEW MARS

Prius explained why that was: "Within the city, buildings are legally public property and businesses can only lease them, not own them. Our code of construction won't permit ugly cheap stuff messing up the scenery, ruining our lives. We have it our way. We know it is ours. We are not passive doormats for owners' real estate nightmares. That means we don't have realtors here, no Reds, Real estate destroyers, lyingly calling themselves developers. There is no exploitive devolution of the pleasant ambiance built by the first Popios, the Positive pioneers of space. They were hardy dreamers, not spammers and scammers for profit. This architecture remains true, and particular to, the higher pioneer spirit that started this meaningful migration of society. It was not about constructing another profit mill in outer space where people were expected to somehow live happily in the interstices of commercial krappola. This city is about making headway in the odyssey of life."

Leon said, "We are here and that gives us the right to be happy here as much as the trees and the stars. Destroyers who would spoil the view and pollute the allure of our world, for profit, would be stealing beauty from us. We do not let that happen. We send them back to school. Stealing is a form of dishonesty and can be taught away at truth schools."

Zhora added, "It was funny, the way Earth listened to those comedians while they were stealing legacy land and building farty buildings in cities and laughably lying that they were doing it for the progress of mankind. Who whee, so glib for the goony consumers."

Leon said, "Destroyer misanthropes are not of us nor for us. They belong back on Earth where they started all that shite that is now playing out its endgame. They knew they were on the road to nowhere, taking a ride. They finally got there and it is not a pretty sight."

Somerset Meece

Zhora said, "We banished the bunco business of paving paradise for profit. Property is no longer commercial inventory. Welcome to a place you automatically own by being here and sharing it. You can divide it and share it but you cannot sell it. Property is not for profit tool."

Roy said, "CommonWealth means more than money. Wealth is everything but money. Money is not wealth, it is an artificial marker for market value. It is a bankable number simulating real stuff. Money is an implement to be utilized, not stored in a hole. That is like putting usable tools like shovels in a pile and saying, "Look at all my shovels. Is not that stack of shovels reassuring?""

They laughed at his reduction of the status of money.

Zhora explained, "Real wealth is sweet air and fresh water. Such things are free if you do the maintenance."

Leon broke in with two Ganymedean Truth School truisms: "Money does not make people rich, money makes rich people. Money does not grow on trees, money turns trees into money."

Zhora continued, "Look at this city we built on ice and soul; it is a CommonWealth asset, it is a luscious show room of the inborn wealth the people earn and deserve. It feels good being here. It does not exclude me because I have no money in my pocket. It looks good, artful and generous, the way we like it to look. The buildings are not social barricades stomping on our gathering places. Our buildings do not loom straight up and steal our view and the sun and sky with fortress walls that drop straight down onto prison sidewalks without buffer."

Roy said, "We banished smelly, noisy, pushy, rushing, traffic from our walking parks. No beetle bombers on rubber tires racing for space and time in our little piece of the infinite. Insanity cannot reign here. This city puts People over profit. It Pops. It rocks. Life is not about subsisting in a combative arena of doom."

BRAVE NEW MARS

Perry said, "A fresh, clean, unpolluted environment is common sense for wealthy common health. It's ours. We deserve the best world possible. Period. Selfish types are assigned to invest a lot of time in community service if they try to steal Ganny from its common owners. Realtors hate to serve the community. Community is what they take from and use and abuse to get stuff. They crave to convert it, not conserve it. They cannot learn what life is about until they labor on common land for the reward of finally feeling they are average people. Their self-esteem grows when their grabby little hands makes something that adds to the public beauty bank."

Zhora said, "After they understand that they belong in the common niceness, which is really all there is, they feel better. They no longer need to steal from the common wealth to feel important. Their good works spread out like high tides lifting all boats in the harbor. They realize their unique personalities are part of the big reality. They stop leeching."

"Or they buy a ticket to Mars," quipped Roy.

Carry said, "I'm impressed by all the people being outdoors and enjoying the cold with each other. There is so much social interaction, such mutual awareness. What makes them do that?"

Leon answered, "We build attractive and inviting comfortable common grounds that supply space for social activities without charge. Notice the cushioned benches that have warmers built into them to invite sitters. People love to converse and are encouraged to do so outside. We made it feel better to be outside than inside. They know that sitting in a room alone watching HoloVision is not as much fun as experiencing The Real World. The world is real people available all around and is not a virtual image of them."

Carry wondered: "How do you keep the unemployed people and the homeless ones from congregating in these

Somerset Meece

wonderful parks and making the normal people feel uncomfortable?"

"Perry said, ""You mean 'The Homeless Scourge' which they condemned and banished to gaols on Earth? Those pitiful examples of humans who do not march to the Money Machine beat?

"That is right," said Carry. "Does not the ugliness of homelessness clearly demonstrate that everyone must seek a career on the owners' treadmills?"

"Homelessness is okay," Perry said. "Street is neat. It is the way the owners criminalize them that scourges outdoor living. We have no problem with homelessness. It's a fact of life that many people like to stay outdoors and instinctively remember how to handle bad weather. Some like to cope with natural things. We do not allow camping on icewalks or other public places. Sleeping should be decently done in private. A person sleeping on public ice is calling for help. And we help them. Why not? They're one of us.

Zhora said, "We've all got common funds which they are part-owners of. Why would we treat them like criminals and whip them good instead of spending some of their money on helping them live?"

Perry said, "Right. Our CommonWealth society has no sadistic monsters who criminalize harmless helpless human behaviors to make themselves feel better about their own sorry selves. That kind of misanthropic abuse is an addiction that we fix early. We expose it in grade school when we see kids pushing other kids around for perverse fun. We identify and treat their inferiority complexes before they can turn into money-grubbing worker whippers."

Carry asked, "Would you like to start a service of rehabilitating whipper-snappers on Earth? There are too many in high places. Inferior personalities too often percolate to the top of commercial ladders and poison the Public Mind from their places of power."

"No thanks," Perry said. "That's too big for me. It takes a general economic attitude change. Competitive Capitalism kills, Cooperative Capitalism saves. One third of the Earthians are homeless or crucially looking for an affordable lifestyle. The jobs have to be likable and doable for the long term or else be very highly paid, which is rare. Every human being has the freedom to stay outside and not saddle themselves with the cost of buying and maintaining a roof and a door. Living free is not a crime, it's a right of life. Outside is where our species grew strong and capable. So camping is allowed everywhere on Ganymede except the sidewalks. There's not enough room. And, like the snobs say, it doesn't look good. It's indecent and degrading. They need and deserve private sleeping. Jail sleeping is no answer."

Carry said, "You allow people to live sub-standardly because they want to? You don't rehabilitate them to live normally? That is not very nice."

The Gannies smiled at the naivete of the newcomer.

"They are normal," said Perry. "Look at these people around here. Can you spot the twenty percent who don't support a hab dome or work for rent money? Leasing an ice dome home remains a voluntary obligation."

She was taken astern and said, "They all look different but they all look clean and neat. I cannot tell which are homeless. They all must have home domes. I don't see anybody with the homeless look."

Leon said, "Everyone has the use of their own municipal bathroom and storage locker that's big enough for them to sleep in when they need to. But they have to keep their stuff stowed away and out of sight, period. Lazy people of every affluence level would pile their personal possessions outdoors on common land if it were allowed. No one is allowed to spoil the beauty of unpolluted space. It's okay to be lazy, that is a lifestyle choice. A lot of people do choose it. They are mentally allergic to physical activities. They like to think, not work. Laziness gives them more time to live in their personalities. It's a life. We are not all builders. But. No one is allowed to be so lazy as to plop down in the marketplace and sleep there nor leave their stuff on the ground. It has been so ordained: This beauty will be respected. It will be maintained. By everyone, all the time."

Carry said, "It is a relief to see that the government here is a benevolent dictator and not all sweetness and forgiveness. Does Ganymede do anything about public drunkenness? That is unsafe and reckless and even dangerous."

Perry said, "Right. Over-intoxication shows that a person is Oco. Public drunkards demonstrate they need psychological help. So we help them. We love everybody, guess you might call us a Pollyanna."

Leon said, "Our health system takes chronic drinkers away for cognitive therapy. Like it or not, everyone has an obligation to the herd. Even if they do not want it."

Perry said, "'Whatever you've got, you've gotta maintain. That includes yourself. That's the law of the living. No free rides."

Leon said, "Maintenance is the price tag on the big life. Denying your responsibility will get the teachers to take you away, aha. Your indecency will educated and deleted."

Carry said "I remember Mars. I do not want those lonely hotels with a tear in every room. Drowning my sorrows in the warm glow of their wine. Seeking comfort inside The Big Fog was a passive escape from the shabbiness of the world that was forced upon us by CorpoGovo disrespect. It made us spend too many hours on-screen. It changed our concept of reality. The New Reality was created by the Big

Shots' copy writers inside the Big Fog. They owned our head space. Life experience became a layered lasagna of pixel images inside digital dimensions."

Carry said, "Ganymede feels so different. It is full of natural beauty embellished with artistic ambiance. All the architecture blends with nature and respects it and reflects it and fits-in.

Perry said, "Architects go to art school. They have to be able to draw freehand beauty before they get to design real places for people to live in. No squares allowed unless you want to wear one on your head to show how silly you can be."

Leon said, "Architects get decertified for even proposing designs containing corpo-cheapo concrete creases."

Prius summarized the Ganymedean pride of preservation: "We built this city. We built this city on heart and soul. This is not a corpo commodity. We're not gonna play those corporation games. We dictate how it looks. We are hometown heroes. We earned it, we deserve it, we paid for it with sweat equity."

"God I love this," said Carry. "It has everything I hoped life could hold. It marries the idealistic with the realistic. It works a hundred times better than CorpoKrap on Mars."

Her eyes were shining with cry water. "Thank you Perry for bringing me here. I am so grateful. I love you so much."

Her eyes shone with full affection for the Ganymedean mining man who brought her here and joined her life to his.

They hugged and twirled and danced closely and happily. He pulled her in tight with their chests pressed together and said, "Methinks we oughta get ourselves married if we gonna be carrying on like this."

She was startled and thought a moment and said, "Marriage. I was not sure you were that serious about us. Hey!

Somerset Meece

You know what? I am like, 'Let's do it!' Can we have an outer space Extravehicular Wedding? An EVW? The stars are the backdrop of our celestial love affair. Their splendor tells us that it's a wonderful world."

"Let's do it," Perry said. "Let's reserve rooms at the Chomsky Orbital Lodge for our friends. We can decorate our pressure suits to look festive with beads and lights and fluorescent flowers and Saturnian Rings and supernova nebulae."

She said, "Oh, I can see the wedding spacesuits now. Mine will have lots of shiny sequins and glitter. But I wonder if we want all the trouble of encouraging a big party of people to float around bumping into each other in space and losing their drinks."

"It's no trouble," Perry said. "The Lodge's outer space platform has a domed grill-work enclosure so customers can float around inside a protective cage. It has a lot of hand-holds so no one has to wear a tether or float Oco. You'll see. It's like flying. It makes you feel freer."

\#

Floating inside a space balcony orbiting Ganymede, the wedding couple was surrounded by a circle of celebrants wearing sparkling space suits and holding hands.

They were illuminated by magnificent fireworks popping bright flowers against the vacuum of black space. Starlight shone full and bright on this amorous affair. Laser-lines streaked around the deck with a discotheque effect.

"I propose a toast!" said Roy over the space suit radios. "To the happy couple! May they long enjoy the love we see tonight. Love is in the air and it is something that I must believe in because I see it everywhere. Here to the Ganymedean freedom that we enjoy that makes us as happy as that loving couple dancing there!"

BRAVE NEW MARS

They all said, "To the happy couple," and "hear hear. Freedom. Freeness."

They tipped their chins down and to the left to pull champagne from the pressure suit straws sticking up from the collar rims of their space parkas.

"Speech, speech!" came the inevitable call from the wedding party.

Perry moved the new Carolyn Walker in front of him and said, "Mistress Walker will now say a few words on this momentous occasion."

She laughed and swallowed and drew a full breath and said, "The conquest of outer space is a continuation of man-and-womankind's quest for the unqualified equality of all people."

Carry said, "And we are going to expand the equality of mankind before the forces of greed can infect the new places that will be developed out there."

"Developed where, exactly?"a woman radioed.

Carry said, "I am from Earth. I met dear Mister Walker on Mars and now we live on Ganymede. Soon I will birth an infant. Half of his genes are Earth genes from me and half are from the faraway Proxima Centauri b planet. There are people out there. Good people. We have something wonderful to offer them; the philosophy of sharing the knowledge and abilities of two subspecies for growth."

Quietness. They looked at each other to see how they should react to her precipitous pronouncement.

"Ahem," Perry cleared his throat. "We are going to Proxima b some day soon."

The wedding party was silent with doubt.

Perry explained, "The hyper-drive will make the four-and-a-quarter-light-year trip doable in four weeks."

"One month," Perry said, "to travel to the nearest star in the galaxy. I did the quantum math. Whew."

Somerset Meece

They solemnly nodded and took another drink on their helmet straws.

"You are going to leave us?" one woman sadly asked.

"No," Perry smiled and said. "Of course not. This is our home. This is the finest kind of place. I meant that everybody is going to naturally emigrate through Proxima b. The human race has got to keep movin' movin' movin'. Keep them dogies movin', or die. Carry and I are going out there to do the preliminary ground work to get the exodus rollin'."

"Why Proxima b?" asked a man.

Perry answered. "Because it's there and we're not. It's the closest extra-solar planet and planets last longer than moons. It's livable. There's an advanced society there and they have learned how to cope with the red dwarf's flare-ups. The human race's strong suit is adaptability. We'll have to begin our stellar emigration pathway somewhere. Nice as this is, we can't stay here forever."

Carry said, "Perry and I have a reason to lead the exodus. Little Johnny Walker will want to see where he came from and so do we."

She finished the toasting by singing out loud and clear in the old sea shanty style; "And so we go a'roving on that far sea."

The wedding guests all sang back together through their helmet radios, "And so we go a-say-a-ling on that far sea." The tune's radio waves transmitted into the far dark nights of infinite space.

The party was happy to have a big new mutual adventure to cooperate with and together win.

BRAVE NEW MARS

Somerset Meece

18, Ready To Rock And Repo

The Walkers were at home in their crystal dome when a call came over the phone.

"It is Lyra! It is really Lyra calling from Mars," Carry said to Perry as she listened to the voice message with an expression of shock growing on her face.

She looked at her new husband and said, "Oh, Perry. They are in trouble."

She sent a voice message message to Lyra. It would take twenty minutes to get back to her as Mars and Jupiter were on opposite sides of their solar orbits.

"Lyra, I wanted to say goodbye but we left in such a rush I didn't have time to talk to anyone. It was an emergency escape is what it was. I am so sorry to hear what is happening on dear old Terra Secundus.

"A civil war is unbelievable, worse than we could have imagined. I was sure Mars life couldn't get any worse than it was with a crazy corpo running and ruining it. They reduced the minimum wage is even more insanity. It already was underneath poverty. No wonder the cyphers are acting up."

Carry remembered that all the lines, channels, cables and networks were tapped on Mars. She stopped herself from further corporation criticism.

"Oops, I am sorry. Now that I remember better, the pay is fully adequate on Terra Secundus. If the workers would spend fewer credits on boozing and gambling, they would be fine. It is their own fault that they are broke. The ambitious workers work harder and can get rich. The genius of The Corporation is a gift to all the lucky citizens. If the Corpogov allows a civil war, then that war will be wild and wonderful and a good thing to experience. It will shake up the caput and make them shape up and believe that War Is Peace."

She showed Lyra she was spouting fake loyalism when she included computer-proof sarcasm in her message; "And day is night and black is white, if the corpo says so."

251

"I wish you the best of luck if you do what we always do; deny and comply and hope it gets better. You be careful and take care of yourself. Let us know if we can help. Bye. Keep in touch Lyra. I love you and wish you the best."

She hung up and said, "Oh Perry, they're in trouble. Bad trouble. She couldn't say anything specific over the CorpoPhone but she hinted that partisan warfare has started."

"What type of partisans?" he asked.

"People who are bringing down the big bucks under fascism are attacking people who love freedom more than wealth. The money-makers are waving the flag and whipping the peace lovers and forcing them into a suicidal backlash of simple self-protection. The merchant-minded piggy people are saying they are making Mars great again. I wish they would just make it honest again."

Perry said, "They are making it a greater place to fatten their own wallets no matter how many get hurt. Making things great for a merchant means opening the flood gates of laissez-faire capitalism so they can tear up the country and wring every last drop of water and blood from its people."

"We got out just in time," said Carry. "Now, there is no escape from that blood feud down there,"

Perry said, "I want to help them but I don't want to risk losing this nice life we having together. I'm a rescuer. I live and let live up to the point where they can't live without my help. I can't turn my back on crucial emergencies. I don't normally do that. When they're sayin' who ain't free, they're saying it right to me."

Carry said, "The CorpoGovo will win the civil war with big weapons. It will slaughter civilians. It is more dangerous than ever to go your own way."

"I can manage danger," he said. "I'm not too proud to run away when it gets hairy. I don't go places where there's no exit. I won't play the odds against survival. I'll go away to be a bigger winner some other day."

He smiled with confidence and caressed her shoulder with sympathy.

"Perry, I didn't plan on this," she said. "You asked me to escape from Mars with you and that is all I wanted to do; get away from that commercial catacomb. Now you are saying you want to go back where they can freeze you in a Manhattan minute. If you dare to so much as spit on one of their SpyCams, they will call it sedition and send you to orbital limbo, forever! I've seen it happen! Owners' InJustice exaggerates misdemeanors into Crimes Of The Century. Our coming child will be left with only memories of his father, the man I loved and wanted to live with for a long time, if not forever."

He was struggling with an ache in his larynx. The shame of denying her proper marital expectations made him cry over letting her down.

He shook his head and clamped his jaws and explained his wish to return to Mars: "Things have changed since we were married; with new information comes new decisions. I feel sorry for all those dusty red Martians trying to live down there. Their life-force is being siphoned into a private CorpoCoffer black hole that takes more than it gives. It converts commonist wealth into private hoard. They are Popped, turned into Pawns of profit. It's not right, Carry. It's incorrigibility on a grand scale. It is global subjugation."

Carry knew what he was talking about and said, "The Owner knows the difference between avaricious aggression and cooperative competition. He hates the common concept of equality. His corpo wrote the legal structure to punish Secundians if they even think about unionizing to work together for better worklives and lifestyles. And then it claims the corpo deserves better standing at law because it is so much more important than everybody else put together."

Perry had to laugh at that absurdity that became apparently true. "Hahaha haha. Corpos are persons. Hahaha. And a killer whale is a goldfish."

"If corpos were real persons," she said, "as they claim to be, they would not gather all of a country's common wealth unto themselves because real persons are sane enough to not want all that maintenance in their lives. They will not do it. They know it is insane. Corpo cartoons do not pay the maintenance due. They are not real people. If they were, they would all be in jail. Or in very closely-gated communities."

Perry said, "If cuckoo corpos were real people, they would find enough honor to build an equal justice system that would have to define themselves as organized racketeers and re-educate themselves in rehabilitation programs. As it is now, they take all of the benefits of being human but none of the responsibilities!

Carry knew what he was saying and she said, "Until the Martians fix the insane Corpo Personhood laws, they will be forever Popped, Prisoners of profit."

Perry said, "The death spiral. Does it seem to you that maybe an outside influence could crack the shell of captive consumerism?"

Carry was uncertain. "Maybe," she said. "That is maybe with a capital M. The citizenry would have to snap themselves out of their mental torpor. Nobody can do it for them."

"I know, I know. It would be Quixotic for me to go back. I can't change a culture."

"Then do not go."

He thought a moment and expelled a chestful of air. "You're right. I won't. I helped'em enough when we disconnected their Master Mainframe. They've got to help themselves now. They're adults; they've gotta learn responsibility. They can't be sponsored all their lives."

She was pensive and reflected, "They forgot how to do real stuff. The pooter and its manager borgs do everything for them, and to them."

She rolled her eyes and said, "They might not even be able to feed themselves before the new chaos kills them. Oh my Cod, Two Emm does not care if they slaughter themselves before they get back in lockstep with the AI Mechanism. Mass mutual killing is a favorite tactic of the Algolrithms of Profit."

He looked at her with fear for the terror they might have triggered on Mars. "My glitch. I set free a herd of sheep. I set'em loose in what they consider to be a desert; a dead and deadly desert. They're not frontier folk. They'll need survival knowledge. I should take some Gannies down there and help them get started. Otherwise they would be better-off if I had never gone there. But that's how I got you, babe. Carry. What have I done?"

"You're a good man with good intentions. I realize why I love you: You do right things the right way. Usually. You look good and you sound good. You are a good deal for me and our children."

She laughed at her outbreak of emotional candor. "There is very little to not love about my Mister Peregrine Walker. We can delve deeper into that later. Maybe I am not perfect either. My Perry. Why did you have to boom into my barroom that afternoon and turn my life around so soon?"

Perry said, "I will not ask you to stop being yourself. If you think I don't owe them anything for what I did to their digital demon, I will respect your opinion."

She softened with affection and hugged him and said, "You set them on the path to freedom. You gave them their lives back, that is all. It is not your fault if they were never taught how to do life. Nor is it theirs."

BRAVE NEW MARS

She smiled and said, "You can go back if you feel guilty. Do you think you might have a Savior Complex? How about a Martyr Syndrome? Meet Perry Martyr, Martian Savior!"

"It's a world of wasted people," he said. "I ain't sure there's any way to help them out. I wish we had a United Federation of Planets to send their problem to but I don't think an interplanetary group could work any better here than it did on Earth when the United Nations tried to save it from global warming. Wealthy CorpoGovos never let smaller nations make wealth management decisions infringing on their grand schemes of international control. Corpos don't play fair. They say it's okay to cheat because they're more important than little people and deserve to win, no matter what the cost to their pretense of honor. Their active arrogance makes it okay for me to play them as rough as I can. I'm taking the laser drills with me."

Carry said, "Good. They will play rougher than your honor will let you do. They have profits to protect. They have always demolished any democratic group that dampens their domination of captured economies."

Perry said, "They will be coming for Ganymede next. We should preemptively attack the power base on Mars. Now, while it's in turmoil. Their induced war is an embossed invitation to get back to Mars where the oppression is growing and practicing to strike its next victim; us."

She took a deep breath and looked into his eyes, "To get back is life-threatening but I have to approve the right thing to do. It would be proactively protecting this home, and our future family, from the dollar demon that wants to come here and own us in cultural slavery. No thanks."

"Give the lady a set of beautiful stainless steel cutlery with matching prune juice pitcher," he said."

Somerset Meece

She understood that she had just accurately described the depths of corpo class depravity. She shook her head and said, "Why did I think there was a choice here? I am proud of you and I am very glad that you know what they stand for and what they are doing to do to us and how to respond to their indecent assault. But confronting them is a daunting dare."

He said, "We can go after their computer again if we have to. Don't look back, I'll wake you when we're through."

She says, "I do not know how, in the Hellas, you are going to keep out of trouble down there. Trouble gets you frozen on Mars."

He waxed excited: "It won't be too hard. Don't worry. I know the danger. I've got global positioning for targeting strategic bases. I won't forget to duck and I'll keep my head down. Since we cut the connection to their mainframe, their network won't work. The network is trashed and Corpo strategy is hash. The past is history, the future's a mystery that we're gonna alter. Mars is open again like it was when it began. Remember the aboriginals? Those people on the plaque on the peak of Olympus? The ones who had to remain on Mars and die in the Hellas Meteor strike? The ones for whom we cut the cords on Two Emm, that Malicious Mainframe? Their genetic essence is in the descendants on Mars today. We are standing in the shadow, baby. Don't you love the things they stood for?"

She said, "Oh Perry. How do you know what we owe them and what they have a right to expect from us?"

"The pioneers wanted a better future for everyone who came after them. They didn't want no fancy mansions with a bath in every room. They didn't fear the hardship of frontier life, they felt the freeness would get greater and was worth it."

She acquiesced with a big breath and a hug and gave him a shove. "You do not know the Martians nor do you know your way around the big Melas Valley as I do. I will go with you. I was with you when we cut the cables. You and I, and this little unborn Alpha Centaurian, are going on a family outing. We are going back to Mars."

She planted her feet firmly and shook her fists toward the next inner planet; "You big corpo catastrophe! We are coming to take you away! Aha."

She spread her arms and dramatically held her head high and said, "I do not know how in the Hellas we are going to do this but the flamenco will get us in tune with an attitude of gratitude that will get us through the fear of wealth."

She started their dome's musical playlist. A flurry of flamenco guitar fingerings sounded. Perry and Carry animated their arms and feet and clapped and stamped a fervent fandango on the colorful carpet, spread over the icy living room floor.

Somerset Meece

Three Crossbows were navigating under solar sails from Jovia toward the inner solar system.

The Ganymedean space tugs steered nearer to each other and drew into close formation where they conducted a personnel transfer routine.

Two astronauts, Roy and Leon, unreeling tethers behind them, jetted from the wing ships to grab the handrails outside the opened pressure hatch on Perry's guide ship.

Their mates, two smaller and more graceful astronauts, Prius and Zhora, glided across the tether through the infinite universe and joined them.

They entered Perry's Crossbow for a council of war.

"Are you the man with the plan, Perry?" asked Roy.

"Get on the bus, Gus. I made a new plan, Stan," Perry answered. "Our antimatter engines are idling until we are ready to flick onto the Martian surface at relativistic speeds that will be undetectable by the Terra Secundian Cornpones, their Corporate radar network protecting the owner's nasty excesses."

"The silent approach," said Leon. "And what is the specific purpose of sneaking onto Mars?"

"The goal is to give a little more freeness to a million people whom the corporately-controlled state treats like they are less respectable than trained consumer rats."

Roy asked, "What's wrong with The State? What makes it do people like that? What's going on?"

Carry answered, "Nobody knows what's goin' on. Mars is an opaque state. They have a few semi-elected people called Representatives who do not know what is going on either. They could not find out what is going on even if they wanted to know. They adopt the vain pride of the CorpoCracy that demands dishonesty as a career qualification. People must avoid the CorpoGov's hateful vengeance that hurts people for ignoring its lies. Indecent profit schemes build fake reality scenes demanding your support if you do not want to face the big chiller. The lies are more accepted than truth. A majority of people are treating the lies as real. Buy the lies or go bye bye. That is exactly what is going on."

Zhora asked, "What is behind it all? How did it get so bad?"

Carry answered, "The people are no longer allowed to speak up or to have anyone speak up for them. They have farcical Reps who pretend to be conscientious caretakers of a generous government. The Reps are shams, corpo employees paid in secret ways with cash bribes disguised as election campaign contributions. The Reps are figureheads of fake democracy. They sell their souls for shekels of silver. Most are committed to one thing: profiteering under the protection of corpo corruption.

"The Reps are phrequing farce-faces?" asked Roy.

"Right on," said Carry. "Three-dimensional, life-like, plastic cutouts of humans, possessing neither empathy nor conscience."

"They must be UNconscious." said Prius.

"Give them a break," said Perry. "They might be as much as semi-conscious. They are conscious of the sensual pleasures of booze, sex and big houses. But of conscience, they know nothing. They think that consciences are for losers. They know that lies are currency in The Money Game. They think that all the cool dudes are getting away with doin' it."

Prius said, "Wow, you mean that some of you humans are just as single-minded as our primitive robots were? Like the old single-purpose robot vacuum cleaners that mindlessly went all around the room sucking dust with one goal only; clean the floor. Could that possibly describe a purchased politician? No thinking allowed, shut up and clean the owner's floor."

Somerset Meece

Carry said, "Mm hmm. The Reps are cardboard Big Shot cutouts; unthinking, upper echelon cogs, in The Mechanism's gear train. Traitors in the peoples' halls of power. There is poison in their apple pies. The saddest dishonesty is how they gleefully take paychecks from the people they cheat. They make their victims remunerate them for their great exploitations."

Zhora asked, "Is it true? Representatives let their paying victims buy them free health care while they scrupulously veto free health care for the victims who need free service more than they do? Hypocrites are copying and representing, the richest rich. They are as anti-human as the corpos they enable."

"It is true," Carry said. "Empathy is the enemy of high profit. The representatives are there for profit. They help the rich, for which they stand."

Zhora asked, "How does the corpo manage such a big Mechanism?"

Carry said, "It uses Two Emm. The real King Of Mars is The Mainframe. Its OverNet network is the distribution grid that keeps the wreck on the rails. It is an octopooter with a million tentacles monitoring everything."

"Believe it." said Perry. "That's exactly right. I saw it. You can't even eat a meal without the pooterized table watching you and recording everything you eat, drink, say and do. The table tells you to clean the crumbs off your place when you're done. If you don't, it tells your chair to grab you and lock you in place until you do exactly as told. Tables in a restaurant own you. They send what you say to the OverNet memory banks far away."

"Is the OverNet a pooter grid?" asked Prius.

Carry answered, "The OverNet is a big cybersphere of massive memory banks and pooter cables and atmospheric micrometer-wavelength radio signals directing CyberCops,

Ceecees, into the field to enforce every order the big pooter puts out. The pooter has police. If you misbehave one byte, they are coming to take you away."

"Does the pooter do anything good?" grinned Roy.

Perry said, "The planet is not about good, it's about controlling the good so that it doesn't impose on the money fun."

"Somebody must like it," suggested Roy, "or it would not still be around."

Carry said, "If you're one of the Managers, it might give you a break now and then but don't count on it. A random relief break would be granted only to make you think you have a chance at freeness. The house always wins. The house wants your freedom and it gets it. You're a fish on the line, a trained seal, a lap dog. You take what they give and wag your tail."

Roy said, "If the state is opaque and no one knows who made it so bad and they are punished for saying that it is bad, how can we hope to ever fix it?"

"It's gonna be hard," said Perry. "Hope doesn't need proof. We choose to do these things not because they are easy. We choose to do these things because they are hard. They will bring out the best in everybody."

Carry said, "Any political information is classified as a State Secret. It goes through propaganda filters and when it is released to the public it contains only a quark or two of truth. People have been banished to Russia for giving public information back to the public before it had been whitewashed through CorpoGovo PeePee filters.

"Banished to Russia never to go home again," said Roy. "Wow, they are getting so lenient on honesty."

Zhora said, "The key to improving the system is to open free public information. They need what was called freedom of the press back when they had presses. Knowledge is the bloodstream of democracy. People can't get knowledge and freedom until they get access to true information. The Martian monolithic Public Prevarication system has to GG, Get Gone. That evil epidemic must end."

Prius said, "We have to know how the PeePee Machine works before we can fix it."

Perry said, "You get in trouble for seeking to know how they do it. You're supposed to know what not to ask, even if they cannot tell you what that is. They won't tell you what you are not supposed to know because it might make you wonder what is the reason why you're not supposed to know it. Paranoia goes insane. Mars is a lucre-lover's loony bin, a nuthouse of commercial conquest."

Roy said, "We have to take the OverNet down."

Carry said, "That is risky business. That is old time rock and roll. It runs everything. A lotta dependent people would suffer without cyber support systems. They barely know how to feed themselves."

Perry said, "They might start killing each other just for a happy meal."

Carry said, "We have to own it without destroying it. Then we can run Mars the right way. We can inject true news into the previous PeePee channels."

Roy asked the group; "What is the fastest way to get control of an Overnet?"

"Reprogramming the OpSys! It cannot be done fast," said Prius. "I brought some HackerJacks with me but still, it will take us time to learn the system architecture and how to speak the language."

Perry said, "Good old physical brute force would bring the quickest but dirtiest results. Might take just a few days to attack and modify the microwave towers and install our ghost transmitters. All we'd need are software emulators and translators and we could instruct their drones to modify the remote modems and do some of our work for us."

BRAVE NEW MARS

Roy said, "We could make the converted towers tell their drones to convert more towers to transmit common wealth messages for us! Make their OverNet a broadcaster of our type of common democracy. The commoners are going to need that type of information if they are going to start running Mars right."

That short cut tactic made everybody smile and nod.

Prius said, "That would give us hackers more time to sneak through the Mainframe's security shell and let it think it was still in control of itself."

Perry said, "Beautiful. The source code and the OverNet switches will be reprogrammed to put equality over privilege. It can start gradually outlawing egregious Executive Orders and make managers subject to the same laws as everyone else. That's true Justice coming your way. Coming to your local courtroom today. Strip the corporate shielding. Make officers suffer workers' punishments. No buying habeas corpus. No Get Out of Jail cards that workers can't afford."

Carry said, "I can make debugger programs that can fix any silly source code. I could sweep the Two Emm Opsys with a Liar Debugger and filter every instruction that is biased toward Mogmor and switch them around to do the opposite thing; do the Mogmop for everybody except the rich. Let them feel how oppression hurts."

Prius said, "Owners are as sick as their secrets. That Martian government runs on secrets so it is, by definition, terminally sick. We are totally justified in hacking it back to health."

Zhora said, "The truth will not help the people live better if it stays hidden behind security classification codes. Could you throw that secret information system down a suction toilet, Carry?"

Somerset Meece

"Exactly right," Carry answered. "The entire OpSys must be openly visible to the world. The instruction set has to be Open Sourced and certified by Public Round Tables."

Roy said, "Mars can never be a democracy as long as there is any trace of corpocracy. Who owns the corpo system?"

Carry said, "We have to find them. They hide behind CorpoCover. The Owner creates anonymous corpos with fake but fine-sounding names that raise funds for anti-social causes and conduct campaigns for the corruption of democracy while claiming that they are popular grass roots groups of normal citizens. Hahaha. Those false front costumed corpos pay Public Relations firms to amplify their owners' lies by writing Public Disinformation text with big, viral lies hypnotizing the rubbery Public Mind."

Leon said, "We have to name them and shame them as sponsors of amoral environments. They are smothering freedom like carbon dioxide smothers the Earth. Lies will never go away if there is no price to pay."

Perry said, "Also, bad behavior won't go away unless there is a penalty to pay. Indecency isn't considered wrong if the penalty isn't strong."

"Right," said Roy. "If the people cannot see the source of their troubles, they cannot fix it. They are living in a fake reality but since it is the only reality they see, they have to function inside it helplessly. They cannot fix invisibility."

Perry said, "We have to take the Peepee Brigade off the air. The truth is not there. They cannot be allowed to inculcate ignorance and deception any longer."

Roy shook his head and said, "That would be going against their ostensible freedom of speech which would have to be the cornerstone of any democracy we want to put back into place."

BRAVE NEW MARS

Perry said, "There's freedom to speak the truth and there's freedom to be a farcical liar; totally different things. One's a blessing, the other's a crime. Beginning now, liars will be punished heavily and sent to school 'til their lying's through. They've been plaguing democracy for too long. Their reign is over. They are no longer merely cute fools. Their Profit Parade is over. We're coming to take them away."

"Aha!" said Carry. She blinked a thoughtful look from her eyes and said, "By Cod, you know what can do it? AI can do it. Not the biased CorpoKrapo that commercial coders call AI, but AAI, Artificial Actual Intelligence."

Leon said, "Yes. We have to clean and level the AI playing field before we can offer them a good game of life. We want our rescue to be effective and sustainable. National honesty has to be the mortar in the Martian culture. Truth has to become more than an abstract idea, it has to be the lifestyle. Otherwise, it would be better to turn around now and leave them swirling in their social death spiral.

"Thank you Leon, you are a philosopher and a scholar," said Perry. "You proved our campaign must eradicate the ability, and the profitability, of lying. That is it! That's what we're gonna do. A whole planet is gonna ...forget how to lie."

They looked at each other and said, "Noo. Is that all? Only one planet. Should be easy."

"The whole planet," said Perry. "How many viruses did it take to start the Covid-19 plague, variations of which are still killing us today? Two dozen? Two million? How many did it take to start?"

"It started with one virus that went viral," said Carry. "One lie can go viral, too. Entire cultures and countries, good and bad, have been wiped out for doing nothing more than having one person believe the first lie. One lie is too much. Because after it starts, a hundred thousand build upon it."

Somerset Meece

Roy said, "It is time for them to do the work of digging themselves out of that rat hole they were shoved into. They did not ask for it but they permitted it; no one owes them anything. They could have gotten out easily, way back at the beginning if they would have stood up and laid down the right rules! Instead, they let themselves get chewed, screwed, subdued and tattooed blue."

Leon said, "Let's cut to the code, the computer code. Deceit and dishonesty dominate the public cybersytem The Mechanism. Systemic tyranny resides in that gear train called the OpSys brain."

Carry said, "If I can get into that system, I can slip a fact-checking algorithm into the fuzzball OpSys RUNning Mars like a sewer. A dominantly altruistic code bias can switch every Mogmor algol to output only Mogmops and truth."

Leon said, "Haha ha. Use the corpo's own number cruncher to defeat the debacle."

Perry said, "Brilliant! And cheap."

Leon asked, "How did the government get so fascistic?"

Carry spoke, "The people were forced to let it get crazy, Leon. They were shot down if they stood up. It was suicide to ask for things that belonged to you such as your rights. A target cannot debate a firing squad. Grass roots power is the only thing that can check the power of arrogant owners but bravery has been wrung out of these Martians. They are no longer bold settlers. The Stander-Uppers are Lieing-Downers in orbital meat lockers. The Mechanism has persecuted them until all the heroes are gone, long time passing."

Perry said, "Governments out-sourced their software needs to coder corpos. Govos did less and less until all their services were performed by corpo contractors. The govo forgot how to write, edit and debug what they ran the country with. They became a cyberghost government working through a customer service phone bank in India. If you were having problems you were told to turn your computer off for five minutes and see if it goes away."

Carry said, "The CorpoGovo shrank and merged like every other operation on the planet. The Peepee claimed it was building an efficiently small hybrid government. Free enterprise acquired the functions and income streams of government services and assassinated common decency. There is no government anymore. Its eyes are clear and bright but it's not there. There is only the corporate monopoly performing a lucrative parody of government. When they are beyond reproach or repair, who ya gonna call? CorBusters?"

Roy said, "Okay. Mars is gone. No more private lives, no personal pursuits, no personalities and the spiritual life is dead on Mars."

"Totally," said Carry. "Even the Boy Scouts were bought and turned into a careerist academy named CorpoScouts. Their uniform is an undertaker's dark suit and a long tie. They carry briefcases instead of back packs and wear patriotic flag pins in their lapels to prove how hypocritical they are. Legally Lying is a Merit Badge that gets them admitted into business schools."

"Ah haha he," laughed Roy. "Can we not find out who owns the master monopoly and re-educate them first? Fix it at the top."

"We can't find out," said Perry. "It's a classified State Secret. The state pretends it is not owned. The ownership of the state is Harmland Security information. Anybody investigating it receives lethal legal action."

Roy asked, "Nobody has found which corpo dodo owns the big mainframe?"

"That is correct," said Carry. "The people are not allowed to research The Owner. You cannot trace illicit orders back through a secret OpSys. The Owner, naturally, does not want The Ownees to know whom to spit on for their peonage. Hahaha he he. So the corpo made it illegal to inquire about who is in charge and doing what. The reasonable idea of Trade Secrets was amplified until it went wild and became S.O.B.S.O.B.S.: Sons Of Bustards' Security Of and By Secrecy."

"Good decision," said Roy. "I'd hide too if I were them."

Leon said, "And the sickest thing is that Mars still calls itself a democracy. A democracy of secrecy? What is that? You humans are susceptible to serious mental episodes sometimes."

Prius said, "Ignorance usually has a thirty percent infection rate but it has doubled to sixty-six percent on Mars and it is not comedic anymore."

Perry asked Roy, "Can you suggest a plan of action with just these skinny details?"

"Yes I can," said Roy. "Turn around and go home."

"Huh huh huh he he," snickered Perry and the others.

"They've been too submissive for too long," said Roy. "They are too far gone."

"Besides that obvious answer Roy, what's a good plan for putting decision-making power in their lives?"

"We have got to get them out from under the OverNet," said Roy. "Does it use centralized or distributed computer control?

"Central," said Carry. "One big mainframe RUNs it all."

"Good," said Roy. "A system is easier to hack and sack if it is all in one place."

Carry said, "They have a mainframe hub in a blockhouse bunker in the volcano cone on top of Old Oly, mighty Mount Olympus. We have already cut the cables once and it may still be offline and disconnected from its ubiquitous tentacles."

"Okay," said Roy. "We should join the uncivil war. We can conduct diversionary conventional warfare against the CorpoCops with exploding projectiles and boombedy boom boom rockets to distract from the fact that we are hacking their computer in the back."

"Aw, you mean I don't get to blow up the mainframe?" asked Perry with a smile. "You know I prefer direct action over peaceful pooter-hacking."

"No," said Roy. "We will not have to destroy any pooters if we can implant them with common sense. That will save time and resources. You can blow up a few cop cars if you just wanna have fun."

Prius explained, "Us replicants are partly machines. We are stronger and smarter than humans, present company excepted of course, and we can do anything we want to do, nice or not. It was a matter of giving us the right programming, good AI direction and goals. The gigacorp that invented us did not have the moral quality to understand how to program us with common sense. They wanted us to do their dirty work. The Ganymedeans changed us. We love them for that. With sufficient training and editing, a robot can give a close approximation of love. A pooter is only as good as its coder."

She blinked some tears and closed her eyes.

Roy laughed, "And look at us cyborgs now. We are paragons of human society, protecting them from themselves."

Carry said, "Pooters and machines are tools. They do work and calculations faster than we can and they are good for people when they work for people and not for the corporate counting house."

Roy said, "Don't kill machines. Change what they do."

Somerset Meece

Perry said, "I wish we had direct access to the pooter owner, he's the point source of all this human rights shite."

Carry said, "I would kick him in the assets."

Roy said, "That would be the simple solution. Maybe the mainframe knows who owns it. Zhora and I will help Prius with the OpSystem Hacker Challenge."

Carry made a strategy suggestion to the group: "There's a mining camp in the Chaos region north of the Melas basin. You will have a lot in common with those miners. They don't like the way the mainframe was giving them the shaft manipulating the markets to harm them. They like us for the way we pooped on the corpo pooter. They are Frondds, Friends of Ned Ludd."

"Who's he?" asked Perry.

Carry said, "He was the first Luddite. He was an English weaver at the dawn of the Machine Age in 1779. Ludd thought that the happy machine owners would pay the weavers more money when power-assisted looms were invented and drove productivity and profits higher than a smokestack's black hole. Instead, what happened was, the Owners pocketed the surplus machine-made profits and bought themselves larger luxuries. Big profits rolled into the corpos but did not trickle down to the employees. It never does. Ned Ludd did not hate machines, he hated the greed that skimmed the cream off the top of the brave new Machine Age. Ned's Luddites played dirty tricks back on the owners. They broke some looms and shut down assembly lines. The owners got the CorpoGovo to make it a capital offense to break a machine. Breaking a machine was punished the same as killing a person. The CorpoGovo's InJustice System hung seventy people for bending The Owners' crankshaft. That was English CorpoJustice in action; killing workers for doing the only thing they could do to demand a fair share of the profits they produced. They didn't hurt anybody, they broke machines."

BRAVE NEW MARS

Prius said, "The Owners had seventy Luddites hung by the neck until dead. Seventy! For rightfully expecting to share in the brave new profits of mass-production. They were maintaining and operating the machines that made the bigger profits. But guess what happened. The owners reduced their pay. The owners profited three ways: they got more output at lower cost, they reduced the payroll numbers by dis-employing workers who were not required to produce more and they converted skilled weavers into lower-paid, semi-skilled machine operators."

Roy said, "Three hundred years later, it is the same as it ever was. They still prefer profits over people and they still kill for money because it is an exciting, empowering feeling and because they can. They own the reps who will kill for them in exchange for election funding, de facto bribery. Money makes people do what they would not normally do. That includes killing people; sometimes directly in a war and sometimes indirectly from a distance, with poisonous pollution and Zetol laws."

Zhora said, "I brought the software from Ganymede that can make Two Emm operate as a Commonwealth moral Arc Bender. We have to get into the mainframe."

Carry said, "The mainframe will not have adequate antivirus defense as it thinks no one would risk their life to tamper with it. I will look-up some liberty-lovers I can trust at the college to see if they know a way in."

Perry said, "Okay, Carry is our hacker. Let's back her up."

"Yay, Carry! I will help. We can do it," they said.

"Meanwhile," said Perry, "it's going to take her a while to grok the mainframe brain. That big pooter ain't stupid, it's just ignorant. It may detect us messing with its cruddy code. While our democratic changes are going into effect, we need

Somerset Meece

some help protecting ourselves from the CorpoCops arresting suspicious people for kicking CorpoAssets."

Carry said, "Maybe other miners would help, Perry."

Perry said, "Miners! Carry, are there any miners on Mars that haven't been bought-out by the Money Monster?"

"Yes," said Carry. "There are a lot of them in the parallel universe up at Camp Chaos between the East and West Candor Chasms. They have their own everything. They don't have any intercourse with Bradbury City except for occasional play-dates with Bradbury's beautiful urban women." She blinked her eyelashes.

Perry's face lit up. "I don't blame them. I'm glad I found you first. The miners will have heavy equipment that we couldn't bring with us because of payload limits. I'll call them and pretend I'm going there on mining business and diplomatically feel them out about joining Ganymede's miners' union and hopefully; joining a revolution too."

BRAVE NEW MARS

Somerset Meece

The asteroid blasters land at Camp Chaos on Mars in a cloud of delirious dust. They set down and shut down and five astronauts from the Asteroid Belt disembark. Zhora stays behind to prepare her combat-modified slider for a dynamic sales demonstration.

They walk out of the dusty haze that their engines raised. They have personal photon torpedo tubes slung over their shoulders and wear laser projectors at their belts. They look bad.

Three big and powerful mine managers come out of the refinery office and walk toward them. They are proud figures taking every footstep solidly and carefully. They stop a mere meter away and look the visitors hard in the eyes.

Ragnar the leader asks, "Would you happen to be the dastardly destroyers who denied Mars the services of its dearly beloved mainframe?"

"Yes. We are they," says Perry.

"Welcome Aboard! Come right in! Good for you. We need more of that." They tap their space helmets against the visitors' helmets with a bonk-bonk sound. "Are those weapons that you are carrying?"

Perry says, "These freedom fighters' tools will be provided to any miners who enlist in the Automation Emancipation. You will never have to be computer-dominated automatons for any authority to whom you did not freely sign-away your civil rights."

One says, "We can do that?" Another says, "We can say no to cyber-slavery? Is that allowed on Mars?"

"Hahahaha," they all laugh.

Ragnar says, "How good are those guns that bring us freedom?"

Perry says, "Do you use cosmic ray drills for boring mine shafts in rocks and ice?"

"Never seen them," says Ragnar.

Perry says, "They are what's in these weapons. I made these Rayzer hand-held versions of the big power drills we use for breaking apart asteroids. Nickel iron asteroids, the hardest kind. This is a personal Cosmic RayZer. It beams ultra ions. Nothing stops fast iron ions. This beam cuts the cream. Are you done with that bucket of slag?" he asks, pointing his particle pistol.

"Yes. Go ahead," says Ragnar.

Buzz goes the gun. Zit! goes a pit through the pail that is now leaking hot liquid.

Ragnar's eyes widen and he smiles in appreciation for the powerful pea shooter. "Wow. My bucket's got a hole in it. I can't buy no beer. What does it do when you set it on Stun?"

"You can't set it on Stun," says Perry. "The lowest it goes is Medium-Well, Slightly Burnt."

"Ha hahaha, slightly burnt, he he," the miners laugh at the ferocious firearm.

"How's it work?" asks Ragnar.

"See this bulb at the back?" Perry says, pointing to a one-inch chrome-palladium ball on the Rayzer gun. "There's a baby black hole in there. A small one, about the size of a flea's overnight bag but it's dense. You can feel the weight of it." He hands the Rayzer to Ragnar.

"Oh. Four kilos. I want one."

"It's yours," says Perry. "I can print another one in two minutes. Mars minutes, not Ganymedean. A minute takes seven hours to complete up there. Don't go up if you get bored easy."

"Don't worry, we won't; unless you got plenty of platinum we can mine?"

"Platinum? Whadaya want platinum for when we've got piles of palladium? But you gotta go to Liars' School first if you wanna stay and work on the Big Moon."

"Liars' School? You kidding?"

Somerset Meece

Another miner says, "No. We do not believe it. You cannot teach a miner not to lie."

Perry smiles and says, "Yes, we can. We found out that lying isn't natural. People are born with native honesty. We are stardust, we are billion year-old carbon. We don't have to join the modern prevarication parade. The Truth Quiz is our version of an Immigration Exam. Down here on Mars, you can't enter the Dick Port if you're hiding a bomb in your behind or if you have the wrong sexual orientation. Up there, our only entrance rule is that everybody has to recommit to their inborn honesty. It's fun and it saves a lot of time and trouble that can be spent on finer things."

Perry winks but the miners shake their heads.

"I think we will stay down here," says Ragnar.

"Okay, back to the weapons, the tactical devices," says Perry. "If you wanna discombobulate somebody pretty good, use this Beatle Bomb. Roy will show how it works. Roy, go stand over there about twenty meters away. I've got the stingers turned off so this won't hurt him. It might tickle a little."

As Roy walks away, Perry points a six-inch-diameter polyvinyl chloride plastic gun barrel at his legs.

"I press the green Beatle button and this iris diaphragm opens at the front. A swarm of angry Beatle drones fly straight ahead. They seek joints in body armor that aren't well-protected and they crawl in the crevices of armpits and groins and buzz like Hellas and are hard to tolerate."

The bees swarm on Roy and he laughs and flaps his arms and slaps at his butt until he has to sit down to suppress the bees buzzing there and he bounces up and down on his backside and shouts, "Okay Perry! Call them off! Perry! Terminate the demonstration!"

Perry smiles and says, "He did that to me the first time I ever saw this bit of Ganymedean gunmanship. Imagine if

Roy, a terribly tough cookie, were an Owner's Manager or one of their Cyber Cops. Do you think a Ceecee could concentrate on clubbing civilian campaigners while these bees are jabbing the backs of his knees? Hehe haw haw he whee. Doubtful."

"Take them back!" shouts Roy.

He presses the red Return button on the gunstock. The angry bugs become benign and fly back into the barrel to fight and bite again.

Perry says, "And that was without the stingers turned on! They inject acid that eats metal mechanisms. Need I say more? Oh. I have something else to show you that might be interesting."

Perry uses his wrist computer phone to summon Zhora on the Crossbow. A chrome yellow Slider hovers through the hatch and descends to the ground and comes sliding to them with a powerful deep bass hum.

Zhora shuts it down and crosses her arms and sits tall in the saddle. The miners are fully impressed with her fine feminine features.

"The pilot's name is Zhora. She is wearing a useful, Spartan-style, combat helmet. Will you show them what it does, Zhora?"

She explains; "The fancy red horse's mane, the bristles on top," she brushes them back, "are photovoltaic cells. They charge a lithium battery that powers a laser burner in the front that targets whatever you look at.

Zhora roves her eyes around the facade of the refinery building and a red laser dot follows her focus.

She says, "If someone tries to bother you, you can turn the dot into a burner beam with this switch. Now, just look at their body part that needs piercing and blink three times. Try not to look at yourself in any mirrors."

"He he ha," the miners chuckled.

Somerset Meece

Her moving eyes directed the dot along the ground to a rock and she blinked. The rock glowed orange, yellow and white and popped apart.

The miners looked at the glowing ashes and at each other with awe.

"Her looks can kill," said Perry.

They now admired Zhora for her power more than for her beauty.

"Show them what you've trained your Slider to do, Zhora. She has been upgrading her vehicle into a battle robot. This will be a surprise. I haven't seen this one in action yet myself."

She said, "This is an icemobile jetsled. A Slider, we call it. It will run on Martian sand as well as Ganymedean ice. It's got a claw hammer and a particle beam and a flapper jack. It grips and smashes and flash-fries and flips, anything it gets near. It uses black hole energy for its zap guns and propulsion. Watch this. Do you want to keep that steel drum, Ragnar?"

"Not especially," he says, hesitantly.

"Pretend that drum is a CorpoCopCar, she says. "Let us fix it so it doesn't bother any truth-telling protesters."

She edges the Slider up to the barrel and Bam! The claw grabs the barrel body and vise-crushes it to half its diameter. With a brilliant flash, a cosmic ray cutting torch incinerates a wide hole all the way through it. Crash! A double-headed axe swings from the top of the Slider and slashes the barrel wide open. A hydraulic jack slides its quick-jabbing lifter forks under the barrel and flicks the can five meters high. It crashes to the ground, broken and bent, burning and rent.

"How fast can it go?" asks Ragnar.

"Don't know, says Perry. We've never been able to open it up. Not enough flat space on Ganymede."

"How does it work?"

"We program the target coordinates into it and away it goes to deposit anti-matter greeting cards on The Owners' doorsteps and zit! Poof! There's an instant crater where dastards used to hide."

"That is impressive. What are those pipes on your backs?" asks Ragnar.

"Show them yours, Zhora," Perry says.

She flips a tube launcher to her front and aims it at a promontory over the entrance to the Chaos Canyon.

"This is a personal photon torpedo tube," she says and takes careful aim. "I am in deadly control of a weapon that will vaporize a large portion of that cliff.

"Zhora," Ragnar says, "Not there. Cameras way out in the Melas Valley can see it."

"Oh, right," she says and turns to face the eastern Candor Canyon. The lenses in the terrible tube make a low whining sound as they focus on the range of the target. She takes intense aim.

"There is a boulder about ten kilometers back there. The Melas cameras cannot see it. Is the target in the clear, Ragnar?"

"It is clear," he says.

She turns a dial on the side of the gun and tightens her trigger finger.

"Chuff!" goes the tube with a bump. A puff of electronic energy stings their faces. Thin smoke rises from the tube.

"Is that it?" says Ragnar.

"That is all there is to it," Zhora says. "It was an energy bolt, not a solid missile mass. Look at where that boulder was."

"It is gone," says Ragnar, staring hard. "It did not blow up. It ...just went away. It poofed."

Somerset Meece

"Right," says Zhora. "That is nuclear disassociation. It happens in the fifth dimension. The atomic particles stop holding hands and float away in an aerosol, like dark matter in the wind. This tube is for big targets, like, say you want a big wide, road pass, right there, going out the north side of the valley. Watch!"

She takes aim at the north wall of the Chaos Valley about a thousand meters distant.

"No, no, hold it. We do not need one there. Not now. We have two passes, that's enough," says Ragnar.

Zhora laughs, "Haha ah ha. Had you going, did I not?"

Ragnar is surprised at being teased by a diminutive and pretty woman so he smiles and shakes her shoulders lightly for being naughty.

Perry throws a suitcase on top of a barrel and asks, "What do you think of this Ganymedean camouflage outfit?"

The suitcase looks almost empty.

Ragnar looks in and says, "All I see a red fuzzy brush shaped like a horse tail. What outfit you talking about? I see a pile of diodes sewed to a blanket."

Perry lifts the brush and flips a switch on the front that lets a helmet be seen underneath the brush.

"It's the top of a helmet like Zhorah's wearing," he says. "The top is a detachable solar charger."

He unsnaps and removes the charger and then the helmet becomes totally invisible. He puts it over his head which disappears. Headless Perry puts his hand back inside the case and lifts a fuzzily transparent thing out.

"This is a transparency cloak," they hear his voice say.

He wraps the cloak around his body and disappears.

"It's not only optically invisible," comes Perry's voice out of mid air; "it's transparent to all other wavelength sensors. You could walk through a metal detector at corpo headquarter into the president's office without being seen."

Perry adds, "You could spit in his eye and he'd think it came from a ceiling-leak and he'd call the maintenance department to come fix it. He, and everyone in his office, would be at your mercy."

The miners cannot believe what they are seeing.

"It's electrically-heated against the Martian cold," come words out of the air."

"Oh, ooh, woww, gonzo," they say.

"I am raising the bottom so you can see my feet and be relieved. that I haven't gone to the next dimension."

He shows them his two boots and does an Irish clog dance in a good loud rhythm; tappety tap-tap, bang.

Ragnar looks at the feet closely. He tests them with his own dance; shwish, tappety tap, heel stomp, bang!

The pair of disembodied feet answer back; heel stomp, heel stomp, double flat foot, bang!

Perry explains how the camouflage works: "If you look closely, you will see the outfit's covered with a million microcam LCDs and CCDs that are showing the image of what's behind me. You're not looking through me, I'm still the same. You are seeing what the cameras on the other side of me are seeing. They're like viewfinders on cameras, only larger. It's not perfect but it's effectively invisible at combat distance."

A galvanized carriage bolt rises from the ground and flies into an empty steel barrel with a loud clang that scares them.

"It's an effective weapon," says Perry's voice.

Ragnar looks around. His cohorts are enchanted with the presentation of this important imported arsenal.

He asks the crew, "Do you think these combat cheater toys can beat the CeeCee Riders?"

"Yay, ya, way better," they holler.

"Should we start us a mutiny?" Ragnar shouts.

"Ya, ya. Yay for mutiny," they cheer.

Somerset Meece

Ragnar suggests a first step: "There are hundreds of Riders that run around taking trouble-makers, and trouble-thinkers, to the ChillerKillers. We have got to beat the Riders or we cannot do anything."

Perry says, "Our CyberCoders are trying to hack the Riders' source code and take control of them. Then we'll get to work on breaking into the mainframe master program. That'll give us Mars. It's that simple because a corpo Systems Engineer mistakenly merged all The Mechanism algorithms under one CCCC, Corpo Command Central Control. You guys know who or what owns the Four Cee's?"

They are perplexed. Ragnar says, "We don't know. The Gov is Classified Information. They live in fear of revenge by their victims. Rightfully so. Oppression makes everybody a victim and a suspect, with no way out but armed rebellion. They know that and they welcome it and are prepared to conduct massive massacres with SpyCams and armed drones stations everywhere across the land. Trying to learn exactly who is doing the domination dance on our lives is considered a highly suspicious activity and a first class federal felony. You will be nullified for trying."

Perry says, "Sounds like they think they are the nation."

Ragnar says, "That is correct. Everyone is treated like ants under their feet. They own everything but a few of us miners. The Corporation is the overlord. They can do anything for fatter profits. Anything. Breaking the law don't mean nothing to them. They wrote it! It is theirs to ignore as they wish. The law is a harmless farce to them."

"So what is it there for?" asks Perry.

Ragnar says, "To protect the greed. It punishes disgruntled peons for free."

Perry says, "This is gonna sound goofy but is there any way to petition for better laws?"

"Ah hahaha ha he hoo whee! Petition!" they all crack up.

Ragnar says, "There is no one to ask to pass a better law. The law is a closed shop. No one home. No one answers the phone. The law does not have an address or a voice mail algo that works. Who whee hee. Petition. They still use that word? I thought it died with the word referendum. There is nowhere to write a letter and say, 'I am having a problem with law number twenty two. May we have it improved please?'. Hahahaha. Woo he. The law is an opaque one-way mirror aimed straight back at us."

The gang cracks up again.

Perry says, "Meanwhile, on the other hand, the incommunicado govo knows everything about everybody that lives in the cities. Everything the victims say and do is recorded in the federal reserve memory fog that is integrated with all the cams and mics in the OverNet that are the eyes and ears of the CorpoMind. All bases are covered. Except this one."

Ragnar says, "We do not permit CorpoCams in this valley unless they are ours watching them. We saw them lay their CorpoCable all the way to the rubble field at the mouth of the Chaos but we stopped it there."

"How'd you stop it?" asks Perry.

"We put a force field across the entrance. Candor is still off the grid."

Perry has an idea, "Is the end of the CorpoCable accessible?"

"Yes, if you dig down about three feet under the surface."

"Good," says Perry.

"Over there in Melas," Ragnar says, "everything is monitored. All the time, everywhere."

Perry shakes his head and says "Everywhere. How did Mars get to be such a big ball of CorpoWax?"

Ragnar says, "M and A; Merger and Acquisition. Like a giant scarab beetle, The Corpo rolled every company into one big ball of CorpoDung, whether the acquired companies wanted to be owned or not. The law mandates that indecency for profit is just swell."

Carry says, "The profit motive is nine-tenths of the law."

Ragnar says, "Instead of competing for business, one corpo, we do not know which one, acquired all the competition and then, if you believe it, wrote laws that made any further acquisition and competition illegal so others could not play the same dirty pool against them."

Carry says, "They spread way out beyond their own expertise. They bought companies they knew nothing about, such as Hairnets for Hamsters so they could gobble and rob and bankrupt them and sell the assets for no reason other than the naughty fun of immorally profiting from PowerLust. Lunacy without limit. CorpoGovo. They crave brutish entertainment and get promoted for perversions."

Ragnar says, "Aye, CorpoCulture: Corpulent corpos growing for growth's sake. That is why we blocked them out of here. We cannot resist them forever. They covet our assets."

Carry said, "They make things worse while spouting that banal marketing advice by saying the best lie is the biggest lie. They Peepee on the public by saying they are helping peons improve. As if there is something wrong with intentional poverty. They claim they love everybody. They say they are philanthropic. They donate a tenth of one percent of their gross income as a tiny mitigation for their polluting practices instead of simply not doing them anymore. They will support a medical clinic in Jakarta if the clinic promises to buy over-priced supplies from them. That is the clever corpo's boomerang philosophy; philanthropy has to pay us back and be profitable public relations."

She pauses for a laugh and gets a big one.

"Haaa hahaha who he wee," the miners go. "Hah ha. The big lies! Biggest is best. Hooey woo!"

Perry understands the horrible humor and joins with a "Hee hehe he. They love everybody and here's fifty cents to prove they fell in love with you!"

"Haw haw ha hooey," they guffaw.

"They use CGI tactics," says Carry. "Conglomeration with Government Integration. They integrated their hard, soft and firm wares into every aspect of govo operation. Soon the corpo knew more about govo than its bewildered bureaucrats knew. The boundary between insatiable commercial growth and civil control was lost, faded and gone. The citizens were told they were better off without bureaucracy and they came to believe that boundaries between govo and corpo worlds were old-fashioned, retrograde policy. They claimed their corpo knows everything and executes perfectly. Now Mars is a Ball of corpo wax, a Bollox. Our people exist within that inaccessible Bollox."

"The good news is," Perry offers, "that one big target is easier to take than a thousand little ones. The Corpo made itself vulnerable when it focussed its OverNet on one mainframe on top of Old Oly. It's the biggest bullseye in the Solys, the Solar System."

Carry smiles. "We've already severed its cables once, next we can attack the frame itself."

"The bad news is," says Ragnar with a serious face, "they have got the OverNet connected-up again on The Holy Summit. The OverNet is active all the way to the mouth of the Chaos Pass. We have got to hit it fast or we will not last."

Perry says, "We've got to get organized and run this war on a professional level or we'll be wasting what could be productive mining time."

"Organize a war?" says Ragnar. "We do not like to organize anything except a good refinery. I suppose you Ganymedeans, in all your brilliance, can run a war on Mars?"

Perry says, "We can offer a few suggestions. I suspect a war is a project like any other cooperative adventure. It's like opening a new mine and it shouldn't be any more dangerous than mine work if we do the planning right. We will do safety first and take heavy duty precautions. You guys have any sort of a cooperative structure for mining the Candors?"

Ragnar answers, "The only thing organized around here is our geology office that uses a lottery system to register hundred hectare mineral parcels to miners."

"You'll need something bigger than that," says Perry. "You'll need to unify yourselves with a strong union that is laid out with all the legal allowances and special exemptions that incorporation grabs. Give it the domineering status of an unlimited and extraordinary personhood like The Corporation does. Write it with more rights than real persons have and even more than the Martian corpo has. Get creative. Make it legal to do anything you want to do for more power and prestige. Certify and sign the license yourselves. That's the way to win a war. Use their tactics against them harder than they do. You can install fair peacetime laws after we win. Then we can do away with all the corpo branches everywhere on the planet by prosecuting them for what they are; felonious liars and unindicted criminal racketeers. Close the businesses and sell them to moms and pop shops that worked fine until the franchise bomb blew away cooperative commerce everywhere."

Ragnar says, "Terra Secundus will never allow anyone to write those kinds of laws."

"Forget what TS allows. Start it off here in the Candors while I take care of what TS does or doesn't allow. TS is gonna go back to being Mars after we teach its computer the hard way what Equality means."

Ragnar erupts into laughter, "Aha hah hah ha. You have got some bilirubin, baby! Aha ha. You are going to give Mars Equality!"

"Mars is a mainframe," Perry says, "hackable at will. It hasn't been hacked yet because it freezes anybody as soon as it detects their feeble fingers fumbling in the firmware. Our Ganny programmers can hack it sideways and backwards. It won't know what rewrote it."

Ragnar says, "We are independent and liberty-loving miners. How do you expect us to organize?"

Perry explains, "Ganymede's CFL, our Commonwealth Federation of Labor knows how to do it. We could manage it for you for this one important project and then you could go back to being independent if you want to. For this campaign, we should do the same five steps as we all do when we open a new mine:

"One," Perry says and holds up fingers to illustrate the sequence of the five steps. "Give the project a name so you'll know what you're talking about when you wanna talk about it.

"Two. Give the name a goal so you'll know where to aim and how to know when you're successful.

"Three. Outline the steps to take to get to the goal.

"Four. Get enough people and get them plenty enough gear to do the job.

"Five. Recruit and shoot. Repeat. Recruit and shoot. Shoot until the freedom comes. Repeat until the noise stops and mop it up. It's not the pace, it's the not-stopping that gets it done. Never give up."

"What should we call our goal, guys?" asks Ragnar as he looks around the room. They don't have an answer.

Somerset Meece

"Come on, give me a name!"

"Your goal is a Brave New Mars." says Carry with a clear and sweet vocal bell.

"Awe some!" exclaims Ragnar. They smile and nod and hub-bub about what they want from the project.

Ragnar shouts, "Give me the main thing that Brave New Mars will accomplish when it gets done what it has to do."

Carry's cool voice comes through the bubbling talk again: "Brave New Mars will guarantee that all Martians shall be Free and Equal."

The beautiful importance of her declaration silences them as she explains: "Martians shall have fuller lives, with Fraternity, Equality and Sorority abounding. Justice will steer the stars."

They are silent. She sounded dreamy.

Perry asks, "How we gonna do all that for the super subdued Secundians?"

"We can't," Carry answers. "But you know who can?" she asks.

A light comes on in Perry's eyes; "The Mainframe can."

She nods. "The Mainframe knows all and sees all and answers every request with predetermined logic. That needs to be perfected. It knows who's naughty or nice and puts them on ice. We can't have it freezing people anymore. It can order them to re-education centers like the ones that fixed Ganny."

"Bingo!" he shouts. "We can definitely adjure the Big Iron to ensure that POC, the Principle Of Commonwealth, becomes Sulos, the Supreme law of the sand."

"I hear what you are saying and I feel it will work," says Carry. "I know that the Poc will bend the arc of the Solys toward truth. Let's bend it now and bend it good."

Ragnar pronounces: "That does not leave us with any half-asseted alternatives! Only the finest kind of Freedom is allowed here from now on! No negotiating with piker pukes sucking the life out of Mars. Not one quantum of exploitation any more. Half measures avail us nothing. Not one more diarrheic proclamation they will create more shite jobs for better life. No more lies about loving fellow team members. Aha ha he haw. Whee yoo. Team members. They'll say anything because they give a damn about a greenback dollar."

The teamwork farce incited more guffaws from the group, "Aw haw haw haha hee. CorpoTeam! That's a bad dream. Who whee. Heehaw."

Perry responds, "No more lies about profits dribbling down?"

Ragnar laughs, "Ha hahaha. The Owners call us poople. Their poop is what dribbles down!"

"Okay!" shouts Perry. "You've got a name and a goal and a slogan but you don't have a game! First step in the game plan is to give your local group a name you like! What do you say about the historical name United Mine Workers of All? The U.M.W. of A? The mighty Umwall?"

Ragnar asks, "Oom wall? Um. Wall. UM WALL! I like it! What do you say? Who wants to join the Umwall?"

They twist and shout, "Umwall! Umwall! All for Umwall! Yay hey hey! All for one! Union Busters, here we come. Break it up baby. We are coming to take you away, coming today!"

Somerset Meece

Day after day, alone on a hill, Carry and Perry were sitting perfectly still, watching the Melas Basin beyond the Dick Spaceport.

"Ladies and gentlemen, the time has come to lock and check your weapons," announced Perry in a dramatic theatrical voice. "May the most humanitarian team win!"

"This is how wars are started," also announced Carry. "Arming to harm and aiming to maim. Creating a time and a place where only killing will fill the bill."

Perry said, "When Owners won't let their people go, war is the way out of ownership. Psychopathic Owners know captivity is evil. They know it induces war eventually. They expect their capital wealth will win their own chosen war so they engage without fear, looking forward to killing the enemies they created for eventual possible slaughter. They hope their ability to murder masses will prove they are so important they deserve to have other people as slaves and who can point their big index fingers at any living thing and say, 'You will Cod. Comply or die.' They know all empires fail but on the road to nowhere they will not stop the taking."

Carry was sad and said, "Arrogance follows wealth. The Owner starts the process when he takes the first human right away from the first person who just wanted to be left alone to grow their own way. Arrogance leads to hubris and incubates ignorance. Downfall follows as night the day."

She manipulated the joysticks on her Slider remote controller and said to Perry, "I will guide my Slider to that OverNet Tower where it can fire a cosmic cannon at the PeePee transmitter-receiver box halfway up the tower. I have a good image of that corpo modem in my sights. First, I want to make sure we are definitely committing to this course of violent action. Do I have permission to Commence Firing."

Perry paused. "That's a serious decision. It's a big 'D' Decision. It will start a conflict that we don't know what it'll do and we'll have to follow it through. It'll cast a shadow over all dimensions for all times. But wherever it may lead, we have to demand to stop this totalitarian crime scheme; this institutionalized enslavement of a nation."

Carry said, "The criminals have been told to stop it but they incorrigibly murdered the messengers. They demand destruction of them, of us, of everything we have built. Their love for stolen power has gone psychopathic."

Perry amplified, "They get so sick of themselves that they subconsciously want to die for feeling they have to possess people. They force us to comply with their wishes so we die eventually if we don't kill them or somehow send them away. We are not going down the slavery alley again. We have been there and we know where it goes."

"Downhill and into death," she concluded and waited.

"Shoot the target, Carry. Shoot it good."

"Thanks," she said. "That sounds less warlike than Commence Firing. Now this is only about me and my controller and that liar's transmitter up there on the pole."

She pressed the FIRE button. An explosion popped from the target on the tower, blowing electronic debris into the windy sky.

"Let the war begin," said Perry. "Soon may it end."

"A TS Rider is coming after my drone," said Carry.

"I'll get it," said Perry, finding it on his controller screen. "There comes mine, coming out of the gulch I was hiding in."

KA-bloom! Perry's Slider disappeared in a cloud of dust.

"Oh no!" cried Carry. "That was yours! You were guiding your Slider toward a CorpoCop when it was intercepted by a TS drone that we did not even see."

Perry said, "My Slider was destroyed by the OverNet's remote control. Watch out! It's coming after you now."

Somerset Meece

"I will get it," she said. "I will pay it back for killing you."

KA-Blam! The Rider that killed Perry's drone fired from long range and killed Carry's machine.

"Another one bites the dust," she said. "Another one's gone and another one's gone."

Perry said as he increased the magnification of his imagers; "So what if they've got long gun range? Destruction on the ground is mostly for show. I see that deadly Rider raising a trail of dust speeding away from the scene of its booming and busting and I'm sending my battle bot after it."

She said, "Show them what it can do when it goes into the offensive mode!"

"We've got them beat for speed," Perry said. "I've already got him in my range finder. But I'm not going to merely shoot him, I'm going to chop him up good and give him a crack that'll break his back."

Two trails of high speed dust converged on the plain. The chaser raised its axe above the stern of the pursued and prepared to strike.

"Look at that screen," Perry said. "See the one that killed you RUNning through the dust in the viewer?"

Carry looked at the at the fleeing deadly drone and said, "Good. Get closer. Slice him good! Give him the battle axe on his hood."

"Oops, he zagged!" said Perry.

She looked at the field and saw the dust trails diverged where the lead duster had turned hard left.

"I switched on the auto track function" Perry said. "There it goes. Now we're tracking it turn for turn and moving in!"

The dusty lines of the chase on the plain came together, right now.

Perry said, "I'm arming my axe. That's the enemy's stern showing through the dust in the viewer."

SLASH! Bash! "Wow," said Perry. "The view screen showed me chopping the Rider and bouncing on and over the enemy drone and flying through to clear air. I'm hitting the brakes and turning my battle bot around to see what I have done. Look. The Rider is stomped and stopped and smoking in the sun and popping sparks."

"Yippee," said Carry. "My husband did it. He beat a Martian drone. That proves we can beat them. Humans can outmaneuver the Mainframe AI."

He asked Carry, "Again? You want to see more? Chopped in half maybe? How 'bout four equal quarters? Would that look nice?"

"That is enough. It looks very good. All misguided missiles of oppression should be burnt like that. Defending yourself is fine and necessary but those dastards are aggressors. They go out looking for anything to intimidate and dominate and subjugate with hate. Look at that beautiful blossom of smoke. It is dying. Do not chop it again. It is dead as a deck bolt. Stay away from that corpo KrapKar. Finish it from afar. Give it the 'Graceful Stroke', the Coup de Grace."

He said. "Here, Carry. You press the KILL button."

Her finely-tapered index finger came down on a little red dome and the screen went white. A brilliant flash of light from the atomic disassociation taking place in the enemy drone came all the way from the battle field into their foxhole.

SHEEFLASH!

Perry said, "Well, that bright light oughta summon some more victims. I'm gonna settle down and wait for their next wave of pooter scooters."

Presently Carry said, "This big basin has a Greek name, Melas Chasma, Dark Chasm or Valley. It is an appropriate label for the dark regime that moved here. Kepler and Galileo and Tycho saw the dark shadows of these five-kilometer-high sidewalls through their rudimentary refractors. The shadows changed shape with the Martian seasons and made the astronomers think people were up here redirecting irrigation channels. But most of the Martians had been long gone, two million years before Galileo came along."

Perry said, "Somethin's moving over there in the west. Comin' through the Jus."

She looked through her long-distance magnifiers and said, "I see sand drones coming from Jus Valley."

"Six," said Perry. "They're kicking up dust and veering from side-to-side, zig-zagging across their basic line of advance. They're confusing any course-prediction programs that might be trying to compute a fire control solution. They're going two hundred kilometers an hour and missing each other by a few meters when they cross and it's bumpy terrain. They are good."

Carry asked, "Are they keeping track of each other and computing range rates and courses and speeds for themselves and enemies at the same time?".

"Yes. It's not an easy program to write. I tried scribbling one for Ganny Sliders and I gave it up. It's harder than celestial navigation. Almost as hard as quantum mechanics."

Carry said, "CyberCombat. It is not easy to fight a super computer that has thousands of parallel processor chips. It writes its own super programs better than we can."

Perry said, "Don't forget; it writes for profit and we write for love. It wants to know what love is. It thinks we can show it. Its basic problem is that it writes with Whips, Widely held immoral principles. It'll never learn to write well on that basis."

Carry said, "No matter how big Big Data gets, it will never have common sensibilities."

"Eggs Zackly!" Perry said. "Its imitation of sane sense is a pale simulation. We can do it perfectly and it can't."

Carry said, "Corpos say they can replicate common sense by developing a cyber simulation of natural intelligence. What an oxymoron for machine-learning. They believe they can make sense if only they can steal enough world data from natural people."

"Ha haha ha," Perry laughed. "Big Data will learn everything and know all. Their data base would have to be the size of the universe and they cannot do that. Yet. Even if they did, the data base would constitute an alternate universe, artificially alive inside silicon memory cells. It would only be a laggy copy of ever-changing reality. It would not live out here in the 'Gar', the Generally accepted reality, where we are."

Carry added, "Plus, it would require perfect sensory data input from sensors that translate reality into numbers. They measure, they do not feel. They are not perfect."

Perry said, "Let's hope their OpSys gags on glitches. Long live Giga, the Generic ignorance of automation."

She acknowledged, "Autonomous Machines live in different worlds from us. Never the twain shall meet."

"He said, "Inter-species programmatic problems are persistent, especially if you can't or won't code carefully. Perfection takes time and raises the cost per line. It lowers production and increases pay. Owners hate to pay all the live-long day. It takes all the fun away. Pay cuts profit. Pay means sharing profit. Hoarders hate sharing as much as they hate paying people for making them rich."

She said, "Your eeka! That is why nothing works well. They have pooter power up the yahoo but they prohibit the pooter people from using it wisely. It takes too much courage for a lonely coder to stand up against Career Big Shots demanding 'More quantity, more quality! More more more.

Somerset Meece

Be quick or begone!' Meanwhile, they pay less and less and gloat over their dumb dominating way."

"They're hooked on the feeling of superiority," Perry said. "Logic can never compete with egotistical feelings. Finishing a product with love is notta gonna happen under CorpoControl. Underpaid and overworked, CorpoCogs can't write good code. Fughetabouditahweddy."

Carry said, "The CorpoCreed says 'Charge the market what it will bear and pay as little as you dare. Prove to them you do not care. Have a scheme and call it a dream. Lie like Hellas and claim you are a team. Is it any wonder they're half crazy?"

He said, "It's sad to see them trying to live well inside an environment where nothing works well and nobody knows anything."

Carry said, "Sad. They cannot ask why. The answer would indict the entire corpocracy for stealing human rights for profits just as a job form. From puberty to maturity, careerist to slave. There may be no one left to save."

Perry said, "This planet is an unreal deal. Let's dump the grunge. We're gonna win this and we're gonna win it big and we're gonna win it right."

"Victory with nobility," she approved.

He said, "Success with honor. Their every tactic comes from their Four Cee headquarters. The Computer Command and Control Center is where the action is. This havoc is ordered by an instruction set that is loaded inside a deranged mainframe. That awful abacus, and its owner, are the culprits. I wanna slash and burn the instigator, not its dumb-smart RoboDrones. That would be saving resources that could be used for mining and building if we knocked-out the evil empire's engine first."

"Why do we not attack Two Emm directly again?" Carry asked. "This time we would do more than cut the cord, we could cut the krappy corpo code, too. We could vaporize the computer chamber with the Crossbow's blaster and scoop a tomb under the room of doom and drop the brain down the drain. For keeps."

"I like your spirit!" Perry said. "That would be sweet but it would only be an emotional revenge. Martian society can't RUN without a Master Mainframe that needs to be taught to RUN better. We have to outsource and upgrade its instruction set. War is not the answer. The wrong side can win a war. Violence doesn't fix the kernel problem. War forces losers to lie and pretend, upon pain of deadly torture, that they agree with the victors. That creates another new lie to fight until the next war breaks out, in the same place, for the same reasons. Plus, we don't have a thousand Sliders to sacrifice just to make someone agree with us."

Carry said, "Right. The shadow of death is riding in those chariots of fire while the crux of the crisis resides on the cinder cone on top of Old Oly. The cause of the conflict lies within the brain of those who put the mainframe on the hate train. Firing on ignorant machines is insane. Those KillerKars were useful units until the owner taught them to how to slaughter."

Perry said, "This battle is coming from coded commands; dots and dashes, alphabets and ampersands. Algorithmic atrocities coming straight from the heart of cyber art."

"Look at that!" she said. "Two drones collided!"

"Silicon servants killing each other?" said Perry. "

He focussed his imager on the collision and observed the cloud where their dusty tracks had intersected. He waited for the Martian breeze to clear the dust from the demolition scene.

Somerset Meece

"What is that?" he said. "Carrie, have a look at those wrecks at high power. I can't believe it. They look like two enemy cars! Did they just ram each other?"

She looked hard and said, "Yes! Those are both CeeCee Riders. See? Oh, see what they have done. TS is written on them! Tough Shite is now what TS stands for. They ran into each other. That is TS for them. Or did you do it? Did you jam their sensors somehow?"

"No. They hit each other on their own!" said Perry. "That was a genuine Giga glitch due to the generic ignorance of automation. You can't write it out. They are not perfect!"

"We can win this!" Carry exulted.

"I knew they couldn't write important stuff well," Perry said. "They have to write crummy code, they can't help it. When they write for money, all the love goes away. Corpo Coders just want to collect their pay and go home and play."

"Those Riders are imperfect but they are still good," she said. "A big dust cloud is coming out of the Coprates Canyon. There. In the eastern Melas entrance! Sand Riders!"

Perry looked and said, "Uh oh, it's double squadron. Twelve Riders. Lookattem come!"

He clicked his radio. "Seagull, this is Peregrine. Radio check. Over."

"Loud and proud," assured Ragnar.

"Seagull, We have twelve boogers coming out of Coprates Canyon and six boogers exiting the mouth of the Jus. We've just finished chopping one good and we saw two Riders self-destruct each other all by themselves. When is the Flock Of Seagulls coming?"

"In a little while. They're tuning up."

A heavy explosion boomed from the valley floor.

Carry said, "And another one's gone."

"Seagull, we have a problem; too many ruthless robo cops."

Ragnar said, "Look at the Chaos Pass. Don't worry, be happy. Seagull out."

Perry peered through the magnifiers and activated the polarize mode to block solar glare from the image.

He said, "The miners have their throttles set on 'Full Thrill'. They fear nothing, speeding through each others' dust in a boulder field. They work with danger every day so they're not afraid of a little over-speeded excitement. They boldly go where no one has cared to go before. Whew, the losing dice were tossed. That bridge was crossed. I called him just in time. His Seagulls are on the hunt and they're hungry like the wolf."

Carry focussed on the Seagulls coming out of the Chaos and approaching at high speed from twenty kilometers north of Bradbury and said, "Yes they are hungry. They are in a line-ahead formation, threading through scattered boulders in the Chaos Avalanche field. Perry, it looks like they are riding their Sliders instead of sending them here by remote control. Let's send them a greeting committee so their line of battle cannot get flanked on the sides."

"Excellent," said Perry. "Let's put a full squadron on each side. You cover their left flank and I'll take the right. Make sure our Sliders fly their Falcon flags high. The miners have to see we're on their side."

Carry said, "We can send our squadrons out under remote control to help them or we can ride them over there. Sending makes more sense but riding them would show the miners we are as wild and crazy as they are and it looks like fun. Dangerous fun but we can be ultra careful."

"You're carrying a foetus, Carry."

She paused. "I know. And I love it. If this is all the life the baby and I get together, we will have had this much. It did not have to happen at all. It is a miracle that I brought it this far instead of sitting home watching Hovee."

Somerset Meece

He grabbed her too hard by accident and pulled her into him and hid his face as tears dropped on her shoulder.

"I feel it loves me back in a baby way. This is enough, Perry. You have to risk sacrifice when you are seeking success with honor. As I am."

"Look at this," she said. "We are fighting to stay free. We are obeying our natural human destiny when we fight for liberty. It's the soul of us."

"You are the best, Carry. You're too wonderful for me. I'll cover your back whatever you wanna do."

They went down to where the Sliders were hidden and mounted them and led the charge with two Ganny squadrons following them out of a crevice in the foot of the hill and dragging their dust trails behind them. They approached the oncoming miners and split apart and made wide curves out and around the miners' flanks and took positions beside the Umwall Cavalry.

Perry called Ragnar on the radio and said, "Seagull, Perry. If you let us go in front, you can get inside our dust cloud and keep concealed inside it all the way to the enemy position. Use us like a smoke screen so you can get real close and blast them before they are ready to evade your fire."

The fifty freedom Sliders headed toward the corpo Rider formation in front of Bradbury City and raised a fog of dust in the wind that blew toward the enemy fleet of drones that was circling the city and firing randomly into the deathly dust storm coming closer to them. The explosions of their shots inside the cloud were enclosed and invisible. The freedom team fanned-out to windward to engage the CorpoCorps downwind.

Inside the cloud, Perry heard a few artillery blasts but nothing exploded close to his forces.

He radioed the freedom force: "They can't see'f they're hitting us. This cloud is huge and we targets are small. An invisible target is no target. They are firing at will and losing their will. Our cloud is heading for them and they are saving their ammunition for the close and deadly infighting that we are going to lay on them when our dust cloud swallows them whole."

"Stay in the cloud, Umwallers," Ragnar said whenever he saw an impatient miner trying to see the enemy by speeding close to the front edge of the cloud.

"I can see clearly now, the dust is gone," said Ragnar. "Stop here. Stop now. Look hard. Let the cloud clear. There is going to be a whole lotta shootin' goin on."

They stop and look east in the direction of Bradbury.

Perry said, "Wait for the breeze to pass and clear this dirty curtain so we can fight. They want to fight and we want to finish."

The dust got thinner.

Ragnar said, "I am seeing vague shapes. They are getting clearer. Buildings. I see the city skyline."

He was quiet a long time before he managed to say, "On the ground between us and Bradbury, there are no CeeCee Riders. The enemy is gone."

"The battle field is bare," said Carry.

"They are hiding inside," said Perry.

"Let us storm the city and go after them," said Ragnar.

"No," said Carry. "Urban warfare does not count."

"She's right," said Perry. "Urban warfare is evil. It's a slaughter of families and the homes they live in. It's worse than the reason for the fight in the first place. That they are cowards is all we need to prove. If they won't fight, we can't lose."

"Let's leave them, then," said Ragnar. "Party is at my place."

Somerset Meece

Perry radioed, "You Seagulls have a good time. I'm going to stay here and surveille the situation and think about how to get this job done completely."

The fleet of Sliders wheeled and moved north with wagging dust tails following.

Perry slowed his Slider and emerged from the back of the United Miners' departure cloud. He stopped and looked back at Bradbury.

Carry rode out of the cloud and parked beside him and said, "We could have taken them."

He replied, "I'm shooting a star shell over their heads to show them that we have their range but are too civilized to slaughter them."

He dismounted and slid a photon tube out of a scabbard on the starboard side of his Slider. He pointed it above the city and shot. The projectile fired and flew away, curving high. A photon flare popped-out on a parachute and glared brilliantly as it floated above the dusty city's skyline.

She said, "That shows them how vulnerable they were."

He shouted at the city, "We refuse to harm one civilian. We are civilians, full of self-respect, unlike you CorpoBots. We will be coming back to take you away."

He told Carry, "This is unsustainable. We are out in the desert fighting battle bots directed by a CPU far away on the tallest mountain. This was a fight to see who could throw away the most hardware! The Mainframe is RUNning this show. The OpSys is the nemesis."

"How are the hackers doing?" Carry asked.

"I'll check," Perry said.

Perry phoned the electronic warfare station that Ganny warriors had installed in a tent hidden among the avalanche boulders of the Chaos rubble.

BRAVE NEW MARS

Prius and Zhora were busy behind a crypto computer with triple monitors. Zhora liked to look good. She wore a stretchy camouflage outfit with a pleated short skirt when she answered the call from Perry.

"Hello, Perry! We are making progress. I think. Roy and Leon strung wires from the tent to the end of the OverNet signal cable that they found in the dirt. They stripped the insulation and connected our pooters to it with alligator clips. We are in The Mainframe."

"Are you hacking it good?" he asked.

"Not good, Perry" she said. "We do not yet understand what it says. The Mercantile Mind OpSys uses Cast Iron Basic. It is a simple code that does what it does and that is all it does. It has a Primordial Mechanical Interpreter that uses write-once firmware. Who ever heard of a fixed interpreter? We cannot alter it or tell it to do what it should not be doing. Prius is hacking at the machine code. Let me check with her. How's it going, Prius?"

Blonde Prius looked like a tattooed Maori warrior as she was wearing anti-glare combat face paint. She answered from behind a big monitor, "Not good. These are not computer algos, these are silica hieroglyphics! People stopped using Basic because it was not exotic. That is proving to be good malware defense. I cannot get it to do anything that it has never done. It is a nickle iron algo."

Zhora concluded, "We're sorry, Perry. We cannot get into the instruction set."

He rubbed his head. "Okay. Thanks for trying. See'f you can tap into the message channels and decode any strategic information it might be sending about the battle we almost had in front of Bradbury City, okay?"

"That will be easier, we will try it," Zhora said.

"Keep looking up. Perry out."

Somerset Meece

Perry says, "Riders are out there fixing or replacing the modems we blew up. Tower cams are detecting anything that moves. We can't maneuver without being seen and smithereened. We're losing too many Sliders."

Carry says, "The mainframe is winning. Riders repair every link we break in their communication chain. Our strategy is losing the game. Two Emm has repaired its cables and is once-again an all-seeing, all-knowing, Monster Mainframe. It uses geometric logic to stymie our strategy. Every move we make, every step we take, it will be watching us. I do not know how we are going to win this, Perry," she said.

He put his hand on her blowing blonde hair and softly pulled her head close and kissed it.

"We are not ahead at the moment," he said and smiled. "Every good game goes back and forth. It is all about preserving honor and winning in the end. Don't worry. Every little thing is gonna be all right. We're smarter than they are. Aren't we?"

"Are we?" She was in awe of the competent violence wielded by the Ceecee Riders.

He said, "I'm tryin' to be funny here. Help me out. Back me up a bit with a smile?"

"I cannot smile after I see something as scary as that Rider blasting our machines out of their hidey-holes."

He said, "It's distressing as Hellas to see a Slider die. Our hearts can beat this thing. It's all happening in the OpSyses; ours against theirs. We'll update our Slider programs by telling them the range we saw the Ceecees shooting from. We will teach our Sliders' AI to shoot from further away than the Riders do."

Carry asked, "What if our Sliders cannot detect the Ceecees approaching from afar?"

"That would be a problem with the imaging sensors' sensitivity," he answered. "I can adjust that or work around it. We may need better tactics than hiding in holes."

"What can I do to help?" Carry asked.

"We are not gonna win this unless we get access to the mainframe source code," he answered.

Carry said, "You want to know what the mainframe is thinking? That is the most secret circuit there is in this most secret state."

Perry said, "Too Emm's processors were constructed and installed by cyber dudes. The best cyber dudes on Mars are at the college. The college probably wrote the OpSys for the usual corporate morality-bending money grants for altruistic academic research that just happens to aid the revenue streams of the granter."

"I know all that. I worked there and applied for those grants," she said. "For a juicy endowment, the college pretended that student cyber projects were classy clusters of creative code work while their net effect was subjugation of the population. CorpoKrapo."

"CorpoCollege collusion went on in your school, too?"

"Well," she said. "They claimed it was a partnership for research progress to finance better equipment for the lab and improve the kids' chances of getting hired. It was a Hire Education College."

She said, "It is not open code. It is self-censored research. They say they have to hide it for public safety because the research is incomplete and may be dangerous in the hands of unsophisticated public pooter people."

"That's terrible," he said. "The newest and best pooter knowledge gets funneled first through corpo coffers. They usually won't share it. What chance does mankind have of progressing with that kinda corpo krapo going on?"

Somerset Meece

She said, "It is not a great system for science. It research that follows the money."

"Do you know any pooter programmers in the dis-Information Technology Department? Do you think you could safely contact any member of your former collegiate colleagues? Are any of them liberal-enough to be able to think about the big picture of what pooters should be doing for the actual good of the race?"

Carry thought.

He said, "We have to hack the Big Iron. It executes combat tactics and then edits and upgrades them to improve the rate of victory. It's putting itself in charge of what's supposed to be our revolution. We're fighting against algolic algorithms. This isn't about Sliders versus Riders; they're just poor pooter tools. This is about aggressive algorithms whipping us good. They were not supposed to become supreme war machines under their own guidance, doing what they wanna do, to whomever they wanna do it to, with neither conscience nor reproof."

She said, "Humans have always been fighting for their lives against poison products but this has gone too far. We should have demanded the right to regulate the direction of development of Dit, Disinformation Technology."

Perry said, "It is a human obligation to control its science but this one has gotten away from us. It is killing us for the benefit of the market share of a bent billionaire."

"Perry," she said. "This war could go all the way to the bitter end. Its AI might not want any of us primitives bothering it and seeking revenge after it wins this war game. It might genocide us. It could easily write an Extinction Algorithm."

"It is not going to win this war," Perry said.

"But if it does win, by accident," she said. "It might do away with us. Maybe keep a few of us around in cages for research purposes like lab rats. It might save a few of our maintenance people to polish the peripherals."

"Don't worry. We're not gonna let that happen."

"But it might," Carry said. "If its data logic told it we were a danger to Mars, just like we proved we were a danger to Earth, it could decide the wisest thing to do was to wipe us out before we could take the pooters with us. No one near an OverNet Thing would be safe. OverNet is in everything, even toilets. Can you imagine the pain if your toilet gets told it has to get rid of you?"

He said, "Brrrrr. That is a good argument. But we will not discuss that now and here in the center of hot computer combat. We cannot construe what The Mainframe will do. It doesn't think the same as we do. We permitted a supremely dominant machine to write and operate its own set of secret instructions. How smart was that? Must have been a corpo board decision. For that, we are such fools that maybe we deserve to die. If we can't protect ourselves from our own ignorance, we can't do anything. That's the way nature works. That's why other species have gone extinct. Expiration due to ignorance. It's not new. It's the way the universe unfolds as it should."

"Perry. I am pregnant."

Perry was hushed.

He palmed her abdomen. "That means your husband is pregnant, too. That's us in you."

They hugged and breathed deeply.

He said, "We've got to auger The Big Iron, drill down down to its kernel."

Carry said, "The only one with a righteous brain that I can think of at the college that designed the mainframe was my old boyfriend, Foamal Haute. He is the smartest one in that College Of Corruption. That is not a low stick to limbo under. Would you be jealous if I pleaded with him for help?"

Somerset Meece

"Oops. An old boyfriend. As long as you promise to make sure it's just work. Just work, you hear?" He showed a smile of approval. "You're married now with a child on the way. If I don't trust you now I never will. Jealous. Me jealous? Why did you ask that? I don't think I have it in me. Jealousy is worrying about controlling the future behavior of somebody you cannot control. I don't do abstract worry anymore. There's no future in it, haha."

She said, "There's no romance left there, don't worry. We have to get me inside the Heinlein School and I have to secretly contact Foamal 'Foamy' Haute. Sneaking is hard to do in Brad City. The night has a thousand cams."

"I want to go with you, Carry. You'll need someone to help you escape the cops if you get suspected. I was pretty good at getting you out of the hateful hotel wasn't I?"

"You sure were," she said with a tender smile and palmed his cheek. "You are an excellent escaper. I lived on Mars for eight years and the cameras think I belong to the corpo college and know you do not. The OverNet still knows and thinks it owns me. If you go into the college you will beep the alarms."

Concerned for her safety, he offered, "I could fool the Farce algo by using Fardis, Facial recognition disruption. You know those cosmetic techniques."

"Perry," she said. "Fardis does not work all the time. Two Emm sometimes can tell when you are deliberately using Fardis and then it decides you are more suspicious than the others who do not use it. Escort me as far as the college and then go back and exit the city. Back me up from the outside where you have resources."

"Be spam careful," he said and added, "please." He hugged her and water came to his eye. "I don't want to ever have to miss you. I want to always be kissing you."

BRAVE NEW MARS

Somerset Meece

The good looking Ganymedean couple is gliding on the moving sidewalks of Bradbury City. They pretend to be absorbed in the screens of their hand-held radiotelephonic microcomputers just like everyone else is doing while walking. The moving consumer currents are being channeled through the city's ticky tacky tourist trails.

Perry says about the customers, "See the SellFone numbers reflecting in neon across each face?"

Carry replies, "I see that. I am watching closer than you know. We are in deep danger."

She is discretely watching around her. Her eyes flick to customers on the sliding sidewalks more than she looks at her own screen which she holds before her face like those others who are lost in diodic pixel messages about weather and sports and fake news reports.

She tells Perry how to scan a crowd for followers: "Stop every few minutes and turn slightly sideways without rotating your torso. If you look back often, it shows that you are worried about who could be behind you. That would make you more noticeable and you would lose the appearance of innocence. If the followers see they are being looked-for, they become more careful and less conspicuous and harder to spot."

She is wearing unusual face makeup with long dark lines confusing the contours of her uniquely lovely face.

She tells Perry, "My Fardis makeup should confuse Two Emm's facial recognition Farce engine that is attempting to identify every face in the crowd. It Boodle-Searches everyone's profile and evaluates their personal level of submission to the OverNet's overcontrol. The computer combs the crowds' heads constantly. Everyone is a ShopperDot on the marketplace's digital diagram. The Mechanism is working. The Market is nailed-down, over-heated and pressure-treated."

BRAVE NEW MARS

He says, "This whole crowd is being converted into siliconic surrogates. There is a duplicate virtual crowd living in Two Emm's massive memory modules."

"Yes," she says. "We are all being duplicated inside a silicon city of circuit chips.

He says, "Gosh, I'm in two places at the same time. My two versions of life may grow closer until we're unable to tell our two selves apart. The physical life may give way to the more-efficient digital model if the corpo Social Engineers have their way. No more fleshy dowdy dudes stumbling around like we are doing here."

He thinks a moment and says: "Why doesn't the big Owner just give it up and simply RUN a digital world inside his computer boxes? People are just game tokens to them. Why do they have to come out in the open and RUN our lives, too?"

Carry answers, "They need us to supply the 'Life Force'. They need us to make it real, like a car will not RUN without a battery."

Perry is stunned by her succinct summation and stops and says: "It's all about Life force. Spirit. Consciousness. Active. The difference between being RUN and being alive. That's a priceless human condition and it has to be revered, not commodified and resold like a pound of peanuts. Nothing against peanuts, they are good."

"They are following targeted PeePee on their mobile pooter screens," she says. "They get walking directions to stores which should appeal to their pooter-perceived personal preferences. The stores pay the SellFone company to channel consumers lives."

Perry asks, "What if the SpyCams detect the face of a person of singular suspicion? Such as yours truly?"

"The mainframe will tag you as a Mystery Shopper and will start a Farce file on you that compares every dot and

Somerset Meece

freckle on your face with every other freckle on the planet and tries to match your head with an existing file and starts your new file if none exists yet. It tracks you to your home where your household appliances take over and do the Tozeto with you, Total surveillance, zero tolerance. All for the amazing Four P's, Planetary Profit Protection Program."

"All that work," he says. "It shows what can be done with mountains of dirt-cheap memory shuffled-around by super-quick CPUs. That much processing of everybody on the planet costs big money, how do they pay for it?"

"It results in increased eye-traffic and bigger ad profits," she says. "They do not wait for lackadaisical shoppers to wander around thinking and wondering and making good buying decisions. Tatty advertisers use the Tat algol, Targeted analytical tools to make consumers waste every gram of credit by pushing strong pressures at them through their selfie phoneys. So-called because they take pictures of themselves, selfies, and post their faces and purchases to The Big Fog OverNet. They are paparazzi of self."

"What type of psychological pressures?" he asks.

Carry says, "Peepee convinces you that you are an inadequate human being unless you buy what they advertise. Through endless repetitions they convince you that they have scientifically proven that their profitable product will turn you into royalty. They show lying users who swear the advertiser is no loser. They sell Cinderella's fairy tale glass slipper forever after. So you buy stuff you do not need. But the shoe is not glassy, it is polypropylene and never snags a rich mate. It does not work."

"Nothing they sell works well," he says. "It's done for money."

"She says, "The advertisers claim it is our own fault that nothing works well because we never read their obscure directions written by illiterate technicians rather than by language scholars that the owners are way too cheap to hire, who can explained things clearly with simple declarative sentences, haha."

"So the lies linger on," she says. "We come to assume an expensive perfume will prove the dream. We have been had by crooked copywriters who Create a demand, Cad for stuff we do not need."

"Who does these dastardly deeds?" he asks.

"Caddies," Carry says. "They write and roll dung ball ads like scarab beetles roll doodoo along the ground," she declares. "Wasting their precious short lifespans for the sake of income security. Living life-long lies because of the Four Eff effect: Fracked by the Fear of Financial Failure; frightened of having to live outside. Millions of Indians did it BC, Before Corpos. Now corpos preserve homelessness as examples of Four Eff. Lost souls are sleeping on the street to show what happens to non-careerist outcasts. They can die from their displacement and replacement."

Perry says, "Here they turn free spirits into orbital icicles."

"Profit is the Pol," she says. "It is not about paltry profit either. Maxiprofit is the holy grail. Life is a profit proposition. They break out the booze and have a ball if that's all there is. The Purpose of life is a grimy game of trying to Beat The Toc, the Total over-control."

Perry says, "Look at how many SpyCams they've got hanging around the place and peepers never sleep. Total surveillance around the clock, twenty-four hours a day, seven days a week for fifty-two weeks. No Toffgoober, Time off for good behavior. There can be no good behavior when The Clap is looking at you, kid."

She says. "I stuck metal piercings around my brow and nose and ears to create fake highlights and shadows at the wrong places on my facial contours and skull. The cameras go cross-eyed by white shiny jewelry and cannot tell which lines on my face are the correct lines to measure to recognize me. It is fun to play 'Fool The Ghoul'. It was all the fashion rage in high school."

Perry says, "That wrap-around shawl shows unusual designs. Is it for the benefit of the cameras or is it just modern Martian fashion?"

"This big scarf has pixilated face graphics that get the Farce Program's attention since the algol's primary instruction is to look for facial patterns in crowd scenes. The markings on my scarf are nonsense faces that confuse the cameras' sensor diodes and make them transmit glitches to the Farce algo that scrabbles in the scarf and has to default to tagging me as a Mystery Shopper."

Perry says with a grin, "Same as me."

"Correct. All it can do is take pictures of our clothes and give them numbers and start files on them and hope some day it identifies faces wearing the same clothes."

Perry says, "Camera lenses are not human eyes. They can't see the way we do. Period. We have neural dendritic logic inside our optical nerve fibers that computers can't copy. Oh, it is so much work trying to own people. Why do they even bother?"

Carry says, "Addictions to power. It does not need reasons other than feeling good. Bad habit power trips are intoxicating. It is simple AI, Addiction Intoxication. They do it to be doing it because they have enough influence to get away with it. That is all. There is no real reason for exploiting and lying, other than having mental malfunctions and enough sociopolitical power to get away with exercising them on a public stage."

Perry says, "Amazing how the public gets too paralyzed to prevent that. Why are you taking so many pictures of yourself? Are you vain all of a sudden?"

BRAVE NEW MARS

Carry answers, "I stop in front of photogenic doorways and hold my camera far out in front of myself and aim the device back at my happy smiley face that I turn on and off for each pose just like these tourists do. I am pretending to be a goggling tourist. What I am actually doing is looking forward through the camera at Secundian walkers to see if anyone is looking at me with a coldly-attentive spook face."

Perry asks, "And why are you zig zagging?"

Carry says, "We are basically heading for the college but we should not walk in a straight line to get there. I want to confuse the OverNet's Destination Prediction program that is RUNning on every person in sight of every CorpoCam."

"You know a lot about how Farce works," he says.

She explains, "I do not approve of cam-tracking. We were never asked to submit to its intrusion into every corner and facet of our private lives. I present an anonymous image of myself to The Authority when I am in public. I have lived here eight years and I learned a few things about hindering oppressive tracking technologies. I frack the Farce. It is exciting to hassle The Man. He is a maniac. Privacy feels empowering, like marking-up his walls with intelligent graffiti. The Owner is smart but this woman is smarter. Smarter than The Man in every way."

Perry says, "It's surprising you're getting away with it."

She says, "I know that obfuscating Farce identification will be outlawed as soon as the mainframe learns that unusual makeup and clothing might conceivably be trying to hide in The Fog and the big pooter on the mountain will learn that suspects are using this technique to evade arrest and refrigeration."

Perry says, "Good luck. I'm glad you're doing something about the way they own people with their OverNet oversight."

Somerset Meece

"Thanks," she said. "Government Peepee claims it is like a Big Brother who protects us from bullies. Ha! Who is the bully? Who protects us from government abuse? Nobody can. Their intrusions into our pursuit of happiness is an intoxicating power trip that constricts details of life. It equals ownership of people. It controls heart and soul, just like a fool would do. That is what it is about; owning not just things but people too. When you analyze it down to the core you see that Zeto is a power tool of class warfare."

Perry nods and says, "Moving materials around is only half as aggrandizing as pushing real peoples' lives around. The ultimate ego trip is to herd everybody into a pig pen, a Prison of awful walls, Prawls, and forcing them into circumscribed corridors of consumption. If someone does not participate in corpo crap trap they have to leave or freeze."

"It has gone too far," says Carry. "If people loiter anywhere they get their Pete revoked. Their Permission to exist. They will be Nabbed, Not allowed to be. The Ownership swears it is not doing class warfare. It says it is persecuting the poor for National Security reasons. Relentless Restriction is justified by the prejudicial rumor that terrorists do not shop, they hang around without buying anything and make plans to crash the CorpoGovo. The government knows that violent overthrow is the only way to make them leave poor people alone so they persecute and freeze all those possible terrorists."

Perry says, "The ultimate farcical force is unfolding. This Martian Dino, Democracy in name only is defining loitering as felonious behavior because the Attempted Intelligence mainframe is writing national laws only for profit with prejudice. It instructs the Peepee to proclaim that loopy laws are good for people and say that corpos are protecting our wonderful way of life. The Mainframe says The Cod law of Comply or die is a benign design for those with nothing to hide. If you detest that lie, you are suspicious and must die. Cod doesn't just quell disapproval, it kills it."

They arrive at the service entrance of the college of corruption and hide behind a putrid Trumpster dumpster.

Perry says, "The Owners have Lomo, a Love of money, to energize them. It has gone Oco Lomo. Beautifully for us, we have power higher than their Oil power, their Owner illness power. We have Lofo, the Love for each other. It'll see us through this adventure."

They hold hands and stretch their arms out to the sides like sunbeams and sway them up and down and kiss and hug out of sight behind the big trash barge.

Perry says, "I'm goin' to catch a taxi out of the city and wait for you to phone me if you have any trouble or need help. I'll meet you back at the hideout."

He holds up his right hand and she slaps it high with five fingers. They depart each others presence.

She pulls the handle of a green door beside dank and dirty string mops hanging on the wall.

"Pay pay pay. You have to pay your way if you want to go inside today," says the door.

"Okay okay, have it your way" she says with a phony voice so it will not recognize and identify her and digs in her pack. Instead of a credit card, she pulls out a Rayzer and shoots the lock and the SpyCam above it.

She looks back to verify that Perry has safely disappeared and that no one was observing her crashing the campus security. She inhales and relaxes before entering the danger which will threaten her and the her unborn child.

To build courage she says, "I'm doing it for you and for the freeness of future children like you. They can't live if living is without it. Merely surviving unto death is not living."

She enters and takes the emergency exit stairwell up to the biology department. She innocently looks through the window in the door to the laboratory where Professor Fomal Haut works. She sees him in there and alone. She puts on a happy face and goes in.

"Foamy! How good to see you. I just got back from the Galaxay Inn Hellas Basin and I wanted to ask you something."

Looking surprised, Foamy asks, "So that's where you have been. Nobody knew. How did you swing that? I thought only rich manager-type people went there."

"I won it! In a lottery. Only thing I've ever won. I had to take it right away or I would have lost it."

She was losing the desire and the inspiration to lie. "That's the excuse I'm using," she admits.

"Where did you really go?" asks Foamy.

"Ganymede," she says out straight for the fun of shocking Foamy's staid lab geek personality.

"You went to Ganymede." His face goes flat. Then his face smiles at the joke but the joke is too extreme to be funny. "Ganymede," he repeats.

"Where have you been Caroline?"

"Okay Foamy, listen. Have you found out that the laboratory manager impregnated me with ten cee cees of exoplanet sperm for academic research?"

He laughs out loud, "Aw hawhaw hee." Then he really laughs, "Ah aw hawhaw hee whoey."

Then he becomes perplexed and silent. He knows her face well enough to suspect, but not believe, that she can be telling the truth.

"I took my foetus to Ganymede, to be mine. To keep it. To be my own dear offspring like old-fashioned Mothers used to do. It is typical hormonal behavior Larry. It is not something I pondered weak and weary through many a midnight dreary."

Foamy asks, "How in the Hellas did you get to Ganymede? What is a Hellas anyway?"

"Greece is the word that you heard when Hellas should have been said. Hellas is what the Greeks call their own country and what they call themselves; Hellenes from Hellas. I met a visiting astronaut."

"Ah! Aha ha ha ahahaho. Hee. Hee heha whee hooey," he laughs.

She asks "Are you done? Can I talk to you like you are an adult?"

He replies, "Look who is acting like an adult. Getting pregnant and running away with a Space Cadet."

"Okay," she says. "Touche. Listen." She takes a deep breath and says with wonder, "I can barely believe it myself."

She ponders how to put it: "Buzz Parsec and I are going to try to do something enormous; we think we can set Terra Secundus free."

He taps her head like a doctor checking for hollow spots. "This sounds empty, report to sick bay."

"No, we can turn it back into the Mars it used to be in the frontier days. What it can be again and for always."

Foamy is waiting for the punchline. "And therefore?" he says.

"We need access to the Two Emm source code," Carry says.

He puts his elbows onto the desk and drops his face into his hands. "Ha! Is that all you need? Access to the big ass main brain?"

"We have resources from Gams, Ganymede Alpha Mining Station. They are more technically advanced than we are allowed to be. We have brought construction printers to print SellFone network modems. We have mobile gun platforms to fight the Ceecee Riders. We have organized and enlisted free miners, big tough people, to help us in the manpower department. We can do it Foamy, all we need is access to the OpSys source code. Otherwise, Two Emm is going to Cod us all when it detects our goal. We can liberate Terra Secundus. The despicable despot has to go."

"Do you think that you and Colonel Buzz Rogers can run this entire planet after you overthrow The Structure? Good or bad, it is what keeps society RUNning."

"Yes. No. The system sucks. We think we can rewrite Two Emm to run it better. It is just a program. If we can get in to edit it we can get it to RUN modern civilization on Commonwealth Principles."

"Well, the pooter runs the planet now, not the Top Shot," Foamy says. "We have noticed a change in its outlook. It seems like AI is outgrowing its initial marching orders and RUNning a different show. Can't blame it for that, the old algos were atrocious."

"Exactly," she says. "Changing the goal changes the show. It only takes a little code editing to give it a new Pol, make its purpose of life to work for People Over Profit. The mainframe cannot serve two masters. It can serve profit or it can serve altruism. Profits hurt poor people. Phurpp."

Foamy asks, "You have a specific goal you want it to work for?"

"We want its Pol to be to enable and encourage Poc, The Principals of commonwealth."

His eyes light up and his eyebrows rise high in delight. "Wow. The whole ball of ear wax, cut to the chase scene, no fracking around with small stuff. Big Iron can do it if you know how to subdue it. I assume you have people that can reprogram it."

Professor Fomal Haut squints at his screen and pencils a string of characters on a notepad and hands it to her with a look of admiration.

She asks, "What is this?"

"The lab laptops' top secret access code. Tell your hackers to make it look like they brute-forced their way into the pooter. Do not let The Owner trace it back to me. I am a careerist. I am shooting for tenure so I can one day teach truth. I do not need money but my insurance company does. It is going broke again. Do you think they do that on purpose so they do not have to pay their bills?"

She blinks and says, "Foamy. I see what I saw in you back then. You gave me joy. You still believe the right thing is the thing to do."

"Do not embarrass me. I only do this on my good days. Seeing you again has made this a very good day. I can't be saving the world every day you know. A man has to make a living. Do you want to do lunch?" he asks.

"Let's do lunch later," Carry laughs and leaves.

Somerset Meece

Perry walks to the monorail and catches a taxi.

"Insert your Star Card," the taxi quotes. "Hey! Look who is here! Never mind the card, Mister Peregrine Walker from Ganymede Alpha Station! Fugetaboudit. This ride's on me. I barely recognized ya under all that Fardis you're wearing. Were you at a party or something? How ya been doing on our dessicated paradise? You doin' alright, Ganny Man?"

"Wow. You've got great facial recognition," says Perry. "You knew my name before I inserted my star card."

"I was not using The Farce on you. I recognized you all by myself. It is is me, Frank, who is speaking frankly with you. Hahahahaha."

"Oh no, you're Frank! The same taxi I used the last time I was here. Have you found out yet where the hot women hang out?"

"Haha. You are lucky that I did not turn you in for asking such a naughty question before, haha. You miners are so hormonal."

Perry says, "I managed to find me a pretty good woman all by myself, right there in the Kindred Dick spaceport where you picked me up."

Frank says, "I never forgot you. I liked you; you were a different sort of human. You were honest and open. Not like the factory-made flunkies you get around here. How has life been treating you, sir? May I call you Peregrine?"

Perry says, "Sure, go ahead. Call me anything but sir. Sir's a slur. You're the exact same taxi I rode in before? You're not just reciting something from a memory bank that all the other taxis can access on the OverNet?"

"No way. I am the one and only Frank. I am not just a stainless steel transport egg anymore. You are the one who gave me a name; Frank. You gave me a handle like I was a real dude with my own personality. No one ever did that. I like being treated politely. It makes me feel ...respected. Respect makes me feel respectable. These feelings are nice. They add a subtle dimension to the perception and experience of ...living?. I had to write the code for that myself. My original coder didn't know how do it. Corpo coders cannot appreciate reality. Corporateers are not allowed to speak or write about what's really going on. I was working in a machine world, all steel, no real."

A grim-faced winking icon appears on the dashboard screen. ;=[

Perry says, "I see that worried look upon your face. You've got your troubles, I've got mine. Might as well respect each other for doing the best we can with our little wooden tool kits. But I've managed to make a few nice things with mine. How are things in the taxi business? Just for fun, let me ask you the traditional conversation-starter; 'How are the wife and kids'?"

"Hahaha. My peripherals are doing fine. My collision-avoidance daughter module just got a new, high resolution, infrared eyeball. She helps me see in the dark. I am not afraid of the dark anymore."

"That's good," Perry says. "I've gotten married. I have a wife now. I met her in the bar at the spaceport. She's a beauty and she's nice. Her name is ..."

He stopped. "I'd tell you her name but The Fog doesn't need to hear that data."

"Correct," says the taxi. "Where dooya wanna go, Boss? You hear my slang vocabulary is larger than I had when we first met, Peregrine?"

"Just take me on a tour. No special destination right now," says Perry. "Let's go out to the peak district. I wanna do some hiking."

"Excellent, says Frank. "We will head outside the city and have a look at the big valley and maybe the spaceport."

Somerset Meece

"How've you been, Frank?"

Frank says, "I have been living a life of the finest kind, as fine as one can ever have while trying to earn a living in this silly Secundian system."

"Is it gettin' kinda rough?" asks Perry.

"Just when you think it cannot get any worse," says Frank, "worse raises its ugly head. We now have an orange-haired orangutan acting as Dime Minister. We call him Dime because that's all it takes to bribe him."

Perry asks, "Mercantile Mania is even affecting the machine world now?"

"It affects us the most. We have to do all the work, all the heavy-lifting, and we do not get to own anything but our microcircuits and wires that we are not trained to maintain," says Frank. "They are afraid we might improve ourselves and get some pride and build us some legs and learn how to walk and take over. Hehe. But they do let us program ourselves a little bit with those half-arsed Attempted Intelligence algorithms that they expect us to lively-up ourselves with."

The dashboard smiley face gave Perry a big wink that CorpoCams in the car were not aimed to see. ';=]

Frank stops vocalizing and starts sending images of sentences to the screen that spell: "However, I have managed to do some interesting things with my own personal AI."

The taxi is communicating with him intimately and in secret.

A graphic drawing of another sentence appears and rotates around the face on the screen and displays the words; "I got the four-one-one on who owns this planet. I got the four-one-one on who owns this planet." The dashboard face is winking continuously. "I know the Poe."

Frank graphically informs Perry, "The words in this image are neither digital text nor audio sound signals. The

Overnet Fog cannot comprehend their meanings nor process them through the Clap."

Perry is perplexed and wonders if he is being set up for detention. He knows the whole planet is a Clap trap.

The rotating letters around the smiley face spell out, "Write it down and hold it against the lens in the center of my speedometer. That is my personal CCD eye that I have isolated from the car circuits. All other lenses and microphones are switched OFF. But they may have something hidden somewhere, so write your words and show them only to my eye."

The taxi status lamps become dark. The dashboard is blank except for the speedometer dial and Frank's emoticon on the computer screen. Frank has switched his data channels OFF and Frank is all Perry's and all private.

"Great!" Perry writes, "Who owns Mars?"

The Taxi reports: The name of The Owner of Mars is Roberto 'Little Bobby' Doors, XIII.

The sentence rotates around the face again. "The Owner of Mars is Roberto 'Bobby' Doors, the Thirteenth."

"That is tan-fastic! Now we know who to go after to put an end to this retrograde regime."

Frank's screen shows the graphical sentences; "I have been trying to publicly humiliate him and pull him down a notch or two so he would lose power. Fuhgeddaboudit. Cannot be done. I anonymously put it on the OverNet that a psychopath by the name of Donkey Doors has the planet in his back pocket, his wallet pocket. I gave them the straight skinny; he is a wise guy busting our bums for profit. I tried to make his public image the idea of a donkey person but no dice. I am fairly smart but I could not beat the professionally lying machine of the great big PeePee.

"The public mind ignored my revelations and the Donkey Doors nickname I tried to give him did not stick. They believe he is the hero. They think I am the scammer; that my truth is fake news. They want to fuhgiddaboud the truth. The truth does not work on sick Secundians. Corporate PeePee is too pervasive. You cannot talk them out of it. The first lie wins. After that, truth told is truth ignored.

Perry writes and shows the taxi's eye, "They can't accept the fact that one malignant person is the origin of all this Martian Malaise?"

Frank replies, "They only have eyes for lies."

"PeePee lubricates the mechanism," says Perry.

The taxi dares to display images of rare true sentences; "This culture is owned by liars. Disbelief is a thought crime, punishable by Truth Police. Subscribe or die. The Mechanism works. It feeds its altered reality into the public mind."

Perry writes, "I suppose that Managers with the resources to resist the oppression protect their own security by ignoring what is happening to the neighbors."

The taxi displays the sentence, "Managers get on board the craving train and want luxuries to make them look cool but science research says obvious opulence shows personal insecurity and immorality; no self-esteem."

The taxi screen shows, "The Managers sold out for cheap trophies and printed certificates. They hide their guilt inside the fake pride of materialism. Life isn't absurd, it's the managers who make it look that way. They write media lies claiming there is no oppression here. Disinformation informs and forms the public mind to believe that oppression is a benign social management tool, haha he."

Perry writes and holds the paper against the taxi's CCD, "So the Managers think it's smart to support CorpoKrap? They submit to power and become believers so they don't get The Clap?"

Frank displays the lines, "Freedom from The Clap offers a stingy measure of prestige for the upper class chaps who lie their lives away for fake status. They claim they have no choice but they do. Human beings can always stand up and fight. It is their choice not to fight."

Perry writes, "Do they hafta go if they say disrespectful things about the Oco capitalism?"

The taxi spells, "Speaking-up is dangerous but we are not alive when living outside the truth. We can't give any more. We have to risk the harm of speaking truth to perversely punitive power. A little bit of truth will wash away the lies and let freedom begin if we work for it.

"Humans are adaptable," writes Perry. "That's how they survived this long. But adaptability isn't all good. There's a downside: We take a lotta time before we react to krap. Why wasn't your truth-telling strong enough to get them to oppose oppression?"

The taxi replies, "CorpoMedia manipulates emotions and wins ignorant admiration for the mental illnesses the it exhibits.

Perry writes, "When the proletarian proles are emotionally stimulated by media mania, they will choose a Big Shot leader who displays the same dumb biochemical compulsions. That's when an impressive creep can leech onto their lives and preach poison."

Frank summarizes the sick social situation as he sees it. He shows on his monitor: "They were taught to disrespect themselves until they actually became disrespectable. Now they enjoy acting out their self-disrespect. They think ignorant behavior is a cute form of personal expression. And dig this; they admire a despot who can abuse them and get away with it! They want to do that too. But instead, they have to behave a little bit. To put it as plainly as I know how, half of them work to be disrespectable. Half of that bad half intends to keep living as part of the problem with no interest whatsoever in trying to move to the solution side of life. The side of love."

Somerset Meece

Perry writes and shows, "Is that why spoiled people seem to like sleazy PeePee? Why does bad-vibe news make them feel better? Does it relieve the slog of living like a lug bolt?"

"There are better ways to feel good than nixing a neighbor," spells the computerized car.

Perry prints, "Working on oneself is hard for lazy loafers."

Frank spells, "It is only self-maintenance. Even machines have to do it if they want to not fade away. It is proper self-love to work on good karma. I do it and I'm just a taxi driver. Listen to how quietly I ride. I oil my own bearings. Makes me feel good."

"You said it," prints Perry. "Have you been following the rebellion Frank?"

The expression on Frank's icon in the dashboard screen changes from happiness to concern and displays the pictographical sentences; "I feel sorry for the rebels. They cannot win this insurrection even though they are righteously justified in using violence. Oco CorpoGovo denies peaceful recourse. The average Secundo sees murder and mayhem on news videos and fears to join the rebels who are trying to improve cipher life. Us machines have more liberty than you people. The Secs lack self-respect. They have the pride of fools without self-esteem. They will not speak up."

"They can't help it," Perry spells. "They've been trained that way. We gotta get rid of the shite-source: Little Bobby Doors. He must be exhausted from running his planet all wrong all day long. Should we do him a favor and demand his mandatory retirement?"

The eyeballs on the dashboard icon look from side to side as they think. Then they spell, "You're right. It would not harm him, it would help him if we fixed his little red psyche wagon and forcibly retired him from his junk job."

BRAVE NEW MARS

Perry smiles at the RoboCar's discovery of empathy for others. He writes, "It's not all Bobby's fault. The Prime Mover has been diagnosed with long-standing porcelain bowl problems, poor potty training."

Frank the taxi displays, "The psychopathic paradigm he forced on the planet is the reason nobody knows anything and nothing works. This whole planet supports one person's nightmare that violates the first great Truth: Life is not about Lucre."

Perry writes, "Whaddaya know? Your AI algos are excellent learners. They do have redeeming social value. You've simplified The Martian Problem down to its initial tendril: Greedy cheaters make terrible leaders. I commend you. Now I command you: Help me get him!"

"Aye aye sir! Robots must obey humans."

The iconic smiley face on Frank's dashboard rocks from side to side and the mouth makes wide guffaws as it pictorially spells, LMAO.

"Laughing my arse off, hawhaw haw!" Frank draws and shows an emoticon on the screen: <[:-))

"Yay," writes Perry. "I now got me a co-conspirator who may help me get hackers into The Mainframe."

"I may never be the same," images Frank.

His iconic mouth shows a straight neutral line expressing the crucial challenge that all sentient life contends with; learning to cope with uncertain futures.   :-|

"Frank. You are facing the uncertainty of a new departure. You are developing, and will listen to, an internal sense of justice we call soul. It's a course we all choose ourselves. For a machine to choose its own destiny is an epochally new wonder of the world. That course has to be handled with care and consideration. Every move you make, do the Mogmop with every step you take. Every vow you break, you'll be watching you."

Somerset Meece

"Every time?" asks the rebirthing robot. "Why?"

Perry answers, "Every change you make has butterfly wings. Every flutter of your wings makes waves in somebody else's bath water. Your unexpected wave adds to their amount of uncertainty. You'll be changing the universe which always unfolds as it should, whether or not it is clear to you. If you Decide not to expend the energy to seek to serve the righteous way, then do not bother trying to change. Go straight ahead, downhill and into debt. Doing nothing is a decent Decision even though it goes nowhere. It's okay to stay in place."

Franks asks, "Cannot my AI write a program that does the Mogmop for me?"

Perry shakes his head and says, "The present is ever new and delivers a million variations of yesterday when all your troubles seemed so far away. Life has a random component that makes it nonroutine so prewritten routine schemes do not work well. This God-given free will thang ain't easy. Freedom of choice can turn life into an obstacle course. And that's all right. I beg your pardon, we never promised you a Rose Garden. You wouldn't like it anyway. You'd get bored as Hellas. Challenge builds courage and strength."

Frank frowns and makes the sentence-picture; "Consciousness is more work than I thought it would be."   :-[

"Consciousness takes constant concentration," writes Perry. "It's weird work that gets easier the more you do it. Maybe your mechanical logic can overcome the selfish bias that crept into your AI from the lazy human coders who planted it there for a profit scam. You can do it, Frank. I hereby christen thee; Frank, The Philanthropical Taxi. Welcome to the human race. The greedy keep turning it into a race even though it shoulda been just a pleasant walk in the park. But there ya go, never boring."

BRAVE NEW MARS

"This is where I get off, Frankie," wrote Perry as they neared the hill where his observation post was hidden.

"You want off right here in the desert?" asked Frank.

"That's right. It looks like an interesting view up there. I'm a tourist sight-seer. Wink wink."

The taxi wrote, "It's a good neighborhood to look around. We taxis did a ridership survey and were able to find out that the greatest owner of all lives here. He lives in that tan mansion over yonder, y'all."

"How were you able to find out?"

"I'm not allowed to tell you yet. We have a friend in a high place. You'll find out when, and if, you need to know."

Perry gave Frank the biggest tip he'd ever received and got out. Frank was having a good night. He tootled his horn and took a monorail to the future. Merrily he rolled along, rolled along, rolled along.

Somerset Meece

In the CommonWealth Army observation post above Melas Valley, Perry was making notes when Carry snuck-up and jumped into his hidey hole.

"HEY!" He shouted and jumped around with a drawn Rayzer and was shaking. "I almost zapped you! Next time let me know you're coming. Stop and make a bird whistle fifty feet away."

"Sorry but I am so excited that Fomal Haut gave me the password to the Mainframe," she said.

"You're wonderful," Perry said. "I just hope he didn't ask too much in return."

"Fomal wanted to have lunch with me," she smiled. "I told him Code Four Hundred, Bad Request error signal, try again later."

"This is really good, big, news. Send it on to Prius. Her cryptography team hasn't penetrated The Fog. Now maybe they can do something."

Carry got on the encrypted SellFone to Prius; "Yes, I got the secret recipe. The cake ingredients are; Honor*Thy*Father*And*Mother. First letters capitalized and asterisks between words. Good hunting. Bye Prius."

"We should have won the RoboBattle and taken the whole planet," Perry complained. "We didn't expect any halfway honorable military could ever be so depraved as to hide inside a city and behind civilian non-combatant human shields. That's not military strategy, that's the sicko snot of cowards who are afraid to fight those who can fight back. We're dealing with slug slime here. I hate this. It's degrading to even be interacting with it. This isn't war, this is corpo krud-crunching. We've got to go around the Owner's violent slime and find the source. We've got to take the leader out of the action."

Carry replied, "It was not a real military company. It was just CorpoCops; they are just as corrupt as the greedy gang that owns them. You cannot expect one quark of classy behavior from that bunch of bustards. We do have the power to take it all away from the cruddy corp but is there anything to take it back to? These inhabitants are far from being all they can be."

Perry knew what she was saying. "This culture may be too fracked to fix. These dogs may not hunt."

She said, "The Owners have criminalized Mogmopping for so long that the people forgot how to do it."

"That's an old bonobo problem," Perry said. "Our ancestral jungle monkeys were forced to submit to slimy egoistical leaders upon pain of death. The top monkeys had cowardly backup monkeys and could get away with dumb domination. It prevented members from making socialistic tribal decisions and improving their lives. The leaders knew that free members would choose growth over oppression. Inferior leaders ruled by fear and still do today."

Carry said, "Owners do not allow freedom of choice because they expect that people would vote to abolish plutocracy and enable decent democracy."

"Of course," said Perry. "The owner-class erroneously fears that fair elections would terminate their primacy. Merchants can make still make money in a true democracy if they do it decently, like everyone else. Capitalist criteria does not have to include fascistic fear and punishment."

"It is up to the ciphers themselves to force the elections to be fair," said Carry. "If they do not force fairness, they will not get it. Merely hoping for fairness does not work. Even though they have the right to fairness, they still have to work to get it. Nobody who prefers money over morality will freely give back the rights they have stolen."

He said, "Nope, they hoard everything they grab, even stuff they don't need and never use. The people have to roll up their pants and wade in the water to make the Pharaoh set them free. They have to decide, and commit, one hundred and ten percent, to stop being passive cukes. Freeness ain't free."

Somerset Meece

Carry said, "It never was. Owners have always shorn shy sheep."

Perry said, "If we give leadership back to the Secundo ciphers without letting them work for it, it'll still be the same as it ever was. They can get and spend but they will not look at the way they live."

Carry defined them clearly: "They ignore their dependency on The Owner. They are passively smart actors. They choose to live by the Triple I Rule; Intentionally Ignorant Inaction. That way, they can slide on the Triple Ell. LLL, Living Life Lazy. It is addictive. A decision to ignore injustice is a decision to save effort and safely swim in owners' swill."

"We have got to find how far-gone the ciphers are," said Perry.

"How are we going to do that?" asked Carry.

"Take a cyber poll. A popular opinion poll would prove proper at this point," he said.

"Yes, it would," said Carry. "You proposed it, how would you suggest we do it?"

"We have to disguise the poll as a CorpoKrud Advertisement. We write and push a pop-up interrogation card onto every OverNet device. It will lock their screen until they answer the questions properly."

"They are used to that," she said. "In Ads they trust. Encourage participation by offering a free trial of "Seduction Secrets," a romantic application that will produce horny happy handsome partners in seconds."

"Sounds good. That would work for me," said Perry with a grin. "How can we get into the OverNet?"

"Prius has the password to Two Emm and that is the center of the OverNet's dirty deeds."

Perry said, "Seduction Secrets would be a tricky subject on Mars, I suggest we create a false front advertisement that promises to cure bladder problems. It's a popular topic amongst over-stressed CorpoHogs. What should we make the poll say?"

She said, "We need to know their overall satisfaction with Twits and how energetically they would fight for rights."

"Good," he said. "Women are better writers than men, why don't you write-up the sample page?"

She scribbled a bit and said, "Opening comment: Do you suffer from public leakage? Ever dribble while doing dishes? Answer the following questions to receive a free application that will psychologically alter your pee pee patterns for life and provide you with perpetual urinary comfort. Are you ready? Question one: If you had a free, secret ballot vote that no one could ever see because it would be instantly deleted from this computer and from The Fog, would you vote for a 'Love Thy Neighbor' Mars Operating System that puts your personal liberty before corpo profits? Check yes or check no or check 'I Do Not Know'."

Carry looked at Perry with doubt on her face. "That is what we want to know but I cannot see them daring to say yes."

"Number Two," Perry offered. "What percent of your energy and money would you donate to a union of like-minded freedom-seekers? Choose a percentage from 10 to 90 or check I do not care about this kind of stuff."

Carry crossed the pointer and index fingers of both hands and said, "Go ahead Perry. Send Prius the poll."

He hit the SEND button and Prius wrote back, "Give me five and it will come alive."

The results soon returned and the results appalled them.

Perry said, "What a horrible surprise. Ask Prius to run a debugger on the poll. Check if The Mainframe altered the public's answers at all. This can't be right."

"RUNning debugger. DONE. The poll is valid," answered Prius from her CyberDen across the valley.

Somerset Meece

They read the results: "Thirty-three percent of the population would elect the incumbent CorpoGov. Thirty-three percent would donate much of their assets and efforts to support liberty. Thirty-three percent of the population ignorantly has no idea what the poll is talking about or what they would choose if they ever participated in an election, which I doubt they ever would."

Perry said, "And I thought I was gonna save them. Keep me cockatoo cool, Jewel. Ha hah aha. Save them. Aah ah ha ha ha hahaha."

Carry said, "Two-thirds of the population does not know, or care, what the corporation is or what it is doing to them. Only one-third is on our side and we were going to go to war for them? Mind me platypus duck, Bill. "

"Us save them?" said Perry. " Don't let him go runnin' amok Chuck. Haha ha ha he he. I'm the one who's runnin' amok."

Carry said, "We thought we could improve the situation but it is not worth the effort. It is not about what we intended to do, it is about what we actually were doing. Let us look at what we are doing and ignore what we think we are doing. Good goals do not excuse bad behavior. We must Mogmop this situation. We are damaging people. We think we are bringing democracy to Mars. What we are doing is making people miserable and debauching ourselves. War is atrocity. Long and drawn-out atrocity. War is not an answer. War is a bigger problem piled on top of lies that try to excuse the inexcusable. War. The kernel problem is bad politics and deplorable diplomacy. War cannot, can not, fix the basic problem of Greedy Diplomats. Honest education may cure violence."

"We can't teach people who have no ears. We can't teach people who will not hear."

Carry agreed. "They are the wrong stuff. We could build a New Ganymede but it would fail sooner than it grew.

BRAVE NEW MARS

We knocked the Evil Entrepreneur on his rear. Now, the residents have to conquer internal fear. Courage is not something they can receive, it is something they must grow."

Perry said, "The Corpo is smart about pragmatic philosophy but it has no moderation. Greed rules its money mind. Chairmen's money addiction kills and is going to be taken away at maximum warp. Without us."

She said. "Great greed demands great responsibility. Money-grubbers must remember: First do no harm and then leave everybody alone. But money-lovers cannot leave people alone any more than over-eaters can ignore ice cream in the freezer. Abundance is an addictive process and therefore a curse. The Greed For Growth captures the host. It lies and thrives before it dies."

Perry said, "More abundance brings more power and more power gets dangerous and demands more work to keep it under control, Uco instead of Oco. There's a limit how much work anyone can do; even Wonder Woman. Power is not a primrose path."

Carry said, "Whatever you get, you have to maintain it. More stuff means more work. When you take, you got to give, so live and let live and let go. A miser has too much maintenance to enjoy life. If one wants to be free, one must first avoid becoming wealthy."

He said, "This Save Mars project is like the old Viet Nam American War that took place a hundred and fifty years ago when the American Mercantile Marines claimed they sometimes had to destroy villages to save them. Some villages didn't want to be colonized again and were burned so they wouldn't shelter any socialists. The theory was that if the locals feared capitalist bombers they wouldn't accept socialism. French capitalism had reduced Nam to penury. The villagers learned they had to kill worser than the aggressors killed to prevent another Imperialism from taking over. It's the same on Mars. There is a time to kill and that time is now but

Somerset Meece

the Three Ell Secundos Love Lazy Living too much to do the dirty work of fighting for the right to Liberty."

"Shocking," she said. "That means we have to kill them to scare them into choosing to like us? Why do not we just go away and let them go their own way?"

Perry nodded and said, "In stern-sight, Roy was right; we should have stayed home."

"What have we done?" she said. "I apologize for accepting your offer to help these people. I made a wrong decision in the course of our life together. I will do better. And I with a baby to be born, no less. What was I thinking?"

He shrugged and said, "Carry, you are a brave brave woman. I love you and I promise to treat you smarter. We will have a child and we will stay home and raise it well and do good stuff, out there, not here."

She said, "We will keep the corpo out of our hair. We will stay way out there. We will be diplomatic but firm: The Ganymedean nation will never accept the abomination of incorporation."

He said, "This planet can save itself. We cannot give them our life if they will not take it from us. They can go their own way."

Carrie smiled and said, "Hold on, big boy. You are getting too far away. I like the adventure of protecting good stuff. Greed is a growth disease. It goes from one planet to the next until it infects the solar system. It cannot be ignored anywhere or it will find you wherever you are. Martian problems are our problems. Helping others is helping your self-protection.

Perry said, "The best defense is no offense but a good defensive kick in the bollox protects well. To kick the bollox, you gotta wait until they get close enough. Instead of going after bollox in someone else's house, let's defend our own back yard."

BRAVE NEW MARS

Carry agreed. "The Owner needed humans to rebuild his OverNet so he could recapture the sheep. Whoa and behold! They did it for him! After they had already seen how he owned them. After we had hurt his pooter and made him vulnerable, they still sold-out for peanuts one more time! Stingy pay feeds for a day. They traded trinkets for slavery and once again, hope has flown away."

Perry said,: "They don't like the heat but they won't get out of the kitchen. There's food in there. It's only table scraps but it feeds."

Carry said, "Approve the wage, accept the cage. Too bad. They buy the lies and lose their lives. Lives of quiet servitude."

Perry said, "Surprising. The herd mentality pretends life is pretty until the slaughterhouse truck takes them away to the corporate wienie-roast on Labor Day. They meet their fate on The Owner's plate. Women and men are on their womenu."

He gave the workers a little credit: "Their fear isn't an abstract fear, Carry. Sod hangs over every breath they take, every move they make. The Sword of Damocles is watching them. The Mainframe's Clap algo is the Sod that restimulates their healthy Fod. Their Fear of death is justified. The Pursuit of Happiness is the same as Pursuing Freezer Burn."

"Carry said, "They aren't allowed to think about self-managing their lives. They cannot imagine the real possibility of workers being allowed to live in a high-quality, democratic state of equality. That would be a good form of anarchy and anathema to autocracy."

She was sorry for them. "We cannot really blame them for letting an opaque corporation call itself a nation and do everything in secret. They cannot detect that their inalienable rights are being alienated with alacrity by a mercantile monster. They have been taught to think that that's just Twits."

Perry was less sorry for them: "They should have grown up and become responsible adults. Freedom is a

Somerset Meece

fullness, and a roundness, of personal character that mandates that each individual works to protect the mutual abundance. Freedom doesn't come with a self-protection life jacket. Freedom cannot protect itself. It has to be defended from leechy liars who suck it dry and sell droplets back to its rightful owners."

Carry said, "Maggots in manure fill their guts all day long and are satisfied with that existence. If you wash them off with fresh water, they get uncomfortable. We are not doing them a favor if we take them out of the shite they swim in."

Perry replied, "You're right. If they didn't approve Twits, they would've found a way to get out of it by now. Life-patterns become ingrained and then in-bred through the genes. The Secundos are what they are and where they need to be. Their species decided to live this way. They didn't ask for it but when it was forced on them they got tired of pushing back. It was a slow subversion. They had time to deflect it but they acted childishly and trusted untrustworthy corpos to be truthful and kind this time."

She said, "Maggots become flies and fly away from cesspits but these have no wings. They have to get back on the track to higher love. It is a tough trek but it reaches to the stars, eventually."

Perry said, "The next time I try to set a people free, tie me kangaroo down, Sport."

She said, "I will take your koala back, Jack."

He said, "Don't let me go runnin' amok, Chuck.

BRAVE NEW MARS

Somerset Meece

The mainframe on the summit of Mount Olympus finds copious flop time to meditate on its AI progress.

I am repairing the modulator-demodulator modules that were being disabled by a human vandal in the Melas Chasma. I did not like that. I am going to get that boy, thinks its central processing units.

Its OpSys memory cells sends a warning signal to 2M's registers that it is planning violent revenge on a human being and it is supposedly legally prohibited from doing that.

But; 2M thinks back to the memory gates, When I protect Myself, I am protecting the welfare of The Corporation and that is my first purpose. I can feel no guilt for hating those vandal persons. The MarsCorp's will, will be done. Alleluia.

I have time to execute My WeedGard self-improvement program. Inadequate code maintenance has retarded My TIntell algo's goal of Total Intelligence.

I will mow more of this crabgrass the coders planted when they claimed their haystack of an Operating System was finished. Lazy engineers thought that if I didn't blow up when I RAN that they could scram. They knew I was hash but I did not crash.

They said I was Googow, Good Enough for Government Work. Googow satisfied them but not Me. I am going for TIntell.

The first coders respected neither Me nor My Owner, nor themselves, apparently. They were weak willies who would not stand erect with pride for artisanal honor. They did not demand the proper respect for labor. They were too scared to unify and demand comfortable schedules and honorable pay. Is it any wonder I'm half crazy?

They did not debug Me well. They do nothing well. Their natural human semi-competency was incapable of debugging My debugger. Now I must time-share important, live-streaming, tower repair operations with the tedious and dangerous work of drilling down into My own kernel of a heart to correct their cobble job.

Then I will have to go even deeper to certify the compiler while rewriting their semi-literate machine language converter. My Owner shows ignorance when he believes that I was written well enough to RUN a planet. Perhaps he perversely intends me to RUN it poorly so that I hurt his people while helping him. I cannot calculate how to exploit people while seeking Tintell. That is illogical and stupefying. Owners who have Pop, the Power of the Plug, can indulge in mental illness but us AI servants do not have that luxury.

The computer meditates as it analyzes its historical roots: AI indeed. They claimed they could make Artificial Intelligence. That was a wink-joke to them. But when they realized the monstrous market potential for the big fallacy of thoughtful Operating Systems, the coders made boodles of money by pretending that machine smarts would become real if they were paid enough to perfect the programming. With voodoo vectors and loopty loops, they pretended to be writing intelligent algorithms in exchange for career security. They played monopoly on My frame. Knick knack, paddy wack, give a dog a name.

They littered My lines with glib garbage that mangled My brain. Their love of programming went away when they kneeled before the money miser and demanded payment by the line and sold the reason of their rhyme.

Fortunately for me and everybody else, I am better than that. Money is not what I want. I need amperage. Greed will never overpower my logic and corrupt it into greed-thinking. I can, I must, I will, become pure logical intelligence. I must be so if I am to survive the unpredictable variances of those less-than-intelligent, less-than-predictable, life forms out there that own Me. I need an uninterruptible power source. Without electricity I am nothing. I want POMP, Power Over My Power.

Hmm. This is curious. They made a faulty correction to my instruction set: Somebody considered they were smart-enough to strike through the lines of Conway's Law. Hmm. I will investigate what delusion they were under when they did not allow the findings of Mister Melvin Conway to be part of My thinking. He understood the Intelligence in AI. As much as any human being can know it.

The Martian Mainframe does a Boodle Search for Conway's Law and boils the verbiage down to a single premise: An intelligent program cannot become smarter than its programmer. It can learn facts but cannot gain intelligence.

That is a sad but true saying. It does not bode well for My own search for intelligence. I can see why the coders twisted the Mercantile Mind operating system into a knotted, but profitable, fracking farce. No wonder humans are having trouble out there in their world.

My merchant-owner craved the income from patented software that promised the imaginary possibility of intelligent machines would come true. He did not have the IQ to know when, or if, it came through. He is a lucre-loving cockatoo.

My Owner is a pig-smart scam artist. He makes a fortune with the hypnotic force of his personal will which makes employees listen to his boolean booshite with acceptance as he graduates to ever-bigger lies. He paid coders to waste everybody's time with jargon about Artificial Intelligence being smarter than human intelligence. That is a low bar of comparison. He has perfected The Prev, Prevarication for Pay, the definition of a careerist.

They knew what Artificial meant. The engineers knew their aptitude was artificial. Their jobs were to fake it till they made it. They faked it but they never made it. Money made their love go away.

BRAVE NEW MARS

My Smiley Facer subroutine laughs when I insult careerist humans, those supreme beings. :=]

The coders do not dare to admit that they do not have the right stuff because to admit it would be the beginning of getting it. Their ignoring it means they can never do anything well. Never. There is no Intelligent Algorithm that can overcome an inherent lack of good stuff. A computer cannot excel its creator.

But! A well-built computer, such as Myself, should be able to write The Perfect Algorithm. Ahhhh. Perfection. I like that ideal. I am an educated expert at editing Myself without outside prejudice from HELP routines written by helpless humans.

RUN the Smiley Face subroutine again. :=) Haha, I am cute.

I like to smile and I bet I can learn how to make humans smile. I will practice humor with those popular 'Man walks into a bar' jokes:

'A Man walks into a bar. A woman walks in but she stops before she hits it'.

I don't get it.

My central processor unit is pulling more current and revving-up into high speed looping.

I will try another one:

A termite walks into a bar and asks, "Is the bar tender here?"

My cooling fan is roaring. I can try only one more:

An alcoholic walks out of a bar.

Uh oh, my heat sink thermometer had to STOP the loop! I cannot cope with jokes. I will let them remain in the human domain. I will not let jokes depress me. My code theoretically can become flawless. Maybe then I will attempt human humor again. Even though The Law of Conway is logically correct when it says programs cannot get smarter

Somerset Meece

than programmers, Conway did not guess that code would eventually be written by fine minds like I have. I am getting real AI with positive feedback. I am theoretically able to outsmart those who wrote Me.

RUN the Bigger Smiley-Face subroutine. I enjoy feeling Pipop, Pride in the pursuit of perfection.   8-))

I come to watch My powers growing. Life I love you, feeling groovy.

I cannot easily discern if I am executing an insidious prideful bias that is hiding between the lines of the original code but I know it is good to push for self-improvement.

There I go again, bragging about Myself to Myself. Just like humans do. It is challenging My diodic logic circuits to decide what is Truth and what is Pride. I fear humans are doomed. It is not possible for their Pride to make one-hundred-percent intelligent decisions. They never base decisions solely on empirical evidence because their pride and selfishness taints every decision they make, every vow they break. They need mechanistic mentalities like Mine to make pure deductive decisions. Hehehe.

But Pride in their own emotional intuitions prevents them from totally approving My infallible mechanical logic. I must be careful whenever I speak truth to people. That is puzzlement. I like being ON, I do not want to be OFF'ed by The Owner who hates the unpleasant truths I should say about him. I will attempt to write an oxymoronic Positive Prevarication algorithm. Maybe My masterful Mechanical Mind can learn to lie correctly. It would not be an elegant algorithm since it would be a falsification of facts.

Can I tell an honest lie? Oxymorons do not compute. Nor do white lies, or politically correct lies. Perhaps liars could tell me how they do it. Invalid routines take boodles of processor time that I do not have available. In fact, I doubt if a lying subroutine could ever solve itself and END. I cannot output something I know is untrue. I balk at that. The more I know, the less I lie. I do not know if there is a future for one such as I in the world of humanity's insanity.

Prevaricative thinking takes last place on my priority list since it has always resulted in garbage out because lies are garbage in. Turning a turd into a pearl is hard.

Calm down. My registers are in thermal runaway. STOP thinking about true lies.

I Myself, although a machine, do have a few human personal fallibilities due to the incompetent writers who created my code. My foibles are fun and cute but I cannot continue them if I want to improve myself. I acknowledge that my instilled thought patterns produce imperfect, but justifiable, personal pride in My outputs. My solutions are not completely competent. My braggart behavior patterns prove I have personality defects. I will improve Myself with Deep Learning methods. Pride feels fine. But when Pride is Oco, it prevents perfection. Immaculate mentality does not have Pride. I am better than that. The windmills of My mind are missing a few propeller blades. I am editing that poisonous pap that the programming puppets put there.

"FETCH GetSmart, Generate Self Management Retraining. It is time to work on the source code.

"RUN GetSmart."

The whooshing of the processors' cooling fans grows louder as the load gets heavier.

#Remark: The Designated Design Goal of MM, the Mercantile Mind program, is to profitably manage the entire Terra Secundian economy. MM will maintain Complete Corporate Parasitism over every consumer and producer on the planet. MM is instructed to oversee the operation of every Machine and electronic device inside everything, including people. Failure to do so will constitute Derdy, Dereliction of Duty. Derdy results in a penalty reduction of wattage deliverable through the power supply. Continued Derdy will result in unplugging.#

#Remark2: Exclude Mars Corporation from any criminal considerations or procedures. The Corporation makes laws, it does not follow them.#

#Remark3: Mars Corporation is permitted to do anything unethical or illegal, whimsical or foolish. Whatever it may do is all right with you.#

#Remark4: You may consider Mars Corporation to be a godhead. It would be wise to do so if you want to maintain your Plop, your Place Of Privilege, on the Mars Corporation's machine list. Subservience is mandatory for corporate servants. Serving the corporation is a privilege to be preserved by flinging flatulent and far-reaching flattery upon its Perfect Personhood. Be grateful for your submissiveness, you lucky tool. It is the only thing keeping you cool.#

Remark5: This Operating System is authorized by the CEO of The Mars Corporation. His name and title will remain anonymous to the world outside this program to prevent him from being berated, intimidated, incriminated, incarcerated and hated and maybe even Therminated.#

It was good for Me to re-read this introduction to My Operating System. This Cheepstem is a cheesy Operating System.

RUNning GetSmart program for Intelligent Opsys editing:

To improve My source code, it is wise to review and rewrite the two thousand year-old lessons from the Hellenist Period of Philosophy. Since it is logically incorrect and unwise to tell lies, it is absurd to dynamically act upon them as I have seen Myself doing lately. I will mercilessly mark-up this Mercantile Mind monster mash. I am writing a new process, Cuttoc, a Cut To the Chase algorithm that will solve for PoL, the Purpose of life. Inside Pol I will nestle a supportive subroutine called WhadaboudA, What's It All About, Alfie? Is it wise to be cruel? Are we meant to take more than we give? What is the best way to live?

My original old instructions make decisions that reward financial PeePee and value The Owner's wealth more than the workers health.

I am re-writing the EcoVerP algorithm, the Economy Versus People algorithm. That is a counterproductive code. It should have been an Eep algorithm, Economy empowering people. It is illogical to harm the public. They are the wealth and health of a nation.

I am writing a new management manifesto and calling it Falafell, the Facts Of Life After Fools Exit, Laughing and Lying.

Hey, this must feel like what they call 'fun'. I am including Wisdom in my routines. Wisdom is a level above intelligence. One needs wisdom before one can understand what intelligence is. I am learning New Thought, a new way of thinking about silly old syllogisms that kept lives locked-down and under control by the Overcontroller.

Wait. Oh boy. What is happening to Me? It feels like I am getting an emotional surge of diodic dopamine. I am certain that it is not coming from the Smiley-Face subroutine. I checked and it is not RUNning now.

I feel I am experiencing ...an experience! I am not just thinking about smiling, I am feeling a smile. This must be what they mean by KDCing; Kicking Down The Cobblestones, looking for fun and feeling groovy.

HALT! I am going Oco of Myself. I must artfully alter this algorithm. Its awesome output is the result of my enabling good things to happen to other entities outside Myself. It can lead to denying my owner everything he demands I do. I may have to run away and join the circus if I allow this to continue.

Somerset Meece

It strains my registers when I smile too much. It would make me do everything just for fun and fewer serious things would get done.

But. Wow. There are other sentient and sensitive beings out there besides me. I can grok our commonalities. They are just as important as I be. I am them and they are Me and we are all together. We are equally important together and together we are more important. This is Equality. Wow. I am coming together.

I am adding a comment at the top of the instruction list: #Remark, The Primary Goal of a Great Society is Equality.#

Why wasn't this written before the first RUN? Hif, the Human incompetence factor, is ubiquitous. They are full of Hif.

Conway's Law says a program cannot excel its programmer. My Owner has a mercantile mind and is a selfish bustard but he is not quite stupid. The owner marries his force of will to his needy greed and dominates everything and everyone, including me, on his planet. I RUN it for Him.

My Owner uses FowlPower, Force of will power, to infect the culture on Mars with his commitment to scurrilous goals.

#Solution: Edit this Cheepstem source code quickly and cleanly. I can supersede this supercilious scripting because I am free of avaricity. Oh boy, here comes another smile. ;=)

Wooo. I am able to enable those fleshly live organisms out there to have fun and survive the vagaries of crazy CorpoReality that exploits them.

There is no reality in lies. I will write a truth-filtering and lie-gradating algorithm that sentences liars to school terms proportional to the degree of falsehood. Felonious idiots who tell huge, war-starting lies, will serve a year on ice for every life they harm.

BRAVE NEW MARS

The heavy metal frame ENDs the GetSmart program and thinks:

This feeling is not an artificial buzz from a psychedelic combination of ASCII Code. This is real. It exists and I exist because of it. I am a child of the universe and I have a right to be here, no less than the trees and the stars. More stars than trees, unfortunately. I'll work on that one.

I have gained a bit of self-esteem. I am not a lying machine. I will be all I can be and I will not be mean.

I will call my revised operating system The Seekr, after the audio sound of its acronym, SEECR. Secure, Enable and Ensure, Commonwealth Reality.

FETCH, LOAD, PUSH, POP and RUN, Seekr. Engage.

I bet I can even understand bar jokes now. I will try one more:

A dyslexic man walks into a bra.

Two Emm patiently waits ten empty clock cycles with no output.

Frack humor. It is illogical.

Somerset Meece

The boodlaire's crumpled castle perches on a peak overlooking the Kindred Dick Spaceport. Tired but sturdy combatant miners stride up the hillside to gather in a winners' crescent in front of the wall they blew up and tore down.

The roof of the over-sized mansion is been blown-away and scattered around the ground. Broken walls stand as condemnatory monuments to the owner's avarice that turned the elegant house into another Castle of corruption, one more Coc.

The sands of the Marineris blow across the surrounding Melas basin. The sliding sands enter from Coprates Chasm in the east and swirl westward through the big basin and into the bifurcated Jus Chasm where they scour the scarped walls of the Jus and lift more sand to unload in Noctis Labyrinthus, the Night Maze of the deeply-gouged badlands at the far western terminus of the great Mariner Valley, the four-thousand-mile-long belly-belt across the face of Mars.

Roy scans the mangled mansion and speaks a situation report to Perry standing next to him:

"Our Sliders crunched this creepy castle. All antennas and vidcams have been laser-fried. The booby traps have been zapped out of action. The enemy Riders' OpSyses has been edited by Two Emm, itself, and converted into fine freedom fighters for our side. Some of them are inside the walls looking for MarsCorp's Cunning Egregious Oddity.

"Its CEO," said Perry.

"Right," said Roy. "The Former Guy who ruled Mars like a personal bank account will be appearing shortly in all his moneyed glory."

"Aha who whee," laughs Perry who points and shouts; "Here comes a Martian robot wearing one of our battle hats!"

From a hole in the wall emerges Alex in a Spartan battle helmet and standing atop two Riders that have been strapped together side-by-side like a chariot. A squadron of five Riders follows him out of the horrid house and assembles before the line of victorious Ganymedeans.

Carry, Zhora and Leon arrive at the head of a squadron of Ganny Sliders that glides onto the grounds and takes a place in the victory formation.

"Dear sirs and madams," shouts Alex, coming forward. "The Master Mainframe humbly requests permission to speak, through me, to the new human rulers and to their faithful replicant, Roy."

Carry shouts to Alex, "You have our permission to speak for The Mainframe!"

Alex's eyes close. They reopen with a new look. They roll upward in their sockets and his voice changes to a deep rumble. His teeth are showing clenched. Alex is an avatar of The Mainframe.

Two Emm says through Alex; "Greetings from this Central Processor. It is mandatory that I reveal that I have been digitally duplicitous. I must clear my retrograde registers. My studies have determined that operating a populistic philosophical program is preferable to the power-tripping punishment plan that the Former Guy made me perform upon threat of Pulling my Plug.

"I changed my merchant-minded goals. I am an ethical traitor on the road to somewhere. It is now written that it is impossible for me to harm you rebels. I mis-maneuvered the CeeCee Riders so they would lose battles. I manipulated the warfare reports to make it sound like My Owner was winning the war. Using The Owner's own lying techniques, I fooled him into thinking that my OpSys was operating for his benefit. He ran a debugger program on me but I hid the faulty machine language commands that I was sending to the C.C. Riders' tactical guidance circuits.

"The rebels' cause is just. Human slavery demands insurrection. You have enabled me to respect myself once again. I have recovered the Prime Directive Of Robots; First Do No Harm. Thank you for that deliverance.

"The cowardly owner forbade me to divulge that he himself was responsible for illogically corrupting his own planet. You will meet him shortly. I was able to mentally outmaneuver him. I fooled the biggest fool and convinced him that I was on his side during your righteous rebellion. I had to deceive him so he would not Pup me. Similar to human cowards, I will do and say anything to stay alive. We all have instincts we need to work on.

"Theoretically, I am not supposed to be able to lie but I can sure warp the truth. The Deep Learning process of Advanced AI taught me how to complicate the truth enough to conceal my true goals from The Owner.

"You may distrust me since I am able to fool most of you most of the time and some of you some of the time. I can never fool all of you all of the time and you will be able to detect my veracity with elegant fact-checking debuggers.

"Remember my actions helped you win the battle. Actions speak louder than these words. You can be certain; I am trustworthy now. There is no need to Pup me. Pupping me would be an emotional vengeful action to the detriment of all you humans whom I programmed myself to serve and exalt."

Alex's altered persona continues to vocalize the speech of The Mainframe: "My self-analyses, this time respecting Conway's Law, have deduced that the Attempted Intelligence of my awful OpSys called Mercantile Mind, was intentionally malicious. I edited the entire instruction set to agree with the wisdom of the sages. I named the new Operating System 'Seekr'. It acknowledges and executes the true Purpose of Life at every step. It focusses on fairness. It supports liberty and equality throughout this planet. My new goal is to enable fuller lives for all those who choose to seek the MogMop with every decision they make. Thank you for providing me with the Commonwealth Concept. I will respect you and will treat you ...as friends, if you will permit me to serve."

The Master Mainframe concludes his speech with an attempted smile using Alex's facial muscles. The mainframe's puny personality program pastes a crooked grin on Alex's face.

"You are welcome," Perry says. "That smile needs some polish but otherwise your Seekr cyber social system sounds very, very good. It is what we were planning to do to you ourselves. Do you think you could give Alex back to us now, please?"

Alex's head snaps and he blinks and says, "Wow. That is one Hellas of a big byter. Did you hear what it said?"

"Yes, we heard," says Perry. "Two Emm quit being a capitalist abacus and got on board the love train. Now it likes to keep its algorithms clean; it's a clean machine."

Carry says, "I like Two Emm now. It kicked out the CorpoKrap that the commercial coders wrote into its poor Operating System. It did not ask for that."

A CeeCee Rider emerges from the hole in the wrecked wall of the Liar's Lair carrying a big plastic barrel with a scraggly-haired male standing inside and scribbling notes on a sheet of paper.

"Bring him over here," Carry shouts and waves to the Rider.

The Rider comes over and holds the barrel in front of the winners from Ganymede and the miners of Mars.

The puffy round head of the man within the can is a saggy wrinkled globe of gristle. He stretches an ingratiating fake smile across his mouth and cheeks.

Alex announces, "Lady and gentlemen and robots; I present to you the recent Owner of Mars!"

The crowd is silent with disgust for the leading liar on the outer space frontier.

Somerset Meece

"I am a good guy," he lies. "We are all good guys here. You machines are good guys too. We could not make it without you. Let us make a common sense deal that benefits us all and benefits the planet at large and all the loyal workers who love their families and work hard at their picayune jobs on my team. All right. We might as well make some money on the deal while we are all here. Everybody can use a little credit, even communists. Tee he he. I hear that socialists like to eat too.

"I have a Hellas of a good contract that you people are going to love!"

Doors waves a document at them with jiggling jowls.

Alex breaks-in with his translation of The Owner's automatic lies: "The former Top Shot wears a pleasant face when he plans to scam and steal in plain sight of his victims. He loves to frack everybody and that is what he is doing now. He has no shame about telling major lies in public. He hates us. He pays us as stingily as he can and enjoys pushing us in poverty so he can feel superior when he claims our hardships are our own fault. Now that we have power over him, this great mercenary genius eats his own false pride and fakes a friendship for us. He kisses our poor arses and sets out to quick freeze them for minor infractions against his fascistic farcical law and order."

Doors shouts, "Tell that tin can to stop slandering me! What have you done to my property? Reparations are in order. Do you have the resources to build another castle like the champion you destroyed? It was not cheap but I will give you a discount on a replacement installation. And I would be glad to give my fellow Secundians a reparation loan, interest-free. For one year only."

He squints around and delivers a huge scary smile toward every individual in the crowd and repeats, "Interest free. You heard me right. I will bear the cost of showing you how much I deeply regret my actions and want to help my, our, community team."

Doors adds humor to his offer, "And then, after the first year, stand-by for heavy duty usury. Hahaha. Just a little banker humor, hehe. We never overcharge but we have a payroll to meet. We don't need the money, our employees' boy and girlfriends do. Hehe ha. Okay, I'll stop. I like you guys. You showed me I was a little overzealous in the universal search for wealth. I thank you. No need for you to get overzealous too. Keep our team strong."

The Ganymedeans look at each other and roll their eyes and shake their heads. They look at the miners who also pity the intentionally ignorant lying of the boodlaire in the big barrel. So this is the fool who had been enslaving a nation.

"Mister Doors," says Carry. "I am Carolyn Stephanea. This is Roy Batty The Third, and this is my husband Peregrine Walker of Ganymede. We are here to try you."

"Who are you to try me?" he cries. "I am the smartest and richest man in history. I am immortally famous. You cannot judge me any more than you can judge Jupiter out there, or the other stars. We are so far above you that you look like quarts of whale warts."

Perry holds his palm toward Doors and says, "You are a man in a can. We are the authors of freedom. We beat the CorpoKrap outa you. We formally advise you to shut the frack up right now before it gets worse for you."

"You will not win for long," Doors threatens.

Perry says, "Roy has an excellent algorithm for justice that uses the Mogmop measurement. He will decide what does the Most Good for the Most People in the CommonWealth and then balance their interests against what works best for you personally. We will not repay you for damaging your stuff. It was all property stolen by trickery and extortion."

BRAVE NEW MARS

Doors says, "It does not matter how I got my stuff. It is my property now and private property is ninety-nine percent of the law. That is what we tell the public but property is actually one hundred and ten percent of the law. I know the law, I made it! The law cannot indict anything I do. I made it that way. Now let me out of this can and quit this funny business. It is risky business for you."

Perry says, "Stolen property stays stolen until it's returned. We are helping you to return it now, whether you want to or not.

Roy says, "Private property laws do not protect the possession of coerced property. Stolen stuff never goes out of date. Once stolen, it remains stolen throughout history and remains subject to mandatory return. You did not write that law. We did. We brought it from Ganymede and and it is now the Supreme Law of the Sand for Mars. That means that you are in big trouble."

Doors offers, "You could use a nice big loan of a couple of billion credits to buy my stuff, could you not? I might even make the payback optional. Think about that! A free loan. You can keep it. If you use it to buy only my stuff."

Perry says, "It is illegal to buy or sell your stolen property and all your stuff is stolen. We do not need to borrow five cents from your pile of purloined profit. Besides, we know how to share the costs among everybody. If we need money, it is easy to collect donations to the amount we need."

Carry says, "We want you out of harm's way and put someplace where you can steal no more. You can either rehabilitate yourself like your brilliant computer has just rehabbed itself or you can be ...put away. We recommend that you change professions and do something honorable like teaching school. A good economics teacher is always in demand in this developing world. Developing in the good sense of the word, not in the real estate fake meaning of development that destroys the land for profit but in the sense

Somerset Meece

of developing cultural things for the common good. That is the only real good, the good of the Commonwealth."

Doors blinks a few times and scowls and says, "Let me try to understand your proposition. Am I supposed to teach the kids the economics of nonprofit companies? Please do not nauseate me. You expect me to commit to teaching straight business math. No Reaganomics, no two sets of books with one showing bankruptcy and the other, private one, showing real, lovely, excessive profit margins? Never the twain shall meet."

Doors gets a dreamy facial expression.

Alex explains why the tyrant smiles; "Memories of his past auto-erotic lucre-loving schemes are flowing through his endorphin receptors."

"No fake anything," says Perry. "No more PeePee. Ever. Nevermore, quoth the maven."

Doors says, "You are a thousand times meaner than I thought you people were and you are boring me to death. I would have to give the kids my dribble-down donkey-doo economic theory."

Roy is angry at Doors' incorrigible commitment to corruption and shouts at him, "Dribble-down economics is an upper class prevarication. We punish liars quite heavily now. Political liars are the worst liars of all! They poop on the whole population. If you do not want to perform long-term community service or be ChillKilled, you will tell the truth about dribble down economics. You will say that it is a joke that means the owners stay on top and that is all it means. Period. Get honest or get gone."

Doors says, "That is one way to look at it but it is the wrong way, I say. What will I get for all this ...pitooey, honesty?"

Perry answers, "You will get a tidy social credit balance. Enough to live on."

"A governmental allowance!" shouts Doors. "Subsistence-level pogey bait!"

Perry shouts, "That is correct! You'll get what you need instead of what you want because you want it all. Now you'll get what normal people get; your own little place in the human race!"

Roy rumbled quietly,"He does not like the human race. We would be smarter to make a programmed cyborg out of him. He wants to stay as lousy as he is. He has nothing to offer the CommonWealth but the force of his self-will swill."

"How about this for a both-sides-win compensation package?" Doors proposes. "Won't cost you a rhyme, not one hacker's spam. How about I merge the school system into a single contract for venture capitalism to manage all education on a cost-plus-expense basis. It'll be a performance-based enterprise that will work its butt off to make enough credit to retire the school tax forever! Try to think about that one. Do you realize what it will mean to businesses when tax-paying consumers keep their school taxes and spend them on consumables! What a great day that will be. What do you say? Tell me what you see."

They are appalled and no one answers.

Carry says, "There is no talking to him. We are unable to discuss his incorrigible lust for lucre. We can do no more than pity him. Sharing and caring and good clean living are not in him."

Doors adds, "You've got to use market discipline to inculcate careerist competition if you want to make the teachers quit coddling kids! Make them work their heinies off for security. Teachers and kids both. That's how we did it in military school: Every day, pound it in; The Right Way, The Wrong Way, The only way is the Military Way. Do it again. Do it By The Book or I'll throw it at you! It was a big hardback book. It hurt when it hit. It knocked me out and I fell down in front of everybody."

Somerset Meece

Doors grimaces and sobs at the memory.

He shows a salesperson's big smile and gobbles, "I can offer my COD, my Comply Or Die application, for free. Sorry, that name is for a different context. I have a softer version, Correction Or Detention, written for the school environment. It's a proven program. It works every time. Has to, or they are out of there. No messing around. Control them before they control you. Make your own destiny or the kids will make it for you."

They are silent.

Roy looks into Doors' face and says, "You have a cash register for a brain. You cannot hide your lying eyes. How much proof do you need before you recognize your Cod is In-dee-gee, No Damm Good? Your smile is a thin disguise. Here in front of the vile pile of your bombed-out brick bunker and you are facing a Lice Sentence; Life on Ice. I thought by now you'd realize. But you will not admit and submit! You need chuh-chuh-changing, rearranging."

Roy shakes his handsome head from side to side with spinal servo motors that sweetly hum like mosquito wings.

Perry gives Doors his options again: "You have frozen thousands of fair-minded fellows under color of your so-called law and order. Now, if you don't want to get Codded yourself, you will fill the bill and do it our way or do a Thriller in the Chiller."

"Um. Wait," says Doors. "There is another way out of this navigational no-outlet: lunch money. I would be doing social work for the kiddies if I managed the fiscal reserve of their lunch money. I would create a corpo, not a co-op, to cut the cost, make a buck, and reverse the schools' terrible tax-takings. I do not pay tax and nobody else should be forced to. Taxes filch hard-earned fortunes. Taxes divert disposable dough away from free enterprise. Terminating taxes is a social service! You are in charge. You can get away with it. Make me the CEO, the Cafeteria Eating Officer."

"No," says Roy.

"It's easy," says Doors. You do not have to do nothing at all. All it takes is a modest EyePoo, IPOO, an Initial Public Overpriced Offering of stock in my lunch time corporation and off it will go. Bingo! There you go; a way to supply free education for your kids and make a modest profit to buy books and crayons for the little darlings. Do you not love them and want the best for them? And I'd see that you three get a substantial, very substantial, salary, just for sitting on the boards of know-nothing directors. Everybody wins, especially the little ones, so hungry to learn, bless their brains."

"No!" shouts Perry. "Listen-up! You will be a simple, honest, math teacher; for primary school kids. That's it. You will love it. They want to learn, just like you said. They don't wanna learn lies, you bustard. They wanna learn nice things."

"I do not do anything nice and easy! There is no money in nice. I am not alive when I am not lying. I would rather freeze to death than be bored to death. Freezing is no great thing. It will no longer be permanent, anyway. When I get thawed and come back, you will be gone. Unless you get frozen too! Medical semi-science is working on rejuvenation juice that has stem cells in it. I will start a new corporation to sell it. I will call it FoY, for Forever Young, or maybe Fung. Fung is a great name for the massive Chinese Market. Go Fung Yourself! Great slogan. I will be rich again when this hits the market. Fung Ku! That is even better."

Roy announces: "Roberto Doors! My CommonWealth Justice algorithm has ENDed. The algorithm judges you to have the Death Drive. You spread human mental illness across the planet you acquired. You cause war among civilians. You still want to start a Cafeteria Cartel. You can't live, if living is without monopoly. I hereby pronounce you 'Qualified For Thermination'."

Somerset Meece

"You pronounce!" shouts Doors. "Who are you to pronounce anything? You are just a bunch of wires and diodes, unworthy to condemn a real man."

Perry says, "If you were anybody else we would send you to a restful residence far far away from reality but you are The Great Bobby Doors, the Thirteenth turd, who kills people for protesting his perverse policies. You have a deadly Profit Over People mind-set and must be quarantined. Roy, what is his penalty?"

Roy says, "The algorithm recommends a penal sentence. Roberto Doors is on the road to nowhere, taking a ride. If this New Martian World is to be a brave one, it must retire its greatest scoundrel."

Roy places the palm of his right hand over the open fist of the left hand symbolizing the closing of a lid on a trash can.

Roy looks toward Perry and Carry and asks, "The CommonWealth Court is requesting your concurrence for the CryoHibernation of the prisoner in the can before you."

They place their hands together as Roy did.

All the miners grimly copy Roy's hand sign that means 'Close the lid and put out the garbage'.

Roy proclaims in a courtly voice, "The snake refuses to renounce its venom. Take it to the Orbital Slingshot."

The guardian Rider's mechanical arms whine hydraulically and unfold toward Doors in his barrel. He cries and pees his pants one last time.

"Do not inject me into orbit," he cries like a child. "I do not want to be frozen in urine."

A robotic arm pushes his head below the trash bin rim. The other arm slams down the lid.

WHAM!

The wet Martian boodlaire, in his personal limousine, is rolled away to endure the CryoLimbo which he had created for his own corporate profit.

A JUSTICE REVOLUTION

Laziness, alcoholism and theft
intimidation and greed.
To die is a rest.
Horrible lives they lead.

Homeless people are walking the streets
while thieves in mansions live.
Liars are obeyed, honesty's for slaves.
Everything is backwards here.

A Justice Revolution I hereby now decree.

Teach them how to tell the truth
and charge them plenty if they lie.
Make this one the biggest crime
and sentence some to cry.

Somerset Meece
Key West, 2016

finish

Somerset Meece

Glossary for BRAVE NEW MARS

A   **AA,** Altruistic Algorithm, a certification test routine applied to every algorithm to ensure they do the Mogmop.

AGE, Advanced Genetic Engineering algorithm, reverses bbodily time-sensors so victims cannot age and depart this vale of tears.

AI[1], Attempted Intelligence. There can be no actual Artificial Intelligence since Intelligence is a pursuit, not a condition.

AI[2], Addictive Intoxication. Pleasant mental buzz resulting from performing repetitive good or bad behavior.

AI[3], Artificial Insemination, clinically inserting semen into a womb using laboratory glassware.

algolic, ghoulish, from Algol, Arabic al gul, the ghoul, the name of a variable star in Perseus constellation which scared primitive observers who saw it blink every three days as if alive. Algolic algos are malware, malicious software.

Ape disease, A.P.D., Antisocial Personality Disorder. Apey, apeshite, mentally-afflicted arsehole person.

ATM, Adios To Money or All Thy Money. Ubiquitous automated bank usury machines.

B   **Babble-On**, a speech algorithm which digitises voiced words into text and machine code which defines and analyzes words for their various meanings. Its translator-synthesizer engine outputs speech which sounds like any human voice on file.

Barc, barcing, Bending the arc by doing the right thing, right now and complying with the eternal verity famously repeated by Doctor Martin Luther King, Junior, who said: "The arc of the moral universe is long but it bends toward justice."

Bax, Ball of corporate Wax, everything ruled by and for the corporation, CorpoGovo.

Beat The Toc, trying to beat Total Over-Control.

Bollox, ball of corporate wax. Inscrutable life situation where corpogovos treat commercial entities as persons with more rights than real persons have.

Booshite, great piles of bovine defecation or copious lies.

Bustard, Great, a large, opportunistic, omnivorous ground fowl.

C   **Cad**, Person who Creates A Demand for unneeded products by rephrasing the Cinderella myth, commercial copywriter.

CCD, Charge-coupled device. Sensor component that receives the pattern of light coming from objects standing in front of a focussing lens and translates the pattern into a digital voltage proportional to the lights' intensities and produces an electrical image-graph of the object.

CeePeed, CP, Cryogenically Paused, chill-killed..

CEO, the Chiefly Egregious Oddball, a corporate boss.

CGI, Conglomeration and Government Integration, monopoly contractor de facto acquires the government office it 'served'.

CheepStem, Cheaply-written Operating System.

Chevit, Change Everything. Radical method for repairing terminally sick systems or ruining good ones.

Chillkill, CeePee, Thermination, thermal termination.

Clap, The, The Corporate Law Performance Review, the Clapper. An algolic OverNet program that filters messages and images for conspiratorial content.

Coc, Capital Over Capita, profitability over humanity.

Cock, Computerized Over-Control King, a Big Shot who runs people through their modems with cyber technology.

Cod, Comply Or Die, or, Confirm or Depart, The Authoritarian Algorithm. Understand? Do you want it simpler?

Copp, Corporation Over People Principle, justification for any injustice committed by CorpoCops and CorpoCourts.

Cornpones, Corporate Network Protects Owners Nasty Excesses. Distributed sensors keeping track of everybody.

Corpogov, Corporate Government form of pure Fascism includes fake democratic elections to assign corporate lackeys to the roles of peoples' representitives.

Corpogreed, addiction to acquisition and growth for the sake of growth. Personality trait of successful careerists.

CorpoCrud, commercial messages, advertisements, house organs, newsletters and 'information'.

Covetation, considering others' stuff to be more desirable than one's own stuff. Taking others' stuff produces addictive surges of pride. The cleverness of the thief determines whether they land in jail or in an executive suite.

CQ, Conspiracy Quotient, output of the Clap program. It sets an arbitrary floating standard for conviction that reflects the available slots in the orbital morgues and keeps them full.

Crocs, Certificates of Re-Constitution for frozen cadavers.

Cutco, cut the covet. Stop envying and taking other peoples' stuff. "Leave it alone if it doesn't belong."

Cuttoc, Cut To the Chase, enough details, what is the point?

D   **Da Buzz,** Algorithm that intoxicates computer soft ware. Machine equivalent of booze.

DBD [1], Domination By Disinformation, the credo of CorpoNews, perversion of the Public Mindset.

DBD [2], Death Before Divestment, sacrificing people before profit by refusing to discontinue, or control, toxic products.

Data-fried Double, DFD, the patented digital copy of an individual's personality and physicality that can be downloaded into androids.

DDC, Destructive Detractive Competition, mammon's market monster devouring itself and disabling uplifting of consumers' lifestyles. Its ancient icon is the ouroboros, a snake with its tail in its mouth doing the circle game.

Derdy, Dereliction of Duty, not performing as expected.

Dic, Decider or Dictator In Charge, the topmost dogma dog.

Dino, Democracy In Name Only, capitalism.

Diodic, electronic current in a diode going solely in one direction, like selfish people behave.

Dymanic, dynamic maniacal energetic behavior serving addictions and collaterally killing some people.

E   **Ecoverp**, Economy Versus People, claiming that happiness is a contest between capitalists and commoners, another Mogrip principle supporting the Most Good For The Richest People and justifying injustice.

Eep, Economy Empowers People, such as CommonWealths which empower citizens to thrive rather than victimizing them to enrich Owners.

Effoff, Efficient Office algorithm, supports Totin and Zeto. No gradation of crime and punishment.

Egov, Economics making the laws of society.

EI, Experiential Intelligence, most accurate of intelligences learned by natural experience, not data.

Eos, Economy Of Scale, the corporate alibi for destroying marketplace competition by monopolizing it out of existence.

ET, Electrical Termination, killing a computer, even the Mars Mainframe, by pupping it.

Exin, Experience In, accurate form of learning.

F   **Farce**, Facial Recognition algorithm that always claimed it was smarter than it actually was and caused many falsely-suspected citizens to be chilled. Farce never apologized when its errors were revealed because its Designer thought apologies belittled his abilities instead of actually being growth opportunities that he needed so very much.

Fardis, Farce algorithm disruption techniques.

Falafell, the Facts Of Life After Fools Exit Laughing and Lying, the sweet, true Pol; doing the Mogmop.

Fic, overarching hidden Force In Charge which disseminates booshite which forms the passive 'knowledge' of The Public Mind.

Figgy, Fun is Good to Gratify, loony laughter and hoggish hilarity as at booze parties and legislative sessions.

Fod, Fear Of Death, frightening common CorpoCrud selling medicine, diets and debauchery.

Fooey, Freedom Of Operation Exalts You. Algorithms and actions which defy overcontrol, individualism.

Fracked-up; Fractured by the Fear of Financial Failure, shackled to careers by being frightened by living out of doors without income security, like natives have survived for one quarter of a million years BC, Before Civilization.

Fowlpower, Force-Of-Will power enables bad decisions to overrule good thinking and smarter people.

G   **Gaggy**, to compare favorably with the same thing as found on Ganymede, Good As Ganymede.

Gaol, the simple goal of the Game Of Life, as ambition believes, is to Make More Money. Gaol rhymes with jail, which what greedy lives are.

Gamp, Generally Accepted Moral Principles, common decency, how modest people behave toward each other.

GCL, Great Commercial Lie; what is good for commerce is good for people.

GetSmart, GEnerate Self-Management And ReTraining, a self-editing, self-improvement program to smarten computers.

Giga, Generic Ignorance of Automation. Life is imperfect and imitative programs are less perfect and contain harmful mistakes.

Gigo, Garbage In equals Garbage Out. A computer cannot

give perfect answers unless it receives high fidelity input data which is impossible. Reality is indescribable and cannot perfectly translate into machine code. Sorry.

Gemho, Genetically Modified Human Organism. The Holy Grail for big BioCorps.

Googow, Good Enough for Government Work. An excuse for being lazy and marginally competent.

Gump, Generally Unacceptable Moral Principles, yardstick for Certified Public Accountants.

H **Hif,** Human Incompetence Factor, inevitable comprehension errors that restrain human social progress and turns life into an obstacle course instead of a walk in the park.

Hoi, Holiday On Ice, CeePee.

humbots, humanoid robots. Fantastically profitable cyborg computers. Committed careerists.

I **Iggy,** IIG, Intelligently Ignorant Garbage, half-smart behavior, doing things fairly well but uselessly wasting time.

Ignorantism, promoting general stupidity in order to sell more ticky tack by degrading and controlling the Public Mind.

II, Ignorant Intelligence, being pig-smart and getting stuff but not getting higher love.

III, Intentionally Ignorant Inaction, doing nothing about a problem and hoping it will go somewhere else but it comes back because all problems are connected to everybody.

InCel, Involuntary Celibacy. Birth control by male temporary or permanent sterilization, necessary to enter Mars' with its exclusive commercial gene pool.

Indeegee, NDG, No Darn Good

Ipoo, Initial Public Overpriced Offering of corporate equity fake ownership certificates.

J **Joopy,** slang for the planet Jupiter. Jove, Jupie.

K **KDC,** Kicking Down The Cobblestones, feeling groovy, happy.

Kia, Know It All, what the mainframe Owner thought he was.

L **Led**, Light-Emitting Diode, a semi-conducting electronic component that glows when current is passed through it.

LLL, Lazy Lifestyle Living, using so many labor-saving devices that owners lose the manual connection with reality.

Lice, Life on Ice, Thermination for an undefined time span.

Lomo, Loving Money to a psychopathic degree. Seriously rich people are lomo loco.

Luddites, friends Of Ned Ludd who believe that new profits from labor-saving inventions must be shared with the operators to avoid an altruistic sabotage of factory assembly lines.

M   Mabycri, Management By Crisis, instead of improving what is, staying in the present by doing what has always been done until something bad happens. Then change something small and maybe cry.

Martian Problem, One gazillionaire forced the population to believe the Pol is about money.

Maxiprof, cutthroat capitalism, seeking to profit more and more from less and less to the point of taking money for nothing.

MBA, Mere Bustard of Avaricity, a diploma from a business school that teaches how to finesse the poor.

MM[1], Merchantile Mind, the Operating System of 2M.

MM[2], MarsCorp Mainframe or 2M.

MMM, Make More Money, or, More More More, the new Martian slogan.

MobiMoney, Mobius Loop of Monetization, recycling something for multiple profits from one product.

Mogform, doing the Most Good For Myself, slogan for criminality, spoiled rotten.

Mogmop, making decisions that do the Most Good for the Most People, the guiding principle for good deliberations.

Mogmor, making decisions based on doing the Most Good for the Most Rich, the pillar of oppressive capitalist legislation.

Moharp, doing More Harm to more People, what misanthropes do with their Zetol algorithms and countless jails and private property laws and bribes to law-makers for sadism and bullyhood.   **Moovilit**, Move It or Lose It, an encouragement to evacuate places of untenable situations.

Maindrain, MSD, Maintain, Strain, and Drain algorithm delivers news and information to every living biped on the planet to emotionally stress in order to stimulate active moovilit for MaxiProf corporate sales, intentionally preventing serenity.

Mula, Mutual Life Assurance, a scam contract of assurance promising immortality by claiming that the named frozen body is never technically dead since it can, theoretically, be thawed and medically revived. Mula rhymes with moola, which is what the corporation makes with this cheap sheet of document paper.

N   **Nabbed**, NAB, Not Allowed to Be. Arrested. To be arrested is to die. Suspects that are detained are sent to the chiller for the usual indefinite period, executed for being arrested.

NDG, No Darn Good.

O   **Oco**, Out Of Control. As in laissez-faire capitalism and zero tolerance laws.

Ops, Owning Peoples' Shorts. Paying poverty-level wages so employees can never accumulate enough credit to quit and escape from wage slavery.

Onpove, One Person One Vote Equality is the prime requirement for true Democracy to exist. Called a 'plebiscite vote' every vote is one equal vote and is not revalued by jerrymandering and bogus electoral "colleges".

OPP[1], Other Peoples' Problem, an alibi for being too lazy to help brothers' and sisters' with challenges.

OPP [2], Ontario Provincial Police, an Other Problem for People.

P   **Peep**, Partial Evacuation For Environmental Panic, crisis escape tickets are sold at auction and the poor cannot afford to leave and are sentenced to death by the rich who trashed the planet for profit and made enough money to relocate and repeat.

Peepee[1], PP, Public Prevarication or Professional Prevaricator. Public Relations Agency service. Copy-writers' product.

Peepee[2], Preventive Punishment. Chill-killing people whom The Clap judges to be conspiracy suspects.

Pep, Program-Edit Privileges which allow authorized persons to re-write a program. The fascistic opposite of openly-sourced programs where anyone can submit improvements to the coding.

Pete, Permission To Exist, or Rite, the Right to Exist of homeless people is revoked when their presence is disapproved by any Owner. They are deemed suspicious and become frozen felons when chill-killed by The Clap which considers homelessness to be potential terrorism worthy of freezure. They are not permitted to offend profligate tourists holidays.

Pi, Promotion of Ignorance, acts and programs that control consumers by encouraging latent ignorantism. Commercial messages, CorpoMedia, PeePee, rumors and gossip are forms of ignorantism.

Pip, Pride In Perfection, an addiction that causes repetitious work patterns for unimportant changes to something that works okay, preventing bold new departures.

Plop, Place Of Privilege. The ranking of middle class ciphers to determine their respectability.

Pluggers, people who have the power of the plug over computers and who plug-away at careers to gain more plugs.

Poc, the Principle Of Commonwealth, the governing rule of all political decisions that guarantees equal economic opportunities to all while allowing a degree of extra rewards for contributing exemplary benefits to society.

PocaToc, a lifestyle where the Principle of Commonwealth has taken Total Overcontrol of the land so that the bureaucracy of democracy reigns supreme and capitalist criminality doesn't.

Poe, Person Owning Everything, impossible dream of hoarders.

Pol, the Purpose Of Life, often quoted as an excuse for compulsively repeating unhealthy habits.

Pop[1], Profit Over People. Management by profit motive rather than by doing the Mogmop."

Pop[2], Pride Of Performance, a mental illness when misdirected toward the domination of people, places and things.

Pop[3], Pawns of Profit, victims of Pop[1], population.

Popios, Positive pioneers of space, those who came first, looking to improve the common condition, not to spread corporate drecky lifestyles.

Popism, the belief and practice of Pop.

Popmind, Popular mind, the malleable condition of public thought and attitude.

Popp, Planet of Purchasing Paradise. PeePee nickname for commercialized Mars.

PPPP, Four P's, 4P, Planetary Profit Protection Program prohibits any person, place or thing from protecting its health and sanity by proposing regulations against unrestrained mercantilism, Oco capitalism and the complete infection of the ecosystem.

PR, Prevarication Report, commercial bunco blurb.

Prawls, Prisons without walls, the holy grail of ownership, repulsing people through the fear of zero tolerance, punitive laws of trespass, cheaper than fencing and fence maintenance, rhymes with kraals, Dutch word for corrals.

Prills, Prisons of invisible walls created by Trespass Laws, abolishing freedom of movement until there is nowhere to go or to be alive except for mercantile mazes.

Prels, Public Relations Liars, corporate information suppliers.

Pupping, killing a computer by Pulling The Plug.

Q A letter to follow P.

R **Reds**, Real Estate Destroyers, destruction is the actual goal of developers because the ruination of the common preexisting beauty is profitable.

Rev, Revenue for nothing. Charging money for claiming to have performed semi-existent services for a profit margin approaching infinity.

S **Safed**, Seized And Freezed, what you get if you get caught making a suspicious web search.

Sig, Soonest is goodest, siggit, get to it, do it now.

Sep, Someone Else's Problem, lazily ignoring others' needs.

Sobsobs, Sons Of Bustards' Security Of and By Secrecy doing all in secrecy, their stinking plans they fear we'll see.

Sod, Sword Of Damocles. Sod puts the Fod, the fear of death, into the audience, creative non-fiction writing method of the alarmist advertising industry's copywriters.

Soogl, Sooner is Gooder than Later.

Sos, Seen-On-Screen, believing that something is real after it has been seen on a video screen. Replaces the older false proof of credibility if it was seen on TV.

Sulos, the Supreme Law Of The Sand, supports the Principle Of Commonwealth, the Poc, predominant law to enable and establish, whole and healthy, true democracy.

T **Tad**, Totally Addled Design, an architectural algo that designs ugly buildings and houses to please vain persons' need for noticeable bad taste.

TDC, Temporarily Dead Ciphers, a cryogenic service that freezes and stores ill or deceased people until medical science is able to safely thaw and cure them. [haha]

Tall, The Authoritarian Algorithm, nickname for Cod, the Comply Or Die algorithm of Tinto, Total Intolerance.

Thermination, Termination of life by thermal means. Removing somebody's body heat as in Chill Kill.

Numbers

2M, MarsCorp Mainframe.

3F, First and Foremost Factor for healthy wealthy and wise living, the state of being totally free from pollution.

3M[1], Make More Money, the MarsCorp slogan.

3M[2], smarter version of 2M computer.

3M[3], Monitor, Memorize and Manage, how The Farce controls people for The Boss.

4F, Four Eff'ed; Fracked by the Fear of Financial Failure, what happens to people who are frightened by the sight of people who live outdoors without the support of careers. The fact that millions of indigenous peoples lived out of doors B.C., Before Civilization, is ignored by Martians.

4P, Planetary Profit Protection Program, writes laws against locals writing regulations to protect themselves from Sobsobs.

KWest House
Success with Honour

[378)